10/14/09   124269 3805

INTERTWINED

GENA SHOWALTER

HARLEQUIN®
TEEN

HARLEQUIN®
TEEN

ISBN-13: 978-0-373-21002-2

INTERTWINED

www.HarlequinTEEN.com

Printed in U.S.A.

To the real:

Victoria, Riley, Haden, Seth, Chloe, Nathan, Meagan, Parks, Lauren, Stephanie, Brianna and Brittany. I love you all. But just remember that your characters can sprout horns and tails at any moment....

To Jill Monroe. I sent you coal and you found the diamonds. This book would not have been possible without you. *I* would not be possible without you. So I'm just gonna say it: I love you. And yeah, you were right. But if ever asked in public, I'll deny that last one.

To Kresley Cole. If I could live anywhere in the world, it would be inside your books. Or your house. I could move in tomorrow. Just sayin'. After all: Kresley − Gena = Sadness. Kresley + Gena = Happiness. And yes, I love you, too.

To P.C. and Kristin Cast. I pull a muscle every time I'm with you because I laugh so hard. My life is a better place with the two of you in it! Because…what? I love you.

To Max, my husband, sweetheart and (as I've been told) the greatest guy ever. I love you.

To my amazingly supportive family. Mike, Vicki, Shane, Shonna, Michelle, Kemmie, Kyle, Cody, Matt, Jennifer, Michael, Heather, Christy, Pennye and Terry. I'm the lucky one who gets to enjoy (and love) you. You guys just got stuck with me. Suckers!

To David Dowling. Thank you for creating Crossroads. You are NOT a fool.

To my agent, Deidre Knight, who really went to bat for this one.

To my editors Tracy Farrell and Margo Lipschultz. You are with me every step of the way, no matter what I decide to write, supporting me, lifting me and making me better.

And to myself. Because this one almost killed me.

ONE

A CEMETERY. No. No, no, no! How had he ended up here?

Clearly, wearing his iPod while exploring a new town had been a mistake. Especially since Crossroads, Oklahoma, perhaps garden gnome capital of the world and definitely hell on earth, was so small it was practically nonexistent.

If only he'd left the Nano at the D and M Ranch, a halfway house for "wayward" teens where he now lived. But he hadn't. He'd wanted peace, just a little peace. And now he would pay the price.

"This sucks," he muttered, pulling the buds from his ears and shoving the shiny green distraction into his backpack. He was sixteen years old, but sometimes he felt like he'd been around forever, and every one of those days had been worse than the one before. Sadly, today would be no exception.

Immediately the very people he'd been trying to drown out with so-loud-your-ears-bleed Life of Agony clamored for his attention.

Finally! Julian said from inside his head. *I've been screaming for you to turn around for, like, ever.*

"Well, you should have screamed louder. Starting a war with the undead was not what I wanted to do today." As he spoke, Haden Stone—known as Aden because, as a kid, he apparently hadn't been able to pronounce his own name—backtracked, removing his foot from the graveyard's property line. But it was too late. In the distance, in front of a tombstone, the ground was already shaking, cracking.

Don't blame me, Julian replied. *Elijah should have predicted this.*

Hey, a second voice said. It, too, came from inside Aden's head. *Don't blame me, either. Most times, I only know when someone's gonna die.*

Sighing, Aden dropped his backpack, bent down and palmed the daggers he kept anchored in his boots. If he were ever caught with them, he'd be tossed back into juvie, where fights erupted as regularly as lunch was served and making a trustworthy friend was as impossible as escape. Deep down, though, he'd known carrying them was worth the risk. It was always worth the risk.

Fine. This is my fault, Julian grumbled. *Not like I can help myself, though.*

That was true. The dead had only to sense him to awaken. Which, like now, usually involved Aden accidentally placing his foot on their land. Some sensed him faster than others, but they all eventually rose.

"Don't worry about it. We've been in worse situations."

More than leaving the iPod at home, he mused, he should have been paying attention to the world around him. He'd studied a map of the town, after all, and had known what areas to avoid. But as the music had pounded, he'd lost track of his surroundings. He'd been momentarily liberated, seemingly alone.

The tombstone began to rattle.

Julian sighed, the sound an echo of Aden's. *I know we've endured worse. But I caused those worse situations, too.*

Fabulous. A pity party. This third, frustrated voice belonged to a woman—who also took up prime real estate inside his head. Aden was only surprised his other "guest"—as he sometimes thought of the souls trapped inside him—didn't pipe up, as well. Peace and quiet were not something any of them understood. *Can we save the festivities for later, boys, and kill the zombie before it emerges all the way, gains its bearings and stomps our collective butt?*

"Yes, Eve," Aden, Julian and Elijah said in unison. That was the way of it. He and the other three boys would bicker and Eve would step in, a formidable mother-figure without a finger to point, but a formidable mother-figure all the same.

If only that mothering were enough to fix the situation this time.

"I just need everyone to zip it," he said. "Okay? Please."

There was grumbling. And that was as quiet as things were going to get.

He forced himself to focus. Several yards away, the headstone teetered back and forth before tumbling to the ground and shattering. Rain had fallen this morning, and droplets sprayed in every direction. Handfuls of dirt soon joined them, flying through the air as a disgustingly gray hand poked its way free.

Golden sunlight poured from the sky, highlighting the oozing skin, the rotting muscle…even the worms slithering around the enlarged knuckles.

A fresh one. Great. Aden's stomach rolled. He might puke when this was over. Or during.

We're about to smoke that fool! Is it bad that I'm hot right now?

And there was Caleb, voice number four. If he'd had a body of his own, Caleb would have been the guy taking pictures of girls in their locker room while hiding in the shadows.

As Aden watched, waiting for the right moment to strike, a second oozing hand joined the first, both straining to heave the decayed body the rest of the way from the ground. He scanned the area. He stood on a cemented walkway, high on a hill, lush trees helping to form a path and block him from prying eyes. Thankfully, the long span of grass and head-stones looked deserted. Beyond was a road where several cars meandered past, their engines humming softly. Even if the drivers were rubberneckers and failed to keep their attention on traffic, they wouldn't be able to see what happened below.

You can do this, he told himself. *You can. You've done it before. Besides, girls like scars.* He hoped. He had plenty to show off.

"Now or never." Determined, he strode forward. He would have run, but he wasn't in a hurry to ring the starting bell. Besides, these encounters always ended the same way, no matter the sequence of events: Aden bruised and broken, sick from the infection the corpses' tainted saliva caused. He shuddered, already imagining yellowed teeth snapping and biting at him.

Usually the battle lasted only a few minutes. But if anyone decided to visit a loved one during that time… Whatever happened, he *couldn't* be seen. People would assume he was a grave robber or a body snatcher. He'd be hauled into whatever detention center this hole-in-the-wall town offered. He'd be forever labeled a no-good delinquent, exactly as he'd been labeled in every other town he'd ever lived in.

Would have been nice if the sky darkened and rain poured again, shielding him, but Aden knew he didn't have that kind of luck. Never had.

"Yep. I should've paid attention to where I was going." For him, walking past a cemetery was the epitome of stupid. A single step on the property, like today, and something dead would awaken, hungry for human flesh.

All he'd wanted was a private spot to relax. Well, as private as a guy with four people living in his head could get.

Speaking of heads, one peeked through the now-gaping hole, swinging left, right. One eye was rolled back, the white branched with red, while the other was gone, revealing the muscle underneath. Large patches of hair were missing. Its cheeks were sunken, its nose hanging by a few threads.

Bile burned Aden's stomach, threatening to double him over. His fingers tightened around the hilts of his blades, and he finally quickened his step. Almost…there… That haggard face sniffed the air, obviously liking what it smelled. Toxic black saliva began dripping from its mouth and its struggle for freedom increased. Shoulders appeared. A torso quickly followed.

A jacket and shirt bagged around it, torn and dirty. A male, then. That made what he had to do easier. Sometimes.

One knee shot onto the grass, two.

Closer…closer still… Again, he increased his pace.

Aden reached it just as it stood to full height, a little over six feet, which put them at eye level. His heart slammed in his chest, a frantic drum. Breath blistered his lungs, scalded his throat. More than a year had passed since he'd had to do this, and the last time had been the worst of all. He'd needed eighteen stitches in his side, had worn a cast on his leg for a month, spent a week in detox, and had made an involuntary blood donation to every corpse at Rose Hill Burial Park.

Not this time, he told himself.

A hungry growl burst from the creature's ruined lips.

"Lookie what I have." Aden held up the blade, and the silver glinted in the light. "Pretty, isn't it? How 'bout a closer look, hmm?" Arm surprisingly steady, he reached back and struck, going for the neck. To kill a corpse—permanently— the head had to be removed. But just before contact, the corpse gained its bearings, as Eve had feared it would, and ducked. Survival instincts were something that never died, apparently. Aden's knife whizzed through empty air, his momentum spinning him around.

A bony fist pushed him face-first to the ground, and he soon found himself eating dirt. A hard weight immediately pounced on him, crushing his lungs. Fingers encircled his wrists and squeezed, and he lost his hold on the blades. Thankfully—or not—those fingers were disgustingly wet and couldn't maintain a strong enough grip to keep him still.

No, it was the teeth in his neck that subdued him, chomping toward his artery, wet tongue sucking. For one pained second, he was too dazed to move, burning up, dying, awakening, burning some more. Then he snapped into focus—win, had to win—and used his elbow to crack the fiend's ribs.

It didn't budge.

Of course, his companions just had to comment.

Wow. Are you out of practice or what? Caleb said.

Laid low by a toe tag, Julian scoffed. *You should be embarrassed.*

Do you want to be dinner? Elijah added.

"Guys," he gritted out, his struggles increasing. He managed to roll to his back. "Please. I'm fighting here."

I wouldn't exactly call this fighting, Caleb replied. *More like being spanked like a girl.*

Hey! I take exception to that.

Sorry, Eve.

"Don't worry. I've got this."

Guess we'll see about that, Elijah said grimly.

Aden tried to squeeze the creature's neck but it kept moving, kept pulling from his grip. "Be still," he commanded as he punched it in the cheek with so much force that what was left of its brains rattled—but that didn't weaken it. Actually, the action might have strengthened it. Aden had to anchor both of his hands against its jaw to prevent it from swooping in for another bite.

"You, more than anyone, know this isn't the way I'm going to die." The words were broken with the force of his panting breaths.

About six months ago, Elijah had predicted his death. They didn't know when it would happen, only that it would. And it wouldn't be in a cemetery and his killer wouldn't be a corpse. No, he would die on a deserted street, a knife in his heart, the tip cutting the organ every time it beat, until life slipped from him completely.

The dire prediction had come the same day he was told he was being sent to the D and M Ranch just as soon as there was an opening. Maybe that should have deterred him from moving here. But...

At the same time, he'd begun having visions of a dark-haired girl. Of talking and laughing with her...of kissing her. Never before had Elijah foretold anything other than a death, so Aden had been shocked to know—or rather, hope—the girl would one day enter his life. Shocked but excited. He wanted to meet her for real. Was desperate to meet her, actually. Even if that meant coming to the city of his death.

A death that would happen all too soon, he knew. In the vision, he hadn't looked much older than he was now. He'd had time to mourn his own passing, though, and had even had time to accept his fate. Sometimes, like now, part of him even looked forward to it. That didn't mean he'd roll over and take whatever the undead wanted to dish.

Something stung his cheek and he blinked into focus. Unable to get its yellowed teeth within range, the corpse was now clawing at him, nails cutting deep. That's what he got for allowing another distraction.

You've got this? Really? Well, prove it, Julian said, the challenge probably meant to strengthen him.

Roaring, Aden reached for one of his fallen blades. Just as the corpse broke free from his hold, he slashed forward. The blade slid through bone…and caught. Useless.

There was no time to panic. Hungry and oblivious to pain, his opponent made another play for his throat.

Aden threw another punch. There was a growl, another baring of teeth, and a stream of that thick, black saliva seeped from the corpse's mouth onto his cheek, causing his skin to sizzle. He struggled, gagging at the fetid smell.

When a long, wet tongue emerged, inching toward Aden's face, he once again grabbed the corpse by the jaw, fending it off while reaching for his other knife. Mere seconds after his fingers curled around the hilt, he began sawing at its neck.

Crack.

Finally, the head detached from the body and fell to the ground with a thud. The bones and tattered clothing, however, collapsed on top of *him.* Grimacing, he swiped them off and scrambled to a clean patch of grass.

"There. Proven." He, too, crumpled.

That's our boy, Caleb said proudly.

Yes, but now isn't the time for rest, Eve added, and she was right.

"I know." He had to clean up the mess or someone would stumble upon the desecrated remains. News stations would swarm the place like flies, begging the entire town to help locate the evil, twisted person responsible. Plus, others were going to rise whether he stayed here or not. He needed to be ready for them. But as he lay there, squinting up at the sky, hurting, the sun glared down at him, draining what little energy he had left.

By the end of the day, the saliva's poison would have worked through his system and he'd be hunched over a toilet, his cornflakes nothing but a fond memory. He'd sweat profusely from fever, shake uncontrollably and pray for death. Here, now, though, he had a moment's respite. It was what he'd been searching for all day.

Up and at 'em, sweetheart, Eve urged.

"I will, I promise. In a minute." Aden didn't know his real mother, his parents having signed him over to the state at the age of three, so he liked—sometimes—that Eve tried to fill the role. Actually, he loved her for it. He did. He loved all four of the souls, in fact. Even Julian, the corpse whisperer. But every other kid in the world could walk away from their families for a little "me" time. They could do things other sixteen-year-old boys were doing. Things like...well, *things.* They could date and attend school and play sports. Have fun.

Not Aden. Never Aden.

Whatever he did, wherever he went, he had an audience. An audience that liked to comment and critique and offer suggestions. *Next time do this. Next time do that. Idiot, you shouldn't have done that.*

They meant well, he knew they did, but Aden hadn't even

kissed a girl yet. And no, the beautiful brunette from Elijah's visions didn't count. No matter how real those visions felt. But God, when was she going to arrive? Would she?

Only yesterday, he'd had another vision of her. They had been standing in a forest, the moon high and golden. She'd thrown her arms around him and hugged him tight, her warm breath stroking his neck.

"I'll protect you," she'd said. "I'll always protect you."

From what? he'd wondered ever since. Not corpses, obviously.

He drew in a breath, then grimaced. Hello, stinky. The scent of rot seemed glued to the inside of his nose. Probably was. He'd have to scrub himself with a Brillo pad from head to toe.

He released the dagger he still held and wiped his hands on his jeans, leaving streaks of that poisonous goo. "What a life, huh?"

If you want to get technical, this really isn't our fault, Julian said, obviously no longer willing to shoulder the blame. *You're the one who absorbed us into that fat skull of yours.*

Aden ground his teeth. It seemed like he received a similar reminder a thousand times a day. "I've told you. I didn't absorb you."

You did something, 'cause we sure didn't get bodies of our own. Nooo. We got stuck with yours. And no control button!

"FYI, I was born with you already swimming in my mind." He thought so, at least. They'd always been with him. "It's not like I could stop what happened. Whatever happened. Even you don't know."

Just once he'd like a flash of total peace. No voices in his head, no dead rising to eat him—or any of the other unnatural things he had to deal with on a daily basis.

Things like Julian waking the dead and Elijah predicting the death of anyone who passed him. Things like Eve whisking him to the past, into a younger version of himself. One wrong move, one wrong word, and he would change his future. Not always for the better. Things like Caleb forcing him to possess someone else's body with only a touch.

Just one of those abilities would have set him apart. But all four? He was in a different stratosphere. Something no one, especially the boys at the ranch, let him forget.

But despite the fact that he didn't get along with them, he wasn't ready to be sent away so soon.

Dan Reeves, the guy who ran the D and M, wasn't too bad a guy. He was a former pro-football player who had given up the game because of a back injury, but he hadn't given up the disciplined, by-the-book way of life. Aden liked Dan, even though Dan didn't understand what it was like to have voices chattering inside his head and vying for attention he couldn't hope to give. Even though Dan thought Aden needed to spend his time reading, interacting with others or pondering his future rather than "rocking out and roaming." If he only knew.

Uh, Aden? Julian said, bringing him back to the present.

"What?" he snapped. His good mood must have died with the corpse. He was tired, sore, and knew things were only going to get worse.

Just another day in the life of Aden Stone, he thought with a bitter laugh.

Hate to be the one to tell you this, but...there's more.

"What?" Even as he spoke, he heard the shattering of another tombstone. Then another.

Others were indeed rising.

He pried his eyelids apart. For a moment, only a moment, he didn't breathe. Just pretended he was an ordinary guy whose only concern was what to buy his girlfriend for her birthday.

Where *was* the brunette? he wondered. When was her birthday?

Aden, honey, Eve said. *You still with us?*

"Still here." For him, concentrating was the equivalent of counting to infinity, and Eve knew that. "I hate this. I'm at the edge, and I'm either going to jump myself or kick someone in the—"

Language, Aden, Eve said with a *tsk.*

He sighed. "Kick someone in the butt and force *them* to fall," he finished properly.

I'd leave you if I could, but I'm stuck, Julian said, solemn.

"I know." His stomach protested and his neck wounds burned from strain as he pulled himself to a crouch. The pain didn't slow him; it, too, angered him and that anger gave him strength. He saw four sets of hands breaking through the dirt, uprooting grass and the colorful bouquets left by loved ones.

He swiped up one of his daggers. The other was still embedded in the first corpse's neck, and he had to jimmy it free. He might have been hesitant to battle in the beginning, but he was mad enough now to sprint in swinging this time.

Besides, there was only one way to handle four at a time... Eyes narrowing, he dashed to the corpse closest to him. The top of its head had just emerged. It was completely bald, no skin remaining. A living skeleton, the kind of thing nightmares were made of.

You can do it, Eve cheered.

Arm up...back...waiting...waiting... Finally, its shoulders came into sight, giving Aden the canvas he needed to work his magic. He struck, in one fluid motion rendering the dead...dead. Again.

"I'm sorry," he whispered. Not that it could hear him. Made him feel better to say it, though.

One down, Julian said.

Aden was already running to the next grave. He didn't slow when he reached it, just raised his arm and slashed.

"I'm sorry," he said again as this newest corpse fell, head one way, body the other, its bones separating on impact.

That's the way, Elijah praised.

Instinct was finally kicking in. His hands were soaked, sweat pouring from his face and chest, and as he hurried to the third, battered grave, pride blended with his guilt and sadness. Feral red eyes watched him.

We should be paid for this stuff, Caleb said, every word dripping with excitement. Clearly, he was hot. Again.

A growl sounded behind Aden a split second before a skeletal weight landed on his back and sharp teeth sank into his shoulder, ripping through shirt and skin and hitting muscle. Stupid, stupid! He'd missed one.

He groaned, propelled to the ground. Another bite, more poison. Later, more pain.

He reached over his shoulder, grabbed the fiend by the clavicle and jerked. Rather than tug the carcass off him, his hand wrenched away with a piece of lace and bone. A woman this time. *Don't think about that.* He'd hesitate, and that hesitation would cost him.

Those sharp teeth latched onto his ear, drawing blood.

He pressed his lips together to cut off his shout. God, that hurt. Reaching back once more, he managed to grip its neck this time. But just before he jerked, the corpse fell to the ground, motionless, and all four voices inside his head began screaming as if in pain, then fading…fading…silent.

Frowning in confusion, Aden quickly shimmied out from under the lifeless body and jackknifed to his feet. His neck, shoulder and ear throbbed and burned as he whirled around and looked down.

The corpse didn't move. Its head was still attached, but it didn't freaking move.

He spun in a circle, gaze roving, cataloging, searching. The other corpse, the one he'd been racing for, had fallen, too, despite the fact that it, too, still possessed its head, and now remained immobile. Even the light in its eyes had died.

O-kay. What the hell had just happened?

Oddly, none of his companions had a smart-ass comment.

"Guys?" he said.

Still no response.

"Why were you—" His words trailed off. In the distance, he caught a glimpse of a young girl and forgot about everything else. She was dressed in a white T-shirt streaked with dirt, faded jeans and tennis shoes, strolling just in front of the cemetery. She was tall and thin with straight brown hair anchored in a ponytail, tanned skin and a pretty—very pretty—face. She had earbuds in her ears and seemed to be singing.

All that dark hair…was she…could she be the girl from Elijah's visions?

Aden stood in place, covered in mud and grime, confused, excited, and trying not to panic. If she spotted him and the carnage surrounding him, she'd shriek. People would come gunning for him. They'd track him, wherever he went. They always tracked him. As he'd feared, he'd be sent away and the kinda sorta freedom he now had would be a thing of the past.

Don't look, don't look, please don't look. The prayer was his own, the souls still strangely quiet. And yet, part of him *did* want her to look, to see him, to be as intrigued by him as he was by her. If she *was* the girl he'd seen in those visions… finally…

She was almost past him. Would soon disappear around the corner. And then, as if she sensed his secret desire, she threw a glance over her shoulder. Aden tensed, catching a glimpse of big hazel eyes and pink lips she couldn't stop chewing.

She scanned the area.

A second later, their gazes met. There was a blast of sound as the world suddenly zoomed in on them—and then nothing.

There were no movements. Not their heartbeats, not even their lungs filling with air. There was no yesterday or tomorrow, only here and now.

They were the only two people who existed.

This was peace, Aden thought with shock. True peace. Calm and quiet, no voices in his head, pressing him down, pulling him under, vying for his attention.

Then, everything exploded. There was another blast of sound, as if the world's focus expanded this time. Cars started back up, birds began chirping and wind whistled through the trees. A sharp gust of it slammed into him and tossed him backward. He landed with a thump, chin jarring his sternum.

That same wind must have hit her, because she stumbled to her butt with a yelp.

There was a twinge of sickness in his stomach, and as he stood his limbs hung loose and heavy. A need to run to her filled him—followed quickly by a need to run *from* her.

She scrambled upright. After another silent glance, she turned away and rushed down the pass, soon disappearing from view.

The moment Aden lost sight of her, everything returned to normal.

Caleb growled, *What the hell?*

Pain. Darkness, Eve said, voice trembling. *Horrible.*

They'd been hurt? How could souls with no bodies feel pain? "What do you mean?" he asked them, though he suspected part of the answer. The girl. Somehow, some way. That odd stillness when their eyes first met…that strange gust of wind…

She'd approached and the dead had fallen. The voices

inside his head had faded. She'd looked at him and a peace he'd only dreamed about had encompassed him. She'd left and boom, everything had kicked back to terrible life.

He had to experience that peace again. Could she really be responsible? Was she the one he'd been waiting for?

Fearing the corpses would rise again, he hurriedly removed the heads of the remaining two. But rather than clean the mess, hiding the evidence of what had happened, he found himself gathering his backpack and chasing after her. There was only one way to find out whether she'd done what he thought she'd done. Only one way to find out who exactly she was.

Dude, tell us what happened before I start screaming, Julian said.

"I don't know what happened. Not exactly." Truth. He was determined to find out, though. "Are you okay?"

Multiple shouts of *No!* rang out.

Go back to the house. I have a bad feeling about this, Elijah said, sounding more afraid than Aden had ever heard him.

Aden slowed. Elijah'd had "bad feelings" before, and while they hadn't been actual predictions, Aden had always heeded them. But what if this was his one and only chance to meet the brunette from those visions?

"I'll be careful. I swear," he said.

Aden spotted the girl a block from the cemetery. Once again a strong wind jolted him, sickness seeped into his stomach, and then the world around him became all that he'd ever dreamed. Silent, his thoughts his own.

Dear Lord. She *was* responsible.

His palms began to sweat. She rounded a corner, heading into a busy intersection. He stuffed his hands into his backpack and dug out his wet wipes, quickening his step and cleaning his face as best he could. He withdrew a clean shirt and stepped into the shadows, then changed, never taking his gaze from the girl.

Would she run screaming if he approached her? Bones had been piled around him, after all.

He waited for his companions to toss out answers, but all remained quiet. It was odd, not having someone tell him what to do, how to do it, or how badly things would end. Odd and strangely agonizing, when he'd thought for years it would be freakishly cool.

For the first time in his life, he was truly on his own. If he messed this up, he'd have no one but himself to blame.

He squared his shoulders and prepared to approach the girl.

+WO

MARY ANN GRAY SPOTTED her friend and neighbor, Penny Parks, and raced toward the outdoor café. "I'm here, I'm here," she said, pulling the plugs from her ears, Evanescence fading. She stuffed her iPod in her purse, gave her Sidekick a quick check—only one e-mail from her dad asking what she wanted for dinner. Replying could wait.

Penny *tsked* under her tongue as she handed Mary Ann a capped mocha. "Just in time. You missed the raging power outage. I was inside and all the lights flicked off. No one could get cell reception, and I heard a lady say that all the cars on the road died."

"There was an outage that caused *cars* to die?" Weird. Then again, it had been a day for weirdness. Like that boy she'd seen in the cemetery on her way here, who'd somehow caused her to fall—without touching her!

"Are you listening to me?" Penny asked. "Your face totally

blanked. Anyway, like I was saying. The outage happened about fifteen minutes ago."

The exact time she'd been at the cemetery, iPod momentarily silent, unexpected wind blowing. Huh.

"So what took you so long?" Penny asked. "I had to order on my own, and you know that's not good for my codependency."

They plopped into the chairs Penny had been saving for them, the sun shining brightly on their table. Mary Ann inhaled deeply, the scents of coffee, whipped cream and vanilla flooding her. God, she loved Holy Grounds. People might approach the stand frowning, but they always emerged with a grin.

As if to prove her point, an older couple walked away from the register, smiling at each other over the rims of their cups. Mary Ann had to look away. Once, her parents had been like that, happy just to be with each other. Then her mother had died.

"Drink, drink," Penny said. "And while you're savoring, tell me what held you up."

Mouth watering, she sipped at her grande white chocolate mocha. Ah, de-freaking-licious. "Like I said, I'm sorry I'm late. I really am. But sadly, my tardiness isn't the worst of it."

"Oh, no." Expression pinched, Penny fell back in her chair. "What's going on? Don't break it to me gently. Just rip the Band-Aid."

"Okay. Here goes." Deep breath. "I'm not actually done for the day. This is only a thirty-minute break. I have to return to work." She cringed, waiting for the shouted—

"What!"

And there it was. A small infraction, really, but Penny would see it as a grave offense. She always did. She was a high-maintenance friend who expected their time together to be uninterrupted. Mary Ann didn't mind. Really. She actually admired the trait. Penny knew what she wanted from the people in her life and expected it to be given to her. And it usually was. Without complaint. Today, however, couldn't be helped.

"The Watering Pot is providing the floral arrangements for the Tolbert-Floyd wedding tomorrow and all of the employees have to work overtime."

"Ugh." Penny shook her head in disappointment. Or was that disapproval? "When are you going to quit your loser job at that flower shop? It's Saturday, and you're young. You should be shopping with me as planned rather than slaving over thorns and potting soil."

Mary Ann studied her friend over the rim of her cup. Penny was a year older than her, with platinum hair, bright blue eyes and pale freckled skin. She liked to pair lacy baby-doll dresses with flip-flops no matter the weather. She was carefree, experienced, had no thoughts for the future, dated who she wanted, when she wanted, and skipped school as often as she attended.

Mary Ann, on the other hand, would vomit blood if she even considered breaking a rule.

She knew why she was the way she was, but that just made her determination to be the "good girl" worse. She and her dad only had each other, and she hated to disappoint him. Which made her friendship with Penny all the stranger, since her dad (silently) objected. But she and Penny had been neighbors for years, had even attended the same preschool when they'd lived miles away from each other. Despite their differences, they had never stopped hanging out. Never would.

Penny was addicting. You didn't walk away from her without wishing you were still with her. Something about her smile, maybe. When she flashed it, you felt as if all the stars had aligned and nothing bad could happen to you. Well, girls felt that way. Boys caught a glimpse of it and had to wipe away their drool.

"Could you please, please, please call in sick?" Penny begged. "A little dose of Mary isn't going to be enough."

When she flashed that smile this time, Mary Ann steeled herself against it. "You know I'm saving for college. I *have* to work." Only on the weekends, though. That's all her dad would allow. Weekdays were devoted to homework.

Penny traced a perfectly manicured fingertip over the rim of her espresso. "Your dad should pay for your education. He can afford it."

"But that wouldn't teach me responsibility or the value of a hard-earned dollar."

"God, you're quoting him now." A shudder rocked Penny's petite frame as she grimaced. "Way to ruin my mood."

A laugh escaped Mary Ann. "If he paid my way, he'd be screwing with my fifteen-year plan. And no one screws with my fifteen-year plan and lives to tell about it. Not even my dad."

"Oh, yeah. The fifteen-year plan I can't get you to rethink no matter what temptation I throw your way." Penny anchored a strand of hair behind her ear, revealing three silver hoops.

"Graduate high school, two years. Bachelors, four. Masters and Ph.D., seven. Intern, one. Open your own practice, one. I don't know what I'm doing tonight, much less in fifteen years."

"I can guess what you'll be doing tonight. Or rather, who. Grant Harrison." The pair had been on and off for six months. Currently they were off, but that didn't stop them from hooking up. "Besides, there's nothing wrong with a little preparation."

"Little. Ha! I suspect you have your life mapped out to the second. You probably even know what underwear you'll be wearing in three years, five hours, two minutes and eight seconds."

"A black lace thong," Mary Ann responded without hesitation.

That gave Penny a moment of pause. Then she chuckled. "Almost had me, but the thong gave you away. You're cotton briefs, baby, all the way."

And all that coverage was a bad thing? "Honestly, I don't have *everything* planned. Not even I'm that anal."

"You said anal." Penny snickered. "Look, I've known you most of your life, and asking people about their feelings wasn't always what Mary Contrary wanted to do when she grew up. She wanted to dance a ballet to a packed house, kiss whichever celebrity she was crushing on and tattoo her entire body with flowers so she'd look like a garden. You didn't decide to become a shrink until after your mom—" Realizing she'd taken a wrong turn at Foot In Mouth Lane, she finished with, "You just didn't!"

Slowly Mary Ann's smile faded. Deep down, she wasn't sure she could refute her friend's claim. She *had* been a rambunctious girl at one time, giving her parents fits, talking and laughing too loudly, always desperate to be the center of attention and throwing tantrums when she didn't get her way. Then her mom had died in a car accident. A car accident Mary Ann had been part of, as well. She'd spent three weeks recovering in the hospital. Her body had healed, yes, but not her soul.

Upon her release, the Gray household had fallen into a spiral of sadness, Mary Ann and her father whirling further and further away from the loving if combative family they'd once been. Over time, that sadness had bonded her and her dad. He'd become her best friend, making him proud her biggest goal.

When she'd told him she thought she might like to be a clinical psychologist like him, he'd smiled as if he'd just won the lottery. He'd hugged her. Spun her around, and laughed for the first time in months. No way she could've chosen a different path after that. No matter how much she hated studying. Still. Now she couldn't imagine herself being anything other than a doctor of the mind. And for Penny to give her grief about it, well…

"Let's talk about something else," she said stiffly.

"Great. I've pissed you off, haven't I?"

"No." Yes. Maybe. Usually, they stayed away from the topic of her mother. Though several years had passed, the memories were sometimes too fresh, too raw. "I'd just prefer it if you looked out for *your* future, not mine."

Penny sighed loud and long. "I shouldn't have gone there, and I'm sorry. It's just, all work and no play makes Mary a dull girl, and I want my sparkly girl back." When Mary Ann offered no reply, Penny reached out and squeezed her hand. "Come on, Mary Contrary. I can still see the hurt. Forgive me. Please. We've only got, what? Fifteen minutes left, and I don't want to spend it fighting with you. I love you more than anything or anyone and you know I'd cut off my leg and kick my own ass if I could. Maybe even cut out my tongue and nail it to your bedroom wall. And then I'd—"

"Okay, okay." She laughed, the silly images her friend's words evoked soothing her. "You're forgiven."

"Thank God. But seriously, girl. You really made me work for that one, and you know how I hate to work for *anything*." Grinning that irresistible grin of hers, Penny dug a pack of ultrathins and a lighter from her beaded purse. She lit up, inhaling deeply. Soon a thick haze of smoke surrounded them and Penny was reclining in her chair, legs extended. "So what do you want to talk about? Girls we hate? Boys we love?"

Mary Ann cradled her mocha against her chest, leaning back as far as she could go. "Why don't we discuss the fact that smoking kills?"

"No need. I'm indestructible."

"You wish," she said with a grin. But her amusement faded as a short but forceful gust of wind nailed her in the chest. She rubbed the spot just above her heart and gazed around.

That stray wind hadn't seemed to affect anyone else.

Only one other time had she ever felt such a strong kick. Her stomach began to churn.

"If you won't put the cigarette out for you, then put it out for me," she said. "I don't want to return to work smelling like an ashtray."

"I have a feeling your roses will love you, anyway," her friend said dryly and took another drag. "Take pity on me. I've been stressed and I need this." As she spoke, she flicked the ashes on the pavement, attention wandering.

"What have you been stres—"

"Oh, oh, oh. Boy. Three o'clock. He just sat down at the table across from ours. Dark hair, movie-star face and muscles. Dear God, the muscles. Best part, he's totally scoping you. Best part for you, that is. Why isn't he scoping me, too?"

Mary Ann's heart immediately soared into hyperspeed. First that strange wind, and then a dark-haired boy nearby? *Please be a coincidence.* Leaning forward, shielding her mouth with her hand, she whispered, "Is he dirty?"

"You mean, perverted? I don't know, but I'm willing to find out. He's hawt!"

"No. I mean dirty, as in mud and some kind of black gunk all over him? Like motor oil? Are his clothes ripped?"

"His face is dirty, yes. Well, kind of. It's smeared, like he tried to clean up. But his shirt is clean and oh, so perfect. God, his hair is dyed black but the roots are blond. I wonder if he has a tattoo? That's sexy. How old do you think he is? Eighteen? He's tall enough to be legal. And oh, my God, he just looked at me! I think I'm going to faint."

Besides the shirt, the description fit. Maybe he'd changed.

An emotion she couldn't name skittered through her. That he might be here…

She'd meant to stop by her mother's grave before meeting Penny. It was along the way, after all. But she'd taken one look at the boy, experienced that strange gust of wind, and had only wanted to escape.

"I saw him earlier," she said. "I think…do you think he followed me?"

Eyes widening, Penny shifted in her seat and unabashedly peered over at him. "Probably. A stalker, do you think? God, that's even sexier!"

"Don't stare!" she gasped, slapping her friend's arm.

Unhurried and unrepentant, Penny faced her. "Well, I don't care if he's the Tri City Butcher and keeps human hearts in his locker. The more I look at him, the more I like him. Very—" she shivered "—bad-boy chic. I might *offer* him my heart."

Bad boy. Yes, that fit, too. Mary Ann didn't have to turn to remind herself of what he looked like. His image was burned into her mind. As Penny had said, he had black hair with inch-long blond roots. What she hadn't mentioned was that his face was as perfect as the Grecian statues she'd seen in her world history book, even with the grime. For the briefest of moments, when a beam of sunlight had hit him, Mary Ann would have sworn his eyes were striped with green, brown, blue and gold. But then the ray had disappeared beyond a fluff of clouds and the colors had melted into each other, leaving only an intense black.

The color didn't matter, though. Those eyes were feral, wild, and she'd felt that undeniable shock of wind—bizarre wind that had ended as quickly as it had begun. For a moment, she'd felt hooked to a generator, the eye contact jolting her, unnerving her. Even hurting her. That's when the nausea had begun.

Why had she experienced all that again just now, albeit in a muted way? *Before* she'd seen him even? Why had she felt any of it at all? This made no sense. Who was he?

"Let's pick him up," Penny said, excited.

"Let's not," she replied. "I have a boyfriend."

"No, you have a horny jock who sticks around because he's desperate to get in your pants even though you keep saying no. Which, by the way, is a guarantee he's knocking it with someone else every time your back is turned."

There was something in her tone…Mary Ann pushed the boy from the graveyard out of her mind—best that way—and frowned over at her friend. "Wait. Have you heard something?"

Heavy pause. Another drag. Then a nervous laugh. "No. No, of course not." Penny waved a dismissive hand through the air. "And anyway, I don't want to talk about Tucker. I want to talk about the fact that you and this Mystery Guy should totally hook up. You like him, I can tell. Your cheeks are flushed and your hands are shaking."

"I'm probably coming down with a cold." Was it bad that she hoped her words were true? When a girl couldn't get a boy out of her mind, she, well, couldn't get him out of her mind. Schoolwork was forgotten. Goals were abandoned. The brain became mush. She'd seen it happen, time and time again. She wouldn't let it happen to her.

That's one of the reasons she dated Tucker. He was safe. Cute and popular, but safe. He was busy with football and didn't mind how often she skipped out on him to work or study.

"Don't be a prude. Give me permission, and I'll call him over here. I'll have his digits in five flat, and you guys can go out. I won't tell Tucker, I swear."

"No. No, no, no!" She shook her head for emphasis, ponytail slapping her cheeks. "One, I would never cheat on Tucker."

Penny rolled her eyes. "So break up with him."

"And two," she said, ignoring her friend's remark, "I don't have time to juggle another boy. Even as a friend. Grades have never been more important. SATs are coming up."

"You have straight As. And you'll nail the SATs, guaranteed."

"I want to keep the As, and the only way I'll nail the SATs is if I stay the course. You know that stuff doesn't come easily for me."

"Fine. But when you die from stress and disappointment, you'll think back to this moment and wish to God you'd taken me up on my offer." Penny splayed her arms and peered heavenward. "Who would have thought I'd be the smart one in this relationship?"

Now Mary Ann was the one to roll her eyes. "If you're the smart one, what does that make me?"

"The dull, pretty one." Penny grinned, but for once the expression lacked its usual dazzle. "You can't help it, I suppose. What with the psychobabble your dad is always feeding you.

There's good in everyone, blah, blah, blah. I'm telling you, Mar, some people are as worthless as an empty bottle of beer and Tucker is one…of…them." The last was said on an excited gust of breath. "Swweet! I didn't have to do anything and he's coming over! Yep, you heard me right. Your stalker is coming over here!"

Mary Ann turned before she could stop herself. It *was* the boy from the graveyard. She barely hid her grimace as another of those jolts swept through her, burning her like acid.

At least the world didn't seem to implode on itself this time, leaving her with a strange sense of nothingness.

Steadier now, she studied him. His jeans were ripped but he had indeed changed his shirt. This one was clean and free of holes. His face was just as perfect as she remembered, too flawless to be real. He had thick black lashes that perfectly framed his eyes. Perfectly sculpted cheekbones that surrounded a perfectly sloped nose. Perfectly shaped lips, now dipped into a frown.

This close, she realized he was taller than she'd assumed. If they stood next to each other, he would tower over her. His features were tight with determination.

One step, two, he hesitantly approached. When he reached them, he stopped and dropped his backpack at his feet.

Mary Ann tensed and her mouth dried. What would she do if he asked her out? Tucker was her first and only boyfriend. The first and only guy to ask her out, really, so she'd never had to turn someone down before. Not that this boy wanted to ask her out. *Please don't ask me out.*

Aren't you an egotistical one? Most boys want your study notes, not your body. Oh, yeah.

"This day couldn't get any better," Penny said, clapping.

He waved shyly. "Hi," he said. Then he frowned and rubbed at his chest, just as she had done a bit ago. His gaze narrowed, and he glanced all around them.

"Hi," Mary Ann said, dropping her focus to the iron tabletop. Her tongue suddenly felt huge and glued to the roof of her mouth. Worse, her brain seemed to have taken a vacation and she couldn't think of anything else to say.

Awkward silence bloomed between them.

Penny released a heavy sigh. "Fine. Allow me. Her name's Mary Ann Gray, and she's a junior at Crossroads High School. I'll give you her phone number if you ask nicely."

"Penny." Mary Ann slapped her friend's shoulder.

Penny ignored her. "What's your name? And where do you go to school?" she asked the boy. "Wild Horse?" Disgust dripped from her tone.

"I'm Aden. Aden Stone. I just moved here. And I don't go to public school." Pause. "Yet. But what's wrong with Wild Horse?"

His voice was deep and oddly shiver-inducing. She forced herself to focus on his words, though, rather than his tone. He'd said he didn't go to public school. Did that mean he attended private school? Or that he was homeschooled?

"Hello, it's only our biggest rival and home of the worst humans on earth." Penny kicked out a chair. "But since you don't go there, would you like to join us, Aden Stone?"

"Oh, I—I—if you wouldn't mind?" The question was directed at Mary Ann.

Before she could reply—not that she'd known what to say—Penny preened and replied, "Of course she wouldn't mind. She was just telling me she hoped you'd join us. Sit, sit. Tell us about yourself."

Slowly Aden inched into the chair, as though he feared having it shoved out from under him. The sun stroked him lovingly, practically worshipping his beautiful face. And for a moment, only a moment, Mary Ann saw those different hues in his eyes again. Green, blue, gold and brown. Amazing. But as quickly as they appeared, they vanished, leaving that blazing onyx.

The scent of pine and newborn baby drifted from him. Why a baby? From a wet wipe, maybe? Anyway, dirty as he was, she would have expected a more unpleasant odor. Instead, the sweet smell reminded her of something…of someone. Who, she couldn't place. She just knew she had a sudden urge to hug him.

Hug him?

From attraction to curiosity to distaste to affection? Seriously, what was wrong with her? And what would Tucker say? She'd never flirted with other boys—not that she was flirting now—so she had no idea how Tucker would react if she did. He might be a piranha on the football field, but he'd always been nice to her.

"I was wondering…I saw you outside the cemetery," Aden said to Mary Ann. "Do you, uh…did you…notice anything that disturbed you?"

So hesitant, he was. It was kind of cute. Sweet, too. The urge to hug him increased. But she merely blinked over at him, unsure she'd heard him correctly. Had he felt that bizarre wind, too? "Like what?"

"Never mind." Slowly he grinned, and it was a grin that not only rivaled Penny's, but surpassed it.

Guess he hadn't, she thought. "Were you visiting a loved one there?"

"Uh, no. I, uh, work there. Just so you know, news stations will probably be blasting stories about the desecration of several graves soon. I was…cleaning things up."

Was her mother's grave okay? It had better be!

"How wonderfully morbid." Penny blew a puff of smoke in his direction. "Are you ever tempted to do a little digging and steal a little bling?"

To his credit, he didn't cough or flinch. "Never," he said, turning to shield his face as a pudgy man walked by their table.

Hiding? Maybe that was his boss and he wasn't supposed to be on break.

She studied him, wondering what he— Her gaze caught on the bruise on his neck and she gasped. "Oh, ouch! What happened to you?" There were two puncture wounds, both a mix of blue and black. Teeth marks, she realized then, and blushed. He could have gotten them from a girl. Probably had. "Never mind. That's personal. You don't have to answer that."

He didn't. He covered the wounds with his hand, his own cheeks heating.

"Great, two prudes at one table." Penny released a long-suffering sigh. "So what do you do for fun, Aden? Where do you go to school, if not public? And do you have a girlfriend? I'm assuming the answer is yes, since you've been nibbled on, but I'm hoping you'll tell us it's about to end."

His attention returned to Mary Ann. "I'm more curious about Mary Ann. Why don't we talk about her?"

Way to dodge the questions, she thought.

"Yes, Mary Ann." Penny rested her elbows on the table, expression mockingly rapt. "Tell us about your *exciting* fifteen-year plan."

Mary Ann knew what her friend was doing: trying to force her to voice her supposed dullness so that she'd realize she needed excitement. How many times had Mary Ann told her that admitting a problem was the first step to fixing it? Penny must have been listening because, for once, *she* was acting as the shrink. "Another word out of you and I'm going to take you up on your earlier offer. Your tongue will look nice above my bed."

Palms up and out, Penny projected her innocence. "Just trying to lighten the mood, sugar." Grinning, she dropped her cigarette to the concrete and smashed it with her foot. "Maybe the only way to do that is to leave. You two can get to know each other."

"No," Mary Ann rushed out when her friend stood. "Stay."

"Nah. I'll just cause more trouble."

Aden watched the exchange, head zinging back and forth between them, expression bemused.

"You won't." Mary Ann gripped Penny's wrist and tugged her back into the chair. "You'll—" A thought occurred to her and she gasped. "Oh, no. What time is it?" She set her mocha on the tabletop, pulled her cell from her pocket and glanced at the clock. Just as she'd feared. "I've got to go." If she didn't hurry, she wouldn't make it back to the Watering Pot in time.

"I'll walk you wherever you're going. I don't mind." Aden jumped up so quickly, his chair skidded behind him and knocked into a man who'd been walking past. "Sorry," he muttered.

"I'm in a mad rush, so I…I think I should go on my own. I'm sorry." Best this way, she told herself. Her blood was still burning in her veins, her stomach still clenching. She leaned forward and kissed Penny on the cheek before standing herself. "It was nice meeting you, though, Aden." Kind of.

"You, too." He sounded despondent.

She backed up a step, stopped. Backed up another step, a dark corner of her mind shouting for her to stay, despite everything.

Aden moved toward her, saying, "Can I call you? I would love to call you."

"I—" She opened her mouth to say yes. That dark corner wanted to see him again and figure out why she felt both pain and affection in his presence. The rest of her, the rational side of her nature, listed all the reasons to stay away from him: School. Grades. Tucker. Fifteen-year plan. Yet still she had to fight to work, "No, I'm sorry," out of her throat.

Whirling, she headed back to the Watering Pot, wondering if she'd just made a huge mistake. A mistake she would regret for the rest of her life, just as Penny had predicted.

✝HREE

ADEN WATCHED as Mary Ann walked away from him.

"Here's her number. If you still want to call her, that is, considering her rudeness," the girl named Penny said, sliding a piece of paper toward Aden. "The second number is mine. In case you decide you want someone a little more available." Then she, too, stood and walked away from him.

"Thank you," he called. He grinned as he stuffed the paper into his pocket. The grin didn't last long, however. He didn't know a lot about girls, but he knew that he'd made Mary Ann Gray uncomfortable. Knew she'd wanted nothing to do with him.

Had she sensed how different he was? He hoped not, because that would make convincing her to spend time with him impossible. And he had to spend more time with her. Had to talk to her, to get to know her. She really was responsible for his newfound sense of peace.

It was strange, too. The more time he'd spent in her presence, the more he'd had to fight the urge to run away from her. Which made absolutely no sense. Up close, she was even prettier than he'd realized, cheeks bright, eyes a mix of green and brown. She was smart, well able to hold her own against her friend. Any other guy would have wanted to date her, yet when they'd begun talking, he'd first experienced a wave of affection, as though he should be mussing her hair and teasing her about boyfriends. (As if he needed more proof that he was weird.) And second, that stupid desire to flee for his life.

He could think of no reason good enough to run from her. The moment he'd spotted her at the café, the voices had screamed again—he had hated that—then quieted again, and he had loved that.

How did she do it? Did she even know she did it? She hadn't seemed aware, her pretty face innocently unconcerned.

He hadn't decided yet if she was the girl in his visions or not. She certainly *looked* like her, but the thought of kissing her…he grimaced. It just felt wrong. So very wrong. Maybe, hopefully, after he got to know her, that would change.

He kicked into gear, heading home, careful to stay first on the sidewalk above the graveyard, and then the main roads. Twice he tripped over trash, stumbling forward, and every wound on his body throbbed.

Ugh, we're gonna hurt tonight, Caleb said.

Yep. Beyond the ache of the existing bruises, in a few hours, the poison would begin to break him down, chew him up and spit him out.

You're really starting to annoy me, Ad, Elijah suddenly

said. *I do* not *like the airstream or whatever it is that tosses us into that black hole.*

"Tell me about it. The black hole, I mean."

Dark, empty, silent. And just for the record, I'd like to know how you're doing it.

A girl. I caught a glimpse of her, Eve said.

Julian sputtered. *A girl? A dumb girl is sending us away? How?*

"Is she the one I've been dreaming about, Elijah?" Duh. He should have asked before.

Don't know. I didn't see her.

Oh.

Well, I did see her, and I'm positive I know her. There's something familiar about her. Eve paused, clearly thinking things over. She pushed out a frustrated breath. *I just can't place what, exactly, is familiar.*

The others never saw the images Elijah projected inside his head. Only Aden did. So Eve wouldn't have seen her in the visions. "We've only been here a few weeks and haven't left the ranch until today. We haven't met anyone but Dan and the other dregs." Dregs, his name for the other "wayward" teens at the D and M.

I swear. I know her. I do. Somehow. And she could have lived in any of the towns we've been sent to.

"You're righ—" Realizing that he could be caught talking to himself, Aden searched his surroundings, making sure no one was within hearing distance. He would have thought his replies, rather than speak them, but there was such a constant stream of noise in his head that the souls had trouble differentiating his words from everything else.

He was outside, the sun finally beginning to fall, the ranch on the horizon. It was a sprawling structure of dark red wood surrounded by windmills, an oil rig and a looming wrought-iron fence. Cows and horses grazed all around. Crickets chirped. A dog barked. It wasn't the kind of place he'd ever imagined living, and he was as far from a cowboy as a person could get, but he found that he liked the open spaces better than the crowded buildings in the city.

In the back was a barn, as well as a bunkhouse where he and the other dregs slept. Usually they could be found outside with their tutor, Mr. Sicamore, or baling hay, mowing and scooping manure into a wheelbarrow for fertilizer. The chores were meant to help them "learn the importance of hard work and responsibility." Only taught them to hate work, if you asked Aden.

Thankfully today was everyone's day off. As he strode past the gate, no one was out and about.

"You're right that she could have lived in a different town at the same time as me, though the odds of that are pretty bad. Still, I promise you, I never saw her, *really* saw her, until today," Aden said, picking up their conversation where they'd left off. If he and Mary Ann had crossed paths before, he would have experienced that sweet silence. That was not something he would have forgotten.

Caleb laughed, though there was a sharp edge to his amusement. *You keep your head down and your eyes averted every-*

where you go. You could have met your mother and you wouldn't have known it.

True. "But I've been shuffled from one mental institution to another, and even juvie, where no girls were allowed. This is the first time I've really been out in public, no matter what town I've been in. Where would I have met her?"

Eve's breathy sigh drifted through his head. *I don't know.*

I still think you should stay away from her, Elijah said solemnly.

"Why?" Had the psychic already divined Mary Ann's death and now hoped to save him from the heartache of her loss? Aden fought a rush of dread. When Elijah told him when and how someone was going to die, that someone died, exactly as Elijah had said. No exceptions. "Why?" he rasped again.

Just...because.

"Why!" he insisted, the question harsher than he'd intended. He needed a good reason or he'd be hunting her down at the first opportunity. Anything for another taste of that silence.

Well, I for one don't like how powerless I feel when you're around her, Julian said.

"Elijah?" Aden insisted.

I just don't like her, the psychic grumbled. *All right? Happy now?*

No impending death, then. Thank God.

Aden tripped as one of Dan's dogs, Sophia, a black-and-white Border collie, tangled around his ankles, barking for attention. He petted her head and she continued to dance around him. As he stood there, an idea took root in his mind. He didn't speak it, not yet. But he did say, "Well, I do like her, and I want—*need*—to spend more time with her."

Then you're going to have to find a way to set us free, Elijah said. *Any more time in that black hole and I'll go insane.*

"How?" They'd already tried a thousand different ways. Exorcism, spells, prayer. Nothing had worked. And with his own death looming, he was becoming desperate. Not just for the peace it would give him these last years—months? weeks?—of his life, but because he didn't want his only friends dying with him. He wanted them to have lives of their own. The lives they'd always craved.

Let's say we did find a way out. Eve paused. *We'd then need bodies, living bodies, or I fear we'll be as insubstantial as ghosts.*

True. But bodies aren't something we can order online, Julian said.

Aden will find a way, Caleb replied, confident.

Impossible, Aden wanted to say, but didn't. No reason to destroy their hope. When he reached the main house, he muttered, "We'll finish this conversation later," and meshed his lips together. All the lights were dimmed, no shuffling feet or banging pots echoing. Still. No telling who lurked where.

He knocked on the front door. Waited a while. Knocked again. Waited even longer. No one appeared. His shoulders sagged in disappointment. He really wanted to talk to Dan and put his as yet unspoken idea in motion.

Sighing, he made the trek to the bunkhouse. Sophia barked

and finally raced off. Inside, the warm but fresh breeze died, air thickening with dust. He'd shower, change, maybe grab a bite to eat, then head back to the house. If Dan wasn't back by then, he'd have to wait until next week to talk to him. He hadn't forgotten that the poison even now swimming through his veins was going to start pummeling him in the next few hours, at which point he'd be no good to anyone.

This was just the calm before the storm.

There was a murmur of voices in the background, and Aden tried to tiptoe to his room. But a floorboard creaked, and a second later, a familiar voice was calling, "Hey, schizo. C'mere."

He paused, staring at the fat wooden beams stretching across the ceiling and wondering if he should just sneak out. He and Ozzie had never gotten along. Maybe because every word out of the guy's mouth was an insult. But still. Any more fights, verbal or otherwise, and he'd be kicked out. He'd already been warned.

"Yo, schizo. Don't make me come after you."

A round of laughter.

So Ozzie's sheep were there, as well.

Leave. I can't deal with another upset today, Julian said.

Walk away and they'll think you're weak. The pronouncement came from Elijah, therefore had a greater chance of being true. *Then you'll never have a moment's peace.*

Wrong. Go to the woods and you can have peace right now, Caleb said. *Besides, you can't fight them in your condition.*

Just get it over with. Eve's determination made her voice

harsh. *Otherwise you'll worry about being ambushed all night. And sick as you'll be, you don't need that on your mind.*

Jaw clenched, he stalked to his room, tossed down his backpack and then crossed the hall into Ozzie's room.

You always listen to Eve, Julian whined.

Because he's smart, Eve said.

Because he's a teenager and you're a female, Caleb muttered.

You've never complained about my being female before.

When Aden appeared in the doorway, a grinning Ozzie looked him up and down. The grin soon became a sneer. "What have you been doing? Making out with the vacuum since no one's desperate enough to actually touch you? Or maybe you and one of your invisible friends hooked up. Was it a guy or a girl this time?"

The rest of the dregs snickered.

"It was a girl," Aden said. "She'd just left you, so she *was* desperate enough."

"Burned," the other dregs laughed.

Ozzie stilled. His eyes narrowed.

Ozzie had been here a little over a year, which was months longer than everyone else. From what Aden had gathered, he'd gotten busted for drugs and shoplifting on more than one occasion and his parents had finally washed their hands of him.

"I'm outta here," Aden said.

"Stay right there." Ozzie held up a half-smoked joint. His blond hair was spiked, as if he'd tangled his hands in it one too many times. "You're gonna take a drag. You need help with your crazy."

More laughter.

"No, thanks." He didn't need "drug use" added to his already-lengthy record.

"I wasn't asking you," Ozzie snapped. "Smoke. Now."

"No. Thanks." Aden studied the bedroom. It was a mirror image of his own. Plain white walls, a bunk bed with matching brown comforters on both the top and the bottom, a dresser and a desk. Nothing extra. No wall hangings or framed photos. To help them forget the past and concentrate on the future, Dan liked to say about the lack of frills. Aden suspected it was because dregs came and went so quickly.

"Come on, m-man. Just d-do it." Shannon, black and the biggest of them all, lounged on the pillows they'd strewn across the floor. His green eyes were red-rimmed, one of them swollen. From a recent fight? Probably. Usually, he would stutter, the dregs would make fun of him, and then he'd lash out. Why he still chose to hang with them, Aden didn't know. "Y-you could forget what a nut j-job you are."

Seth, Terry and Brian nodded in agreement. The three of them could have passed for brothers. Each had dark hair, dark eyes and similar boyish faces. Their individual styles set them apart, though. Seth colored thick red streaks in his hair and had a snake tattooed on the inside of one wrist. Terry wore his hair long and shaggy and dressed in baggy clothes. Brian was all smooth polish.

Saying no again was hard. Especially when it would help dull the pain he knew was coming. But he did it. If he got high, he'd forget more than who he was; he would forget about talking to Dan. And he had to talk to Dan. If Dan agreed to Aden's plan, Aden would get to see a lot more of Mary Ann.

With that kind of incentive, he'd give up anything, everything.

"Whatever, man." Ozzie's cheeks hollowed as he inhaled, and smoke wafted around his face. "I knew you were pathetic."

Do not react. "Where's Ryder?" The sixth member of their crew.

"Dan found a bag in his room—empty, of course, or he'd be out—and took him into town for drug testing," Seth said. "They'll be gone for hours. Hence the party."

"Parties are like cupcakes," Terry said with a grin.

Uh, what?

"No, parties are like peeing in a cup," Brian said and everyone burst into loud guffaws as if the funniest joke ever had just been dropped.

Had he been this stupid the few times he'd gotten high? Aden wondered.

A knock suddenly sounded at the front door, followed by a creak of hinges.

"We're back," Ryder called nervously. He must have known what they were doing.

"Gone for hours, huh?" Aden said.

Ozzie cursed and scrambled to hide the joint, tossing it inside a metal container. He slammed the lid over it to contain the smoke.

Seth grabbed a can of air freshener and sprayed in a circle. Terry tossed the pillows back onto the bed. Brian scrambled around, looking for a way out. And Shannon remained in

place, resting his head in his upraised hands. Then Ryder was
striding inside the room, red hair standing on end, lips peeled
back in a scowl.

Dan was right behind him. He stopped in the doorway
beside Aden, thumbs hooked in his belt loop, baseball cap low
on his head. Disapproval clouded his deeply tanned features
as he sniffed the air.

"I'm trying to save your lives, boys. You know that,
don't you?"

A few of the dregs gazed down at their feet in shame. Ozzie
just smirked. No one spoke.

"Finish cleaning up and then I want you to do something
useful. In fact, each of you will pick a book from the box I
gave you last week and read at least five chapters. You'll tell
me what you read tomorrow morning at breakfast."

Groans erupted.

"None of that, now." Dan studied each of their faces, one
by one. When he reached Aden, he blinked in surprise, as if
he hadn't realized Aden was there. "Let's take a walk," he said.
He didn't wait for Aden's reply, but pounded out of the bunkhouse, the door slamming shut behind him.

"Tell him where my stash is," Ozzie growled at him, "and
I'll cut your throat."

"Try," Aden said, and pivoted on his heel.

Did you have to antagonize him? Eve asked, clearly
frustrated.

"Yes." He didn't react well to threats.

Outside, clean air once again enveloped him, and he

breathed deeply. The sun had fallen some more, casting a gloomy haze around him. It was the perfect contrast to his suddenly bright mood. For the first time in perhaps forever, Aden was hopeful his life could change for the better.

Dan was a few feet ahead, strolling toward the north pasture, and Aden rushed to catch up with him. Even though Aden was just above six feet, Dan towered over him.

A few times over the past week, when Aden thought no one inside his head was paying attention, he'd pretended Dan was his dad. They certainly looked like they could be related. Both of them had pale hair (when Aden didn't dye his to stop the blond jokes), lips almost too full for a boy and square jaws. When he'd realized what he was doing, though, he'd forced himself to stop. Surprisingly, stopping had made him depressed.

What did his real father look like? Aden didn't have any pictures. Didn't even have memories of him. Only thing he knew about the man was that he'd given Aden up. Which meant, he, too, had considered Aden a freak. At least Dan didn't treat him like a mentally unstable child in need of confinement.

"Let's get to the heart of the matter, shall we?" Dan said when Aden reached him. He tipped his hat for a better view of the land. "What have you been up to today?"

Aden gulped. He'd expected the question, had even planned his answer. But the only word he could force out of his mouth was, "Nothing." He hated lying to Dan, but it couldn't be helped. Who would believe he'd been battling corpses?

"Nothing, huh?" Dan arched a brow in disbelief. "Nothing

is the reason your face is smeared with gunk and your neck is eaten up with bite marks? Nothing is the reason you've been gone all day? You know you have to keep me informed."

"I left a note telling you I was exploring the town." There. Truth. He *had* explored. Wasn't his fault he'd stumbled upon the living dead. "I didn't do anything illegal or hurt anyone." Again, truth. There was no law against killing people who were already dead, and you couldn't hurt a corpse. "You have my word."

Dan removed a toothpick from his shirt pocket and anchored it between his teeth. "Exploring on your day off is fine, encouraged, even, *if* you gain my permission first. You didn't. I would have sent my cell phone with you, so I would be able to get a hold of you if necessary. But you didn't give me the opportunity. You dropped the note on my kitchen counter and snuck out. I could call your caseworker and have you picked up for this."

His caseworker, Ms. Killerman, was the reason Aden was here. She was hellishly old, probably thirtysomething like Dan, and struck Aden as, well, cold. She'd been assigned to him while he'd been wasting away in the last institution. He'd had a tutor, of course, but he hadn't been able to leave the grounds.

He'd complained. When Killerman told him about the D and M and placed a request for his admittance, he'd been shocked. And when a spot had finally opened up, he'd been overjoyed. To think that he could now lose that spot as he'd feared earlier, *without* Dan even seeing that decimated graveyard...

"Aden. Are you listening to me?" Dan asked. "I said I could call your caseworker about this."

"I know." He peeked up at Dan, whose features were hidden in shadow. "Are you?"

Silence. Dreadful silence.

Then Dan reached over and mussed his hair. "Not this time. But I'm not always going to be a pushover, you got me? I believe in you, Aden. I want good things for you. But you have to obey my rules."

The gesture was unexpected, the words wonderfully shocking. *I believe in you.* Something burned his eyes. Aden refused to believe it was tears, even when his chin started trembling. There might be a girl inside his head, but he wasn't a wimp.

"Are you still taking your meds?" Dan asked him.

"Yes. Of course." A lie. Truth, half truths or even omissions wouldn't work this time. To Dan, admitting he flushed his pills down the toilet would be worse than sneaking into town. Besides, he didn't need the pills. They made him weak, tired, his mind foggy. Which he was starting to feel anyway, he realized, swaying as a wave of dizziness assaulted him. Stupid corpse poison. Still, with the dizziness came a sense of urgency. "I actually came looking for you when I returned. I—I—" *Do it, just say it. Put it out there.* "I want to go to public school. Crossroads High." There. Done. There would be no taking the words back.

Dan's brow furrowed. "Public school? Why?"

There was only one explanation that sounded believable. "I've never been around normal, average kids my own age, and I think it could be good for me. I could watch them, interact with them, *learn* from them. Please. I haven't missed a therapy session since I got here. Twice a week. Dr. Quine thinks I'm doing good." Dr. Quine was the latest to try and fix him. Aden actually liked her; she truly seemed to care about him.

"I know. She keeps me apprised."

Which was why Aden guarded his words around the well-meaning doctor, as well. Another wave of dizziness hit him, and he rubbed his temples. "If you'll just call Ms. Killerman, she can sign the necessary papers and I can be in class by next week. I'll only have missed the first month, and it'll be the beginning of my new, normal life. A life you said you wanted for me."

Dan didn't even take a moment to think about it. "Good in theory, but... No matter what you tell Dr. Quine, you're still having conversations with yourself. Don't try to deny it, because I heard you just this morning. You stare out at nothing for hours, disappear, and even though I just found you with the other boys, you were stiff and angry, so I know you haven't made friends with them. I'm sorry, kid, but my answer is no."

"But—"

"Nope. That's my final verdict. In time, maybe."

"I haven't made friends because no one here is interested."

"Maybe you're not trying hard enough."

Aden's hands clenched at his sides, a red haze clouding his vision. He didn't know whether it was from the poison or his anger. Maybe he *wasn't* trying hard enough, but why should that matter? He didn't *want* to make friends with Ozzie and his sheep.

"I know you're angry, but this is for the best. If you were

to hurt one of the students, you'd be incarcerated, no more chances. And like I said, I don't want that for you. You're a good kid with a lot of potential. Let's give you a chance to reach that potential and shine. Okay?"

Some of Aden's anger drained. How could it not, in the face of Dan's kindness? His determination, however, only strengthened. He *had* to attend that school, had to spend more time with Mary Ann. Yeah, he could "accidentally" run into her in town, but when? How often? School was in session five days a week, seven hours a day. There, he'd have a better chance of learning about her, about how she, well, temporarily fixed him.

And, for those seven blessed hours, he'd be at peace. For *that,* he'd do anything. Even… He gulped, not liking where the thought ended.

"Are you sure?" he asked, giving Dan one last chance.

"Very."

"Okay, then." Aden scanned the pasture, then glanced behind him to gauge just how well the dregs could see him from the bunkhouse if they happened to be watching from the windows. A direct view. That was unfortunate but couldn't be helped. Hopefully, if they were watching, they would assume the drug they'd just smoked was causing hallucinations.

Are you really going to do this? he asked himself. A million things could go wrong. People could learn the extent of his abilities, decide to test him, lock him away forever. A tremor slid the length of his spine, and he nervously licked his lips. Yes. Yes, he was. There was no other way, the outcome too important.

I know what you're planning, Ad, and it's not a good idea.

Had Caleb possessed a body of his own, he would have been gripping Aden's shoulders and shaking. *Actually, it's a terrible idea. I don't have to be a psychic to know that.*

Last time he'd done something like this, he'd spent a week in bed, cold, shaking, afraid of every noise, every touch against his skin too much for him to bear. And with the toxin even now traveling through him, the aftermath could be a thousand times worse.

Aden, Eve begin, a lecture clearly imminent.

"I'm sorry, Dan," Aden said…just before stepping *into* Dan's body.

He screamed at the agonizing pain of morphing from solid mass to inconsequential mist, which in turn caused Dan to scream. They fell to their knees, dizzy. Colors were blurring together, the green of the grass with the brown of the cows, the bright red of the tractor with the yellow of the wheat. He was panting, sweating, his stomach threatening to revolt.

Deep breath in, deep breath out. Several minutes passed before he found a center of gravity. The pain ebbed, but only slightly.

Now you've gone and done it, Caleb snapped.

"He won't remember this." It was weird, knowing he was talking but hearing a different voice come out. "We'll be fine." He hoped.

Well, do what you want to do and let's get the hell out of here, Julian said. *God, I can't believe you sometimes.*

Elijah moaned. *If anyone ever learns you're capable of doing this…*

"They won't." Again, he hoped. Aden forced Dan's hand to dig into his pocket and remove his cell phone, as if the body were his own. The hand was shaking but he managed to scroll through the address book and find Tamera Killerman. Her number was on speed dial.

Gulping, nervous, Aden connected them.

"Hello?" his caseworker answered after three rings.

You can still walk away, honey. You don't have to do this, don't have to risk being found out.

"Hi, Ms. Killerman." He experienced more of that dizziness, more of that churning in his stomach. *Concentrate.* "This is Ad—Dan Reeves."

A pause. A giggle.

A giggle? From calm and collected Killerman? He'd known her over a year, yet she'd rarely even cracked a smile. Aden blinked in surprise.

"Ms. Killerman, is it?" There was a breathless quality to her voice that made Aden's stomach curdle. "Yesterday you called me sweetheart."

"I—uh…"

"So how are you, baby, and when will I get to see you again?"

Baby? Why would she— Realization slammed into him, and he scowled, nearly overcome with disappointment and anger. Dan was married. Dan should only ever be called "baby" by his wife. A wife Aden liked. Meg Reeves cooked wonderful meals, had a smile for everyone and had never scolded him. She even hummed while she cleaned her house.

Just then, Aden wanted inside Dan's memories; he wanted

to know why the man would betray such a wonderful woman. But mind reading seemed like the only ability he *didn't* possess. *Doesn't matter. Finish what you started before you're too sick.* "Listen, Ms. Killerman. I want to enroll Haden Stone in the local high school. Crossroads High."

"Haden?" Shock dripped from her now, and Aden imagined her pretty but cool face pinching in confusion. "The schizophrenic? Why?"

His teeth ground together in irritation. *I'm not schizophrenic!* "Interacting with the other students will be good for m—him. Besides, in the short amount of time he's been here, he's improved so much I'm not even sure why he's here." Too much?

"That's great, but are you sure he's ready? When we talked yesterday you said he was progressing slowly."

He had, had he? "Yesterday I wasn't talking about Aden. I was talking about Ozzie Harmon." Take that, dreg. "Aden is totally ready."

"Totally?" She laughed again. "Dan, are you all right? You sound a little…I don't know, unlike yourself."

He swayed, barely caught himself. "I'm fine. Just tired. Anyway, if you could set this into motion for me, I'd really appreciate it." Surely that was something Dan would say. "Okay?"

"Okay. I guess. But do you still want Shannon Ross to attend Crossroads, as well?"

Shannon? Why Shannon? And why had no one been told? "Yes. Talk to you later," he added before she could ask more questions. "Baby."

Click.

For a long while, Aden stared down at the phone, struggling to breathe, his shaking intensified. Thankfully, Ms. Killerman never called back.

Later, when Dan was alone, he'd remember his chat with Aden yet think he'd made the phone call of his own volition. He'd wonder at his motives, but would not recall the way Aden had stepped inside him. They never did. Maybe because their minds couldn't process it. Maybe because Aden took the memory with him.

Either way, he wondered if Dan would call Killerman back and tell her that he changed his mind. And would Killerman follow through on her promise to set things into motion?

Only time would tell.

Now all Aden had to do was wait. That, and heal, he thought, as he and Dan hunched over and vomited. Great. His battle with the poison had finally begun.

FOUR

ADEN SPENT THE NEXT SIX DAYS in and out of consciousness. Several times he wanted to give up, just end it all and float away from the scalding mass of pain that was his body. But he didn't. He fought. Fought harder than he'd ever fought for anything, one thought driving him: the peace that came with Mary Ann.

A few times, he'd even hallucinated and thought he saw her hovering over him, that long dark hair tickling his chest. Or maybe Elijah's ability was expanding and he'd had another non-death vision, catching glimpses of the future. Only, unlike in real life, her skin had been pale rather than sun kissed and as hot as a living flame. What's more, her eyes had been bright blue rather than hazel.

There were a few explanations for the differences. Either his visions had never been of Mary Ann and he still had yet to truly meet his brunette or, sick as he'd been, he'd simply gotten the details wrong this time.

Both were entirely possible. He'd realized that while he had seen his brunette in the dark recesses of his mind too many times to count, he'd never really retained knowledge about her actual facial features.

The face he'd seen this week, well, he would not be forgetting.

"Sleep," she'd said, fingertips gently coasting over his brow and leaving a trail of fire in their wake. "When you heal, there is much for us to discuss."

"Like?" he'd managed to work past the rawness of his throat.

"Like how you summoned my people. Like how I still feel the hum of you. Like how that hum stopped for a little bit of time. Like why you want us here. Like whether or not we'll allow you to live. We will talk, though, when your blood smells less like the living dead."

It was a conversation he couldn't even begin to explain.

Unlike his encounters with Mary Ann, he hadn't wanted to run from this apparition, nor had he wanted to hug her as he would a sister. He hadn't experienced that painful gust of wind, either. He'd wanted to tangle his hands in her hair, draw her close, so close, and drink in the scent of her. Honeysuckle and rose. He'd wanted to kiss her the way they'd kissed in the visions.

Eventually, though, the fever faded, and the hallucinations ended. His sweating ebbed and his muscles stopped seizing, leaving him weak and hungry.

Finally, Aden lumbered from his bed, his only clothing a pair of boxers that were sweat-dried to his skin. He'd hidden the worst of his pain, keeping his moans contained inside his head. Anything to avoid hospitals and doctors, pinching and poking and questions. God, the questions.

He'd been excused from tutoring sessions and barn duty all week. Dan had kept tabs on him, though, flittering in and out of his room, expression concerned yet somewhat suspicious. If they'd had a heart-to-heart about what was going on, Aden didn't remember it. Only thing he remembered was Dan asking if he knew anything about the desecration of the cemetery. Apparently several stations had blasted the story as he'd feared. He'd had the presence of mind to say no.

He swiped up the peanut butter sandwich Dan had left him during his final visit this morning and downed it in three bites. Stomach calming, he quickly showered and changed into a pair of jeans and a plain gray T-shirt. Dan was taking him and Shannon shopping. That, too, he remembered. It was something the big guy had never done before and there was only one reason Aden could think of for such a trip: Dan was going to allow them to attend Crossroads High.

His relief was palpable. So many things could have gone wrong. Ms. Killerman could have changed her mind and opted not to follow Dan's recommendation. Dan could have chalked the "decision" to let Aden loose on the public school system up to a moment of insanity and canceled the paperwork.

A hand slapped his open door frame, the loud boom jolting him, and then Shannon was peeking inside. His green eyes were devoid of emotion. "T-time to g-go." Without waiting for

Aden's response, he pivoted and stalked away. Down the hall, the main door slammed shut.

One by one, the souls woke up, stretching and sighing. Great. *What's going on?* Eve asked sleepily.

"School shopping," he muttered as he strode from his room. "So we'll talk later. Okay?"

Ozzie and Seth were standing in front of their bedroom door, arms crossed over their chests. Everyone had a roommate but Aden. No one wanted to share quarters with the schizo, and that was fine with him.

"Talking to yourself again?" Seth said with a laugh. "Why? It's not like you're all that stimulating."

Aden raised his chin and tried to move past them.

Ozzie grabbed his arm, jerking him to a stop. "Where do you think you're going, Crazy? You've been hiding from me lately, and we've got a few things to discuss."

Aden whipped his attention to the boy, the urge to attack strong. He didn't like being threatened like this. Too many times in too many institutions, he'd been held down and beaten up.

You can't afford to punch it out with Ozzie, Eve said.

If Ozzie continued to push him like this, Aden wouldn't be able to help himself. His patience was used up. He *would* attack. And he wouldn't fight fair. Even now, his daggers were pressed against his ankles, waiting.

"Let go," he snarled.

Ozzie blinked in surprise, but maintained his grip. "You better be talking to one of your invisible friends, freak, or I swear to God I'll cut you to ribbons while you sleep."

Seth snickered.

Aden's jaw clenched.

I'm serious, Aden. Don't engage him, Eve said on a trembling breath.

Continue down this path and you might not make your first day of school, Elijah warned. *And if you don't make your first day, you won't see the girl.*

He jerked free from Ozzie and strode away without another word.

"Look at the little baby run," Ozzie called.

His cheeks heated but he didn't turn around. Better to let them think poorly of him than to prove just how wrong they were. Because, in the proving, someone would be hurt and it wouldn't be him. And, as Elijah had reminded him, Mary Ann and public school loomed on the horizon. He would have to be a good little robot, not make waves, and avoid trouble as if it were a cemetery.

Outside, the brightness of the sun had his eyes watering. He blinked against it, searching for Dan's truck. His gaze snagged on the line of trees beside the main house, zooming in, and his jaw dropped. There, in the shadows, stood the brunette. His brunette. The one from his visions.

Only, she wasn't Mary Ann. He realized it now beyond any doubt.

This girl was taller, with a face that belonged in magazines. Those big blue eyes were framed by long black lashes. She had a small nose and heart-shaped lips that were bloodred. Her skin was as pale as snow. Her hair was long, hanging to her waist and curling slightly. Those curls were so black they seemed tinted with blue, and they swirled around her shoulders with every breeze.

Was *this* a vision? he suddenly wondered. Or was she really there?

A boy stood behind her, tall and menacing, his skin tanned, his body a powerhouse of muscle stacked upon muscle.

Both wore black: The boy a T-shirt and slacks, the girl a robe of some sort. It draped one shoulder like a toga while leaving the other bare, was cinched in the middle by silver links and flowed down the rest of her to dance at her ankles.

Both were staring at him. The boy with menace, the girl with curiosity.

Not knowing what else to do, he waved.

Neither reacted.

"Aden," Dan called. "Who're you waving to? Let's go."

"But—" He turned, meaning to ask for a few more minutes. He had to know if the two were real. But Dan was motioning him to the truck, expression impatient in the hot, glaring sun. Shannon was already inside. Aden faced the line of trees in the distance once more, but the pair was gone. "Did you see them?" he whispered.

Who? Eve asked. *The witch and the angry he-man?*

They were real, then. He almost whooped in excitement. She was here. Finally she was here. Who was she? What was her name? What had brought her here? How had she found him? Why had she found him?

When would he see her again?

Elijah sighed. *You know the bad feeling I got when you followed that girl last week? Well, I've got a worse feeling about these two. But yeah, I know where you're going with this. She's the one from the visions.*

We've had visions of her? Where was I? Because day-um. It's official, Caleb said. *I'm hot.*

Aden rolled his eyes.

"Aden," Dan called. "I'm drowning in my own sweat. I said let's go."

There was still no sign of them in the trees. No hint of that black dress or a lock of hair blowing in the wind. Where had they gone? *Why* had they gone?

"Aden! Last chance before I leave without you."

Though he wanted to stay, he forced himself to trudge to the truck, contenting himself with the knowledge that she would return. One day, they would kiss. Elijah had predicted her arrival, after all, and that had come true. The kiss would, as well. Aden's lips lifted in a grin.

"What?" Dan asked him.

"Just excited," he said, and it was the truth.

"About shopping? What a g-girl," Shannon muttered.

He didn't care. Nothing was going to ruin his good mood today.

They made the twenty-five minute drive to Tri City in silence. Aden used every second to try and piece together what had happened. Since the girl, *his* girl, and the boy were indeed real, truly here, that meant the girl *had* come to him while he'd been sick. She'd cared for him. Had wanted to talk to him, have him answer some questions.

She'd wanted to know how he… What had she said? Summoned her people? His brow furrowed. What people? He had summoned no one.

And what about the boy? Were they siblings? The two had looked nothing alike, but that didn't mean anything. Were they only friends? Or were they *together* together? His hands fisted. Okay. *Something* could ruin his good mood.

Honey bear, I can feel how hard your brain is working, Eve said. *You're giving us a headache.*

"I'm—" He barely stopped himself from apologizing out loud.

When Dan idled to a stop in front of the local supercenter, his hands tightened on the steering wheel. "You've got an hour, boys. Buy some clothes, some school supplies, but do not leave the building. I'm trusting you. If you're not waiting for me when I return, bags in your hands, you're out of the ranch. That's the end. No excuses. Understand?"

Aden didn't meet his gaze. He hadn't been able to do so since that night in the field when he'd learned about Ms. Killerman.

"Understand?"

"Y-yeah," Shannon mumbled as Aden said, "Yes."

Dan handed them each a fifty-dollar bill. "All's I've got. I hope you can make it work."

"Th-thanks." Shannon climbed out.

"Aden," Dan said, stopping Aden when he tried to do the same. "Just so you know, you're not going to class on Monday."

His eyes widened. "What? Why?"

"Don't worry. You're going to the school, but you've got to do the placement tests before you can actually go to class. You'll have results within an hour of turning in your work— computers are a wonderful thing—so we'll know if you even qualify. Shannon took his last week, but you were too sick. I think you'll pass, hence the shopping today so you're all ready come Tuesday."

He nodded, relieved that he still had a chance to attend public school but mad that it wasn't already a done deal as he'd supposed. When he stepped onto the curb and shut the door behind him, he looked around. The place was packed but there was no sign of Shannon.

Would it have killed him to wait for you? Caleb griped.

As he shopped, his friends telling him what clothes would look good on him, he spotted the dreg a few times. Shannon flipped through the racks and pretended not to notice him.

"Like I wanted to spend time with you," he muttered.

"Time with who?" someone asked.

He glanced up and saw that an older woman stood beside him. She had too-bright red hair that was sprayed in what looked to be a beehive. She wore a short-sleeved dress that was far too big. Her face, arms and legs seemed to…sparkle, as if she'd bathed in glitter. Weird.

That, he could deal with, though. It was the zaps of electricity seeming to pour off her, causing the fine hairs on his body to rise, that freaked him out. How was she doing that?

"No one," he said, stepping away to increase the distance

between them. He didn't trust strangers. Even strangers who seemed as well-meaning as this one.

"Oh, posh. Something's bothering you, and I'd love to hear what it is. I haven't spoken to anyone in ages. Frankly, at this point I think I'd listen to a discussion about the mating habits of ants."

Was she serious? "Lady, you're creeping me out."

There's nothing wrong with honesty, Caleb said with a laugh.

A couple walking by glanced over at him as if he were insane. Okay, maybe there was something wrong with honesty.

"I'm sorry you're creeped out," the old woman said, and then continued her inane chatter. Not about ants, but about her son, his wife, their kids, and how she hadn't gotten to tell them goodbye before they'd moved away from her. "Maybe you could, I don't know, tell them goodbye for me."

"I don't even know them."

"Haven't you been listening? I've been telling you all about them!" And she proceeded to do so again.

After a while, Aden did his best to tune her out.

You'll need notebooks, binders, pencils and folders, Julian said when the clothing total reached thirty-five dollars and eighty-three cents. With tax. Eve kept track of the money. No one was better with numbers.

"How do you know what I need?" he asked Julian, glancing around to make sure no one was paying him any attention. The old lady didn't pause in her patter.

A memory, I guess.

He'd often suspected the souls had lived before being

paired with him. Every so often, they remembered things that had happened to them, things that couldn't have happened to them while they were inside Aden's body.

Aden left the men's section with four shirts and a pair of pants, and headed toward the supplies. Of course, the woman trailed after him. Still talking. He would have liked a new pair of tennis shoes, but his boots would have to do. Easier to hide weapons that way.

After he gathered everything and paid, his total for the day six cents shy of fifty dollars, he carried his bags outside to wait. Thankfully, the woman didn't follow him this time.

He had twenty minutes to spare. The sun was high, glaring, and sweat soon beaded over him. He leaned against the side of the building, one lucky half of his body then in the shade. Shannon joined him a few minutes later, stone-faced as always, only one bag in hand.

Aden wanted to ask him what he'd bought but knew he'd get no answer.

"How'd you g-get so much?" Shannon asked without looking at him.

The question surprised him so much that he couldn't find his voice.

Answer the boy, Eve coaxed.

"I, uh, only bought sale items."

Shannon nodded stiffly and said no more.

I'm so proud of you. You're becoming friends already. If she'd had hands, Eve would have been clapping.

Aden didn't have the heart to correct her.

SUNDAY NIGHT, Aden lay awake till morning, nervous, excited, hoping his mystery girl would return. She never did. With two hours until it was time to leave for school, he got up and showered, brushed his teeth, then dressed in his new clothes. He couldn't stop smiling—until he spotted himself in the mirror.

Sometime in the last two days, probably while he'd been out catching up on his chores, someone had sneaked inside his room and written on his shirt before folding it and placing it back in its sack where he'd left it. The words *Hello, My Name Is Crazy* stared back at him.

Aden's hands fisted on the hem, wrinkling the material. That stupid Ozzie! And he had no doubt Ozzie was the culprit, if not the one to do it then the one to order it done.

Oh, Aden. I'm so sorry, Eve said.

You need to punish him, Caleb said. *Maybe wake him up with an introduction to your fists.*

That's one way to settle it, Julian agreed. *If you want to miss your test and your first and probably only chance to go to public school.*

And your chance to see the girl, Elijah added, because he knew the mention of Mary Ann had calmed Aden down last time.

In and out Aden breathed. A quick search of the other shirts proved that they were equally ruined. His jaw clenched. "Doesn't matter," he said. He only wished he believed it.

The kids at Crossroads High will think it's a joke, Elijah told him. *Maybe it will even become the new style.*

Whether his friend spoke true or not, he didn't care. Or rather, he wouldn't let himself care. Today was too important.

On the best of days, he tested poorly, his concentration shot. He needed every thought in his mind focused only on success.

Still wearing the offending shirt, he stomped out of the bunkhouse to the porch. His eyes were narrowed as he scanned the line of trees. There was no sign of the brunette or her friend. That was good, he told himself. He didn't need the distraction they presented, either. He'd only wonder why they hadn't approached him again, whether they meant him harm, and if the girl—what was her name?—had liked being with him as much as he'd liked being with her.

If only she stopped the voices like Mary Ann did, she would have been perfect.

He must have stood there, lost in thoughts he couldn't afford, for his remaining hour, because the next thing he knew, Dan was strolling to the truck with two lunch sacks in hand.

The door behind Aden creaked open, and he turned, spying Shannon. Shannon saw his shirt and gazed guiltily at the ground. Guess that meant he'd been involved. Aden capped his anger again and headed for the truck, meeting Dan at the door.

Dan noticed his shirt and frowned. "What happened?"

"Nothing." A muscle ticked in his jaw. "It's fine. I'm fine."

There was a heavy pause. "You sure?"

He nodded.

Dan sighed, unlocked the door. Aden slid inside, scooting to the middle. By the time Dan claimed the driver's seat and Shannon the passenger's, he felt completely penned in. Thank God it was only an eight-minute and thirty-three second drive—not that he was keeping track or anything. When they were parked in front of the school, Dan faced them.

"Here's your lunch," he said. "Peanut butter and jelly. It'll have to do for today. Tomorrow, Meg will pack you something better. Now, listen. Mess up, and you're out."

Great. They were about to get the same lecture they'd gotten at the supercenter.

"I'm not kidding," Dan continued. "If you skip class, pick a fight, hell, if one of your teachers thinks you're looking at him wrong, I will pull you from school so quickly your head will spin. Understand?"

"Yes," they said in unison.

"Good. Shannon, you've got your schedule and can head to your first class. Aden, you go to the guidance office. School ends at three and it's only a thirty-minute walk home. I'll give you forty-five in case you're held up by a teacher or something, but if you're not home in time…"

You'll be out, Aden finished for him.

Shannon filed from the truck and when Aden tried to do the same, Dan grabbed his arm. Total déjà vu. Only, Dan didn't give him another lecture like he had at the store. He merely smiled. "Good luck, Aden. Don't let me down in there."

FIVE

THE DAY BEGAN like any other for Mary Ann. She crawled out of bed, showered, tugged on the clothes she'd laid out the night before, and blew dry her hair while outlining what she needed to turn in or which upcoming tests to study for. This week's most important exam was chemistry, one of her hardest subjects. Only problem was, thoughts of Aden Stone kept interfering.

Penny had admitted to giving him Mary Ann's number. So why hadn't he called? An entire week had passed. Part of her had expected it and had jumped every time her phone had rung. He'd seemed so eager to talk to her. The other part of her, however, had hoped that he wouldn't contact her. He was gorgeous, but after that first initial attraction, she'd felt only confused and friendly toward him—when she wasn't experiencing that strange urge to run.

Did she even want to be his friend? Being near him was like being punched in the chest; her body only wanted to escape him. Her mind, though…it mourned his loss. Mourned, as if he were somehow dear to her.

Steam began to rise from her scalp, and she hurriedly switched the dryer off. She had to stop thinking of that boy. Already he was screwing with her mind, making it mush— proving that she'd been right to date Tucker and stay with him these last few months. Tucker always made her feel pretty, boosting her self-esteem, but he didn't *consume* her. He gave her the space she needed.

With a sigh, she trudged downstairs. Her dad had breakfast ready: pecan waffles with blueberry syrup. She ate two while he read the paper and drank his coffee. Their usual routine.

"Want a ride to school?" he asked. He folded his paper and set it aside, peering over at her expectantly.

He always knew when she'd finished eating without being told.

"Nah. Walking will increase the amount of oxygen in my brain, which will help as I mentally pore through my notes about synthesizing iodide." Which was also the reason she didn't ride with Tucker, though he, too, always offered. He liked to chat and that would have distracted her. Penny was perpetually late, so she was a no-go, as well.

Her dad's lips twitched into a smile, and he shook his head. "Always studying."

When he smiled like that his entire face lit up and she could see why her friends crushed on him. In looks, he was her opposite. He had blond hair and blue eyes, was brawny where she was slim. The only thing they had in common was their youth (or so he was fond of saying). He was only thirty-five, which was young for a parent. (Again, words straight from his mouth.) He'd married her mom soon after high school and they'd had her right away.

Maybe that's why they'd married. Because of her. That wasn't why they'd stayed together, though. Oh, they'd fought a lot but they'd clearly loved each other. The way they'd stared over at each other, expressions soft, had been proof of that. But sometimes, because of the things they'd verbally hurled at each other, Mary Ann used to suspect her dad had cheated on her mom and her mother had never gotten over it.

"You wish I was *her*, don't you?" her mother had liked to shout at him.

He'd always denied it.

For many years, Mary Ann had resented him for the possibility. Her sweet mother hadn't worked, had stayed home and taken care of Mary Ann, the house and all the chores. But when she had died, his utter despondency convinced Mary Ann of his innocence. Plus, he'd been alone now for several years. He hadn't gone on a single date. Hadn't even glanced at another woman.

"You remind me more of your mom every day," he said, his mind obviously taking the same path hers had. His eyes were glazed with memories, his mouth soft with a smile. "Not just in appearance, either. She loved chemistry, too."

"Are you kidding? She hated math, and chemistry is filled with little equations that would have driven her insane." The only homework her mom had been able to help her with was

English and art. "Besides, who said I loved chemistry? I do it because it's necessary."

Mary Ann knew what he was doing, though. Lying to make her feel closer to her mom, as if death didn't separate them. She leaned forward and kissed him on the forehead. "Don't worry, Dad. I'll never forget her."

"I know," he said softly. "I'm glad. She was an amazing woman who turned this house into a home."

Soon after her dad opened his own practice, they'd had the money to buy this two-story estate. Her mom had been ecstatic. She and her sister, Anne, Mary Ann's namesake who'd died before Mary Ann was born, had grown up poor and this had been her first taste of wealth. Her mom had turned the walls from stark white to inviting colors, and had hung up photos of the three of them. She'd saturated the once stifling air with the scent of her sweet perfume and had warmed the cold tile with plush, multihued rugs.

Her father cleared his throat, bringing them both back from their memories. "I have to work late tonight. You'll be okay?"

"Absolutely. I plan to finish reading that article on ADD and OCD. It's pretty interesting. I mean, did you know that thirty-four percent of kids with—"

"Dear God, I've created a monster." He reached over and mussed her hair. "I can't believe I'm saying this, honey, but you need to get out more. Live a little. Several of my patients see me for this very reason, not realizing the stress they've placed upon themselves has begun to wear them down, that time off heals just as much as laughter. Honestly, even I go on vacation. You're sixteen. You should be reading books about wizard boys and gossipy girls."

She frowned. She'd read the article to impress him, and now he didn't want to hear about it? Now he wanted her head buried in fiction? "I'm expanding my mind, Dad."

"And I'm proud of you for that, but I still think you need some time off. Time devoted to fun. What about Tucker? You guys could go to dinner. And before you say anything, I know I threatened to castrate him the first time you guys went out, but I've gotten used to the idea of you having a boyfriend. Not that you spend much time with him anymore."

"Most nights, we talk on the phone," she protested. "But he has football practice or a game every night of the week, and I have homework. And on weekends, as you know, I practically live at the Watering Pot."

"Okay, well, that doesn't help for tonight. What about… Penny? She could come over and you guys could watch a movie."

He really was worried about her social life if he was suggesting she hang out with Penny. That begged the question of why. Did he feel guilty that she spent so much time on her own? He shouldn't. She enjoyed her own company. There was no pressure to be something she wasn't anymore: bubbly, carefree. "All I can promise is to find her at school and ask her what she has planned," she told him, because she knew it was what he wanted to hear. Most likely, she'd spend the evening with her head buried in her chem book.

"Which means you're not actually going to invite her over."

She shrugged, remaining silent.

Sighing, he checked his watch. "You'd better get going. A tardy will ruin your perfect record."

Classic Dr. Gray. When he wasn't getting the results he wanted, he sent her away so that he could strategize and resume the argument later with a new plan of attack.

Mary Ann stood. "Love you, Dad. I look forward to winning round two when you get home." She gathered her backpack and, with a wave, strolled to the front door.

He chuckled. "I don't deserve you, you know?"

"I know," she called over her shoulder, and could hear his renewed laughter as the door shut behind her.

When she exited her house, she immediately noticed a large, really large—ginormously large—black dog...wolf?... lying on its belly in the shade, only a few feet away from her. No way to miss it; it was like a car parked in her yard. Her blood instantly chilled.

The moment it spotted her, it jackknifed to its feet, lips pulling back from its teeth, revealing long, white fangs. A growl rumbled from its throat, low and menacing.

"D-Dad," she tried to yell, but the sudden lump in her throat muted the sound of her voice. Oh, God, oh, God, oh, God.

One step, two, she backed away, her entire body trembling. Blood rushed through her ears, terror screaming through her mind. Those green eyes were cold, hard... hungry? She spun, meaning to sprint back inside the house. The beast leapt in front of her and blocked the door.

Oh, God. What should she do? What the hell should she do?

Once more, she found herself backing away. This time, it followed, keeping the same, too-short distance between them.

She inched backward another step, and the heel of her tennie caught on something. Down, down she tumbled, landing on her butt with a painful *thwack.* What had— Her backpack, she realized. It now provided a comfy rest for her knees. When had she dropped it? *Does it matter?* she thought with a wild laugh. *I'm as good as dead.*

No way could she outrun the wolf now. Not that she'd ever had a chance, really. And it *was* a wolf, probably a wild one. It was simply too big to be a dog. She swallowed a whimper. Would have been nice to lead it on a chase, though, rather than splaying herself out like an all-you-can-eat dinner buffet.

Her only hope was that someone was outside, watching the confrontation—someone who'd either run to help or call 911. A quick peek to her left showed that Penny's Mustang GT was sitting in the Parkses' driveway, but there was no sign of life outside or even inside the house. A quick peek to her right showed her other neighbor had already left for work. Oh. God.

The wolf was on her a second later, its front legs pushing her shoulders into the ground. Still she couldn't scream, her voice gone, stolen.

Don't just lie there. Do something! She reached up, clamping its mouth shut with one hand and trying to heave it off her with the other. It merely jerked its muzzle from her grip and then batted her other arm away. Never had she felt so helpless. At least it wasn't drooling.

Slowly it leaned down. She flinched, pressing herself as

deep into the ground as she could, a sound finally escaping her: a whimper. Rather than eat her face off as she'd assumed, it sniffed her neck. Its nose was cold, dry, its breath warm as it exhaled. It smelled of soap and pine.

What. The. Hell?

What should I do? What should I do?

Another sniff, this one lingering, and then it was backing away from her. When she was free of its weight, she gradually rose, careful not to make any sudden movements. Their eyes locked, emotionless green against fearful hazel.

"G-good doggie," she managed to get out.

It growled.

She clamped her lips together. No speaking, then.

It motioned to the right with its muzzle. A *get out of here* gesture? When she remained in place, the animal did it again. Gulping, Mary Ann lumbered to her feet, dragging her backpack with her. Her legs were still trembling and she almost toppled over her own feet as she backed away. While she retreated, she unzipped her pack and reached inside for her cell phone.

The wolf shook its head.

She stilled. One heartbeat, two. *You can do it. Just need to press 911.* Now that she'd recovered her voice, common sense was returning. No way she'd scream for her dad and have him come racing to the rescue. He despised guns and would be helpless against such a large creature.

Move it! Mary Ann inched back into motion, finally latching onto her phone. The wolf growled when she pressed the first button. Again, she stilled. He quieted. Her blood crystallized in her veins, an ice shower that only increased her trembling. Even the sun's strong morning rays refused to warm her.

Another button.

Another growl. This time, the wolf stepped toward her, front legs bending, placing it in the perfect position to pounce.

It couldn't know what she was doing. It couldn't know what would happen if she pressed that final button. No matter how much intelligence seemed to glow from those meadowlike eyes.

Her muscles tensed as she applied pressure to her thumb. In the blink of an eye, the wolf launched at her, snagging the cell between its teeth. Mary Ann gasped, momentarily paralyzed with fear, relief and uncertainty. Those teeth…they'd come so close to ripping into her palm, but they hadn't even grazed her.

Forcing herself into action, she whipped around, knowing better than to give the creature her back for any length of time. It was waiting at the base of her dad's favorite plum tree, the black plastic still stuck between its lips, sitting as calmly as if it were picnicking. Once again, it motioned to the side.

Slowly losing her fear, Mary Ann stumbled in that direction. Even though the wolf hadn't hurt her and seemed to mean her no harm, she arced around it, keeping as much distance between them as she could.

She walked backwards, too, keeping it in her sights.

A weary breath left it. A sigh? And then it was loping forward, in front of her, maintaining a steady pace, the scrape of its nails against the ground ringing in her ears. Every so often, it glanced backward to make sure she followed.

Not knowing what else to do, she did.

Somehow it—he—knew the way to school. Though there were three ways to get there from her house, he took the route she preferred. Had he followed her before? Could he scent where she'd been?

Were my waffles sprinkled with crack? she wondered. This couldn't be real.

Smart as he clearly was, the wolf remained in the shadows, out of sight from traffic. Mary Ann suddenly wished she knew more about animals. But she didn't. Her parents hadn't liked them—or their pooping and peeing and shedding—so she'd never really been around them. Perhaps that dislike had even rubbed off on her. Penny owned a Chihuahua named Dobi, but Mary Ann avoided that barking, growling little crap machine as though her life depended on it.

Finally Crossroads High came into view and she breathed a sigh of relief. It was a new building, large and red, winding into a half circle. Cars meandered through the parking lot, *Go Jaguars* written on the windshields. Kids milled around outside, basking in the warm summer haze that would soon be replaced by an ice-cold fall. Except… Some of her relief faded. Would the wolf attack them?

Tucker's truck sped past her, and then his tires were squealing as he jerked to a stop. Thank God! The wolf dropped her phone and backed up. When he was far enough away to ease her mind, she raced forward and grabbed the cell. Her gaze remained locked on him as she backpedaled, throwing open

Tucker's passenger door and flinging herself inside. The wolf disappeared into the thick green trees and bushes that surrounded the school.

That last look he'd shot her had been laced with disappointment. Even anger. She gulped. At least he hadn't sprung forward and started chomping at the truck.

"This is new," Tucker said, deep voice drawing her attention.

He had shaggy, sandy hair and gray eyes, coloring that might have been dull on anyone else. On Tucker, with his boyish face, dimples and athletic body, it was heart-stopping.

She'd never understood why he'd chosen to ask her out, much less why he'd wanted to keep dating her, since they so rarely spent time together outside of school. All the cheerleaders adored him, especially their leader, Christy Hayes, the beloved beauty responsible for wet dreams statewide. But Tucker wanted nothing to do with her, was always brushing her off to be with Mary Ann. Which, she hated to admit, did as much for her self-esteem as Tucker's compliments.

You're so beautiful, he was fond of saying. *I'm so lucky to be with you.*

She would smile for hours afterward.

Tucker chuckled, pulling her from her thoughts. "Now this is what I'm used to."

"What do you mean?" The longer they sat there, the more her trembling faded.

"You're ignoring me, lost in your thoughts."

"Oh. I'm sorry." Did she do that a lot? She hadn't realized.

Would have to make more of an effort to stay focused. So what had they been talking about, anyway? Oh, yeah. "What is new?" she asked.

The truck eased forward. "You're pale as a ghost and eager for a ride. Why?"

To tell him about the wolf or not? Not, she decided without any deliberation. Didn't take a genius to know she would be laughed at and ridiculed. A wolf had escorted her to school? Please. Who would believe it? It wasn't something *she* truly believed.

"Just, uh, nervous about my chem test tomorrow." Lying wasn't something she usually did and guilt quickly began to eat at her.

He shuddered. "Chemistry sucks. I still don't understand why you signed up for advanced studies with Mr. Klein. Guy makes a doorknob look fun." Before she could reply, he added, "You look smokin' today, by the way."

See? Who else would even think of saying something like that to her? She grinned. "Thank you."

"You're welcome, but I wouldn't say it if it wasn't true." Tucker parked.

And this is why I stay with him, she thought, smile growing all the wider.

They emerged, and she immediately searched the side of the school, peering into the trees. No sign of her wolf. That didn't lessen the sudden feeling of being watched, though, and she lost her grin. *Note to self:* research wolves. Maybe fear made prey taste better and this was some sort of new stalk, terrify into stupidity and *then* kill technique. If so, there was no better prey than Mary Ann.

"Come on." Tucker wound an arm around her waist and led her forward. He didn't seem to notice her renewed trembling.

There, resting on the bike rails, was Tucker's group. Crew. Whatever. Mary Ann knew them, of course, but she rarely hung out with them. They didn't approve of her, something they made clear by ignoring her every time she approached. Each of them played football, though she couldn't have named their positions to save her life.

The boys slapped each other's hands in greeting. And yes, they pretended that she wasn't there. Tucker never seemed to notice the disrespect and she never said anything. She wasn't sure how he'd react—whether he'd side with her or his friends—and it simply wasn't worth her time to worry about it.

"Did you hear?" Shane Weston, the school's resident prankster, grinned and hopped to his feet, fairly bursting with the need to share.

Nate Dowling rubbed his hands together. "It's our lucky day."

"Let me tell, Dow," Shane growled.

Nate held his hands up, palms out, brow raised impatiently.

Shane's grin returned. "Fresh meat," he said. "Two witnesses, Michelle and Shonna, saw Principal White greet them."

Huh? Mary Ann gazed up at Tucker.

He gave a grin of his own as he and Shane nodded at each other in understanding.

"New kids," Nate elaborated. "Two of 'em."

While they laughed about all the ways to initiate the newcomers properly, the poor kids, Mary Ann wandered to her first class. Mr. Klien lectured on all the things that would be in their test, but for the first time that year, she had trouble forcing herself to concentrate. She'd caught several whispered conversations on her trek through the halls.

Both new kids were juniors, like her, and both were male. One was tall with dark hair and black eyes, but no one had spoken to him. He'd holed up in the guidance offices. Was it…could it be…Aden? Those eyes…

The other was black, gorgeous, with green eyes—like her wolf?—and a hard but quiet demeanor.

Wait. Had she really just compared a human's eyes to a wolf's? The thought made her laugh.

"Ms. Gray?" the teacher said reprovingly.

Everyone in the classroom turned to peer at her.

Heat flooded her cheeks. "Sorry, Mr. Klien. You may continue."

That earned several chuckles from the students and a glare from the head of the class.

Throughout the rest of the day, she watched for new faces. It wasn't until after lunch that she found one. Shannon Ross was in her history class; she spotted him from the door. He was as beautiful as everyone had said, tall with eyes of light green—yep, just like the wolf—and just as quiet.

Mary Ann had lived in Crossroads for a long time now, but could sympathize with being new, knowing no one. He'd taken a desk in back and she slid into the one next to him. Wouldn't hurt to warn him about Tucker and crew, either.

"Hi," she said. Kids had been gossiping about him all day. Currently, the favorite story was that he was one of the troublemakers who lived at the D and M Ranch owned by Dan Reeves. Oh, and he'd killed both his parents. By this time tomorrow, he would have killed a sister and brother, too, she was sure.

Mary Ann had seen Dan around town and had heard the stories about him. Supposedly, his parents had died young and he'd lived with his grandparents. He'd been wild and in constant trouble with the law, yet he'd also been magic on the football field and managed to go pro. Only a few years in, though, he'd hurt his back and had to quit, at which point he'd decided to open his home to boys as troubled as he'd once been. Still. Most of the people in Crossroads still worshipped him—even though they disapproved of who he allowed to live with him.

Shannon flicked her a nervous glance. "Hi."

"I'm Mary Ann Gray. If you need anything, I—"

"I—I—I won't need anything," he rushed out. A clear dismissal.

"Oh. Okay." Wow, that stung. "Just…maybe stay away from the football players. They like to torture the new kids. Their way of welcoming them, I guess." Her cheeks were hot for the second time that day as she claimed her rightful seat. The rest of the class filed inside just as the bell rang.

Before Mr. Thompson discussed the age of imperialism, he had Shannon stand at the front of the class and tell everyone a little about himself, an exercise he stuttered his way through, kids laughing the entire time. Mary Ann lost the threads of her own humiliation. No wonder he'd sent her away. He didn't like conversing with people. It embarrassed him.

She smiled at him as he made his way back to his seat, but he didn't see. He kept his eyes fixed on the painted concrete at his feet.

They shared their next class, too. Computer science. They sat close to each other, but she didn't try and talk to him. Not again, not yet. He'd probably just reject her again.

Tucker was in the class, as well. He'd sat next to Mary Ann until last week, when Ms. Goodwin had moved him for talking.

"Hey, Tuck," Shane whispered from across the room.

Tucker looked. So did Mary Ann and a few others in the room. Not Shannon, though. As he had in the last class, he kept his head down.

Shane motioned toward Shannon with a tilt of his chin. *Do something,* he mouthed.

Mary Ann clutched the edge of her desk. "Don't," she said. "Please."

"Miss Gray," the teacher admonished. "That's enough from you."

"I'm sorry," she managed to choke out. She'd gone nearly all month without getting in trouble, yet she'd been repri- manded twice in one day.

Tucker mouthed, "Don't worry" and raised his hand, drawing attention away from her.

Ms. Goodwin sighed. "Yes, Mr. Harbor."

"Can I go to the bathroom?"

"I don't know. Can you?"

He glowered. "May I?"

"Fine. But do not loiter or you'll find yourself in detention tomorrow."

"Yes, ma'am." Tucker stood. He walked from the room and shut the door, and Mary Ann's shoulders hunched in relief. Scene avoided.

Only, Tucker never veered from the door.

He peered through its small, square window at Shane. Shane held out his hands and Tucker nodded.

Shane stood, and he was suddenly clutching a slithering, hissing snake. Thin, with yellow and green scales and a bright red head. A lump of fear knotted Mary Ann's throat, cutting off her gasp. Dear God. Where had it come from? How had it appeared seemingly out of thin air?

Shane glanced at Ms. Goodwin to make sure she wasn't paying attention. She wasn't, too lost in showing the twins, Brittany and Brianna Buchannan, how to create a password for their pages. Grinning, he tossed the snake at Shannon. It landed on his shoulder, then fell onto his thighs with a hiss.

Shannon glanced down. He jolted to his feet with a scream, patting down his body with frantic hands. The snake hit the ground and slithered to the wall, disappearing beyond the stucco.

Everyone looked at him and laughed.

"How dare you disrupt my class, young man!"

"B-but th-the s-s-snake."

Ms. Goodwin anchored her hands on her padded hips. "What are you talking about? There is no snake. You may be new, but one thing you need to know. I will not tolerate lies."

Panting, Shannon swept his eyes across the floor. Mary Ann followed his gaze. There was no hole, no way the snake could have escaped, yet it was gone. She returned her attention to Tucker, who was still at the door. He and Shane were smiling at each other, beaming at a job well done.

SIX

"YOU...HELPED ME." Aden emerged from the school building to wait outside for Shannon—knowing the dreg may or may not want to walk home with him but willing to chance it. Good as he felt, he might have waited for the devil himself. Perhaps he'd even see Mary Ann in the crowd.

The last class of the day hadn't yet let out, so for now he was alone. He pressed against the red brick at the side of the structure, partially hidden by shadows.

"Why?" he asked.

You want to attend this school, Eve said, *and we want you to be happy. Of course we helped you.*

"But you hate Mary Ann."

I don't, she said. *Like you, I want to spend more time with her. She's a mystery I'm determined to solve.*

Well, I do hate her, Caleb said. *Girl freaking shoves me into that black hole with barbed wire on the sides. But you like her, and I love you.* The last was spoken in a grumble.

"I love you guys, too."

He'd thought they would fight him every step of the way, screaming while he tried to take the tests, distracting him. Instead, they'd done something they'd never done before: remained quiet for an extended period of time. He'd read without interruption, solved equations without enduring commentary about how he was doing it wrong, and drew no notice from those around him because he was seemingly talking to himself.

He'd more than passed. He'd excelled.

He was smiling as a girl walked past him, her gaze nearly burning a hole in his forehead. She had the same glittery skin the woman at the supercenter had had, and Aden found himself turning away just in case she wanted to talk. And then talk some more. Thankfully, she kept moving.

And who knows, Elijah said on a sigh. *Maybe Mary Ann can help us get out of here and into bodies of our own.*

What a difference! Only last week Elijah had experienced that "bad feeling." Aden wanted to ask what had changed, but didn't, too afraid the answer might sway his companions yet again.

A bell sounded.

I'm proud of you, my man, Julian said. *You're officially a student now. How's it feel?*

Behind him, footsteps echoed. Even from here, he could hear the slam of lockers and the murmur of voices.

"Feels great. But, uh, maybe we could try the quiet thing more often," Aden suggested.

All four laughed as if he'd just told a joke about Caleb getting hot.

He stepped into the sunlight, watching the front door. Kids spilled out in a rush.

Julian was the first to calm. *You, at least, can move around when you're bored. We're stuck. Talking is the only thing we can do. Our only distraction.*

"H-hey," a familiar voice said from behind him.

Aden whipped around, not liking having someone at his back. Shannon stood there, peering at the parking lot rather than Aden. Where had he come from and how had Aden missed him? Then he spied other kids coming out of other doors and realized there was more than one exit.

"Hey," he replied. Bummer. No way he could watch every door for Mary Ann.

"L-listen," Shannon said. There was a hard gleam in his eyes. Rough first day? "I know w-we don't like each other and y-you've got no reason to trust m-me, but we've only g-got each other h-here. And, well, if you'll guard m-my back, I'll g-guard yours."

His eyes widened with shock.

"So, truce?"

Seriously? He didn't know if a truce would mean they'd also look out for each other at the ranch, too, but he didn't care. "Truce," he said. Honestly, could this day get any better?

"Shannon, you forgot your syllabus."

Aden recognized the lilting female voice, but it was the surge of needle-sharp wind over his skin, the moans—and then the silence—that told him exactly who approached. Mary Ann. The day could get *much* better, it seemed.

His gaze quickly found her. Her arm was extended, a piece of paper clutched between her fingers.

Shannon turned. His shoulders immediately hunched, as if he wanted to hide inside himself.

Aden's heart began slamming against his ribs. Finally. He was with her again.

The sun gleamed behind her, framing her in gold. She tripped over her own feet when she spotted him, her skin leaching of color. Thankfully, she didn't hit the ground, just slowed her step and lowered her arm.

"Aden?"

"Hello, Mary Ann." The urge to hug her returned. So did the urge to run. Caleb would have said she was heaven and hell wrapped in the same pretty package. A friend and a foe. Both a hunter and the prey.

Wary, she stopped in front of him. "I didn't expect to see you again."

Had she preferred it that way? Her neutral tone gave nothing away. "As of today, I'm a student here."

"That's wonder—Your eyes," she said, blinking up at him. "They're blue. But I thought they were black. Or rather, lots of colors *then* black. Not one solid color."

So. She'd noticed the way they changed each time one of the souls spoke. He fused his top and bottom lashes, blocking the color from her view. "They change with what I wear," he lied. A lie he used often.

"Oh," she said, but she didn't sound convinced.

How could he ever have mistaken her for his brunette? he

wondered. Even momentarily? Yes, they both had dark hair and yes, both were pretty, but up close, he could see that Mary Ann was more planes and angles; Vision Girl was more curved. Mary Ann even had a few freckles scattered over her nose, while Vision Girl had none.

"I—I should g-go," Shannon said to him, acting as if Mary Ann weren't present.

Mary Ann hugged the paper she held to her chest. Her gaze darted between them. "You two know each other?"

Both he and Shannon nodded.

"Oh." Fear sparked in her eyes, and she backed up a step. Was she *frightened* of him? Why? She hadn't seemed afraid of him at the coffeehouse.

"You live with…Dan Reeves?" she asked.

Ah. Now he understood. She knew about the ranch, feared the boys inside…and what they'd done to be sent there. He didn't want to lie to her—again—this girl he so badly wanted to befriend, but he didn't want to confirm her fears, either. So he ignored the question. "My official first day here is tomorrow. Maybe we have a few classes together." Hopefully.

"S-see you at the h-house, Aden," Shannon said, clearly done waiting. He ripped the paper from Mary Ann's hands.

She gasped as Aden said his goodbyes. "See you, Shannon."

Shannon walked away without another word.

Aden and Mary Ann stood in silence for several seconds, kids rushing around them, brushing their shoulders, eager to reach the buses or their rides.

"He's shy," Aden said to excuse the dreg.

"I noticed." Mary Ann squared her shoulders and her pretty features glazed with determination. "Look, I've felt bad for the past week about the way I treated you at Holy Grounds. I've wanted to apologize over and over again."

"You don't have to apologize to me," he assured her. She might have been in a hurry to ditch him that day, but she hadn't called him a freak or made him feel like one. In his world, that was, like, the royal treatment.

"I do," she insisted. "I was rude. I would have called, but I didn't have your number."

"Seriously, no worries. I would have called you eventually." He stared down at his feet, realized what he was doing, and forced himself to straighten. "I just, well, I was sick. I spent six days in bed."

Sympathy softened the angle of her mouth. "I'm so sorry."

"Thanks." He smiled over at her. This was the longest conversation he'd ever had with someone. Well, without being interrupted by his companions or losing track of what was being said. He never wanted it to end. "Maybe we could meet here tomorrow and you could show me around."

Mary Ann hooked a lock of hair behind her ear, cheeks suddenly blooming with red. "I, uh, well…"

Had he pushed for too much too soon? Had he made her uncomfortable again? Suddenly, he hated not being able to talk to Eve. He needed advice. Needed to know the best way to befriend a girl, the right things to say.

In the end, he opted for the truth. "I'm not trying to score or anything, I swear. Besides Shannon, you're the only person I know at this school and I could really use a friend."

"A friend." She chewed on her bottom lip.

"Only a friend," he said, and he meant it. Vision Girl was the only one he was looking to date.

The chewing continued as she shifted from one foot to the other. "I have to tell you something, but I'm afraid it will hurt your feelings. And you may not want to be my friend once you know."

That sounded bad. Really bad. His stomach twisted into a thousand knots. "Tell me anyway. Please." He could take it. Whatever it was. Maybe.

"I feel…strange when I'm with you." The color returned to her cheeks. "God, that sounds even worse out loud."

He wondered…was it possible? Did she feel the wind and the sickness too? "Strange how?"

"I don't know. Like I'm being pummeled by a freak wind and my skin is crawling, and I know that's a horrible thing to say, and I'm so sorry. I really am. But then when that sensation finally fades, I have the weirdest desire to first hug you like you're my brother or something and then—"

"Run," he finished for her. It *was* possible. They had the same reaction to each other.

Her eyes widened. "Yes!"

"I feel the same way."

"You do?" she asked, relief and confusion giving way to insult. Her mouth curled into the cutest grimace.

He nodded, unable to stop his grin.

"What do you think it means?"

Both attracted and repelled, he thought. Like the magnets he'd played with as a child. One side possessed a positive pole. One side possessed a negative pole. When two different sides were pressed together, they bonded. When two like sides were pressed together, they created pressure, repelling each other. Were *they* like magnets?

And if so, did that mean she was like him? Or his opposite?

He studied her more intently. Did she know anything about the supernatural? If she didn't, and he started babbling about raising the dead and trapped souls, she *would* call him a freak. He would ruin his chances with her.

"I have to get home," he said, opting for escape. Hopefully, he would have figured this out by morning. "I'm on curfew, but I would love to talk to you tomorrow and—"

"Mary Ann," a boy suddenly called. Footsteps clomped, then an arm was wrapping around her waist. The owner of that arm was wide and as solid as a boulder. "Who you talking to, babe?"

She closed her eyes for a moment and pushed out a firm breath. "Tucker, this is Aden. One of the new students and my...friend. Aden, this is Tucker. My boyfriend."

Friend. She'd called Aden a friend. He couldn't stop himself from smiling. "Nice to meet you, Tucker."

Tucker's iron-gray gaze flicked to Aden's shirt and the insulting words scribbled there. He chuckled. "Cute."

Aden lost his grin. He'd been flying so high all day—passing tests, making truces and friends—he'd forgotten about the T-shirt. "Thanks."

"Why don't you beat feet and join your friend S-Stutter."
It was a command, not a question. "Mary Ann and I have
things to discuss."

Message received. He and Tucker would not be friends.
That was fine with him. Only person he cared about right now
was Mary Ann. Well, and Vision Girl, but she wasn't here.
Where was she? What was she doing?

"See you around, Mary Ann," he said.

She smiled, and it was warm and genuine. "I'll meet you
here in the morning and show you around."

A muscle ticked under Tucker's eye. "I'm sure he's busy.
Isn't that right, Crazy?"

Aden knew his next words would define the type of hate-
filled relationship he and Tucker would have. If he agreed,
Tucker would feel superior, assume Aden was properly intimi-
dated and taunt him for his weakness. If he didn't, Tucker
would view him as a competitor for Mary Ann's attention and
attack every chance he got.

He couldn't afford another enemy, but he raised his chin,
refusing to back down. "I'm not busy at all. I'll see you in the
morning, Mary Ann." He nodded to them both and ambled
away as if he hadn't a care.

MARY ANN WALKED TUCKER to the football field for practice,
calmly but firmly explaining that calling people names like
"Crazy" and "Stutter" was how they developed complexes and
why they later needed therapy.

"You should thank me for the future business, since you want to be a shrink," he said, rounding on her.

She was so shocked by his response, she stood with her mouth hanging open. He'd *never* talked to her so sarcastically.

His eyes narrowed. "Well, I'm waiting."

"Waiting for what?"

"First, for that thank-you I mentioned. Then you need to tell me you won't see that guy again. I don't like him and I don't like the way he was looking at you. And if he ever does it again, I will knock his teeth right out of his mouth."

The menace radiating off him was like needle pricks in her skin. She actually found herself backing up. What was wrong with him? Why was he acting this way? "You'll stay away from him, Tucker. Do you hear me? I don't want you hurting him. And just so you know, I'll be friends with whoever I want. If you don't like it, you can…we can…"

"You are not breaking up with me," he growled, crossing his arms over his chest. "I won't allow it."

That hadn't been on her mind, but she suddenly found herself contemplating the idea. The Tucker standing in front of her was not the Tucker she knew. This Tucker wasn't making her feel pretty or special; this Tucker, with his scowl and his threats, was alarming her.

This was the Tucker who had somehow helped throw a snake at Shannon—which she still needed to question him about. This was someone who had laughed at another person's fear. This was a Tucker she didn't like.

"You can't stop me if that's what I decide," she said.

To her surprise, his expression immediately softened. "You're right. I'm sorry. I shouldn't have butted in like that. I just want you safe. Can you blame me for that?" Oh, so gently, he reached out and traced a fingertip along her cheek.

She moved away from his touch. "Look, I—" she began, but one of the football players called for his help.

Oblivious to the tension still rolling through her, Tucker kissed the cheek he'd just caressed. "We'll talk tomorrow, all right?" He didn't wait for her reply but rushed off.

Reeling, she turned and headed toward the parking lot. What was she going to do with that boy? The way he'd treated Shannon and then Aden, and then callously excused his behavior…the way he'd expected her to thank him…she ground her teeth together. Yeah, he'd apologized. But had he meant it?

Penny's Mustang whipped around the corner just as Mary Ann stepped from the curb. There went her ride. She could call her dad and wait for him to come get her. She could walk home alone—and perhaps be a tasty bit of wolf bait—or she could chase Aden down.

"Aden," she called as she rushed forward. She couldn't see him, but she knew he couldn't have gotten far.

The sleek black wolf, taller than she remembered, bigger than she remembered, jumped out in front of her the moment she passed the line of trees that blocked off the school. She screamed, hand fluttering over her heart.

He gave an irritated growl, his green eyes bright. *Settle down. I won't hurt you.*

The word *yet* hung in the air, unsaid but palpable.

Though the voice came from in front of her, she whipped around, expecting to see someone behind her. But no, she and the wolf were alone. "Who said that?" The words trembled from her.

As I happen to be the only one around, I think you're safe in assuming that I did.

This time, the words came from behind her. Once more, she faced the wolf. No one was standing beside him. "This isn't funny," she said, a little more substance to the words now. Her gaze tripped left, right. Breath sawed in and out of her throat. Hot. Too hot, burning. "Who's there?"

I love being ignored, I really do. Look, I'm big, I'm black. I'm right in front of you.

She scanned the bright emerald foliage around her. There was no sign of life. "I told you. This isn't funny."

You're wasting time searching for someone else, little girl.

Again her attention fell to the wolf and she laughed without humor. "You can't be talking to me. You just can't. You're a...you are...you're not human."

Smart of you to notice. You're right about the other thing, too. I'm not talking. Out loud.

No, he wasn't. His harsh voice was echoing inside her mind, she realized, dazed. "This is ridiculous. Impossible."

One day you'll laugh about what you just said, because baby, I'm about to open your eyes to a whole new world. Were-wolves are just the beginning.

"Shut up!" Mary Ann rubbed her temples. More than ridiculous, this was insane. Utterly insane. Or rather, *she* was insane. This had to be a hallucination. Nothing else explained it. A wolf—or rather, a werewolf—who had walked her to school and clearly waited for her. A werewolf who was speaking directly into her mind.

What would her father say?

She thought she knew the answer. That she'd been working too hard, not resting enough, never enjoying herself, and this was her mind's way of taking a vacation. He'd tried to warn her this morning, in fact.

What if, now that she'd fallen over the edge, she needed medication? The thought scared her, and she laughed without humor. She didn't want this kind of breakdown in her medical files; most likely, it would haunt her for the rest of her life, ruining her chances of landing the internship she wanted. Who would trust her to handle their problems when she couldn't handle her own?

Bye-bye fifteen-year plan.

But maybe, just maybe, this is real, she told herself, part of her clinging to the hope. There was only one way to find out.

Mary Ann inched forward and stopped before she bumped into the creature's nose. "There's a difference between a wolf and a werewolf?" she babbled to break the silence. *Do it. Just do it.* Gulping, she lifted her arm.

Of course there is. One is merely an animal, the other is capable of being a man. Now, what are you doing?

Though she'd expected him to speak this time, she was still surprised and jerked away with a yelp. If she was wrong, if he was more than a hallucination, he could bite her. Maim her. Kill her. *Don't chicken out now.*

"Don't you already know what I'm doing? Can't you read my mind? I mean, you can talk inside it." A figment of her imagination would be able to read her mind, right?

No, I can't read thoughts. But I can see auras, the colors around you. Those colors tell me what you are feeling, making it easy to guess what you're thinking. But right now your colors are so jumbled I can't see anything.

"Well, I plan on touching you. If you'll just hold still, please." Great, now she was issuing orders, expecting him to understand. Could this be a joke? Was someone filming this, intending to laugh about her gullibility later? Surely not. No way could someone fake projecting a voice into her head. "If you bite me, I'll...I'll..."

He actually rolled his eyes. *You'll what? Bite me back? With those puny teeth?*

There wasn't a reply that would intimidate so irreverent a beast, so she remained quiet. And he remained in place, not even blinking as she reached out again, her index finger ready to poke. She was trembling and hesitant. Finally, skin met fur. Soft, silky fur.

"You're real," she gasped out. This was no hallucination. He was real, and he was freaking talking inside her mind, reading her aura. How were those things possible? Even more unbelievable, he claimed he was a werewolf, capable of changing into a human. That was...that was... Dear Lord.

A moan escaped him. *Scratch behind my ear.*

Still too dazed to process what was going on, she automatically pressed deeper, harder, massaging him.

He uttered another moan, snapping her back to her senses.

Hello. Anyone home? she thought. *You're willingly prolonging contact.*

Her arm fell to her side, suddenly too heavy to hold up. "You're real," she said again. Which meant she wasn't crazy. She should have jumped for joy, but couldn't force her body into motion. She was talking to a werewolf, person, *thing,* the ordinary world she'd woken up to no longer the world she inhabited. That wasn't exactly cause for celebration.

For a moment, he gave no response. Just closed his eyes, seeming to enjoy the lingering effects of her touch. Then his eyelids popped open, the green fierce and glittering, and he snarled at her. *Let's get down to business, shall we? What do you know of the boy?*

He. Was. Real. "Boy? What boy? I don't know why you're following me, but you can stop. You've got the wrong girl." Were there others out there, watching her? Had they always been here, able to communicate, and she just hadn't known? Wildly she looked left and right, panic building. When she saw no one, nothing, she backed away until she was pressed against the jagged bark of a tree trunk. "Seriously, you can go now."

Last time I'll ask nicely, little girl, and then I'll start demanding. You do not want that to happen, Mary Ann. Trust me.

First, he knew her name. The knowledge jolted her. Second, the words themselves were threatening. But the way he said them, so matter-of-factly, lent them a truth that all the shouting in the world couldn't have provided. If she didn't answer, he would force her. With claws, with teeth. Whatever was required.

He stalked toward her, slow and sure, closing the distance between them. *What do you know of the boy?*

He reached her and rose up, placing his front paws beside her temples, boxing her in.

The blood rushed from her head and pooled in her legs, making her head dizzy and her limbs all the heavier. "What boy?" she managed to gasp out.

I believe his name is Aden.

This was about Aden? "Why do you want to know about him?"

He ignored the question. *You spoke to him. What did you talk about?*

"Nothing personal, I swear. All I know is that he's a new student at my school. You're not going to hurt him, are you?"

Again, he ignored her. *What about the other boy? The one you escorted to the stadium.*

"That's Tucker. I'm dating him. Kind of. Maybe. It might be over. I think. Are you planning on hurting *him?*"

Suddenly the wolf growled, another of those low and menacing rumbles that danced over her nerve endings as delicately as a flutter of wings yet still managed to cut her up and leave her bare. Then she heard why he was suddenly ready to slaughter. Footsteps pounded through the grass, crunching against leaves and acorns. He stiffened and swung around, ready to face the threat.

Aden suddenly burst from the trees, sweat glistening over

his face and causing the shirt Tucker had taunted him about to stick to his chest.

"Mary Ann," he gasped out. "What's wrong?" Then he spotted the wolf and stilled, ready to defend and protect. "Move around the tree. Slowly." Gaze never leaving his foe, he bent and withdrew two daggers from his boots.

Her jaw dropped. He carried *daggers?*

The wolf reared back on its haunches, preparing to attack.

"No, please no," she cried out. "Don't fight." Not once, in all her life, had she ever pictured herself in the middle of something like this.

"Go home, Mary Ann," Aden demanded. He crouched, determined. "Now."

Tell him to leave us, the wolf snarled at her without removing his focus from Aden. Why wouldn't he tell Aden himself? Could he not talk to two people at once? Or did he not want Aden to know what he was? And why was she asking herself all these questions? A battle was about to take place!

"A-Aden," she began, attempting to move between them. The wolf twisted, blocking her path. "Don't fight him," she couldn't help but plead, suddenly unsure of whom she was speaking to. All she knew was that there would be a bloodbath if one of them didn't walk away. "Please, don't fight him. I'm fine. We're all fine. Let's just go our separate ways. Okay? Please."

Neither boy—wolf, whatever—listened to her. They circled each other, intent, panting viciously.

"Stop it, Eve," Aden snapped, his harsh voice like a boom amidst the silence. "I need quiet."

Eve?

Then Aden froze, blinked as if confused. He glanced at Mary Ann to ensure she was there, and frowned. "I can hear them."

She, too, blinked in confusion. "Who?"

Enough! the wolf roared. *Tell. Him. To. Go.*

"He wants you to go," she told Aden on a trembling breath. "Please go. I'll be fine, I swear."

"You can talk to it?" Thankfully, he didn't sound horrified. Didn't gaze at her as if she were insane.

"I—"

Do not say another word to him or I'll tear out his throat. Understand?

She pressed her lips together, a small whimper escaping. Never had she felt more helpless or scared. She had no idea what to do.

"Is he threatening you?" Aden asked, soft but fierce. Not waiting for her reply, he raised his blades, the silver tips gleaming menacingly in the sunlight. "C'mere, big boy, and we'll see if you like playing with someone more your size."

My pleasure.

"No!" she shouted as the wolf leapt forward. Aden met him midair. Only, they didn't collide. Aden disappeared. Actually disappeared. There one moment, gone the next.

The wolf fell to the ground, twitching, moaning. Both blades thumped uselessly beside him. Mary Ann rushed to his side, unsure of what had happened or how to react. Maybe she was in shock. There was no blood, so he hadn't been cut.

With a shaky arm, she reached out and brushed her palm

against his muzzle. *Why are you touching him?* common sense shouted. *Run!* She stayed put, her concern greater than her sense of survival. "Are you okay?"

His eyes popped open, no longer green but laced with all the colors Aden's eyes sometimes possessed. He jolted to his feet, unsteady, swaying. Slowly he backed away from her.

When he passed the line of trees, he swung around and ran.

SEVEN

I SAW HER. SAW THE GIRL.

Me, too.

Did you recognize her? I know I've seen her before.

Sorry, Eve, but I didn't.

Aden wanted to scream. There was too much noise in his head, so much he could barely process it. The glide of wind against the trees, the high-pitched chirps of nearby birds. The buzz of locusts, the song of the crickets. The croaks of the frogs.

Grunting, he forced the wolf's big body into motion. It was hard, moving his front legs in sync with his back legs, but he managed it, only stumbling a few times. He'd never overtaken the form of an animal before and wasn't sure he was doing it right. But there was no time to stop and ponder how to go about it. If he didn't hurry, he would be late. And if he was late, Dan would not allow him to attend school tomorrow.

How did you do that? the wolf snarled, his voice joining the clamor of the others. *Get out of my head! Out of my body!*

The creature knew he was there. Could feel him. That had never happened before, either. He would have thought the animal's more primitive mind unable to process the human language. For the most part, at least.

I'm not an animal, curse you.

What are you? he thought.

Wolf. Man. Werewolf. Now get out of me!

A…shape-shifter?

Aden hadn't known such things existed. Not in reality. Considering what he himself could do, he probably should have. Made him wonder what else was out there. Legends told of vampires, dragons, monsters and all kinds of other creatures.

Out! Now!

Even with those infuriated snarls, the run soon proved to be invigorating. Strengthening. Air danced through his fur, caressing all the way to the hair shaft. His gaze plowed the distance as though it were insignificant, taking in every detail, nothing missed. Colors were more vivid, and dust motes… wow. They were like snowflakes, glittering all around him.

I'll rip out your throat for this.

Still he kept moving, warm air sawing in and out of his nose. His lungs expanded, holding more oxygen than he was used to. It spurred him into a faster sprint, nails clawing at the ground. Scents were strong, nearly overpowering. Pine and dirt, a dead animal a few yards away. A deer, he somehow knew. He could hear the flies buzzing around the carcass.

I'll bathe in your blood, human. That is not a threat but a promise.

Again, the wolf's threats—promises—blended with that of his still-chattering companions. Caleb was apologizing for flinging him inside the body, Eve was asking about Mary Ann, concerned for her, and Julian and Elijah were begging him to be careful. Why hadn't Mary Ann sent them into that black hole this time? Aden had approached her, yet he'd still heard them. And he'd known thanks to Elijah—the soul's power *had* to be increasing as he'd suspected—that if he failed to stop the wolf, the creature would stalk her through this very forest one day, racing after her as she cried.

Mary Ann...

What would she think of him now? She knew he was different, that he could do things others could not. There was no denying it after what had happened. Maybe she would understand. She had spoken to the wolf, after all. Maybe, like Aden, she knew things that others did not. That would also explain how she was—sometimes—able to quiet the voices.

—vision is changing. He's going to hurt you the moment you exit his body, Elijah was saying. *Kill you.*

Yeah, Aden knew that. He also knew he'd be too weak to defend himself. There was only one thing he could do to save himself. He'd done it before, when he'd entered the body of a kid attacking him. He hated to do it, but there was no other way.

When the ranch came into view, he finally slowed, then stopped at the edge of the trees.

You can't stay in here forever. The wolf snarled, and Aden couldn't stop the sound from emerging. *Can you? Can you!* Much more, and they would be foaming at the mouth.

Aden glanced around the area, but didn't see anything that would help him do what needed to be done.

There was another way, he thought with a sigh. He sat on his haunches and extended one back leg. He peered down at it. The muscles were bunched, the fur glistening like black diamonds.

No, Eve said, realizing what was about to happen. *Don't do it.*

I have to, Aden thought. His stomach churned with nausea. There was no time to steel himself against the pain he was about to inflict. Forever wouldn't have been long enough to prepare. He simply bared the wolf's teeth and, with another vicious snarl, lunged at the leg. Those sharp fangs sank past that muscle and hit bone.

There was a scream inside his head, a grunt, several moans. Everyone felt the bite, the agonizing pain spreading like wildfire, affecting every organ it touched.

What the hell are you doing? the wolf shouted. *Stop. Stop!*

Maintaining that razored grip, firming his jaw, he jerked back. Warm, metallic-flavored liquid poured into his mouth, down his throat, and wet his fur. He gagged.

More screams, more moans.

Aden panted as the wolf's body sagged to the grass. The pain was immobilizing, just as he'd intended. Now when he left, he would not be followed or attacked.

It took every ounce of his mental strength to reach out of the animal's body, insubstantial hand solidifying and gripping the nearest tree root. The grip, though weak, held and he was able to tug himself out.

Aden lay there for a moment, stunned, trying to catch his breath. *Move. Move!* His human body refused to obey. He was no longer inside that mangled form, but his mind—or his companions—didn't care. They all knew what had been done and could feel the residual effects. His muscles were clamped down on his bones, holding him immobile.

The silver lining: adrenaline began crashing through him, trying to combat the "pain," giving him strength. Finally he was able to roll to his side. The wolf, he saw, lay exactly as he'd left him, leg extended, blood coating the wound, his mouth.

"I'm sorry," Aden said, and it was the truth. "I couldn't allow you to attack me."

Green eyes glared over at him, glazed with pain and fury.

Aden lumbered to his feet, swayed as a wave of dizziness swept through him. "I have to check in with the head of the house and then I'll come back with bandages."

A low howl promised retribution if he returned. Didn't matter. He was coming back. He stumbled his way to the bunkhouse and climbed through the window to his bedroom. Weak as he was, as little time as he had, he just couldn't deal with the dregs. All windows here were wired to a security system, but it was only switched on at night. Plus, Aden had long since cut and rewired the one in his room so that it *never* triggered the alarm (but looked like it would, just in case Dan decided to check.)

He had his own bathroom and downed a glass of water, then washed his face. Thankfully, there was no blood on his shirt, just dirt and grass stains. His face was completely devoid of color, his hair disheveled and laced with twigs.

He stuffed several bandages and a tube of antibiotic cream in a bag and chucked it out the window. He followed it, plucking the twigs from his hair. After he'd hidden it under rocks, he made his way to the main house.

Dan was sitting on the porch, Sophia sleeping at his feet. The window behind him was open, and through it he could hear the sounds of pots and pans banging together. Meg, Mrs. Reeves, was cooking. A peach pie, from the smell of it. Aden's mouth watered. The peanut butter sandwich he'd had for lunch was only a fond memory right now.

How could Dan betray that woman? Eve asked on a disgusted sigh. *She's a treasure.*

Who cares? Caleb exclaimed. *We've got stuff to do.*

Eve huffed. *I care. Cheating is wrong.*

How bad would it look if he shouted, "Shut up!" Aden wondered.

The moment Dan spotted Aden, he checked his wristwatch and nodded with satisfaction. "Right on time."

"I've been looking for you," Aden said, trying not to pant from fatigue. "Wanted to tell you how I did."

"I know how you did. The school called."

What? Had they complained about—

"Said you aced the tests," Dan finished.

Thank God. He nodded, knowing he should have been smiling but unable to manage it. He felt as if he were standing center stage, a spotlight trained on him, highlighting the signs of his run with—as—the wolf. Or rather, werewolf. It was weird to think like that, shape-shifter versus animal.

"I'm proud of you, Aden. I hope you know that."

Throughout his life, he'd disappointed people, confused them, embarrassed them and angered them. Dan's praise was…nice. "Th-thank you." How could Dan be so wonderful and yet, as Eve was still grumbling about, so slimy?

"Have you seen Shannon? He hasn't made it back yet."

He hadn't? Where was he? He'd gone ahead of Aden. "I haven't. I'm sorry. We left the school separately."

Dan gave his watch another glance.

"Guess I'll go do my chores now," Aden said, though he had no intention of starting them until after he saw to the wolf's care. He managed only one backward step before Dan stopped him.

"Not so fast. I was also told you stayed after school to talk to a girl."

Aden gulped. Nodded. Someone had clearly been watching him, and he didn't like it. He only wished he'd felt the heat of their stare; a little warning would have been nice. If Dan forbade him to hang with Mary Ann he would—

"You treated her right?"

That was all the man was concerned with? His shoulders slumped with relief. "Yeah."

Dan's head tilted to the side. "Not very talkative today, are you?"

"I'm tired, is all. Nerves kept me up all night."

"I can understand that. Go on, then. Do your chores and then make an early night of it. I'll have dinner sent to your room."

"Thank you," he found himself saying again. He rushed back

to the bunkhouse, but didn't enter. He grabbed the bag he'd tossed out his window and headed back into the forest, staying in the shadows so that no one would see what he was doing.

The werewolf was gone.

The only sign that he'd been there was the patch of blood, still wet and gleaming in the sunlight. While he didn't see the animal, he did see Shannon, cut up and bleeding and headed toward Dan.

Stomach once again churning, Aden followed and eavesdropped from a distance.

"They were w-waiting for me. A group of them. Th-they jumped me."

"Who were they?" Dan asked, his anger clear. "Did you get a good look at them?"

"N-no."

Aden frowned. Shannon had green eyes; the wolf had green eyes. Shannon was hurt; the wolf had been hurt. Shannon was here now; the wolf was gone. Had he really been jumped or was that a lie to cover something else? An ability most people wouldn't understand? Shannon hadn't limped, though, and that leg wound wouldn't have had time to heal. Would it?

Later, in the barn while they shoveled horse manure, he tried to question Shannon about what had happened, gently trying to steer the conversation toward Mary Ann and wolves to gauge the boy's reaction. All he received was silence.

ADEN TOSSED AND TURNED for hours, resigned to another sleepless night. His mind was simply too wired. The souls were asleep, finally, so his thoughts were his own—but they weren't welcome thoughts. All he could hear was the gasp of shock from Mary Ann when he'd inhabited the werewolf's body. All he could picture was the werewolf, bleeding... dying? Or was Shannon the werewolf, as he suspected? Had he raced into the woods after school, transformed and sprinted back to Mary Ann before Aden could reach him?

If Shannon *was* the wolf, Shannon now wanted to kill him. Had promised to kill him, actually. He'd have to watch, study and wait. If he could. By now, Mary Ann could have told someone what she'd seen. Most likely she wouldn't be believed, but with his past...the accusation would ruin him.

He could pack up, he supposed. Head out on his own. He'd done it before, three years ago. Living on the streets had been hard. He'd had no shelter, no food, water or money. He'd tried to steal a guy's wallet and, unskilled as he'd been, had been caught and hauled back to juvie.

He was smarter now, he told himself. Older. He *could* survive. For the first time in his life, though, he had something to look forward to, something to anticipate. School, friends...peace. Running away would destroy even the chance of such happiness.

He sighed, closed his eyes.

"Awaken."

The word whispered through his mind, sultry yet commanding. His eyelids popped open. The girl from the forest stood over him, dark hair falling like a curtain over her shoulders. She hadn't been there a moment ago, but she was a welcome and beautiful sight.

Was this a replay of a vision? Because he'd seen this before.

Her, standing in front of him. Soon she would motion him outside. He would follow.

He inhaled deeply, breathing in her honeysuckle and roses scent. No, no vision. This was real.

He smiled slowly and tried to recall the rest of the details to this particular scene. They would walk to the woods and she would close the distance between them. She would reach up, trace her fingertips down his neck. Would her skin be as hot as he remembered or as cold as it now appeared?

He couldn't wait to get started. "Where have you been? What—"

"Shh. We do not want to wake the others."

He pressed his lips together, but couldn't stop the sudden pounding of his heart. The same black robe draped her, revealing one pale, slender arm. A large opal ring glinted from her left index finger. In the visions, she was always careful not to let that ring touch him.

"I'm glad you're here," he whispered.

Her eyes narrowed, but he could still see the crystalline glow of them. She doesn't know you the way you know her, he reminded himself. He had to be careful with his praise.

"Come." She beckoned him with the crook of a finger and walked—no, floated—to the window. Then, without moving another inch, she seemed to disappear. A breeze brushed over him.

He was standing a second later, his body compelled to obey on a level he didn't understand. And hadn't expected. He'd walked in his vision, yes, but he hadn't realized *he* would not be the one in control. His feet moved of their own accord, maneuvering him in front of the opened window. Could *she* possess other bodies? He didn't sense her inside him, but...maybe.

Not even when he climbed through, his bare feet pressed against the dewy grass, was he able to grasp the reins of control. He didn't panic, though. He was with Vision Girl. That was all that mattered.

He scanned the area, finally spotting her a few yards ahead, in the line of trees. She hadn't possessed him, then. But what *was* she doing to him?

"Come." Again, she beckoned him with a finger. Again, she seemed to disappear—but not before her gaze raked him from head to toe.

He fought a wave of embarrassment. The only piece of clothing he wore was a pair of boxers. At least they were plain black rather than the red-and-white pair that were covered in Valentine hearts.

What did she think of him?

Part of him felt as though he already knew her, and that part of him was already comfortable with her, already half in love with her. After all, that part of him knew the taste of her lips, had heard the way she sighed his name and felt the way she melted in his arms.

But the rational side of his brain was growing a bit wary. Last time she'd truly spoken to him, she'd wanted to know things he had no answers for. Last time he'd seen her, she'd been with another boy.

The night was cool, the sky painted with clouds. Crickets

chirped, and in the distance a dog barked. Both soon quieted, leaving only silence. Utter silence, thick and dark.

Until his companions began to wake up, yawning inside his mind.

Outside? Julian asked sleepily.

"Yes," he whispered.

Ugh. We're not running away again, are we? Caleb demanded.

"No."

Eve sighed with relief. *Thank God.*

Want to tell us what's going on, then? Elijah asked.

"We're living a vision." Finally, he reached a clearing, foliage surrounding him, hiding him from prying eyes. But where was Vision Girl? Again, there was no longer any sign of her.

"Stop," she said. Her voice came from behind him and he spun around. And there she was, his beauty. His...killer? She held a dagger in each hand. His daggers. The ones he'd dropped earlier when he'd slipped inside the wolf's body.

He frowned.

A beam of moonlight peeked through the clouds and swathed her, illuminating the thick blue streaks in her hair—not an illusion caused by the sun, then, as he'd supposed last time he'd seen her—as well as the daggers. Surely she wouldn't stab him. She looked too innocent in the haze of shadows and gold, dainty, harmless.

"Where's the boy?" he asked. Now there was someone who wouldn't mind cutting him up. He hadn't forgotten the anger that had radiated from the male. "The one I saw you with?"

She remained in place, head tilting to the side. "Had he come tonight, he would have killed you."

Points to Aden for having figured that out already. "Why?"

"He's jealous of you. Besides, I'm not supposed to be here and had he known where I was headed, he would have stopped me. I *had* to come alone."

A thousand questions seemed to rush through his mind at once. Someone was jealous? Of Aden? Why? And why wasn't she supposed to be here? In the end, he asked the one he felt had the greatest chance of being answered. "How did you get me here? You spoke and I was forced to obey."

She lifted a delicate shoulder in a shrug. "A little gift of mine, you could say. These are yours, I believe." Steps measured, she approached. When she reached him, she stopped and extended the daggers.

Aden was proud of himself. He didn't flinch or even crouch to attack.

Who is she? Eve asked.

I have another bad feeling, Aden. Elijah sounded panicked all of a sudden. *I think you should leave.*

"Quiet," he mumbled.

"Don't tell me what to do," the girl snapped. The more she spoke, the more he detected an accent. Not English, but close.

"I wasn't talking to you."

Confusion washed over her lovely features. She gazed around the forest. "Who, then? We are alone."

"Myself." In a roundabout way.

"I see," she said, but it was clear she didn't. "Here. Take

these." She placed the weapons in his hands before he could take them...touch her. "I'm sure you will need them in the coming days."

Nope, she had never meant to hurt him. He looked down at the sharp metal, fingers curling around the hilts. "You aren't afraid I'll use them on you?"

A laugh escaped her, the sound like bells tinkling. "It wouldn't matter if you did. They cannot hurt me."

Oh, really? "Sorry to be the one to tell you this, but no one can withstand a blade."

"I can. I cannot be cut." Absolute confidence radiated from her.

His arms fell to his sides. "Who are you?" *What* are you? He quashed the second question before it could escape, not wanting to offend her. Again.

Besides, the answer really didn't matter, he supposed. He was glad she was here, whatever she was.

"My name is Victoria."

Victoria. He rolled the name through his mind. Soft, lovely. Like her. "I'm Aden."

"I know," she said, voice now hard.

"How?"

Again using those slow, measured steps, she circled him. "I've been following you for days."

Days? No way. He'd only seen her that once. You're not always the most observant of people, he reminded himself. "Why?"

In front of him again, closer than before, almost brushing

against him, she said, "You know why." Her breath was a lick of heat against his skin, like a bonfire on a winter day.

He liked it. A lot. But he would have given anything for actual contact. "I don't."

Her gaze met his, as hard as her tone had been. "You called us."

On the phone? "I couldn't have. I don't even have your number."

"Are you trying to provoke me?"

"No. I honestly didn't call you."

She pushed out a frustrated breath. "A week ago, you somehow overwhelmed my people with energy. Energy that was so strong, it left us writhing in pain for hours. Energy that latched onto us and tugged us to you as if we were tethered with rope."

"I don't understand. Energy? Sent by me?" A week ago, the only thing he'd done was kill a few corpses and meet Mary Ann.

With the thought, his eyes widened. The first time he'd seen Mary Ann, everything had ceased to exist before the world had seemed to explode in a burst of wind. Could *that* be what Victoria meant? And what did that mean for him and Mary Ann if it was?

"Who are your people? Where do you live?"

"I was born in Romania," she said, ignoring his first question. "Wallachia."

His brow furrowed as he considered her claim. A tutor had once forced him to do a report on Romania. He knew that Wallachia was north of the Danube and south of the Carpathians and that Wallachia was not what the town was now called. He also knew there was no way the wind he and Mary Ann had generated could have reached a place that far away. Right?

"Were you there when the energy hit you?"

"Yes. We move around a lot, but we *had* just returned to Romania. So what game do you play with us, Aden Stone? Why did you want us here?"

Us? No, he'd only wanted her. "If I *was* the one to send that energy, it wasn't intentional," he said.

She lifted her hand and rested her fingertips just below his ear. He closed his eyes for a moment, savoring. Finally. Contact. Her skin was burning hot, static, like lightning. Down her nails raked, gentle, so gentle, stopping at the base of his neck where his pulse hammered.

"Intentional or not," she said, "my father was angered. And believe me, his anger is a terrifying thing. The stuff of nightmares. He wanted you dead."

Aden was too entranced by her actions to be scared of her words. "Is that why you brought me here? To kill me?" Then why had she given him the blades? "You'll understand if I don't lie down and take it, I'm sure."

The harshness of his tone must have jarred her because she backed away until she was no longer within easy reach. I should have kept my mouth closed, he thought darkly. What would it take to make her return?

"I said my father *wanted* you dead," she admitted softly, gaze falling to the ground. "He no longer does. I convinced him to wait, to study you. We still feel the hum of your power, after all."

One part of her speech intrigued him more than any other. "Why?"

She didn't pretend to misunderstand. He wanted to know why she would seek to help him, a boy she knew nothing about. "You...fascinate me." Her cheeks brightened with pink. "That was stupid of me to say. Pretend I said something else."

"I can't," he said. Nor did he want to. "You fascinate me, too. I've thought about you since the moment I first saw you." He didn't tell her that had been months ago, in a vision. Didn't tell her that sometimes she'd been the only thing in his life worth living for. "And when you visited me while I was sick...don't try to deny it," he added when she opened her mouth. "You took care of me, I know you did. I've wanted to spend time with you ever since."

She shook her head as he spoke, tendrils of hair slapping her face. "We cannot like each other. We cannot become friends."

"That's good, because I don't want to be your friend. I want to be more." The words rushed from him, unstoppable. What he felt for this girl was different than what he'd ever felt for anyone else. It was more intense, consuming.

Maybe he should have kept that information to himself, as he'd told himself earlier, at least for a little while. But because of Elijah's death-vision, he knew his days were numbered.

"You wouldn't say that if you knew..." Her eyes narrowed on him. "Do you have any idea of what I am, Aden? Of what my father is?"

"No." And it didn't matter. He had four souls trapped in his head. Like he could really complain about someone else's heritage, whatever it was.

Before he could blink, Victoria was once again in his face, pushing him backward until he slammed into a tree and lost his breath. He'd wanted her near him, but not like this. Not angry.

Her lips pulled back from her teeth, revealing sharp white fangs. "You would be running in terror if you knew."

Those fangs… "But…you can't be. You stood in sunlight. I saw you."

"The older we are, the more the sunlight hurts us. The younger ones like me can stand in it for hours, unaffected." There at the end, her voice rose. "Do you understand now? We use your people for food. Our mobile meals. Our blood on tap. And if we like that food enough, we drink again and again until that human becomes our blood-slave. But they never become our friends. To care for them is useless, for we will live on while they wither and die."

He'd wondered what else was out there, and now he knew. "I can't… I mean… A vampire."

Suddenly, in his mind, one of Elijah's visions opened up and he saw Victoria's head against his shoulder, her teeth in his neck. He saw his knees buckle and his lifeless body fall to the ground. Saw her back away from him, mouth smeared with crimson, horror in her eyes.

He wanted to deny what he was seeing but couldn't. He'd suspected Elijah's ability was growing and this proved it. Victoria was here, real and in front of him. She'd led him into this forest, had touched his neck.

One day, Victoria would bite him. Drink from him. It wouldn't kill him—someone's knife would do that—but it *would* leave him helpless.

Could he stop it from happening? Did he *want* to stop it? Having Victoria in his life had somehow become almost as important to him as breathing.

The vision faded, and Aden blinked, his surroundings coming back into view. He was still in the forest, but Victoria was nowhere to be seen. With a sigh, he made his way back to the house, already knowing he wouldn't sleep.

EIGH†

MARY ANN ARRIVED at school an hour and a half early. Presently, she was the only one outside, the sun barely peeking through the clouds. Good thing. She was shaking, unkempt. All night she'd sat at her computer, researching werewolves and paranormal abilities, replaying what had happened in the woods through her mind.

Though she'd printed hundreds of pages, she had found nothing substantiated, both subjects treated as fiction. In that fiction, werewolves were able to shift from animal to man, but even then none were reported as having the ability to insert their voices into human minds. But she knew, *knew,* that wolf had spoken inside her head.

The ability to make a body disappear was known as teleporting, and she also knew Aden had vanished. Knew his body had gone through the wolf's but hadn't come out the other side. She hadn't imagined it. Her terror had been too real, and the feel of the wolf was still burned on her hand.

Was the wolf okay? The question had plagued her all night long, which in turn caused guilt to eat away at her. She should care more about Aden. Was *he* okay? Where had he gone? Had he returned? *Could* he return? She'd looked up Dan Reeves's number but it was unlisted, so she'd almost driven over there. The only thing that had stopped her was the thought of getting Aden in trouble. That, and the fear of voicing what had happened and being told she was delusional.

I'm not crazy, she thought, pacing in front of the black double doors. She was going to confront Aden, demand answers. *If* he showed up. And if he denied his ability, she'd...what? Her shoulders sagged. She didn't know what she'd do. Telling her dad—or any adult—would earn her a referral to one of her dad's coworkers and perhaps medication. She'd known it in the forest, the first time the wolf had spoken to her, and she knew it now. Her friends would laugh at her, perhaps ostracize her.

A dark blue sedan eased into the parking lot, and Mr. White, the principal, emerged, briefcase in hand. He frowned when he saw her, his steps clipped as he approached. He was an older man with thinning hair and wrinkled features. His glasses were thick, as was his silver mustache.

"You're here early," he said.

She smiled; the action felt brittle. She'd always liked him because he'd always been kind to her, but she couldn't feign her usual upbeat mood. "Just wanted to get away from my house to study for today's chem test," she lied.

His dark eyes filled with pride. "Want to come in? You can wait in the office."

"No, thanks." She'd stand out here all day if she had to, but she wasn't moving from this spot until Aden arrived. *If* he arrived, she couldn't help but add again. Knots formed in her stomach, twisting painfully. "The air out here helps me think." When had she become such a fraud?

"Well, you're welcome to come inside if you change your mind. I'll leave the door unlocked."

Alone again, she renewed her pacing. Her gaze continually strayed to the line of trees, looking for the wolf. She stomped her foot. No. Not the wolf. Aden. Looking for Aden.

An eternity passed before teachers began arriving. Finally, the students showed up. All but Aden.

Penny's Mustang swung into the lot, the tires squealing a little. Her friend had no concept of speed laws and why they were important, which was ironic since she was usually late. Several people had to jump out of the way as Penny parked.

Today Penny wore a sapphire dress that matched her eyes. Eyes that were rimmed with red, Mary Ann noticed. Her pale hair was anchored in a ponytail, as though arranging it into the usual neat style would have taken too much energy. Her skin was pallid, her freckles stark.

Mary Ann met her halfway. "What's wrong?" she asked, concern for her friend momentarily obliterating her worries about the wolf and Aden.

The question earned a strained laugh. "What's wrong with me? Nothing. Tucker called me last night *and* this morning, wanting to know if I knew what was wrong with *you*. Said you'd acted weird after school yesterday. Said he'd called you all evening, but you didn't answer."

Tucker was of no importance right now. Especially the new Tucker who hurt people's feelings and threatened her friends. "Tucker's just going to have to wait." She looked past her friend, watching the trees for any sign of life.

Finally, she was rewarded. Shannon cut through, big and beautiful. The entire world seemed to slow down, her skin tightening over her bones. Aden might be close. And it wasn't disappointment she was feeling, she assured herself. Seeing the wolf should be last on her list of priorities.

"I'll call you later, okay?" Off she rushed, Penny's sputtering ringing in her ears. Her backpack slapped against her, the books inside nearly crushing her spine. "Shannon!" she called.

He spotted her and his eyes widened, a startling green against the darkness of his skin. Once again, those eyes reminded her of the wolf's. Her wolf. *Oh my God.* Could he be her wolf?

The closer she came, the more he tried to swoop around her. Which wasn't like her wolf. Frowning, she jumped in front of him, blocking his path.

"Is Aden coming?"

His brows drew together. "W-why do you c-care?"

Her wolf hadn't stuttered, either. But then, he also hadn't been using his mouth. God, this was confusing. And weird! Picturing a human morphing into a wolf was not normal.

But was Shannon or wasn't he?

"I just do," she finally said. "Is he coming or not?"

"He's b-behind me."

He'd reappeared, then. That meant he was alive and well. Her relief was so great, her knees almost buckled. She was grinning as she said, "Thank you. Thank you so much."

Shannon didn't respond, but he couldn't hide the curiosity in his eyes as he finally maneuvered around her and headed into the school. Knowing Aden was out there made waiting that much harder, but she did it, stood there and waited until he came into view. When she saw him, her knees almost buckled again.

That same burning wind stabbed at her chest, there one moment, gone the next, and she would have sworn she'd been cut open, even though she knew otherwise. Before, that might have freaked her out and sent her racing away. Not this time. This time, she wanted answers. Aden was unlike anyone she'd ever met. His eyes changed color in the light, and he was able to disappear in a blink. How was any of that possible?

"Hello, Aden," she said.

His step faltered when he noticed her. His expression became guarded, his gaze scanning the area behind her as if he expected someone to jump out and grab him. Someone like the wolf? Or an adult? She, too, glanced around. There was no other hint of life, the insects and birds strangely quiet.

"Mary Ann." There was a bite to his tone he'd never used with her before. He stopped in front of her. "What are you doing here? With me, I mean."

Whatever had happened to him, he hadn't changed physically. He was just as tall, just as adorable with his black-dyed hair and swirling eyes. No cuts, no bruises.

"I want to know what happened yesterday," she said.

He uttered a nervous laugh. "What do you mean? Someone's dog escaped and scared you. I shooed it away and went home."

Liar! "That's not what happened, and you know it."

"It is," he insisted. "Your fear has just distorted your memory."

No. No, no. He wasn't going to convince her the entire thing had been a mind-trick brought on by the intensity of her emotions. She'd spent too much time replaying the scene through her head last night. Too much time wondering about that wolf.

"Tell me what happened, Aden. Please."

For a moment, he didn't speak. Then he sighed. "Just let it go, Mary Ann."

"No! One thing you'll learn about me, Aden. I'm stubborn to a fault. You'll give me the answers I want or I'll get them another way." Not that she knew what that other way would be, but still.

"Fine." His stare was penetrating as he gave her his full attention. "What do *you* think happened?"

Going to play that game, was he? Let her voice her version of events so he could tailor his own recounting to either fit or discredit hers. Her dad had used a similar technique on her many times, like the day he'd given her the sex talk. *Tell me what you know,* he'd said, and then blushed when she had.

"Look, I haven't told anyone what I witnessed." She crossed her arms over her chest. "And I won't. It's our secret, yours and mine. But you have to tell me what's going on. I'm in the middle of something I'm completely clueless about, seeing things I once thought were impossible." She was babbling, she knew she was, but couldn't stop. "I don't know what to do or how to protect myself. Actually, I don't know what I need to protect myself from or if I even need to be worried."

His gaze flicked pointedly to the school. "Maybe now isn't the best time to discuss this. We'll be late to first period."

"Let's ditch." She'd never uttered those words before and had never thought to do so. In fact, in the past, when she'd even considered them, she'd gotten sick. Now, all she wanted to do was talk to Aden. Nothing else mattered. "We can go to my house, my dad's at work. We'll have privacy for the rest of the day."

For a moment, his expression was so tortured she had to glance at his nails to make sure pins hadn't been shoved underneath them. "I can't," he said. "If I ditch a single day, I'm—okay, look, I have a confession to make. I do live at the D and M Ranch and if I ditch, I'll be kicked out. I don't want to be kicked out. Besides, this is my first day. My teachers are expecting me."

A dejected breath left her. "Then we won't ditch. But we *will* talk." *Please, please, please.*

He nodded reluctantly. "Come on. Walk me to school. We'll talk along the way. Just be careful what you say, okay? You never know who, or what, is lurking nearby."

Though she wanted to stay right where she was to prevent their conversation from ending before she was ready, she pivoted and they ambled toward the school side by side. Thankfully, they had a while yet until they reached the masses blithely going about their day. As she once had, she thought.

"You don't have to start at the beginning or anything like that. Just tell me *something,*" she pleaded.

There was a heavy pause. Another sigh. "What if I told you there was an entire world out there you had no idea existed? A world of—" he gulped "—vampires and werewolves, and people with unexplainable abilities?"

A whole new world, the wolf had told her. "I—I would believe you." But she didn't want to. She wanted to deny it. Despite everything she'd witnessed, despite the fact that he was saying exactly what she'd expected him to say, denial was her first instinct. The thought of bloodsuckers and shape-shifters was abhorrent. The people with unexplainable abilities she didn't yet understand—but she would. She was determined.

"And what if I told you there was a boy who was somehow a magnet for those things, drawing them closer and closer to him? A boy with strange powers of his own?"

She licked her lips. "Can this boy disappear in the blink of an eye?"

He shook his head, a single jerky motion.

"But I saw—"

"Not disappear," he said, stopping her. "You saw him possess someone else's body."

Dear God. Aden could possess other people's bodies. Just step inside them as if they were an elevator and he needed a ride. She shuddered, fighting the urge to dart away so he couldn't do such a thing to her.

He'd ground to a halt, she realized, no longer seeing him at her side. She whipped around. He was regarding her with that tortured expression again, this one mixed with fear and dread. He *expected* her to run screaming from him.

She might have done so, had she continued to think about him possessing her. This was just so much to take in. Too much, probably, for a girl who had always relied on science to explain the unknown. He didn't deserve that sort of treatment, though. He was giving her what she wanted, what she'd demanded. What he hadn't—and clearly still didn't—want to give.

He must live with a constant fear of discovery, afraid of what people would do to him if they knew. Such stress would have destroyed the bravest of men, and that he was standing there, unmoving, expectant, waiting, proved the depth of his strength. That he'd told her anything at all proved the depth of his friendship.

She softened her expression as she closed the distance between them. Beads of sweat glistened from his forehead, a testament to his nervousness. *I will not fear him. I will not fear him,* she mentally chanted. Without warning him, she wrapped her arms around his waist, giving him the hug she'd wanted to give him since the moment she'd seen him.

At first, he remained stiff, unyielding, then his own arms encircled her tentatively. They stayed like that for several minutes, lost in the moment. As he held her, any lingering qualms she'd harbored vanished. Yesterday he had protected her from the werewolf. He didn't want to hurt her.

He was the one to pull away, as if he didn't trust himself to continue. His expression was blank but his eyes…oh, his eyes. They were brown this time. What did the change mean? She had so much to learn about him.

"So tell me. Is possessing bodies all this boy can do?" she asked softly.

Another shake of his head.

So there was more. Surprisingly, the fear did not return. "What else?"

He tangled his fingers through his hair, and a thick black lock tumbled to his forehead. "Mary Ann, what do you think the chances are that this make-believe boy who can do things others can't has spent most of his life shuffled from one mental institution to another?"

Mental institutions? Poor, sweet Aden. She might be young, but she'd seen how intolerant people could be of those who were different. Look how Tucker had treated Shannon because of his stutter. And a stutter was nothing compared to what Aden could do!

"I think there's a very good chance, but that wouldn't make me like him any less."

He gazed down at his feet, hiding his disbelief. A moment passed. He sighed, grabbed her hand, and spun her around, tugging her toward the school. "How can you accept this so easily?"

"Easily?" She barked out a laugh completely devoid of humor. "I agonized over this all night. Did I—" They were pretending to speak of other people, she reminded herself. "Could a girl actually hear a werewolf speaking inside her head? And if she didn't, was she crazy? Did she truly see a boy disappear? And if she didn't, was she crazy? She either had to accept what she'd seen or admit she was, you guessed it, crazy."

His grip tightened. Warm and strong. Comforting. Comfort she needed as much as he did, she realized.

"What about the wolf?" she asked. "What happened to him?"

"Last time I saw him, he was alive." There was a wealth of guilt in his tone.

Why the guilt?

"Did he tell you anything?" she asked. "Mention why he was following me?"

"No, and there wasn't time to ask him. Had there been, though, I don't think he would have answered me. We weren't exactly on friendly terms when I left him."

"He *is* a boy, though, right?" Goose bumps broke out over her skin as she remembered the husky timbre of his voice inside her head, that warm fur against her skin, those pale green eyes watching her every move. Shivers, not shudders. *What's wrong with me?*

"Yes. A very dangerous one. If he returns, stay away from him. He promised to kill me."

"What? Why?"

Finally they reached the school, and he wasn't able to answer. She released Aden's hand when one of her class-mates, she didn't know the guy's name, spotted them and gaped. She wasn't embarrassed for people to see her with Aden and think that they were a couple, and she hoped he realized that. If she'd been crushing on him, she would have been proud to be his girlfriend. But she wasn't his girlfriend; she still thought of him as a brother-type. And the simple fact was, things weren't settled with Tucker yet.

Tucker. What was she going to do about him?

The last time she'd gone to sleep, she'd seen the world in black and white. A world where a fifteen-year plan had driven her every action. Now, her eyes were open to its vast and vivid colors, to a puzzle she desperately wanted to solve, each minute a surprise she couldn't possibly plan for. Where did Tucker fit in this new life? Did she *want* him to fit?

Mary Ann sighed. Looked like she had more than wolves and secret abilities to figure out.

AFTER THEY STOPPED by the office and picked up a map, Mary Ann gave Aden the promised tour of Crossroads High. Their conversation about the supernatural had ended the moment they'd hit the parking lot and they were careful not to resume it, speaking only of the mundane.

Aden was glad for the reprieve, though he knew it would end soon enough. He wasn't sure what else he'd tell her when the time came. Wasn't sure what she could handle. What little he *had* revealed had caused her to pale and shake. He wanted her help with the souls, yes, but…

Could he trust her not to tell anyone? Again, he desperately wanted to, and she claimed that he could. But people, he'd learned at a very young age, often lied. *We'll always love you, but this is for your own good,* his mother had told him in a note. A note she'd left for him at that first institution and he'd read years later. His parents had never returned for the son they "loved." *This won't hurt,* doctor after doctor had told him, just before shoving a needle somewhere in his body.

People would say anything to get the reaction they desired. His parents hadn't wanted him to think poorly of them or their decision. The doctors hadn't wanted him to fight them.

With Mary Ann, he'd forgotten—or chosen to overlook like the idiot he was—years of lessons learned. The way she'd hugged him...as if he meant something to her, as if they were already family and had to look out for each other. Telling her, though, was the only way to gain her help. If she *could* help, that is.

"Watch out." Mary Ann jerked him to the side.

A group of jocks passed, barely missing him. "Sorry. My mind wandered." And it hadn't been because of the souls. Unlike yesterday in the forest, when he'd heard them while in proximity to Mary Ann, they were once again dormant. He didn't understand it, either.

He frowned—and almost slammed into someone else. His mind had wandered again. How long had he been walking through the school's corridors without really seeing them?

He forced himself to take everything in. The walls were painted black, gold and white—the school colors—and posters that read *Go Jaguars* decorated each expanse. Kids rushed in every direction. Lockers were opened and slammed shut. Girls laughed and talked while the boys checked them out.

"Football season's in full swing," Mary Ann said. "Do you

play? I mean, I know Dan used to, so I figured he would have the boys at the ranch train with him."

"No. I don't play, and Dan doesn't have us practice. We have too many chores." Aden loved watching the game, though, and hated that he couldn't concentrate long enough to experience it firsthand.

"I'm sorry," she said.

"Why?"

"Well, you sounded sad, like you wish you could play but—" Her lips pressed together as she realized why contact sports might not be the best thing for someone who could possess another's body.

She had no idea that was only part of the problem. "Believe me. I'll recover." There were a thousand other things he could worry about. "What will your boyfriend think of you giving me this tour? He didn't want you to, remember?"

"I don't want to talk about him." Before Aden could respond, she added, "Now let me see your schedule."

Apparently, he wasn't the only one who knew how to change a subject. He pulled the paper from his pocket and handed it to her.

She ran a finger down the list. "We have two classes together. First and second period."

"Are you going to let me cheat off your papers?" he teased.

"Maybe I'll cheat off yours. I might have straight As, but I've had to slave for every single one."

"We should study together."

"Like we'd really get anything done," she said with a laugh.

"Wait. We're supposed to accomplish something? I thought the word study was code for getting together and talking."

Another laugh. "I wish."

How normal this felt. And despite everything going on, he realized he was happy.

The wolf wanted to eat him for breakfast—so what. Victoria, the girl he still wanted to kiss with every ounce of his being, would one day drink from him—so what. Someone was going to stab him in the heart—again, so what. He could deal.

No matter what life threw at him next, he could deal.

NINE

BECAUSE OF ADEN'S CURFEW, Mary Ann didn't get a chance to talk to him after school.

So, the next morning, she waited for him at the front doors but Tucker got to her first. Too afraid to let the boys interact, she asked Tucker to walk her to class. He, at least, seemed back to his normal self, solicitous and admiring. Still. She didn't know what to do about him, maybe because her mind had too many other things to ponder. Like Aden and the wolf.

She tried to talk to Aden in each of their shared classes, but the teachers separated them, watching him closely, as if they expected him to be a bad influence. And between classes, there were too many kids in the halls to say anything of importance.

At lunch, he was nowhere to be found. Where he went, she didn't know, but his absence was probably for the best. As always, she sat with Tucker and his crew, as well as Penny and hers. No telling how they would have reacted if she left them to be with Aden.

Sadly a week crawled by in the same manner: Tucker met her in the morning, teachers ensured she and Aden maintained their distance, and he disappeared at lunch. They never again had the chance to chat. She couldn't help but wonder if Aden was relieved not to have to tell her any more of his secrets.

Each day after their final class, he was given another reprieve. She didn't *want* to see him. Her wolf—the wolf who had promised to kill him—always waited for her. Actually, he walked her to *and* from school. The relief she'd felt upon first seeing him again, of knowing he was okay, still filled her every time she saw him.

For the good of everyone, she was careful to keep Aden and the wolf apart. But it was costing her bits and pieces of her sanity. She had to talk with Aden soon. How was he doing in his classes? Was he adjusting? Had he made friends? Where did he go at lunch?

What other abilities did he have?

That was the question that plagued her most.

Soon, either before or after school, she would have to shoo the wolf away so that she and Aden could have a moment of privacy. Not that she wanted to shoo him away. She was beyond curious about him. She kept expecting him to reveal his human form—*today's the day,* she'd think every morning, followed by *any moment now* every afternoon—and tell her what was going on. But he'd maintained radio silence since that first day.

She sighed. Today the sun was high and hot, the shadows provided by the trees only slightly cooling. Any second now and her new friend would—

He jumped out at her.

—show up.

This time, she didn't blink, didn't stumble, too used to his presence. He kept pace beside her, his claws scraping against the occasional stone. The first few days, he'd limped. Now, his gait was smooth and easy. She'd asked him what had happened but, of course, he hadn't answered.

It amazed her that she'd once felt threatened by him. Now, she felt safe, like nothing bad could happen to her. Like he would protect her with his life. Silly of her, she knew. But after only a week, there was nothing left of her former self. Her rigid study schedule had been upended, and for once she hadn't worked all possible hours during the weekend. She spent every spare minute thinking about Aden and this wolf.

"I still haven't decided what to do about Tucker," she said, knowing the wolf wouldn't answer but needing someone to talk to. "He's my boyfriend and I like him, for the most part, but...I don't know. Being with him just doesn't feel right anymore. He's leaving Aden and Shannon alone, at least, so I guess I shouldn't complain too much."

The wolf growled.

For Tucker's benefit or for hers? "I wish I knew your name. I hate thinking of you as 'the wolf.'"

Silence.

"Fine. I'll just call you Wolfie and you can deal with it whether you like it or not."

Silence.

"Why won't you show me your human form? You know I want to see, so it's just plain rude to keep it hidden from me."

Again, silence.

"Are you someone I know? Are you hideously scarred?"

His black fur gleamed like polished ebony as he flicked her a glance. His eyes were as pale a green as ever. "Can you not switch? Are you stuck that way?"

A shake of his head. Which meant, she assumed, that he wasn't stuck.

She grinned. "Miracle of miracles, we're communicating! Do you see how easy it is? I ask a question and you answer it."

He rolled his eyes.

"So why won't you show me?"

Silence.

This was getting her nowhere. "Let's try something else." She maneuvered around a fallen branch. "Do you go to my school?"

A shake. Then, a nod.

She frowned. Which was it? "You can talk inside my head to answer. I don't mind."

A shake.

"Why not?"

Silence.

Frustrated, she tried a little reverse psychology. "Fine. Don't tell me. I'm glad you're not talking in my head. You probably can't do it anymore, anyway."

Of course I can! Silly human, he muttered.

Success, even with animals. She barely managed to hide

her grin. Clearly she was going into the right field. "Then why haven't you been?"

Another round of silence ensued.

"Mangy mutt," she grumbled.

His lip pulled back from his teeth, but the expression appeared more amused than angry.

"Let's try this again. Do you have plans to hurt Aden?"

Rather than ignore her as he had every other time she'd asked this, he gave her a definite, assured nod.

One thing she knew, she didn't want a fight to erupt between the two of them. No telling who would win. Someone would be hurt, though. That much she knew. "If Aden hadn't possessed your body, you would have ripped him to shreds. What he did after that, whatever he did—" neither one had told her "—was not done to hurt you but to protect himself. You can't blame him for that. I'm sure you would have done the same thing."

Again, silence.

"Aden's a really great guy, you know."

That earned her another growl.

They broke through the forest and the high brick wall surrounding her neighborhood came into view. "If you hurt him, I won't be able to hang out with you anymore. Not that you probably care, but I've grown to like you. A little. I mean, you're tolerable. Stubborn, but tolerable. And you know things about the world that I've only just discovered. I have so many questions." Questions he could have answered already, the jerk.

Rather than circle around the wall, Mary Ann climbed the

side closest to the forest. Wolf preferred this route, she'd learned that first walk home when he'd nudged her with his nose until she complied. This way, he could remain in the shadows rather than out in the open for anyone driving by to see.

"We keep this up, and I'm going to develop ginormous biceps," she muttered when she finally reached the top. "That's not very flattering for a girl, so don't think I'm going to thank you."

Wolf simply bent his back legs and jumped, a blur of motion. A second later, he was perched beside her.

Resigned, she peered down at the ground. There was a bed of flowers and two rows of mulch, both of which she'd accidentally rolled around in more than once. "Here goes." She dropped, landing with a heavy *thwack* and stumbling forward.

The moment she straightened, Wolf was beside her, his gait easy.

"Not fair," she grumbled, kicking into motion. Because they were in a populated area, people driving home from work, he remained close to the houses, part of his body hidden by bushes. Big as he was, she was surprised someone hadn't already called the pound to come out and hunt him down. A week ago, she would have.

Mary Ann spotted her two-story house in the distance. It resembled an old train station—all the houses in this neighborhood did. The roofs rose to high points on the sides, yet had flat middles. The homes themselves were long rather than tall, with red brick and shuttered windows. She slowed her steps. All too soon, though, they reached her front yard.

This was the part of her day that she'd grown to hate: her last few minutes with Wolf before he took off for God knew where, not to be seen again until morning. Yes, his silence irritated her. And yes, he was keeping her from Aden. But neither lessened the thrill of being with him.

When she snaked around the large maple, she skidded to a stop, her eyes widening. "Tucker?"

Tucker unfolded from the porch swing and stood. He shoved his hands into his pockets, his shoulders a little hunched. Lines of tension branched from his mouth. "Hey, Mary Ann."

"What are you doing here?" He should be at practice.

"I just wanted to—"

Wolf moved to her side, his large body stiff.

Tucker saw him and scrambled backward until he hit the door. "What the hell is that thing?"

"He's my…" For a moment, her mind blanked and she couldn't think up a single answer. Then, a somewhat rational reply slid into place. "He's my pet."

At least Wolf didn't growl at her for claiming he belonged to her. His attention remained utterly focused on Tucker.

"You hate animals," Tucker gasped out.

"What are you doing here?" she repeated. One, two, three, she pounded up the steps. Wolf followed, remaining close. Did he think to protect her, as she'd imagined earlier?

"I wanted to talk to you." As Tucker spoke, his gaze traveled from her to the wolf, the wolf to her. "In private."

"Okay. Talk."

"Let's go inside."

"No. Here's fine." Last time they'd been alone inside her house, all he'd wanted to do was make out.

He cast another glance at the wolf, gulped. "All right. Well, you've been so distant lately, you know? And I don't like it. I want to go back to the way we were. Where you smile at me every time you see me and answer my calls every night."

She felt a twinge of guilt. She *had* been avoiding his calls.

"I think I know what this is about," he said. "Penny, right?" The last was sneered.

Wait. What? "I don't understand. Penny?"

Some of the scorn drained from him, and his shoulders sagged. "I knew you were too smart to believe her."

"Believe her about what?" Seriously. She was more confused by the second.

"She told me she told you," he said, then shook his head, as if *he* didn't understand the direction of this conversation. "Never mind. It doesn't matter, right? Me and you, that's all that matters."

Me and you. Her stomach twisted.

"Let's go out tonight. Talk. Please," he added beseechingly.

Stomach. Twisting. Again. "Look, Tucker. I didn't mean to hurt your feelings by ignoring your calls, you have to believe that, but my life is in turmoil right now. Maybe we should, I don't know, take a break or something." Yes, a break. How perfect. That would give her time to figure some things out.

"No. We don't need a break." He shook his head violently, his eyes pleading with her. "I *can't* lose you."

Her life's goal was to solve problems, not cause them, so

his sudden tortured expression made her want to apologize rather than continue. Still. She forged ahead. "Why? What can you possibly see in me? I'm not as pretty or popular as Christy Hayes, who would cut off her leg to date you. I hate football and know nothing about it. I choose to read textbooks over spending time with you."

"Listen to me." He approached her, arms extending to latch onto her shoulders. "None of that is important to—"

Wolf growled low in his throat.

Tucker stilled, gulped again. "You're beautiful and smart and I just feel better when I'm with you. I don't know how else to describe it, and I don't know how you do it. All I know is that you make me feel normal for the first time in my life."

Normal? Tucker hadn't always felt normal? That surprised her, and proved just how little she'd ever actually known about him. He'd always seemed like the most put-together, confident guy she'd ever met. Well, besides Wolf, but he didn't count.

"That's not a reason to stay together, Tucker." The words left her of their own accord and she shook her head. Was she breaking up with him now, rather than merely asking for some time apart?

Yes, she thought. Yes, she was. They truly weren't meant for each other. She'd been a terrible girlfriend. Absent, distracted and less than passionate. They'd only ever kissed. Anytime he'd tried for more, she'd always stopped him. She'd thought it was because she wasn't ready, but now, looking back, she realized she hadn't been ready *with him*. He wasn't right for her. They were too different.

Like you've got more in common with a wolf? She brushed that thought aside. She hadn't been thinking about Wolf along those lines, whoever he was. Had she?

"If you don't want to date me, at least be my friend," he said, a desperate edge to the words. "Please. Like I said, I can't lose you. And I swear to you now that I'm not the father of Penny's baby. Don't let her convince you otherwise. Promise me."

Mary Ann laughed. "Penny's not pregnant." A baby was something her friend would have mentioned.

Unless…unless the father really was Mary Ann's boyfriend.

Her stomach did that twisting thing again and her focus intensified on Tucker. He was pale, sweating. "She's not pregnant. Is she?"

He looked away guiltily, then gave a jerky nod. "She's slept with half the football team. Surely you know that. It could be anyone's."

The seriousness of his tone settled like a weight inside her. She thought back to the last time she'd spoken to Penny. It had been in front of the school, more than a week ago. Since then, she'd been too distracted. But she remembered that Penny's eyes had been red-rimmed, as if she'd been crying. As if she'd told the father of her baby that she was pregnant and he had denied responsibility.

Before that, at the café, Penny had mentioned Tucker would cheat on Mary Ann if she didn't sleep with him soon. That he might already be doing so. There'd been something in Penny's eyes, an emotion Mary Ann hadn't understood until now. Guilt.

"She's…you…"

"I'm not the father, I swear! I'm not ready to have kids."

His words sank in, as did acceptance. Penny really was pregnant. And Tucker had slept with her. He hadn't said, "There's no way I can be the father because I never touched her." Just that he wasn't the dad because he didn't want to be.

Slightly light-headed, she covered her mouth with her hand. The fact that Tucker had cheated on her embarrassed her to her very soul, yes. Had everyone but her known? Had they laughed at her behind her back? But what hurt her most, what cut like a knife, what utterly destroyed her, was Penny's betrayal. Penny, whom she loved. Penny, whom she trusted.

"How long?" she asked quietly. It couldn't have been too long ago, because she and Tucker had only been dating a few months. "How many times were you together? *When* were you together?" She couldn't stop the questions from lashing from her.

Wolf nudged her leg with his nose, and her hand automatically sought the warmth of his fur. There was comfort in the action, comfort from simply stroking him.

Tucker shifted uncomfortably. "Like I said, none of that is important."

"Tell me! Or *I* swear we'll never be friends." They wouldn't be anyway, but he didn't need to know that right now.

She'd thought him pale before, but he became chalk-white, the blue lines in his forehead visible. "Just once, I swear. Not that long after we started dating. I came over but you weren't home, so I popped over to her house to ask where you were since you weren't answering my calls. If only you'd answered my calls…" He shook his head, pulling himself from his "regrets." "We started talking and things just happened. It didn't mean anything, you have to believe me, Mar."

It hadn't meant anything to him. Oh, well, that made everything better and negated what he and Penny had done. She wanted to shake him. What they'd done shredded her, left her raw. Of course it meant something.

"You need to go," she croaked past the lump in her throat.

"We can work this out." Expression once more beseeching, he moved toward her. "I know we can. You just have to—"

Wolf snarled as she shouted, "Go!"

A muscle in Tucker's jaw clenched. For a long while, he did nothing but peer over at her. Finally, Wolf grew tired of waiting and stalked forward, sharp teeth bared.

Tucker squealed like a toddler and danced a wide circle around the animal before running for his truck. Which was parked in Penny's driveway, she realized. Had the two spoken before he'd come here? Had they had sex, then laughed about Mary Ann's prudishness?

Wolf nudged her leg again.

"You need to go, too," she said softly. Yeah, she'd wanted him to stay earlier, but she didn't think she could withstand company right now.

Her hand was shaking as she unlocked her front door. Hinges squeaked as it opened. Wolf soared past her. He'd never done that before, and any other time, she would have welcomed him.

"Wolf," she called through clenched teeth. "Now isn't the time for this."

He paced through the house, sniffing the furniture. *If you think you can force two hundred pounds of animal to leave, be my guest.*

"Talking to me again? Lucky me." She tossed up her hands. "Fine. Do what you want. Don't be surprised if my dad takes out his .44 when he sees you." A lie, but he wouldn't know that. "And don't pee on the rug." The last was mean, but the last five minutes of her life had eaten away at her nice-girl filter.

She pounded up the stairs, into her bedroom, and dropped her backpack on the floor. Usually she hung it in her closet, taking pride in the neatness of her personal space. Just then, she didn't care about her routine. Tears burning her eyes, she threw herself on the bed and rolled to her side. She clutched her pillow to her chest. The shock was wearing off, replaced by a burning sickness in her veins.

She could have called Penny, screamed, ranted, cried, but she didn't. That wasn't how she wanted to handle this. Actually, she didn't know *how* she wanted to handle it. Except maybe to go back in time, race past Tucker so he couldn't tell her what had happened and she could continue on, unaware and happy.

Had she truly been happy, though?

Wolf suddenly jumped onto the bed, the mattress bouncing, and snuggled up next to her, soft and oh, so warm. His breath trekked over the back of her neck. *Look at me.*

"Go away."

Look at me.

"Can't you do anything I ask you? Anything at all?"

Please.

It was the first time he'd ever asked her for something nicely.

Absently, she rolled to her back, then her other side, and petted his neck. One of her tears spilled over, and she fought the rest back. No reason to add "sobbing like a baby" to her list of embarrassments today.

I'm sorry you're hurting, but I can't say I'm sorry he's out of your life. You were too good for him.

"Him, I'll get over." Her voice shook, the vibrations affecting her chin. The trembling then spread to her jaw.

It's the girl, then. Penny. She's your friend?

"Was. Was my friend. My best friend." Oh, God. So many years of love and trust, now ruined.

Why not still? People make mistakes, Mary Ann.

That was only the second time he'd said her name. She liked the way he said it, drawing out the A's. "I know they make mistakes. I'm studying to be a psychologist, you know. I'm highly aware that some impulses are harder to ignore than others. I'm aware that fear of consequences causes us to guard our secrets. But it's our actions when faced with temptation that define who we are. It's our courage in admitting what we've done wrong that makes us forgivable. She slept with my boyfriend, and then pretended it never happened."

And you're perfect? You've never made the wrong decision? Never tried to hide your actions from your father?

She stiffened against him. "No, that's not what I'm saying. But I have never lied to Penny or taken something from her."

Wolf snorted. *And what did she take? A piece of trash, that's what. You should thank her, and then pity her, because she's the one who's now stuck with him.*

"That doesn't make it right."

I know. You have been hurt and your sense of betrayal is warranted. But was the boy truly yours to begin with? The entire time I've watched you, you kept him at a distance. You were happier away from him.

Maybe he was right, but that didn't lessen the pain of what had been done. "Penny should have told me."

Did you give her the chance to confess? Not once have I seen you seek her out. And when she approached you, you dismissed her, other things on your mind.

Mary Ann slammed her fist against the mattress. "You are so irritating! You sound just like my dad and I—"

I am not your dad, he growled, planting his front paws on her shoulders and shoving her to her back. Those green eyes glared down at her.

She didn't push him off; she didn't want to. His shoulders were so wide he enveloped her, almost like a curtain that shielded her from all the world's hurt. Dangerous as he clearly was, such a sensation amazed her.

"How do I know?" she threw at him. "You won't show yourself. You could be anyone."

There was a heavy pause. *I can't show you.* He sounded as tortured as Aden had looked while making his confession that day in the forest. *Were I to shift now, I would be naked.*

"Oh." Wolf, naked in human form. She'd never wanted to see Tucker that way, but Wolf... Would he be tall and muscled? Lean? Handsome?

Did it matter? What would she do with a naked boy in her bed? A naked boy who fascinated her? A naked boy who had helped ease her torment over what had happened, she realized, the ache now only a dull throb in her chest. *Time to change the subject or he just might satisfy your curiosity.*

"Why haven't you spoken to me like this all week?"

The more I talk to you, the more I want to do so. And I think about you enough as it is.

"Oh," she said again, a thrill of excitement blazing through her. Wolf actually thought about her. Yes, but what were his thoughts? she wondered, excitement draining.

"Mary Ann," her dad suddenly called. The front door shut with a click that reverberated through the house. "I'm home."

A gasp of surprise left her. What was he doing home so early?

"Mary Ann?"

"Uh, hi, Dad," she called, cringing at the way her voice trembled. Much as he hated animals, he would probably call the pound at the first sight of Wolf.

"Hide," she whispered, squirming out from under him. Frantic, she jolted upright. The mattress bounced her to her feet. She raced out of her bedroom to the staircase banister, where she peered down. Her dad had his head buried in a stack of mail.

"Why aren't you at work?" Great. Now she sounded breathless.

"My last patient of the day called and canceled. I was thinking we could go out for dinner."

"No! No," she repeated more calmly. "I'm, uh, studying." *Please just retire to your office. Oh, please, please, please.*

His gaze lifted, latched onto her, and he frowned. "You study too much, honey, and I don't want you looking back on these teenage years, wishing you'd had more excitement. We've talked about this. So go get dressed in something fancy and we'll go to the city." He tossed the envelopes on the cherrywood wall table beside him and headed for the stairs. "I'll shower and we can be out the door and stuffing our faces within the hour. Maybe we can even catch a movie."

Of all the days to want to spend with her. She couldn't get out of it, not without hurting his feelings. "Okay, sure." No, no, no! "Yeah, that'll be fun."

His frown intensified and he paused, hand resting on the rail. "Are you all right? You seem jumpy."

"I'm fine. Just eager to go get ready." Without another word, she rushed back into her bedroom and shut the door, pressing against it and trying to breathe. "You have to—"

Wolf was nowhere to be seen.

"Wolf?"

No response.

Frowning herself, she raced through the room, searching for him. He wasn't in the closet or the bathroom and was too big to be under the bed. The window was open—it had been shut before—the drapes wisping in the breeze. She hurried to it and peered out. And there he was, sitting in her lawn and staring up at her.

He nodded briefly when he saw her, then turned and headed back toward the woods.

†En

ADEN SAT at his makeshift desk and stared down at his homework, an English paper about why William Shakespeare's plays were still relevant in modern society, wondering why he'd fought so hard to attend public school. He wasn't spending any extra time with Mary Ann, he was no closer to finding a way to get the souls out of his mind and into bodies of their own, and he was more confused than ever about Shannon and the wolf, whether they were one and the same or separate entities entirely.

Since that afternoon in the forest, when Aden had bitten the werewolf's leg, Shannon had been avoiding him, even glared and snarled at him despite their first-day-of-school truce—proof he had to be the angry shape-shifter. But Shannon hadn't once walked with a limp—proof he couldn't possibly be the shape-shifter.

Quite simply, Aden was confused and miserable. His teachers weren't exactly fond of him, but he hadn't made any new friends and the only one he had was currently avoiding him. There was no time to talk at school and she raced away from him and into the forest the moment the last bell rang.

He knew why, too. She feared him. She feared what he was, what he could do. How could she not? He was a freak.

He shouldn't have trusted her.

Perhaps following Mary Ann that day in the cemetery had been a mistake. Elijah had warned him.

You should ignore her, Caleb said, sensing the direction of his thoughts. *Treat her like crap. That's what really gets a girl's attention.*

Don't listen to him. He was a lecher in another life, I just know it. Disgust practically dripped from Eve's voice. *Girls respect boys who treat them well.*

"Still think you know her?" He dropped his head in his upraised palms, Shakespeare forgotten.

I'm sure of it. I have a few ideas percolating about when we might have seen her, but I'm not yet ready to talk about them.

Aden caught the hidden meaning to her words and moaned. Eve was planning to take him back, to travel into a younger version of himself—today's mind in yesterday's body—so that he could revisit the past with this new knowledge. The only reason she hadn't already done so, he suspected, was that she hadn't decided on a specific day. That's what was "percolating," he was sure.

"Eve," he began, then stopped himself. Stubborn as she was, she might take him back in time *tonight* if he irritated her enough.

She hadn't forced him to time travel in years, and they were all grateful. He'd just have to solve Eve's mystery for her. *Before* she resorted to using her "gift."

"Lights out," Dan suddenly called.

Grunts and groans filled the hallways, followed by the shuffle of feet. Sighing, Aden pushed to a stand and switched off his lamp. Darkness flooded his bedroom. He didn't kick off his shoes but lay in bed just as he was. He was tired yet restless. As always. Part of him expected Dan to peek inside the room and check on him, and he waited several hours, the covers drawn to his chin to hide his clothing. Those hours dragged by, alone and uninterrupted.

Silver lining: his companions fell asleep from boredom.

Finally, when he was confident the others in the bunkhouse were sleeping, he moved to his window and climbed outside. The nights were getting cooler, fall well on its way. Sophia and the other dogs slept inside with Dan and Meg, so he didn't have to worry about their barking waking the entire ranch.

As he'd done every night for the past week, he maneuvered through the forest toward the clearing Victoria had led him into. Lack of sleep was making him cranky, but he'd rather have the chance of seeing her again than the promise of slumber. Where was she? Why hadn't she returned to him?

Despite the fact that she drank blood—and *would* drink his—and despite the fact that she could turn humans into blood-slaves, whatever those were, he wanted to see her again. *Needed* to see her.

Gradually he became aware of a murmur of voices—and

for once they weren't coming from inside his mind. The closer he came to the clearing, the louder they became. Excitement hit—had he finally found her?

He positioned himself behind a thick stump and listened. One speaker was male, one was female; their actual words, however, were too muffled to decipher. But he soon realized that the female wasn't Victoria. This one's voice was too high.

Excitement gave way to disappointment. He would have left them to their business, whoever they were and whatever they were doing, if he hadn't known a vampire female liked to traverse the area. They could be vampire hunters, for all he knew, planning to kill her.

He didn't know if people like that truly existed, but he wasn't taking any chances. He slinked out of the shadows and edged closer.

One of them might have said, "Kill." Perhaps, "Pill." The other might have replied, "I could." Perhaps, "I'm good." Either way, they weren't out there planting roses.

Just a little closer... A twig snapped under his boot. He froze. Waited, not even daring to breathe. The voices tapered to quiet.

What should he do? He couldn't leave until they did, just in case Victoria showed up. And he couldn't—

Someone tackled him from behind, sending him face-first into a bed of brittle leaves. The impact startled him, but he was able to roll to his back, then roll again, pinning his attacker under him. He punched the brute in the stomach.

There was a grunt of pain, a whoosh of air. Aden jumped

to his feet, intending to grab his daggers, but as he peered down, he saw who had rammed him and froze. "Ozzie?"

"Stone?" Ozzie stood, spit out a mouthful of dirt. "You're following me now? What, are you trying to get me booted from the ranch? Well, good luck with that, 'cause I won't go quietly." Without any other warning, he kicked Aden between the legs.

Utter pain radiated through him, hunching him over, making his skin feel like fire and his blood like ice. He wanted to vomit. Dear…God…

As he gasped and sweated and combated the nausea, rage boiled inside him. Low blow. Low freaking blow. When he was able to breathe again, Ozzie was going to be sorry.

"Let's see how well you can tattle on me without any teeth." Ozzie pounded his fist into Aden's eye. Bad aim? Then his lip. Okay, not so bad.

His head spun. His rage intensified, spilled over, filled him up and gave him wings. With a growl, he launched forward and grabbed the boy around the waist, propelling them both to the ground. *Crack.* Ozzie's skull connected with a large rock, stunning him.

Aden propped himself on his knees and just started swinging. *Boom,* one fist slammed into a cheekbone. "That's for my first T-shirt." *Boom,* his other fist connected with an eye socket. "That's for the others." *Boom,* he connected with Ozzie's chin. Blood sprayed. He didn't care, was lost to the rage, determined to inflict as much pain as possible. "That's for my nuts!"

Snarling, Ozzie pulled his legs from under Aden, bending

and anchoring them on Aden's chest. A hard push had him flying backward. He hit a tree and sank to the ground. A pile of leaves softened the impact.

What's going on? Eve suddenly demanded, groggy but loud.

Doing his best to ignore her, he hopped up and once more launched forward. He slammed his head into Ozzie's throat. As Ozzie hunched over, gurgling, Aden kicked him in the stomach without a second's thought. One thing he'd learned over the years was that there was no honor in fighting. You did whatever was necessary to win, even kick someone when they were down—especially when they were down—or you suffered.

He joined his hands and bashed them into Ozzie's temple. Ozzie swung to the side, dropped to his knees. A plastic bag fell from his pocket. His head remained bowed, one hand clutching his middle, the other covering his face to protect it.

"Get up! Fight me! Isn't that what you wanted?" This had been a long time coming, and now that they were punching it out, Dan not here to intervene, Aden couldn't stop himself. He settled his weight on one leg, leaned forward and slammed his fist into Ozzie's jaw. "Come on!"

Again, the impact sent him flying. Ozzie quickly righted himself and came up swinging. "Yeah, it's what I wanted. What I'll *do*."

Aden ducked, jabbing the dreg in the stomach yet again and forcing more of that needed oxygen out of his mouth. He raised his leg to do it again.

"I wouldn't do that if I were you."

The female voice was followed by the click of a gun. Slowly he lowered his leg and turned halfway, not letting Ozzie out of his sights but eyeing as much of the girl as he could. She was shorter than him by at least a foot, slight and trembling. And she was aiming a pistol right at him.

He could take her, even panting and sweating as he was. No longer was he in pain, his adrenaline simply too high. Hurting a girl, though, was not a prospect he enjoyed.

Because it's wrong, Eve said, as if reading his mind.

He won't have to hurt her, Elijah said. *This is going to be okay.*

How is a chick with an obviously itchy trigger finger gonna turn out okay? Caleb shouted.

Run, Aden, Julian commanded. *Just start running.*

Aden stepped backward.

Stay still! Elijah growled, and he froze.

Run, Julian commanded again, and he took another step.

Stop.

"Quiet!" he shouted, covering his ears.

"*You* be quiet! And move another inch, and I swear to God you'll be eating every one of these bullets. Now who the hell are you?" the girl snarled. She was cute, despite the gun, with a short cap of blond hair. Her bottom lip was cut, as if she, too, had recently been in a fight.

"It's okay, Casey," Ozzie said, surprisingly calm as he stood. His words were slightly slurred, his jaw already swelling. "He's from the ranch."

She didn't lower the gun. "You always tear into the guys you live with?"

"Yeah, I do." Ozzie bent down and swiped up the plastic Baggies he'd dropped. "He's not a cop, and he's not gonna narc. He knows I'd stab him in his sleep if he tried."

Aden knew a dime bag when he saw one. So Ozzie and the gun-wielding Casey were here for drugs. "For someone who just lost, you sure sound confident about what you can do to me."

Ozzie stiffened. Casey straightened her aim.

Maybe he should have kept his mouth closed. But from the corner of his eye, he'd caught a glimpse of Victoria, gliding toward them, silent as a ghost, and the words had slipped out.

Neither Ozzie nor Casey even glanced in her direction.

Aden would have known she was there even if he hadn't spotted her. Power radiated from her, enveloping the area, charging the air so much it crackled. As she closed the distance, her skin seemed whiter than ever. So white it glowed. Her dark robe was swaying in the breeze.

Told you it would be okay, Elijah said, smug.

Another gut feeling proven to be valid. At this rate, Elijah would soon be able to predict *everything*.

"You will not shoot him," the vampire said in that raspy voice of hers, suddenly in front of Casey. She waved a hand near the girl's face, opal ring catching beams of moonlight and casting rainbow shards in every direction.

Casey froze, so still Aden couldn't even see her breathing.

"You will drop the gun and leave, your memory wiped clean of this event."

There was no hesitation as Casey obeyed. The gun plopped

harmlessly to the ground; she turned and walked away, never once glancing back. Aden was both in awe and embarrassed. Victoria's powers were greater than he'd realized. And he'd just been saved by a girl. *He* should be the one doing the saving.

"What the—" Ozzie began.

"You, too, will leave, your memory wiped clean of this event." The dreg's eyes glazed over and he, too, turned and walked away.

"I need him to remember," Aden said. Otherwise, when they both awoke with bruised and battered faces, Ozzie would know they had to have fought, but wouldn't know he'd lost to Aden. Aden wanted him to have that knowledge. To be afraid of coming after him. Afraid of retaliation.

Reluctant, Victoria nodded. "Very well. I shall return his memory to him by morning."

"Thank you. For everything." Aden's gaze slid over her. Her hair was pulled back in a ponytail, and the long, thick length of it hung over her shoulder. Her lips were pink rather than their usual red. "How'd you find me?"

"You're bleeding," she said rather than answering. Or maybe that was the answer. As she spoke, her eyes began to darken, black pupils overshadowing blue irises. Closer and closer she floated to him. But she stopped herself just before reaching him and backtracked. Looked away. "I shouldn't have revealed myself."

"I'm glad you did."

Her gaze returned to him. Or rather, to the blood trickling from the bleeding cut on his lips. "I can stop the bleeding, if you'd like." Her tongue flicked over her sharpening fangs. "It…it won't mean anything. It's just something I can do."

He wasn't sure how she planned to stop it, but he found himself nodding.

"I won't…will try not to…hurt you. I'll be gentle. Won't be an animal."

He wasn't sure whether the words were meant for him or herself, but once again she approached him. And then her mouth met his, pressing softly, gently, utterly warm, her tongue once again flicking out and wiping the crimson beads away.

He stood very still, savoring the feel of her, that honeysuckle scent. He had to fist his hands at his sides to keep from grabbing her and holding on forever. Where she licked, he tingled…ached…but it was a good ache. Don't stop, he thought. Never stop.

But stop she did. She raised her head, eyelids at half-mast, expression blissful. "Delicious."

"You can have more if you want it," he croaked out, tilting his head to reveal more of his neck. If this was how he would feel when she bit him, he was ready.

"Yes, I—no." She shook her head and backtracked again. "No. I can't. Why did you let me do that? Why would you ask me to do it again? Have you no sense? Do you *want* to be my blood-slave? Addicted to my bite, unable to think of anything else?"

"I won't become addicted," he said, praying it was true.

"How do you know?"

He didn't have an answer, so he ignored the question. "Does being bitten hurt?"

Her shoulders relaxed slightly. "I'm told it can feel quite wonderful," she said—and then she disappeared.

He blinked, tried not to panic. Looked left, right.

"But liking it will be the least of your worries," she said from behind him.

He spun.

Victoria had one shoulder pressed against the trunk of a tree. "You shouldn't tempt me to do it, you know."

He sighed. "Would drinking from me once cause me to become a slave?"

"No. It takes multiple feedings. But I will not bite you." There at the end, her voice rose with determination. "Ever."

"All right." He studied her, doing his best to keep his heartbeat under control. She looked ready to bolt and never return. Dropping the subject seemed wise. For the moment. No reason to tell her that she would indeed bite him, whether she changed her mind or not. "How did you move so quickly?"

"All of my kind are able to do so." With barely a breath, she added, "What are you doing here, Aden? This forest is dangerous for humans."

Why was the forest dangerous for humans? When he realized what he'd just pondered, he shook his head. It was weird being referred to as a human. Even though that's what he was. "I was looking for you. You left so quickly the other night and I have so many questions."

"Questions I probably can't answer." She plucked a leaf from the tree, crumpled it in her hand and dropped the pieces. They floated to the ground, twisting and twirling.

Curious as he was, he couldn't allow himself to give up. Rather than push, however, he decided to ask something innocent, something easy. Hopefully, answering him would become second nature to Victoria so he could then tackle the tougher questions. His doctors had used that method on him a time or two.

"Why do you wear robes? I would think you'd want to wear something modern and blend in."

"Blending in has never been our goal." She shrugged. "Besides, robes are what my father prefers."

"And you always do what he says?"

"Those who disobey him end up wishing they were dead." She turned away. "I should go."

"Don't," he rushed out, stepping toward her. "Wait. Stay with me. Just a little longer. I've…missed you."

That's not treating a girl like crap, Caleb suddenly piped up.

We've talked about this, Eve said. *Your crap theory is crap.*

Aden's jaw clenched. "Please, Victoria."

She stopped, faced him. A thousand different emotions seemed to fight for dominance over her features. Hope, regret, happiness, sadness, fear. Finally, hope won. "Come," she said. "I want to show you something."

She held out her hand. He wondered what had caused such turmoil inside her, but he didn't hesitate to close the distance between them and twine their fingers. The heat of her skin nearly singed him as she led him through the forest, deeper and deeper, the trees thickening around them.

"You're so hot," he said, then, to his horror, felt himself flush. "I don't mean you're pretty. Wait. You are. Pretty, I mean. Beautiful. I just meant your temperature is hot." Could he sound any lamer?

"Oh, sorry." She jerked from his hold.

"No, I like it." Apparently, he could. He twined their fingers again. "I was just wondering *why* you're so…um, hot."

"Oh," she said again, relaxing against his hold. "Vampires have more blood than humans. A lot more. And not just because of what we consume. That's why our hearts work at a greater speed."

They rounded a corner. He didn't recognize the area, the leaves hanging from the branches so bright a red it almost looked as though the trees were bleeding. "Where are we going?"

"You'll see."

He hated adding to the distance between him and the ranch, just in case Dan awoke and came gunning for him, but he didn't protest. Being with Victoria was worth the risk. Any risk.

His ears perked when he heard the nearby rush of water. "There's a river here?"

"You'll see," she repeated.

They broke through a tangle of foliage and what could only be a bathing pool came into view. Boulders were stacked at one side, water cascading from them, bubbling and frothing at the edges. His jaw dropped.

"This was nothing more than a puny pond when I arrived,"

Victoria said. "I worked all week to stack the rocks. Riley, my bodyguard, rerouted the water for me."

Riley. Her bodyguard. He must be the boy Aden had seen her with that morning at the ranch. Which meant they weren't brother and sister. Worse, they probably spent a lot of time together.

He studied the stones, using the time to tamp down a suddenly blast of jealousy. There were too many to count, all so large no one her size should have been able to lift them.

"You both did an amazing job," was all he said.

"Thank you."

It's so peaceful here. I never want to leave, Eve said.

Maybe she brought you here to make out with you, Caleb said hopefully. *Who knew being nice could pay off?*

Uh, I did, Eve replied.

Argh! "Guys. Quiet, please. I'm begging you." His companions grumbled but did as he'd asked.

Victoria's focus whipped to him. She was frowning.

"Not you," he told her. "If you want to know who I was talking to, though, you'll have to trade me for the information." There. That was how he'd get answers out of her. *If* she was curious about him. But if she was and he told her the truth, would she decide he was too weird to hang out with, as Mary Ann apparently had?

"I would be willing to trade," she said, and he wanted to both cheer and curse. She faced the water, her back to him. "We can do so while we swim."

Wait. What? "Swim? With you?"

She laughed. "Who else? I've come here every night. You'll enjoy the water, I promise."

"But I don't have a suit."

"So?" Without turning toward him, she tugged the robe from her shoulders. The material slid to the ground, and once again his jaw dropped. Never had he seen a lovelier sight. She wore a lacy pink swimsuit—the first time he'd ever seen her in color. First time he'd ever seen a girl so bare in person. She was as white as snow all over, her body perfectly curved, all lean muscle, smooth planes and hollows.

Am I drooling? he wondered.

Dear Lord in heaven, Caleb gasped out. *I know, I know. I'm supposed to be quiet. But the words slipped out because—and I could be mistaken here—I think my tongue is hanging out. Never mind that I don't actually have one.*

Aden hated that his companions were seeing her like this. Hated it so much a red sheen of jealousy hazed behind his eyes, and it was far greater than when he'd thought of her and her muscled bodyguard together. All the time. Okay. The red expanded, thickened. He wanted to be the only one to enjoy her. Now and always.

Victoria waded into the pool, droplets splashing, water swallowing her up, not stopping until she reached the center, submerged all the way to her shoulders. Slowly she whirled around, grinning. "Are you coming?"

Hell, yes. The jealousy thing he could deal with later. Aden stripped to his boxers and waded in. The water was cool and caused goose bumps to break out over his skin. He took it like a man, though, and pretended he loved it. No way did he want her thinking he was a wuss. Well, any more of one.

His feet touched in the center, the waterline coming to his shoulders, as well, but he was taller than her and realized she couldn't possibly reach the mossy ground. Still, she seemed unperturbed by her swishing feet, the water not even rippling.

They circled each other, their gazes never wavering.

"Ready to trade?" he asked. He was willing to do anything, even blab about himself, to learn about her.

She hesitated only a moment before nodding.

"First, maybe we should set the rules."

"Like?"

"Like, rule one. You're a girl, so you go first. Rule two. You'll ask me a question, anything at all, and I'll answer it. Rule three. I'll ask you a question, again anything at all, and you'll have to answer it. Rule four. We have to answer truthfully."

"Agreed." No hesitation. "I will begin then. So…who were you speaking to earlier when you said 'quiet'?"

Of course she'd chosen the most embarrassing question to kick things off. But then, his luck would have permitted nothing else. "I was speaking to the souls trapped inside my head." Hopefully she would leave it at that.

Her eyes widened. "Souls? Trapped in your head? What do you—"

"Nope," he said with a shake of his head. "It's my turn. Who do you drink from? And more importantly, do you have many blood-slaves?" In his head, the questions continued. Were those slaves male? And what would he do if they were?

"That's two questions, so you will owe me. The answer to the first is humans. The answer to the second is no. I have none. I prefer to drink from my prey only once."

Thank God. "I know you drink from humans, though. That's not what I meant." He thought back to the last few newspapers he'd seen, the last news at nine he'd watched. "There are no articles about recent attacks in the area. No news stations blaring stories about possible vampire sightings. Nobody but me seems to know you even exist. I don't understand how that's possible if you and your family are, uh, eating many meals."

"There's a reason for that, but you will have to trade me for it." The last was said in a singsong voice. Seemed the vampire was using his own strategy against him. "Now it's my turn. What do you mean, souls are trapped inside your head?"

Yep. His luck sucked. "Souls, personalities, other humans. There are four and they've always been with me. At least, as long as I remember. We've played with a bunch of different theories about how they got there, and the best we've been able to come up with is that I drew them into me. Kind of like how I apparently drew you, only I absorbed them inside my head. They talk all the time." He hurried on before they could protest. "Each possesses an ability. One can time travel. One can raise the dead, one can overtake other bodies, and one can see the future. Usually when someone's about to die."

"That means *you* can do these things, as well?"

He nodded. "And now we're even, question-wise."

Her head tilted to the side, her expression thoughtful. "You are more powerful than we realized."

And that was not a good thing, he mused, judging by her hardened tone. But she wasn't running, wasn't eyeing him as if he were nuclear waste. That was miles above what he'd expected. But then, she was a vampire.

"I wonder how my father will react to that."

Aden wondered, too. The man had wanted to kill him merely because of the wind he and Mary Ann had created. This was a thousand times worse. "Maybe you should, I don't know, not tell him."

"You're probably right. So, tell me more about them, these souls. You said they talk all the time. Are they loud?"

He shrugged, and the water rippled. "Most days, yeah. That's why most of the world thinks I'm weird. Because I'm always telling them to be quiet or, worse, conversing with them. And now, *you* owe *me*."

She reached out and threaded their fingers, almost as if she craved contact as much as he did. "People might think you're weird, Aden, but they think I am evil. Maybe I am. I survive on blood. And at first, when I learned to take it, I was too eager, unable to stop myself, and hurt innocents."

He heard the guilt in her tone, the sadness, and hated that she'd experienced the emotion. He only wanted her happy. And if that made him the wuss he didn't want to be, well, he'd freaking be a wuss.

Which brought him back to the bodyguard Riley. Was Aden the only one who wanted her happy? Surely not. After all, Victoria had once told him that Riley was jealous of him. He hadn't understood at the time. But maybe Riley was jealous of the time Victoria spent with him. Jealous, as a boy-friend would be.

Why did she need a bodyguard anyway? he wondered darkly. "Talking about how people view us is depressing. So let's talk about Riley. Is he also your boyfriend?" Every part of him felt like Victoria was his. If she said yes… "You have to answer truthfully. Remember, you owe me."

She laughed. "No. He's more like a brother. He irritates me, which is why I sneak away from him whenever possible. What of you and the girl I've seen you with? Mary Ann?"

"Friends only," he said, though he wasn't sure the friend part was even true any longer.

Victoria's thumb traced his palm. "What kind of person is she?"

Before he could stop himself—not that he wanted to stop himself—Aden brought her hand to his mouth and kissed it. "Sweet. Kind. Honest. She knows about me. Well, knows a *little* about me. She watched me possess the body of a werewolf, so there was no hiding it from her."

"Vampires and werewolves? What have you gotten yourself into? Werewolves are dangerous creatures," Victoria said huskily. "Vicious killers." Her gaze fell to his lips. "Beware of them."

"I already am." Maybe he'd go hunting, find that werewolf and get rid of it before it could hurt someone. Namely Mary Ann. Whether she liked him or not, she was a good person.

Closer and closer Victoria eased toward him, closing the small gap between them. "Before, you asked about the humans we drink from and why there are no reports of people being bitten. You saw the way my voice affected your friends, yes? Just as it affected you when first we spoke. Well, when we bite a human, we release a chemical into their systems that makes them even more susceptible to our suggestions. A drug, a hallucinogen, I guess you could say. Once we are finished with them, we send them on their way and they forget they were ever reduced to a meal."

If he had to have strange powers, Aden wished they could have been more like hers. That voodoo voice would have made his life a lot easier; he could have sent certain people (cough Ozzie cough) away with no memory of him.

"Are you dead, like legends claim?" He'd lost track of who owed whom an answer. But then, trading information was no longer his goal. Touching her was. He wrapped his free hand around her waist and splayed his fingers on the small of her back. She didn't seem to mind. "I mean, did you die and someone turned you into a vampire?"

"No, I am not dead. I live." She lifted his palm to her chest and pressed. Her skin was as hot as before but underneath, he could feel the steady rhythm of her heart. It beat faster than his, faster than anyone should have been able to survive, racing to a finish line it would never reach. "My father, he was the first of us. You might have heard of him. Vlad the Impaler, some call him. During his first life, his human life, he drank blood as a symbol of his power. So much blood it…changed him. Or perhaps he simply drank infected blood. He has never been sure. All he knows is that he began to crave it until it became all that he could stomach."

Talk about the ultimate punishment for his deeds. "How many of your kind are there now?"

"A few thousand, scattered throughout the world. My father is king to them all."

King. The word reverberated in his head, making him cringe. "That means you're a—"

"Princess. Yes." She stated it so simply, as if it were the most normal thing in the world.

A princess. Suddenly Aden felt even more inadequate. She was royalty, and he was poor, stuck at a ranch with kids too wild for civilization. She was the daughter of a king. He was parentless and considered mentally unstable.

"I should probably go," he found himself saying. Why couldn't Elijah have shown him this? Knowing what she was would have saved him the trouble of caring for her— only to lose her.

Confusion darkened her features. "Why are you leaving?"

Did he really need to spell it out? "I'm a nothing, Victoria, a no one. Or should I say Princess Victoria? Should I bow, too?"

His sneering tone had her swimming backward, out of his reach. "You didn't care that I was a vampire, yet my station bothers you. Why?"

"Just forget it," he said, turning. His hands felt like ice blocks without her fiery heat.

Before he could blink, she was in front of him. Back in his arms. "You are beyond irritating, Aden Stone."

"So are you." He knew he should release her, but couldn't force his hands to obey this time.

"Because I am a princess, I have spent most of my life sequestered. Rules and regulations are mine to follow, more so than anyone else, for I must always act with the decorum such a title demands. I must be everything the people want me to be: polite, polished and above reproach. Then you summoned us and we came to observe you. I saw how you kept yourself separated from those around you. I saw the loneliness in your eyes and I thought you would understand how I feel. And then, when you first looked at me, every time you've looked at me, really, I *felt* your excitement. It causes your blood to flow so swiftly." Her eyes briefly closed, as if she were savoring the memories.

"Tonight," she continued, "you asked me to stay with you. You're the first person to want to spend time with me, to talk and get to know me. Do you know how irresistible that is? Riley is my friend, but it's his job to watch me. And with him, I can never forget who and what I am. But with you…I feel normal. Like any other girl."

Being normal. It was a desire he knew well. And that *he* made her feel that way was astonishing.

"You do the same for me," he admitted. "But I'm—"

"Irresistible, as I said. I should stay away from you, but can't. So now I will be the one to ask you not to go."

He didn't know whether to laugh or sigh. As long as she didn't see him as a nothing, he would try not to, as well. "I'll stay."

Slowly she grinned, and it lit her entire face. "Good. Now. What were you saying about me? About the way I make you feel?"

"Just that I feel normal when I'm with you." *And I think you're the best thing to have ever happened to me.* He cleared his throat. "So what else happened when your dad became a vampire?" he asked, pretending they had never veered off course. Pretending, for them both, that they really were normal. Despite the topic of conversation.

She must have realized what he was doing, because her smile brightened. "He ceased aging, his body strengthened exponentially. His skin lost all remnants of color, becoming an impenetrable shield."

Aden recalled the way she'd laughed when he'd mentioned cutting her with his daggers. *I can't be cut,* she'd said. "Your skin can't be broken?"

She shook her head. "Not with a sharp object, no."

That would be both a blessing and a curse. A knife couldn't hurt her, but no doctor could operate on her if needed. *Was* it ever needed? "Do you ever get sick?"

"Once," she hedged, then sighed and released his hand to pluck at the fingers. Some contact was better than none. "Aden."

Clearly, the newest question made her uncomfortable. "If your father ceased aging, does that mean you're almost as old as he is?" he asked, and she relaxed. "No, wait. You can't be. You told me older vampires can't tolerate the sun and you can tolerate it."

"Yes, I'm younger than he is. I'm only eighty-one years old." She tangled a hand through his hair, clearly liked the feel, and did it again. "But don't think I have looked as I do now all that time. My siblings and I age slowly, very slowly. Our mothers despaired of ever getting us out of the terrible toddler stage."

He remembered the few toddlers he'd encountered at various foster homes. The tantrums, the "all mine" mentality, and the way they drew on everything, even his walls. "Where's your mom now?"

"In Romania. She was not allowed to travel with us."

He wanted to ask why, but didn't want to have to answer anything about his own parents. So instead he said, "Eighty-one. Wow. You're like my grandma. If I had one."

"What a terrible thing to say," she said, but was smiling again.

"In all your eighty-one years, you must have had a lot of boyfriends, huh?"

For some reason, that wiped away her amusement. She looked away guiltily. "Only one."

Just one? And why the guilt? "Why so few?"

"He's the only boy my father has ever approved of."

Which meant her father's approval mattered to her. Sadly, approval was not something Aden was likely to get. So how long did he have before Victoria gave up on him? How long before she left him, never to return? How long until she started dating someone her father did like?

As the questions hammered through him, a sense of urgency overwhelmed him. He had to show her how good it could be between them. Had to bring a vision to life—before it was too late.

"I told you I see the future, yes?"

She nodded reluctantly, probably confused by his sudden subject change.

A tide of nervousness swept through him. *Just say it, tell her.* "I've seen us together." Good. Now for the rest. "I knew you'd come to me before you arrived."

She stilled, frowned. "Wh-what did we do? When we were together?"

He didn't mention that he'd seen her drink from his neck. He didn't want to scare her away. She was skittish enough about being with him. "We...kissed."

"You and me, kis...sing." The last was uttered on a wispy catch of breath. "I want to, oh, God, do I want to. But I can't. I'll end up feeding from you, and I refuse to let you see me that way."

Was that the only thing holding her back? "You've already tasted my blood, and you were able to walk away."

"I almost didn't," she admitted.

"So what if you can't this time? I can take it."

"You can, perhaps, but I can't stand knowing that you will have seen me behaving like such an animal."

Victoria? An animal? "I would never think that of you."

Her arms circled his neck, her elbows resting on his shoulders. Sharp white fangs peeked over her bottom lip. "Aden," she said, then sighed. "What am I going to do with you?"

"You're going to kiss me."

Still she resisted—but the determination she'd exhibited earlier was fading. "I could scare you. I could horrify and disgust you." Before he could reply, she pushed away from him. She spun around, refusing even to face him. "We should go."

Waves lapped at his chin, and he fought his disappointment. Soon, he told himself, they *would* kiss. She would bite him, and he would prove to her that such an act didn't disgust him.

"You can't leave yet. It's my turn to ask you to stay and your turn to relent." He didn't want them to part unhappily. When she thought back over this night, he wanted her craving another like it. "Besides, I have one more question for you and you owe me an answer." Truth or not, he didn't care.

She didn't look back, but she did nod stiffly. "Ask."

Slowly he inched toward her. "What do you think of… this." He scooped a handful of water and chucked it at her, drenching her hair.

She was sputtering as she whirled around. Droplets fell into her eyes, catching in her eyelashes. "Why did you—"

Laughing, he tossed another handful. This one hit her dead center in the face.

"Why, you little…human!"

Before he could blink, she had him dunked under the water. When he surfaced, she was laughing, and the sound warmed him body and soul. Like children, happy, carefree children, they played until the sun began to rise. Splashing each other, dunking each other. She won, of course, because she was infinitely stronger than he was, but he'd never had so much fun.

Aden, honey, Eve said, speaking up for the first time in hours. Her voice actually surprised him. The souls had behaved and he hadn't even realized it until now. *You have to go back. We'll be lucky if Dan is still sleeping and doesn't catch you climbing through your window.*

She was right.

But day'um, I wish I could feel what you feel, Caleb said. *I didn't even mind the forced silence. You were pressed against boobs. Several times!*

He barely stopped himself from rolling his eyes. "If I don't return, I'll be caught." He reached out and smoothed the wet hair from Victoria's temple. "I want to see you again, though. More than just once a week. I want to see you every day."

Her smile faded, but she nodded. "I can't promise I'll be able to sneak away tomorrow, and as I've told you before, you'd be wise to stay away from me. But...I'll try. Either way, we *will* see each other again."

ELEVEN

INSIDE HIS BEDROOM, Aden couldn't stop yawning. He glanced at his bed with longing. He had to sleep soon or he was likely to pass out somewhere in public. But there was no time to rest. He'd stayed out so long he only had a little time before he had to leave for school. His gaze swung to his mirror. His eyes were red and burning, his eyelids heavy. Didn't help that one was blackened from his fight with Ozzie.

At least his lip was healed. Victoria's touch had worked wonders.

He grinned, remembering. He wanted her mouth on him again. Only this time he wanted her to linger. Wanted her to wind her arms around his neck, to shift her head so that her tongue flicked *inside* rather than outside.

What are you thinking about? Eve asked. *I can feel our blood pressure rising.*

"Nothing," he muttered, embarrassed.

He showered and dressed and gave himself a once-over.

Thankfully, after a few washings, the writing on his T-shirts had faded. That didn't lessen his pleasure over punching Ozzie for it.

When he entered the hall, Ozzie was waiting for him. One of his eyes was swollen shut, his lip was cut and a lump the size of a golf ball jutted from the side of his jaw.

"Say a word about what happened," he hissed. "I dare you."

Victoria had kept her promise, then, and returned his memory. Well, probably not about her or what she'd done to Casey. "I'm not afraid of you." He grinned and leaned down as if he had a secret to share. "You couldn't win a fight against a sleeping toddler."

Ozzie's mouth floundered open and closed.

"And anyway, we'll have to tell Dan we fought. There's no way around that." Because there was no way Dan would miss their wounds. "We just won't tell him why, when or where it happened."

"And the...stuff?" Ozzie spoke from the side of his mouth, gaze zooming down the hall to ensure the bedroom doors were closed and no one could hear. "About Casey?"

"I don't plan to say anything." Ozzie relaxed—until he added, "Unless you mess with me again. Then I have a feeling every little detail will come spilling out. Understand?" Aden didn't mind blackmailing the dreg. He was tired of being pushed around, abused, and being unable to do anything about it for fear of being sent away.

Ozzie cursed under his breath. "You even think about narcing and I swear to God, you'll regret it." He whipped a steak knife from his back pocket, one he'd obviously stolen from Dan's kitchen, and waved it in front of Aden's nose. "Do *you* understand?"

Aden rolled his eyes, bent down and withdrew one of his daggers. It was bigger and sharper, specks of corpse blood staining the silver. "What I understand is that I could slice you to ribbons. You have no idea how mental I can actually be."

Speechless once again, Ozzie backtracked into his room and slammed the door shut.

Oh, I'm so proud. Eve sounded like a beaming mother. *You stood up for yourself without endangering your circumstances.*

Way to go, Ad! Caleb said. *We need to celebrate. With girls!*

I wish you could have at least punched him again, Julian said. *I hate that kid.*

Don't encourage him, Elijah replied. *We don't want him in jail. Believe me.*

Did Elijah remember being in jail in a past life or had he seen Aden in jail and knew how terrible it would be for them?

There was no time to ask. Shannon peeked his head out of his door, probably wondering what the noise was about. He surprised Aden by entering the hallway.

"H-here." He handed him a stack of papers. "Ozzie came in l-last night and told me he was going to t-take these. I snuck in first and took them myself."

His English paper, which was due today. Aden hadn't even realized it was gone. All the work he'd put into it…if Ozzie had succeeded, he would have received an F. He popped his jaw, wishing he *had* punched the dreg again.

"Thanks."

Shannon nodded. "Owed you. For—" His gaze fell to Aden's shirt. "Y-you know."

When he turned, intending to head off, Aden grabbed his arm. "Wait. You've hardly spoken to me all week, but you just saved me from being kicked out of school. What gives?"

A muscle ticked in Shannon's jaw. He ripped free of Aden's grip, but he didn't race off.

"You might as well tell me now. I'll just hound you till you cave. In the forest. At school. After school. During chores—"

"Th-that day in the forest," was the growled response. "You were right behind me, man. Then those k-kids showed up and you took off, leaving me on my own. I know we haven't always been the b-best of friends, but we had reached a t-truce."

"So you really were in a fight?"

Another nod, this one stiff.

Shannon wasn't the werewolf, then. That left…who? Victoria's bodyguard, maybe? No. Couldn't be. Victoria thought werewolves were vicious. She wouldn't want to be guarded by one.

Aden thought of everyone else he knew with green eyes. A lot of names came up. What if, when a human shifted into werewolf form, his eyes changed color? Aden was living proof that eyes could change hues in the blink of, well, an eye. If that was true, anyone could be the werewolf.

"I'm sorry," he told Shannon, realizing the dreg was waiting for his response. "I didn't know you were ambushed. I didn't see the guys. If I had, I would have stayed with you. Maybe. I mean, I heard Mary Ann scream and rushed to see what was wrong."

"She okay?"

"Now she is." He hoped. Somehow, some way, he had to corner her today and force her to talk to him. "So what made you decide to forgive me for bailing on you?"

"Hard to be m-mad at the guy who kicked Ozzie's ass."

They shared a grin, then gathered their sack lunches from the counter beside the front door where Mrs. Reeves always left them.

Shannon can't be the werewolf, Julian said. *He did you a favor. The wolf would have chewed the paper up, spit it at you and laughed.*

Then lit you both on fire, Caleb added.

Since Aden hadn't spoken his thoughts about this very subject aloud, they couldn't know that he'd already reasoned this out.

Unless this is a trick to throw you off, Elijah said thoughtfully.

Not a trick, he wanted to say, because he didn't want to believe it. His life finally seemed to be on the right track. He'd ruin that himself if he allowed suspicions to poison him. After all, suspicions led to paranoia, and paranoia was classic schizophrenic behavior. He'd be gift-wrapping his doctors' diagnosis when he'd been struggling so valiantly to *dis*prove it.

He has enough to think about, boys, Eve said, probably sensing the intensity of his thoughts. *Let's give him some peace this morning.*

Yes, Eve, everyone said at the same time Shannon said, "You need a good story for your f-face or you'll get kicked out. And maybe don't bring up Ozzie. Do, and h-he'll have the others plan a sneak attack."

Took Aden a moment to sort through the voices and pick out what Shannon had uttered. See? The guy hadn't been faking his gesture of friendship; he was still trying to make things better.

"I can't leave Ozzie out of it because Ozzie has the same beat-up face that I do. We deny it, and Dan'll know we're lying. We'll be in worse trouble."

"Maybe you'll get to put it off. Maybe he's gone." Some mornings Dan was up doing chores, but a few lucky mornings, he slept in or was off running errands.

For the first time since starting school, they headed outside together. The air was cool, the sky overcast. Dan was at the truck, about to open the door when he spotted Aden and froze. As if Aden were cursed, the sun broke through a wall of clouds and spotlighted him, seeming brighter than ever. He had to blink against it, his injured eye burning and tearing. Guess he wouldn't be putting off the conversation, after all.

"Where'd you get the bruises, Aden?" Dan only used that hard tone when he was fighting his anger.

Here goes. He squared his shoulders, even as his stomach clenched painfully. "Ozzie and I had a little disagreement. We're over it, and we're sorry." Short, sweet and honest.

Dan stomped around the truck, bearing down on him. "You know better than to resort to physical violence, no matter the problem. That's one of the reasons you're here, to get a handle on your violent tendencies."

"This was a one-time thing and won't happen again."

"I've heard that before." The big guy scrubbed a hand down his face, some of the stiffness leaving him. "I can't believe you did this. I get you into public school, I buy you clothes, make sure you're fed. All I ask is that you get along."

His companions started screaming inside his head, trying to tell him what to say. Loud as they currently were, he heard only a jumble of indistinguishable words. "We made a mistake. We learned from it. Isn't that what's important?" Hopefully, that fit.

Dan worked his jaw. "Doesn't matter if you learned something or not. Actions have consequences. I have to punish you. You know that, too, right?"

"Punish me?" That, Aden heard. He tossed up his arms, his irritation boiling over with the same potency his rage had boiled over last night. "It's not like you're perfect, Dan. It's not like you haven't made mistakes."

His caregiver's eyes narrowed. "What's that supposed to mean?"

Don't do it, each of his companions shouted in unison. No mistaking their meaning this time.

"You know," he said anyway. "You and Ms. Killerman."

Now his companions moaned.

Dan's mouth fell open. He stared at Aden in silence for several moments, the time ticking away in tune to the crickets' chirps. Finally, his gaze shot to Shannon. "Get in the truck. I'll drive you to school." His tone was no longer hard or upset, but flat. No emotion.

Shannon hesitated only a moment, his expression sympathetic, before obeying.

Dan crossed his arms over his chest. "I don't know how you learned about Ms. Killerman or what you think you know, but I assure you, I've done nothing to be ashamed of. Because that's what you're getting at, isn't it?"

He stuffed his hands into his pockets and nodded, the action tentative. He'd started this; he would see it through.

"Well, you're wrong. I flirt with her solely for the sake of you boys, and Meg is very aware of it. Sometimes she's even in the same room while I'm doing it because it's the only way I can stomach what I have to say and hear. But I do it because it keeps you boys here when you should be pulled in for violence. Or drugs. Or theft. Or any number of other things. I do it because your requests are processed before anyone else's. How do you think you got into public school so quickly?"

"I—I—"

Dan wasn't done. "At first, I couldn't believe I'd called her and asked her to make it happen. But then I remembered your disappointment when I told you it wasn't going to happen. So I called her again and asked her to hurry things along. And you know what? She did. Do you think she does that for everyone? She had to get state and school approval. She had to fight the powers that be. *I* had to fight."

Guilt, white-hot and laced with acid, swept through him. He'd judged and condemned Dan without all the facts. Something that had been done to *him* time and time again. Something he'd sworn never to do to others. As honest and forth-right as Dan was, he should have known better.

"Dan," he began, tortured.

"Appearances are often deceiving, Aden," Dan said softly. "Next time you think poorly of me, I hope you'll give me the benefit of the doubt. Come to me, talk to me."

"I will. And I'm sorry I didn't this time." He raised his chin and met Dan's stare. "I just hope you'll do the same for me. Give me the benefit of the doubt."

Dan crossed his arms over his chest, another of those long silences taking hold. What was going through his head, Aden didn't know. Whatever it was, though, caused his expression to change from suspicion to chagrin and finally to acceptance.

"Get in the truck," Dan said gruffly.

Get in the—what? Did that mean…was he…

"Am I pretending the fight never happened? Yeah. I've been where you are, and I know what it's like to be judged and con-victed when you're innocent. So I'm giving you the benefit of the doubt and trusting that you did what you did for a reason. But it better not happen again. Now, don't just stand there. Move, move, move. You don't want to be late for first period."

Aden couldn't help himself. He threw himself at Dan and gave a quick squeeze. Dan grunted and mussed his hair, and Aden grinned before jumping into the truck.

When they reached the school parking lot, Aden saw that Mary Ann was waiting at the double doors, watching the woods expectantly. For him? He wanted to believe it, but as many times as she'd run from him after school…

The moment the truck reached the drop-off lane, easing forward, that swift, jolting wind cut through him, straight into his chest. The souls groaned, disappearing into their black void. Aden's guilt returned, although for a different reason. They had helped him get into this school and endured the pain of the darkness so that he could find them a way out, bodies of their own. So far, he hadn't done anything to keep his part of the bargain.

That would change. Today. He'd already decided to force Mary Ann to talk to him, hoping to learn what was going on inside her head, but now, he'd take it a step further. He would reveal the rest of his abilities—no matter how he feared she would react—and find out how she sent the souls away.

He studied her more closely. She looked tired, as if she hadn't slept in days, and there were shadows under her eyes. A frown pulled at the corners of her lips. Usually she was bubbling over with energy, had a smile for everyone.

Mary Ann's frown became a scowl as her friend Penny approached. Penny looked worse than Mary Ann, her face swollen as if she'd been crying. Mary Ann said something, head shaking violently. Penny grabbed her hand. Mary Ann ripped it away and disappeared inside the building.

What had *that* been about?

The truck stopped at the curb. "Behave, boys. And Aden, do not resort to violence again. We clear?"

"Absolutely. And…thank you."

Dan nodded, offered him a half smile. "See you later."

Aden and Shannon slid outside and once again walked together as they entered the building. Aden couldn't deny that he liked having someone at his side. Someone who might also watch his back.

"Y-you wanna have lunch together?" Shannon asked him.

"Aw, how sweet," a nearby voice sneered. Tucker's voice. Aden recognized it, hated it. Every time Mary Ann was out of range, Tucker had called him names, tripped him or thrown paper wads at him. "Sounds like Stutter and Crazy are dating now."

A wave of laughter swept the hall.

Aden ground his teeth. He ignored the jock—no more violence, no more violence, no more freaking violence—and said to Shannon, "I'll meet you in the cafeteria."

Shannon gave a barely discernible nod, his gaze falling to the floor, his cheeks pinkening, and was off to his first class.

Tucker slammed into Aden's shoulder as he walked by, knocking his backpack to the floor.

"Watch it," the jock growled, then stopped and whistled, losing all traces of his anger as he studied Aden's battered face. "Well, well, well. Someone must have been a naughty boy to have gotten such a spanking."

How could Mary Ann stand this guy? He was like a pile of manure hidden in a shiny box.

Without a word, Aden picked up his bag and stalked off.

"That's right. Run away, coward," Tucker called smugly.

He could feel hundreds of eyes on him, watching, judging, maybe even pitying. They thought he was afraid of Tucker.

He hated that, but couldn't set them straight. Not just because he had to avoid violence of every kind—and that's what would happen if he challenged Tucker, bloody, gruesome violence—but because of Mary Ann. She might not like it if he ground her boyfriend's face into powder.

Bottling his anger cost him, though. He barely made it through his first class. For some reason, Mary Ann wasn't there. He wished he could follow her lead. He almost stomped from the room a thousand times, his nerves too raw to deal with the lecture and the students. The souls were once again chattering in his mind, trying to comfort him but their voices were only growing in intensity, blending with everyone around him and finally culminating into a roar.

Of course, that's when Mr. Klein pointed to him and asked him a question. He couldn't decipher the words, much less form a coherent reply, so Mr. Klein decided to make an example of him and his inattention and had him stand beside his desk the entire class.

If one more person snickered at him, he was going to snap.

His second and third classes weren't much better. The second, geometry, should have been pleasant, since he had that with Mary Ann, as well, but once again she wasn't there. Had she left? Plus, there was a new kid who'd taken the open desk beside Aden and prattled on the entire hour. New himself, Aden sympathized with the need for a friend—but God, he needed a moment of peace.

"You better stop," Aden whispered midway through the

class. "You'll get in trouble, and you don't want to be on Ms. Carrington's bad side. I hear she bites, and not the good way."

"No worries, bro. No one cares what I do." New Kid smiled. He had shaggy blond hair that kept falling into his eyes.

His skin seemed to absorb the room's light, sparkling. Aden had seen that sparkle before, on someone else. But who—the old lady at the shopping center. *That's right.* And just like the old lady, this kid made the fine hairs on Aden's body stand at attention.

"I'm John O'Conner, by the way. And yeah, I'm highly aware that my name is similar to the guy in *Terminator*. It was my mom's favorite movie."

"Aden Stone."

"Listen, have you seen Chloe Howard around the halls? A brunette with braces, lots of freckles. Very pretty."

"No." He'd been too preoccupied with his *own* brunettes to notice others. He tried to keep his gaze focused on the head of the class. That didn't discourage John.

"Oh, man. You are missing out. But that's okay. You have the rest of the day to hunt her down and—"

"Mr. Stone." A palm slapped onto the teacher's desk, rattling the coffee mug resting there. "Would you like to explain vectors yourself or should I continue?"

He sunk low in his seat as everyone spun in their chairs to face him. "You should continue." Why wasn't John in trouble?

She held his stare for a moment more before nodding with satisfaction and launching back into her lecture.

"Have lunch with me," John told him. "I don't want to sit alone, and I want to tell you about Chloe."

"Fine," he whispered, just wanting the conversation to end. And maybe talking to the guy at lunch would lead to a revelation about that glittery skin and those electrical charges that pulsed from his body. "I'll wait for you by the cafeteria doors."

"Sweet."

Finally. Silence.

All through third period he wondered about Mary Ann, where she'd gone, what she was doing. When the bell rang, he grabbed his stuff and headed for the door, unsure of what to do. He was meeting Shannon—and now John—for lunch, so he couldn't leave and walk to her house to see if she was there.

He'd memorized her number. Maybe the receptionist in the office would let him use the phone and call her. Except...

That now familiar gust of wind hit him in the chest, and he stopped short.

Mary Ann had to be nearby.

He looked down the hall—and there she was, rushing toward him. The intensity of his relief was staggering.

"Aden," she called.

She halted just in front of him, panting a little, shifting restlessly from one foot to the other. "Aden," she repeated more quietly. She offered him a hesitant smile, as if she was unsure of her welcome.

"So now you're talking to me again?" Aden couldn't help but ask. "Why have you been avoiding me?"

Her smile fell. "What do you mean? I wasn't avoiding you. At lunch, you avoided me."

"You kept taking off after school," he reminded her. "I would approach you and you would run."

"I'm sorry. I didn't mean…that wasn't what I…oh, I'm making a mess of this. But I promise you misunderstood my intentions. You're my friend and, well, I need to talk to you." Her gaze darted to the kids shuffling around them. "Now isn't the time to explain, though."

A misunderstanding. Thank God. He was new at this friend thing and clearly had a lot to learn. "What are you doing here? Why weren't you in first or second period?"

"To answer your second question, I, well, ditched." She chewed her bottom lip. "To answer your first, I'm stopping you from running off to wherever it is you usually go at lunch."

He didn't tell her he'd already had to change his plans. "Walk me to my locker," he said, and she nodded. They kept pace beside each other.

"So where *do* you go at lunch?" she asked, still seeming nervous.

"I sneak off campus and search the forest for the…" His gaze circled the crowd pointedly. "You know."

Her jaw dropped. "You do? Why? And Aden, that's not good for you. You need to eat."

"No worries. Dan's wife packs me a lunch every morning. I take it with me and eat in the woods."

"Oh."

Kids still buzzed around them and lockers slammed shut.

"You don't need to do that," she said. "Look for Wolf, I mean. He and I have talked."

First came surprise. Then anger. Then fear. "I told you to stay away from him, Mary Ann. You're lucky to be alive. A…friend of mine told me wolves like that are vicious killers."

The color in her face drained, and her hand fluttered to her throat. "What friend? Someone else knows about what's going on?"

"Don't worry. She's not a…human," he whispered.

Mary Ann's eyes widened. "What do you mean? What is she?"

Should he tell her or shouldn't he? Only a brief struggle was required to reach a decision. He needed her help. Therefore, she needed all the information he could give her, even about Victoria.

Keeping his voice low, he said, "My friend, she's a vampire. And a princess," he added. That fact didn't bother him, not anymore, but it still managed to stun him. *He* was dating a princess. Well, he hoped they were dating.

Mary Ann didn't laugh at him. Didn't tell him he had an overactive imagination and walk away. She gulped and nodded. "You mentioned vampires before but I didn't, I mean, I didn't think you actually knew one." She rubbed her neck, as if she could already feel fangs sinking into her vein. "How did you meet her?"

A group of giggling girls passed him, once again reminding him of their potential audience. "I'll tell you everything, just not while we've got ears all around us. Right now, I need you to promise to stay away from that animal. Besides wanting to kill me, there's something off about him. I shouldn't have been able to...*you know* that day."

Her brow scrunched as she peered up at him through the thick shield of her lashes. "I don't. I'm sorry."

"Possess him."

"Oh. Why not?"

"When I'm with you my abilities stop working. But that day in the forest, every single one of them worked perfectly. Has to be because of him. He was the only variable."

"First, I still want to know what those other abilities are. Second, Wolf isn't dangerous. Not to me, at least. I think he likes me. He's walked me to school every morning and home every afternoon." Again she chewed on her bottom lip, and he realized it was a nervous gesture of hers. She drew her arms around her middle. "He's softening toward you, I just know it."

So said the girl who had a very good chance of being on the morning news one day, her body mangled and riddled with teeth marks.

He couldn't believe he'd spent so much time worrying about her, thinking she wanted nothing to do with him, and she'd merely been playing with a wolf as though it was a pet.

"Is he why you've run from me every day after school?"

Her cheeks flushed. "Yes, but please don't be mad," she said. "I can't seem to help myself. I'm...drawn to him."

That, he understood, even as it worried him. Victoria drew him, too.

They reached Aden's locker and he worked the combination. "I'm sure Tucker will love that you're crushing on someone else. Especially an animal."

"Hey!" She slapped his shoulder. "He's not an animal. Not *all* the time. Not that he's shown me his human form," she muttered. "And besides, it doesn't matter if Tucker likes it or not. We're over."

Aden stilled for a single heartbeat, books frozen midair, unsure he'd heard correctly. "Really? You're broken up?"

She nodded, the blush in her cheeks deepening. "No question. He slept with Penny."

"Ah." He dropped his books inside and slammed the door shut. "That's what you were so upset about this morning."

"Wouldn't you be? They betrayed me, then acted as if nothing had ever happened."

"I'm sorry. I'm not surprised they kept it quiet, though. No one likes to broadcast their mistakes."

"Ugh. You sound just like Wo—" She waved a hand through the air, expression pinched. "Never mind."

Her wolf? Sounding just like a vicious killer was *not* a compliment. Maybe he needed to, like, get in touch with his feelings or something. Act sensitive. "You're better off, you know. Tucker is an…"

"Ass?" she said, and they both laughed.

"Yeah. An ass."

"I agree." She released a shuddering breath as she tugged him forward. "Come on." They walked several steps before she picked up the conversation where it had left off. "If all we've got to look forward to is disloyalty and treachery, why do we even make friends?"

He hated that her usual optimism was gone. "Again, human nature. Hoping for the best is what drives us."

"Now you sound like my dad," she grumbled.

"Well, then, he's clearly a genius."

Mary Ann laughed.

The cafeteria doors came into view. Any minute now, they'd be joined by Shannon and John O'Conner. He pulled Mary Ann aside and peered down at her, a sense of urgency overtaking him. "I need to talk to you."

"What's wrong?" she asked, sobering.

"Please don't take off after school without me. Find a way to get rid of the wolf. There's so much I need to tell you. Not just about the vampire, but about me. There's something I need your help with."

She reached up and squeezed his forearm. "Whatever it is, I'll help you any way I can. I hope you know that."

So easy, and so swift. He had to fight the urge to hug her, and it had nothing to do with his ability or her ability but everything to do with *her*. With how great she was.

With all the people who had cut him loose over the years, part of him had expected her to balk. "All last week I thought you were frightened of me, that you wanted nothing to do with me. To be honest, I wasn't sure how you'd react today."

"Oh, Aden. I truly am sorry about that. I should have told you what I was doing, but I was afraid you'd try to protect me and end up hurt." Those white teeth emerged and she started chewing on her lip again. "And if you'd gotten hurt because of me, well, the guilt would have killed me."

He smiled slowly, relieved, and she returned the smile with one of her own.

"I hope you don't mind, but I promised Shannon I'd eat with him," he said. "Oh, and I told this really talkative new kid that he could join us. I'm supposed to wait by the doors."

"A new kid?" Her brow puckered. "I hadn't heard we'd gotten another."

"Yeah, just today. His name's John O'Conner and he—"

"Wait. What?" Her nose wrinkled in bewilderment. "Did you say John…O'Conner?"

"Yeah, why?"

Rather than answer, she said, "Describe him to me."

O-kay. "Blond hair, brown eyes and his skin looks like he slathered himself with glitter. It's really weird."

Her frown deepened. "Except for the glitter thing, that sounds like the John I knew. But someone was clearly playing a joke on you, because John died of a drug overdose last year."

Aden massaged the back of his neck, his muscles knotting in anger. "A joke."

"I'm sorry."

He wanted to punch the wall as he imagined the laugh everyone was probably having at his expense. "Shannon's somewhere inside," he said stiffly.

Mary Ann regarded him with sympathy before leading him to the cafeteria.

A few minutes later, he found himself parked at a table with

Mary Ann and Shannon. Though they were the only three in that particular section, kids occupied the tables around them, just as he'd seen in movies.

He was very aware of Penny, staring wistfully at Mary Ann, and Tucker, glaring from Mary Ann to Aden with loathing. Shannon kept his head bowed, and Mary Ann kept up a strained, meaningless chatter. Aden looked for "John," but never caught sight of him. No one seemed to be laughing at him, either, so he was able to relax. A little.

Overall, it was an uncomfortable ordeal. He much preferred the isolation of the forest, and that surprised him. How many hours had he spent daydreaming about friends and normalcy? But maybe, in the woods, he would have found Victoria. If only.

Finally the bell rang, signaling it was time to head to their next class. Chairs were scooted back, footsteps began to pound.

"W-wait for me after school," Shannon said to him. "We can all walk home together."

Aden met Mary Ann's gaze. She'd been rendered immobile, half sitting, half standing. Panic flittered through her eyes. After school, she was supposed to lose the wolf so they could talk.

Shannon must have caught the tension-filled undercurrents, because he said, "N-never mind," and tried to shuffle away.

Sensitive as she obviously was to others' feelings, Mary Ann pasted a grin on her face and grabbed his wrist, stopping him. "Walking home together sounds great. I was just trying to remember if I'd told my dad to pick me up or not."

"Oh. Okay." Shannon's posture relaxed.

"See you then," Aden said, trying to mask his disappointment, and strode to his next class. Looked like his talk with Mary Ann would have to be postponed. Again. They couldn't spill secrets with an audience present.

Would they be able to talk in the morning? Or would something stop them then, too? And tomorrow after school was out; Shannon would probably want to walk with them again. At this rate, they'd never have a single moment of privacy. Unless…he could tell her everything without ever having to speak a word.

Determined, he used his next three classes to write. About himself, his past, the things he'd done, the things he'd witnessed and the things he needed from Mary Ann. He didn't skimp on the details, didn't try to paint himself in a more favorable light. He wanted her to know the truth.

I have a bad feeling about this, Elijah said when he finished.

Aden groaned. Not another one. But it didn't matter; he wouldn't let it matter. He was still giving Mary Ann the note. What happened after that would be up to her.

+WELVE

Later that day, Mary Ann read the bottom of Aden's note for the millionth time.

I have to find a way to free them. For them. For me. I'm not mental. They're people, not just voices. But I don't know what to do. Getting them bodies of their own is all I can think of, but that seems impossible, you know? And if I do manage to find bodies—someone who recently died maybe?—how would I pull them out of me and put them inside? ~~Hell, as I'm writing this I'm wondering if I AM mental.~~ You're the only person I've ever met who can cancel out what I can do. I figure you know things I don't, even if you don't yet realize it. Do you? But I'll understand if you don't want to help me.

Mary Ann's arm fell to her side, the paper crinkling between her fingers. Her mind whirled with questions. Four other people swirled inside Aden's head, their voices constant, always distracting him. Except when he was with her. Somehow, she quieted them.

Did she believe all of that? She didn't want to, and honestly hadn't the first thousand times she'd read his letter. Then her doubts had begun to give way to curiosity. The curiosity had given way to uncertainty, and the uncertainty had finally given way to acceptance.

A week ago, she hadn't known werewolves and vampires existed. Now, there was no refuting it. Why couldn't there be a boy with people trapped inside him, as well? People who could time travel and wake the dead. Predict the future and possess other bodies—the last of which she'd seen firsthand.

How was she able to stop them? Why her? She was nothing special.

She nibbled on her bottom lip, no answers sliding into place, and peered up at her bedroom ceiling. It was smooth and white, a blank canvas just waiting to be colored on. *I can reason this out,* she mused, pepping herself up.

Okay, so. Aden thought the best way to free the souls was to find them bodies. *She* thought, drastic as it was and impossible as it seemed, that should be a last resort. Until they reached that point, it made sense to figure out exactly who the people inhabiting his head were. Or maybe who they'd *been.* He'd mentioned that while they didn't recall any life but the one they shared with Aden, they did have moments of déjà vu and recognition. That had to mean something.

Maybe they were ghosts and Aden had unintentionally

drawn them. With that thought, she found herself eyeing her room for any sign of a spectral being, hands clutching her comforter, breath emerging shallow and heavy. Werewolves and vampires were real, so why not ghosts, too? Were there any around her? People she'd known, perhaps? People who had once lived here?

Her mother?

Mary Ann's heartbeat skidded out of control, and tears of hope burned her eyes. She blinked them back. Her mother could be here, watching her, she thought, dazed. Protecting her. Her greatest desire was to see her mom again, to hold her, hug her and tell her goodbye. The car accident had taken her so suddenly, there'd been no chance to prepare.

"I love you, Mom," she whispered.

There was no response.

Concentrate, Gray. You have a job to do. She cleared her throat and quashed her disappointment. *Where was I?* Oh, yeah. If the souls trapped inside Aden's head were actually ghosts, wouldn't they remember their lives fully?

Good point. Either their memories had been wiped when they entered his body or they were something else. Angels? Demons? Were there such things? Probably. But they probably weren't the souls trapped inside Aden. Again, they would have remembered their own identities. But again, their memories could have been wiped.

Ugh. This was getting her nowhere. Could the four be talking to him like Wolf talked to her? Perhaps they weren't truly inside his head but were tethered to him and simply projecting their voices.

She immediately discarded that idea, as well. Aden heard them—if they weren't actually inside him, wouldn't he see them, as well?

Mary Ann tapped her chin. First thing she needed to do, as she'd initially thought, was figure out who the four were so that she could figure out what they'd been. Aden said they'd been together since his birth.

"Which means I need to go back to the beginning," she said, her voice cutting through the silence of her room. To do that, she needed to gather some information. She made a mental list:

Find out who his parents were. Or rather, are.

Find out where he was born.

Find out who was around him the first few days of his life.

The beginning of what?

At the sound of the masculine voice inside her head, she jackknifed to a sitting position, hand fluttering over her once again racing heart. Wolf loomed in her bedroom doorway, huge and black and beautiful. His fur gleamed in the sunlight, and those pale green eyes regarded her almost gently. His ears were perked, pointing like an elf's. Clothing hung from his mouth.

"How'd you get in?" she asked.

I walked.

"Funny."

His lips seemed to twitch around the material. *Last time I was here, I left one of the lower windows open, so I would be able to climb through whenever I wanted.*

"I should have known." She eyed the clothes. Jeans, a T-shirt. "Are those for me?"

No. For me. When I switch forms.

Had she heard him right? "You're going to…"

Show you my human form, yes.

Excitement spread through her veins, encompassing her entire body in seconds and making her shake. "Really? Why now?"

Ignoring her, he paced to her bathroom. The door closed with a swish. Mary Ann set Aden's note on her nightstand and stood. Then she sat back down. Her knees were a little weak. What would Wolf look like? Was he someone she knew? Every time she tried to picture him, all she could see was a hard, muscled body. His face always remained in the shadows.

The phone rang, startling her, and she jumped.

Mary Ann glanced at caller ID, and her trembling intensified. Penny. She crossed her arms over her middle, anchoring her hands under her armpits so that she couldn't reach for the receiver.

Another ring.

As she sat there, Mary Ann was surprised to feel hurt, pure and undiluted, rather than anger. She loved Penny, she did. And Wolf and Aden were right. Making mistakes and then hiding them was human nature. But she couldn't act as if nothing had happened, nor could she trust Penny not to do it again. With someone else. Someone Mary Ann actually adored. For some reason Wolf popped into her mind.

At the fourth ring, her machine picked up.

"I know you're there, Mar. Talk to me. Please. There's so much I want to tell you." A pause. Penny sighed. "Fine. We'll do this over the phone. I wanted to tell you what had happened. I did. Remember at the café, when I mentioned that Tucker would stray? I was trying to work up the courage to tell you but I stopped myself. I was too afraid of *this*. Of losing you. I didn't mean for it to happen." There was another pause, crackling static. "We'd both been drinking and neither one of us was thinking clearly. In my mind, I justified it because I knew you didn't love him. I told myself I would only be hurting you if I told you, that unburdening myself would be selfish. I was wrong. I see that now. Mary Ann…please."

Beep.

Silence.

Mary Ann's jaw started trembling, right along with her body.

The phone began ringing again, and she glanced at the caller ID, expecting to see Penny's number. Would she answer this time? What would she say? She saw Tucker's number instead, and her teeth ground together in irritation. Was something in the air? A call Mary Ann vibe?

Him, she didn't love. Him, she wanted nothing to do with. She wasn't even tempted to pick up the phone.

His message was shorter than Penny's.

"I'm sorry, Mary Ann. If you would just talk to me, I could explain, make you understand. We could be friends, like you said. Just…call me or I swear to God…" The words ended in a growl.

Click. Silence.

She shook her head. They were over, done in every way, and talking wouldn't change that.

"Are you ready?"

Wolf's voice. His real voice. Deep and rough…unsure. Was he as nervous as she was?

"I'm ready," she called, her voice now trembling, too.

The bathroom door creaked open. There was a shuffle of footsteps, and then a boy was leaning against the wall across from her, staring over at her.

First thought to run through her head: she'd never met him before. The second: oh my God. He wasn't exactly beautiful, his features were too sharp, but that only added to his appeal. He looked wicked and ruthless and capable of anything.

He had black hair, as silky and shiny as his fur had been, and his eyes were still green. That, however, was where the similarities with the wolf ended. He was taller than she had guessed, stacked with muscle and sinew, and had wide shoulders and long legs. His skin was a tantalizing golden brown. He wore a plain white T-shirt and faded jeans that hung low on his waist. No shoes or socks.

Her stomach had yet to stop flip-flopping. She'd lain in bed with this magnificent creature. She'd held him in her arms and petted him. She, who spent her spare time reading, who studied no matter how much she hated it and wouldn't know fun if it slapped her across the face. She, whose most defining feature was a fifteen-year plan—a fifteen-year plan she no longer even thought about.

Funny. She'd once thought abandoning her life's plan would be a reason to mourn. Right now, she only wanted to celebrate.

Until doubts took hold.

Had she bored Wolf to death? He ran wild in the woods. He could shift between animal and human. She was plain ole Mary Ann.

What are you doing? Blank your thoughts. He could read auras. Did he know what she was feeling right now? How she was drooling over him? Oh, great. *Gonna be sick.*

"Well?" he said. "Do you have nothing to say? You're bright pink, green and gold. Excited, nervous and nauseous."

Her cheeks heated. Her skin was probably the same colors as her aura.

"So what are you thinking?"

"You can't figure it out?" No way did she want to say it aloud.

"Mary Ann," he said, exasperated.

She'd take that as a no. "I'm thinking you are…normal." Not true, not true, oh, not true.

He popped his jaw. "Normal." His harsh tone suggested that was a very bad thing.

Not knowing what else to do, she nodded.

Silence stretched between them. Neither moved.

Say something. Anything. "Aden thinks I'm some sort of superability neutralizer. If that's true, why didn't I stop you from changing from wolf to human? Or maybe a better question is why didn't you change *back* into a human when you first approached me? Of course, both of those questions hinge on the fact that I'm a neutralizer, which I might not be."

Dear God. She was babbling. *Stop!* "You know, you could stop glaring at me. That might help."

He scrubbed a hand down his face and laughed without humor. "All this time I agonized over the decision to show myself to you, my true self, afraid of your reaction, and this is what I get," he said, and laughed again. "You act as if I didn't do it. As for your ability to neutralize, maybe you can, maybe you can't. Shape-shifting isn't supernatural or magic or whatever you're thinking. It's a part of who I am, how I survive. You can't stop humans from breathing, can you?"

"No."

He nodded as if he'd just proven his case. "My name is Riley, by the way. Not that you asked."

"My name is Mary Ann," she responded automatically, then blushed again. "Sorry. You knew that." God, this was awkward. Part of her wished he'd go back to wolf form. That, she knew. That, she was comfortable with. *That,* she didn't want to drool on—and then subsequently kill herself in embarrassment for said drooling problem. Maybe it was best to change the subject. "So why were you so nervous about showing me your true self?"

"I knew your expectations were high. I wanted to meet— or exceed—them." He didn't wait for her reply but crossed his arms over his chest, pulling the material of his shirt tight against his biceps. "Anyway, you never answered my question. When I first walked in, you were talking about starting at the beginning. The beginning of what?"

Nope. She wasn't gonna go there. "Sorry, but I can't answer you now, either."

He straightened, looking slightly offended. "Why?"

"It involves Aden, and you want to kill him."

"Yeah," he said, not denying it, "but I'm not going to. My friends like him."

"Friends?"

"You. And my charge, Victoria. Vampire princess and all-around pain in my—well, just a pain."

Victoria. The vampire princess Aden had talked about with longing? The vampire princess who had put stars in Aden's eyes? Must be. Friends, Wol—*Riley* had called them. "Aden told me a little about her."

Riley nodded stiffly. "You shouldn't know about her. No one should. My job is to keep her safe and the more people who know about her, the more *unsafe* she is and the angrier her father will be with me."

"Aden and I will keep your secrets, believe me. To talk about them is to paint targets on our backs."

"No one will make you a target," he said, and there was so much fury in his tone she was momentarily speechless. He strode to her, sat beside her. Their shoulders brushed, and she shivered.

There was a beat of silence, of utter tension.

She wasn't sure what she wanted him to do just then; she was only sure she wanted him to do *something*. Anything but move away from her.

"I just meant," she said softly, "that they'll think we're crazy and gossip about us." Another thing to drool over: his protective nature. But did that protective nature mean that he and Victoria were more than bodyguard and princess? More

than friends? Her hands tightened into fists. Was she…
jealous? No. Surely not. "I thought vampires and werewolves
were enemies. I mean, Aden said the vampire told him to stay
away from you."

"She's such a riot, that one."

"So you're not enemies?" And why did she suddenly want
them to be? What was wrong with her? Were the two dating?
Her teeth ground together.

"No. Vlad, the first of the vampires, gave the same blood
he had drunk, the blood that changed him, to his beloved pets.
They, too, began to change. Soon they were able to take human
form, though they retained their animal instincts. In those
early days, they were vicious, ferocious, and would try and
eat everyone they encountered. Those people who were
attacked, the ones that survived, began to change, as well,
though they retained their human instincts. Those are *my*
people. Vlad helped them, nursed them. In return, my people
pledged to protect his."

All that history was fascinating. Scary, but fascinating.
And yet that wasn't what her mind focused on. "So why'd you
decide to reveal yourself to me now?"

"Because," was all he said, eyes narrowing.

"Why?" she insisted. So that he could finally touch her with
his hands? A girl could dream. Her eyes widened. Where
were these thoughts coming from?

"Because. Now, I believe you were going to tell me what
you were talking about earlier."

Frus-trat-ing. But she should be used to his lack of

response. Clearly Riley felt entitled to all the info she possessed, but didn't think it was necessary to return the favor.

He'd said he wouldn't hurt Aden, but would he help her help him? She could use all the help she could get, and she *did* trust him. Sighing, she told him some of what Aden was going through. "I think we need to find out, if at all possible, exactly who the people inside him are. The best place to start is with Aden's parents. From there, we can find out where he was born and who was around him. Only problem is, I don't know who his parents are."

"Call and ask him." He nudged her with his shoulder.

For a moment, she remained unmoving. He'd purposely touched her. And his skin, even through their clothing, had been hot. Wonderfully hot. "I can't. He lives at a ranch for kids who've been in trouble with the law and stuff. A phone call from a girl could maybe get him kicked out since he's not supposed to think about dating, but about improving his future."

"You told me you weren't dating him." Riley said it quietly, but the words were no less intense.

"I'm not. I was just explaining what the man in charge of his care might think." Why did Riley care if she was dating Aden? For the same reason she cared if he was dating Victoria? *Don't think about that now.* She pondered her options with Aden and almost clapped when an idea took root. "*You* could visit him without causing any problems. You could ask him about his parents for me."

Riley was shaking his head before she finished her sentence. "Hell, no."

"Please. You can run to him and run back to me in no time. I've seen how fast you are. Please," she repeated. "Helping Aden will be beneficial to me, as well, you know. The more we learn about his abilities, the more we could learn about mine."

He scowled. "Stop batting those lashes at me. I'm immune to feminine wiles."

She was batting her lashes? And she had wiles? She wanted to grin. "I could find out tomorrow at school, I guess. I probably won't get any sleep tonight, my mind will be so active. And of course, lack of sleep will affect my English test, which is sure to bring down my perfect grade. But I'm sure I'll get over it. Eventually."

For a long while, there was only silence.

"I am such a moron." Riley scowled at her and stood, striding to the bathroom to remove his clothes. "You'll owe me for this," he called.

So she really *did* have wiles. This time, she wanted to laugh.

ADEN HAD THE PAPERS he'd printed off at school, research about Vlad the Impaler, hidden in his geometry book as he lounged on his bed. This was his first peaceful moment since returning home. He'd had homework to complete and chores to do. During said chores, Ozzie had threatened him again—this time with decapitation—if Aden ratted about how he was buying his drugs.

The boy had sounded desperate, and Aden figured it was only a matter of time before Ozzie tried to get rid of him. Not by killing him, of course. Ozzie wasn't a murderer. At least, he didn't think so. But a liar? Yeah. Perhaps Ozzie would hide drugs in Aden's room and send Dan looking for them. Perhaps he'd just claim he'd seen Aden do something vile.

He'd have to stay on guard.

As for now, this moment, he was determined to relax. With a sigh, he buried his nose in the book. But relaxing, he soon realized, was nothing more than a dream. The more he read, the more he realized Victoria was right to fear what her father would do to him if he proved less than useful. A knife in the heart, perhaps, for that was how he would die. Or would the vampire king simply torture him, as was his habit?

Vlad Tepes, Vlad III, Prince of Wallachia, Vlad the Impaler, Dracula, had been known—when he'd been human—for his cruel punishments. He'd loved impaling his enemies and leaving them out in the open to die slowly and painfully. Allegedly, he'd done this to over forty thousand men and women.

Not like Aden could really say anything. He cut the heads off corpses. Still.

Some people believed the warrior had been killed in battle against the Ottoman Empire; some believed he'd been assassinated. Bram Stoker had been the first to immortalize him as a vampire, and Aden had to wonder why. Had the two actually crossed paths?

A scratching at the window had him bolting upright. He glanced at the clock. 9:00 p.m. Could it be Victoria? She'd never come to him so early, but her father could have decided it was time to eliminate him. Had she come to warn him?

What has you so afraid? Eve asked.

"An overactive imagination," he said, forcing himself to calm.

A paw met the glass and the scratching began again. Frowning, he stood and padded over. A stray animal?

When he saw Mary Ann's wolf, he jolted backward.

More scratching.

So. The wolf had finally come for him. The night would only be better if Vlad decided to join the party. Aden grabbed his daggers from the insides of the boots he'd pushed against his bed.

Since Aden had broken the lock, the wolf was able to pry the window open with his paws. Aden remained in place, armed, ready. This wasn't how Elijah had predicted his death, so perhaps he'd just be mauled. That didn't lessen his determination to defend himself however necessary.

Rather than leap at him, though, the wolf remained outside and peered into the bedroom. A tense moment passed in silence. Then: *Do you know your parents' names?*

The voice drifted through his head, but that wasn't what held him immobile with shock and disbelief. His parents? Really? "Look, I'm sorry about your leg. I went back to bandage you up but you were already gone. I didn't want to hurt you that day but you gave me no choice. You were going to kill me. I had to do something. Just like I'll do something tonight if you attack."

You and I will settle that soon, but not now. Now I need to know if you know your parents' names.

Confusion beat against the shock and disbelief. *What* was going on here? "No. I don't. They were just Mom and Dad,

and I was three last time I saw them." He could have asked
one of his caseworkers for their names, but hadn't allowed
himself to do so. They hadn't cared about him, so he wouldn't
care about them. "Now, if you want a fight, you won't walk
away unscathed."

*Could you be any more uncooperative? I'm trying to
help you here.*

"Yeah. Right."

With a growl, the wolf twisted around and raced off.

MARY ANN WAS AT HER DESK running a Google search on
the best way to track down a birth certificate when Riley
reappeared.

He doesn't know.

She rubbed her temples. "I was afraid of that. Did he know
where he was born, at least?"

Riley had been stalking toward his discarded clothes, but
stopped. *I didn't ask him.*

"Oh. Well, I'll ask him tomorrow, I guess. If he doesn't
know that either, it'll be okay. We're going to order his birth
certificate. It'll give us his parents' address, as well as the hospital he was born at. I just need his driver's license. Do you
think he has one? If he does, I can get that tomorrow, too. If
he doesn't…I don't know what I'll do." She pushed out a
frustrated breath. "Waiting is going to be hard. I wonder if I'll
sleep, after all."

Riley ran his tongue over his teeth and jumped back
through the window.

THE SCRATCHING STARTED UP again.

Aden stormed over, ready this time. He had a dagger hidden at his side. "Decide you want a piece of me, after all?"

Do you know the name of the hospital where you were born?

This became more confusing by the moment. "No. Why do you care?"

Do you have a driver's license? The wolf sounded irritated and out of breath.

"Yes. But I'm not allowed to drive. It's only for identification." He'd gotten it a few days before coming to the ranch. He'd been one question away from failing the written test, the souls "helping" him with his answers, but had aced the driving itself. Everyone had loved the illusion of freedom and had been quiet, lost in the moment.

Aden, the wolf snapped. *Concentrate. I need you to give me your license.*

"Why?"

Mary Ann wants to order a copy of your birth certificate. Since you don't know who your parents are, I'm guessing you don't have one handy.

Wait. Mary Ann wanted his birth certificate? That had to mean she believed him. That had to mean she was going to help him. He wanted to laugh—even though he'd told her to stay away from the beast, not recruit it to his cause. "No, I don't. But I'm not giving you the license until I hear from her. I don't trust you."

Well, you'd better start, because she's trying to help you and your friends and won't be able to sleep until she has that license. I don't like the thought of her tossing and turning.

She'd told the wolf about the souls; she'd confided his darkest secrets to his enemy. Aden waited for a sense of betrayal to overtake him, but it never did. She was trying to help him. Nothing else mattered.

"What does the name of the hospital I was born at matter? What do my parents matter?"

You'll have to ask her.

"I will." Aden crossed the room to his desk and dug through the top drawer for the requested item. "Here." He held it out and the wolf clasped it between his teeth. "I don't want her tossing and turning either. If you hurt her—"

She has nothing to fear from me, human. I wish I could say the same about you.

Here you go. Riley dropped the license in her lap.

Mary Ann bent down and hugged him. "Thank you."

My pleasure, he said, purring against her hair.

Now that she'd seen his human form, the action made her want things she shouldn't. Things she didn't want to name, not to Riley and certainly not to herself. But she couldn't help but wonder if Riley wanted those unmentionable things, as well.

Why else would he hang out with her so much? Unless…

She pulled back, a smile frozen on her face. Did she make him feel calm, as she did with Aden and apparently Tucker? Was it part of his job, something that helped him protect Victoria?

That was *not* what she wanted.

The fake smile fell away. She faced her computer to hide her now-pinched expression. "All I have to do is send a note with my request, a copy of a photo ID and ten dollars, then boom, his birth certificate is mine. Can you believe that? I'm going to order mine, too, since apparently my dad lost it."

From the corner of her eye, she saw Riley back away from her, shake his head. *I have to go. The clothes I'll leave behind. Hide them from your dad.*

"He'd freak out if he found them, that's for sure. He'd only just gotten used to the idea of me dating Tucker. If he knew a boy was actually sneaking inside my bedroom…" She shuddered. "I'd be placed on total lockdown."

Your dad's reaction to Tucker's appearance would not have come close to mine. But like I said, hide the clothes. I'll need them next time I'm over.

Next time. He was coming back; she would see him again. Maybe by then she'd have her new, silly feelings for him under control. "I will."

Oh, don't worry that the underwear is missing. I don't wear any. See you tomorrow, Mary Ann.

THIRTEEN

THE NEXT MORNING, Aden did a double take as he arrived at school. Victoria stood just outside the front doors. What was she doing out in public? Everyone could see her—and every boy that passed her couldn't help but stare.

Shock pounded through him, an urge to hide her riding fast on its heels, and he quickened his step. Mary Ann had to run to keep up. They'd met in the forest, halfway between their houses, and had walked the rest of the way together in a rare moment of privacy. Shannon had stayed home sick. The wolf was also absent. She'd grumbled about him the entire way, wondering where he was, what he was doing and why he wasn't with her. There hadn't been an opportunity to thank her for deciding to help him.

"What are you—oh," Mary Ann panted. Was that excitement in her voice?

He followed the line of her gaze. The boy Aden had seen

with Victoria that day in the forest—Riley, the bodyguard—
stood beside the vampire, clearly angry to be there.

But Aden was more interested in Victoria. Today she
wore a glittery black shirt that hung midthigh like a dress,
a pair of black tights and slippers with little bows on top.
Her blue-streaked hair was pulled back in a ponytail that
swung behind her. The only thing that was the same was
her opal ring.

She noticed his scrutiny and shifted from one foot to the
other. "These new clothes are uncomfortable, but for once we
were concerned with fitting in. Do you like them?"

"You're beautiful." And she was.

Her lips slowly lifted into a smile. "Thank you."

"Hello, Riley," Mary Ann said to the bodyguard.

Riley nodded in greeting. "Mary Ann." Was that gruff affection in his voice?

Aden frowned, his attention whipping to her. "You know
him?"

She nodded, gaze not leaving the boy. Man. Whatever he
was. He looked older and harder than all the guys entering the
building. "You know him, too. He's the one you warned me
away from. Don't worry, though," she rushed to assure him.
"He won't hurt us."

The only person—thing—he'd warned her away from was
the werewolf. With that thought, Aden sucked in a breath. The
werewolf. Riley the bodyguard was the werewolf?

He moved in front of both girls, splaying his arms, and
studied the boy, this human version of the big, black animal.

"As Mary Ann just told you, I'm not going to hurt them," Riley said, rolling his eyes.

Aden remained in place. His gaze landed and remained on Riley's legs. There wasn't a bumpy area to indicate bandages.

"I heal quickly," Riley explained with only the barest hint of anger. "Only limped for a day." He shrugged. "Or two."

This was so unexpected. Surreal, unbelievable.

"Eve?" Aden said aloud, and Riley frowned.

Yes, Eve responded.

The only time Mary Ann had failed to banish the souls was when she'd been with the werewolf. That meant the wolf somehow negated her ability, the same way Mary Ann usually negated Aden's.

When he'd considered Shannon the wolf, he'd thought that Shannon, in human form, simply could not affect Mary Ann—and therefore Aden—in any way. But Riley did, even in human form.

Which meant Aden was indeed standing in front of the "vicious and bloodthirsty" creature that hated him. The vicious and bloodthirsty creature that had helped him last night.

Aden? Eve prompted. *Did you need something?*

"Oh. Sorry. I was just checking to see if you were with me or in the black hole," he muttered.

"Who are you speaking to?" Riley demanded as Eve said, *I want to talk about Mary Ann. There's so much I—*

Who to answer first? "A friend," he told Riley. "And Eve, you know I can't talk to you in public. Please understand."

She growled at him, not unlike the wolf had in their prior encounters, but lapsed into silence.

"Actually, I shouldn't be speaking to any of you. Not here." Aden scanned the area, said, "This way," and took Victoria and Mary Ann by the hand, leading them under the towering oak that shaded the side of the building.

A frowning Riley followed. His narrowed gaze remained on Aden and Mary Ann's twined fingers until Aden released her.

"What's going on here?" Mary Ann kicked a pebble with the toe of her shoe, looking nervous, unsure. If Aden wasn't mistaken, she was watching Riley through her lashes.

Poor Mary Ann. She obviously liked the boy, yet Aden knew that wouldn't end well for her. One day soon she would find herself running through the woods, tears streaming down her cheeks, Riley the wolf chasing her. To hurt her?

Or maybe to comfort her, he thought suddenly. Stranger things had happened. Obviously.

"I'll explain in a moment. Introductions are in order first, I think," Victoria said, breaking the awkward silence.

How could he have forgotten? "Victoria, this is Mary Ann," he said. "Mary Ann, this is Victoria. Everyone but me already knows Riley, apparently."

"Nice to meet you," Mary Ann said.

Victoria nodded, her gaze darting between Mary Ann and Aden. "You, as well. I've heard much about you." Her tone was far from welcoming.

Was she…jealous?

"I don't see any… I mean…" Mary Ann's cheeks bloomed with color. "Never mind."

"They are retracted," Victoria explained. "They elongate when the hunger comes upon me."

Mary Ann covered her neck with her hand. "Oh."

"She won't bite you," Aden said.

Victoria didn't offer an assurance of her own. Maybe she *was* jealous. He wanted to grin.

He studied each of the people around him, marveling. How diverse they were. A beautiful vampire, a mysterious shape-shifter, and a seemingly normal teenage girl. They hadn't known each other long, not really. Strange how he'd already come to feel so close to them. Well, two of them, anyway.

"You told me werewolves were vicious," he said to Victoria. "If that's the case, why is one guarding you?"

Her mouth kicked up at one corner. "He *is* vicious. To everyone but me, that is. And that's exactly why he's my guard."

Excellent point. That didn't mean he liked it. "What about Mary Ann?"

"I told you. I would never hurt her," Riley said, offended.

"That's good to know. But if you ever change your mind, I'll make you regret it." He stated it matter-of-factly. Because that's what it was: a fact. He didn't have many friends, and those he had he would protect with his life.

Riley traced his tongue over his sharp, white teeth. "Are you threatening me, little boy?"

"Hey, now," Mary Ann said. "None of that. You two need

to play nice. Riley, Aden is only looking out for me. Aden, you remember how Riley helped you last night, right?"

"Yes," he said grudgingly. Between her questions about the wolf, Mary Ann had told him that when his birth certificate arrived, they were going to hunt down his parents. As grateful as he was to her and as brilliant as he found her plan, he wished he were more excited about it. Actually, any emotion besides dread would have been welcome. But he just couldn't work up a single ounce of enthusiasm at the prospect of meeting the people who had abandoned him.

"Since we're on the hurt-a-girl-and-pay subject, you should know that I take my job seriously," Riley said, the warning clear. "Harm Victoria, I won't just make you regret. I'll hang you by your own intestines while you're still alive."

Mary Ann's eyes rounded, as big as saucers. Had the wolf scared her? Part of him hoped so. She needed to know what kind of person—thing—she thought to call friend.

Riley noticed her expression and offered her a half smile. "Sorry. I'll make it quick and painless, okay?"

"You shouldn't threaten," she said. Rather than fear, he heard anger in her voice. A whole lot of anger. So why was she looking at Victoria now, rather than Riley?

Aden replayed the conversation through his mind and realized she hadn't liked the way Riley had rushed to the vampire's defense. Jealousy must be contagious, because they all seemed to have caught it.

"I would never hurt Victoria," Aden assured him. "You, on the other hand…" He would not back down and Riley needed to know that. He had his daggers, and he wasn't afraid to use them. Even here.

Victoria stepped forward and placed her hand on Aden's shoulder. He felt the burn of it, the sweet sizzle, and his attention swung to her, the werewolf momentarily forgotten.

Her ocean-water eyes glowed. He couldn't have turned away to save himself from a bullet to the head. Just then they were the only two people alive, transported back to their pond, splashing and laughing and brushing against each other. He'd held her, had almost kissed her.

"He will not attack you here," she said. "You have my word."

A gust of wind swirled between them, lifting her hair and casting several locks in his direction. They danced across his cheek, tickling.

"Now. Let's talk about something other than your intentions toward each other," she suggested.

"I'm all for that," Mary Ann said. Her anger appeared to have drained. "What are you guys doing here? Don't get me wrong. I'm happy you're here." She flicked Riley a glance. "I just can't figure out why you are."

A tremor moved through Victoria and she dropped her arm, focus wavering between Aden's face and his neck. "You know how I told you that my people sensed you?"

He nodded. Was she thinking of drinking from him?

"Well…we weren't the only ones. Others have arrived." Concern radiated from her as she leaned into him, careful not to make contact. "Goblins, fairies, witches," she whispered. "They're searching for the source of the lure."

Dear God. More creatures? And they were searching for him? Aden shook his head, wishing the bombshell Victoria had just dropped could be dislodged and lost. Wishing he could forget the trouble that was sure to come. How much more could he take?

"We were raised among them and know how they operate," she continued. "They'll want to capture you. Study you."

"That's why we," Riley said, butting in, "are here to protect the two of you from being taken or injured by these creatures."

He laughed until he realized the werewolf was serious. "I can take care of myself." He'd been doing it his entire life.

"Regardless." Riley shrugged. "Orders are orders. Vlad doesn't want you harmed before he's had the chance to meet you."

Aden tossed up his arms. "Why can't he meet me now?"

Riley ignored him. "And you," he said to Mary Ann, "are Aden's closet friend, which means you could be used to get to him. Which is why you'll be protected, too."

She nodded and it looked like she was fighting a smile.

So did Riley. "The good news is, Victoria and I are now students here. You'll be seeing a lot more of us."

Victoria, with him all day? Okay. Maybe being hunted by goblins, fairies and witches wasn't such a bad thing. Still... "I haven't seen anyone suspicious." Or different, for that matter. Wait. That wasn't true. The old lady at the shopping center, the girl that first day here at the school and then the boy pretending to be John O'Conner. They glittered and pulsed with energy.

What if *they* were goblins, fairies or witches? But they hadn't tried to hurt him or Mary Ann.

Again, Riley shrugged. "You might not have noticed them, but that doesn't mean they haven't seen *you*."

He scrubbed a hand over his face. "What do those creatures want with me?"

"The same thing we did, I'm sure." Victoria twirled her ponytail around her fingers. "To figure out how you blasted that energy, how you hurt them with it. And how you're still humming with a strange sort of power. Except," she added, tilting her head, "when you're with Mary Ann. Only then does it stop. Well, except when Riley is with you. Why is that?"

"I don't know." But he wanted to figure it out. "What can you tell me about those I'm up against?"

"With witches, you must be careful." Victoria clasped his hand briefly in warning. "They can smile while cursing you. Goblins enjoy eating human flesh. Unlike vampires, they do not take only a few pints of blood and walk away. They eat the entire body. Fairies are equally powerful, their beauty a mask for their treacherous hearts." She had spat the word *fairies*.

"Don't like fairies much, I take it?" Mary Ann said, brow arched.

Riley nodded. "They are our worst enemy."

Even though Aden had dealt with weirdness his entire life, he realized anew that there was a whole world he knew nothing about. He might not want to learn it all, but he had to, every little detail.

"I spoke to my father yesterday," Victoria began.

"Victoria," Riley snapped.

"What? He needs to know."

"You father will not like an outsider knowing of his frailty."

"Aden won't use the information against him." Once again she reached out and squeezed Aden's hand. "Anyway, during Samhain—Halloween, you humans call it—my father will officially rise. In honor of that, he is hosting a ball and it is there that he wishes to meet with you."

There was a catch, he knew there was. There was too much guilt in her tone. Then her words sank in and he gaped at her. "You father, Vlad the Impaler, wants to meet with me on Halloween night? And what do you mean, he will officially rise? I thought he was alive and well."

"Yes, he does want to meet you, and by rise I mean just that. For the past decade, he has been in hibernation to calm his mind, to prevent his too-long lifetime of memories from driving him insane. Your energy woke him early, though his body is—and will continue to be—weakened until the ceremony."

Good lord. He'd woken a beast. Literally. No wonder Vlad had wanted to kill him at first.

"I'm asking you to please come," Victoria said. "Do not try and thwart him. You will not like the consequences."

Had she ever tried to thwart the man? he wondered as he peered into her now-haunted eyes. What had been done to her in punishment? Perhaps it was best that he didn't know. If Vlad had hurt her, Aden would want to kill *him*. And if he tried to kill the king of the vampires, even in the man's weakened condition, he'd most likely be chopped into little Aden bits and scattered throughout Crossroads.

Suck it up. Be a man, he told himself. He'd faced corpses before. Yeah, they'd bitten him and yeah, this one was possibly a thousand times more vicious, had sharper teeth, wasn't really dead and still enjoyed the taste of blood, but he liked Victoria. For her, he would face anything. Anyone.

"Please," she said, taking his silence as resistance.

"I'll be there," he said. He had a month to prepare, body and mind.

She grinned. "Thank you."

Inside, a bell sounded, signaling they had five minutes to reach their first class. "You're students, right?"

Victoria and Riley nodded in unison.

"Come on, then. We can't be late."

Reluctantly, the four of them headed toward the school. Their reprieve was over, and they wouldn't get another one for a while yet.

"Do you guys have schedules and should we give you the tour?" Mary Ann asked, shyly glancing up at Riley.

"Yes and no," the wolf shifter replied. "Yes, we have schedules and no, we don't need a tour. We've already looked around."

They had? "When?"

"Last night," Victoria said with another grin. This one was sheepish.

God, he loved when she smiled like that.

His pulse must have spiked because her gaze fell to his neck; she licked her lips. Thinking of biting him?

That didn't scare him anymore, he realized. Not even a little. Good thing, too. Soon, she would do it, unable to resist, just as Elijah had shown him. Finally Aden could lay two of her fears to rest: he would not be horrified by her actions and he would not become a blood-slave.

What if you do? whispered through his mind. He ignored the thought. Not like it would matter. He wasn't going to be alive much longer, anyway.

"Did you see him?" a girl whispered to her friend as they walked past the tree and onto the pavement.

"Oh, yeah. Who is he?" another asked. "He's hawt!"

"I know!"

Just as their voices trailed off, a group of boys passed. "Christmas must have come early. Have you ever seen a girl that fine?"

"Think the new kid's already hit it?"

"Does it matter? There's enough for everyone."

They laughed, then the doors closed behind them, cutting off the rest of their comments.

Aden's hands clenched at his sides.

"Humans," Victoria said with a roll of her eyes.

"Shall I punish them for you?" Riley asked her.

That should be my job, he thought darkly.

She laughed, even as Mary Ann stiffened. "No. Thank you, though."

Just before they reached the doors themselves, something slammed into Aden's shoulder from behind, propelling him forward. Riley caught him with a hand on his chest and pushed him to a stand, keeping him from eating the entrance. He spun around, eyes narrowed—and came face-to-face with Tucker.

"You're in my way," the jock growled.

He raised his chin, the fury he'd felt a minute ago nothing compared to what he felt now. Since Mary Ann was no longer dating him, Aden didn't have to play nice. "So go around me."

You can't fight him, Eve said, no longer content to remain quiet.

Yeah, but he can't walk away, either, Caleb told her. *He'll look like a wuss.*

And if he's kicked out of school... Julian sighed.

Elijah remained strangely silent.

"Get. Out. Of. My. Way." Tucker shoved him again.

The kids in the parking lot rushed forward, expecting a brawl. Wanting it, even. They began chanting, "Fight, fight, fight."

"Tucker," Mary Ann said, grabbing for his wrist. "Don't do this."

Riley grabbed *her* wrist before she could even touch the jock and shoved her behind him. "Oh, no you don't."

Victoria approached Aden's side. When she opened her mouth to speak, he held up his hand to stop her. She could save him from this fight, yes, but Tucker would come back. Bullies always did—until someone gave them a reason not to, exactly as he'd done with Ozzie.

"If you don't get out of my face, jock, I'm going to grind your teeth into the concrete and everyone here will know you aren't the tough guy you pretend to be. That you're just an overgrown baby who runs to his girlfriend's best friend to cry."

Good one! Caleb said excitedly.

Tucker sucked in a breath. "You're going to die for that."

"Ohh. How clever," he said and clapped. "A death threat. You know what's funny? That's not even my first of the day."

For a long while, Tucker just glared at him. Then the glare became a frown of confusion, and the frown of confusion a scowl of irritation. Finally, he pivoted on his heel and stomped into the school.

Okay. What had just happened? Why had Tucker walked away without Aden having to throw a single punch?

The kids surrounding Aden moaned in disappointment but followed Tucker's lead.

"Very strange," Riley said. "I could see spiders springing from the blackness of his aura. It was almost as if he was projecting them at you, as if he expected you to see and feel them all over your body."

"What are you talking about?" Inside that glass foyer, Aden watched as Tucker's attention swung to the boy beside him. A second later, that boy screamed so loudly it shook the glass, patting at his body, ripping at his clothes.

"Yeah, what are you talking about?" Mary Ann asked. "What do you mean, projecting spiders?"

"Demon," Victoria said grimly.

Riley nodded. "You're right. Of course. I should have guessed. Clearly Tucker is part demon. A very small part, but it grants him the power of illusion."

"What?" Aden and Mary Ann exclaimed simultaneously.

"And did you say *demon?*" Mary Ann added, mouth

floundering open and closed. "That can't be right. He was my boyfriend. We dated for months. I might've been distracted for much of that time, but c'mon. I would have known if he wasn't human. Right? I mean, I'm studying to be a shrink. A trained observer. And okay, yeah. Yesterday I wondered if demons could maybe walk among us and that's who Aden had trapped in his head, but I didn't really believe it."

Aden didn't want to believe it, either. "A demon, like, possesses him?"

Riley shrugged. "Either that, or there's a demon in his family tree."

"Penny's baby," Mary Ann gasped out. "Will *it* be a demon?"

Again, Riley shrugged, though his expression was sympathetic. And relieved, if Aden wasn't mistaken. "Only time will tell."

"Shane Weston knows about Tucker, I think, and doesn't seem to care. I wonder if that makes him one, too." She massaged the back of her neck. "Very soon you're going to have to tell me how this kind of thing is possible. I mean, I still don't want to believe you about this demon thing, but I guess it explains Tucker's cruel streak, the way he once produced a snake out of thin air and why he was so adamant about dating me and later, when we broke up, about remaining friends."

"He wanted to stay with you because you are beautiful," Riley said.

"You think I'm beautiful? Not that it matters," she rushed out, then shook her head as if to clear her thoughts. "What I was saying was that Aden once told me I calm him, then

Tucker later told me the same thing. Maybe I'm, I don't know, like a tranquilizer to anyone who's not human."

"Not a tranquilizer," Aden said. "A neutralizer."

"Well, if I negate powers, how was Tucker able to produce that snake? I was on the other side of the door from him, but we were still close."

"Perhaps to do any negating, you need open space between you and the one with the power," Aden suggested.

"Let's not talk about this here." Riley eyed the many cars in the parking lot, the doors in front of them and the students still in the foyer. Anyone could walk up on them at anytime. Anyone could be hiding in the bushes nearby.

They strode into the building, leaving the cool morning behind. Students rushed along the halls. Aden leaned into Victoria and whispered, "Are you going to be okay?" He rubbed his neck to let her know what he meant.

"Yes," she whispered back, her breath warm on his skin. She didn't sound sure.

"If you get hungry—"

"I won't," she said. Again, she didn't sound convinced.

"Well, I'm here for you, anyway."

The bell rang and each of them froze.

"We better get to class," Aden said with a sigh. "We're already late." And just how was he going to explain that to Dan? *Hey, Dan. You can't toss me out because I was talking business with a vampire and a werewolf.*

"I'll take care of it," Victoria said with a grin. "No one will know."

"How—oh." Her voice voodoo. He grinned, too. Hanging out with a vampire princess certainly had its advantages. "Thank you."

"My pleasure."

He expected them to all go their separate ways, but it turned out Riley and Victoria had done more than sneak into the school; they'd ensured Victoria had the same schedule as Aden and Riley the same as Mary Ann.

Victoria. At school with him all day long. He would get to spend more time with her, see her openly, talk with her, learn more about her and her people. Did it get any better than that?

Actually, yes. Mary Ann was helping him and Riley wasn't threatening to kill him.

His optimism didn't last long, though. Something would go wrong and soon. It always did. That wasn't paranoia. That was the simple crux of Aden's life.

"Elijah," he mumbled as he entered first period beside Victoria.

The psychic knew what he wanted. *Bad is indeed on its way, my friend. I told you that before you began this journey.*

Yet he'd embarked on it anyway, so whatever happened would be his fault.

THIRD PERIOD, the boy pretending to be John O'Conner was waiting for Aden, practically bouncing up and down in the doorway. Aden was still furious with him, plus now suspicious of his origins, and pretended not to hear his eager questions.

"Did you talk to Chloe, huh, huh? I couldn't get to the cafeteria for some reason, but I tried."

Victoria claimed "John's" seat, forcing the boy to stand beside Aden. Others were filing inside, staring at her with openmouthed astonishment. He wanted to hit them.

"Go away," Aden growled.

"Who? Me?" Victoria asked.

He motioned to John with a tilt of his head. "No. The pest."

She frowned as she peered over at John. Or tried to. Her gaze never quite made contact. "What pest?"

"Is he…do you think he could be…"

"Come on, man," John said before Victoria could reply. "It's not like I'm asking you to solve world hunger or anything. I just want you to talk to Chloe, see how she's doing."

Aden flattened his palm against John's chest and shoved—or tried to. His hand slipped through as if he were only touching air. Electrically charged air that zapped him as if he'd stuck his fingers in a light socket.

For a long while, he simply peered down at his tingling hand. The teacher started talking, then forced Victoria to stand in front of the class and tell everyone a little about herself—*Hi, my name's Victoria and I'm from New York. I'm happiest when I'm alone and my favorite ice cream flavor is butter pecan. Thank you.*

He raised his gaze to John, studying him through new eyes. The glittery skin, now so clearly an outline of the body he used to have. Not a goblin, fairy or witch, after all. How had he not known? How he had not reasoned it out?

"What? You didn't know?" John asked him. The real John, after all. Killed by a drug overdose and now, apparently, a ghost.

Figured, Aden thought. Were these spirits after him now, too? If so, how was he supposed to be guarded from them?

THROUGHOUT THE DAY, the gossip about Victoria and Riley intensified. One group claimed they were models trying to hide out from the media. Another claimed they were the *children* of models trying to hide out. Everyone thought they were wealthy and a few even speculated they were here to film a reality TV show.

Mary Ann rolled her eyes at it all, not quite sure how money and stardom had entered the equation. She could hardly believe Riley was here. And in human form!

He stayed by her side, watching everyone around her and making sure they behaved. Part of her was still afraid that he only wanted to hang out with her because she calmed him as she calmed Aden and Tucker. Who was a demon. A freaking demon. And she'd kissed him. Did she have demon germs now?

Not that she was complaining about Riley's attention, but she hoped and prayed tranquilization—neutralization—wasn't her only draw. Did he find her attractive? He *had* called her beautiful, but what if he'd said it only to be nice?

He could have anyone he wanted, she was sure. Like Penny, if she'd been here. Mary Ann hadn't seen her all day. He could even have Christy Hayes, head cheerleader, who was currently blowing him kisses as she sashayed by.

"You can go talk to her if you want," Mary Ann told him. Was that harsh tone really hers? "There's time. The third period bell won't ring for another," she glanced at the wall clock, "four minutes and our class is just down the hall."

His brow furrowed, his step never faltering. He shifted the books he held—both his and hers—from one arm to the other. "Talk with who?"

O-kay. He hadn't even noticed the perky and beautiful Christy. Pleasure zoomed through her. "Never mind. So how are you handling the day so far?"

"Fine. We've attended school before. Of course, the students and teachers were just like us, but school is school. You go, you learn, and you kill anyone who gets in your way."

All the heat drained from her face. "You can't just go around killing people. There are rules, laws that must be obeyed or—"

His husky laugh silenced her. "I was only teasing, Mary Ann. I would not harm your friends."

"Oh." Her apprehension faded, and she growled. "Don't scare me like that!"

"Your enemies, however…" he muttered.

She shook her head at him, unsure whether to believe him this time.

They entered the classroom together. Mary Ann took her seat in the far right row, closest to the teacher's desk. Kyle Matthews had the one next to her and he was already seated. As Riley had done in their first two classes, he stood in front of his desired spot and stared. Stared until Kyle was shifting uncomfortably. Stared until Kyle picked up his books and found another seat.

There was such an intensity about Riley, an intensity no other boy possessed. The wicked gleam in his eyes didn't help, either. *I'll do anything necessary to get my way,* that gleam said. Except, he never turned that gleam her way. With her, he was gentle and protective.

He watched her as he placed her books on her desk. "Once again your aura is a mix of colors. What are you thinking about?"

You. She leaned toward him, whispering, "Do you have a girlfriend waiting for you at home? I'm just curious, you understand." *No, I'm a moron.* But she had to know.

His features softened. "No. There is no one. Actually, Victoria is my only friend."

The gorgeous Victoria. Fabulous. Mary Ann hated herself for wishing the vampire princess had flaws beneath that perfect exterior. Anything to even the playing field a little. Not that Mary Ann was going to try for something with Riley. Right?

"I'm your friend, aren't I?" she asked. He'd said so before but could have changed his mind.

A moment passed, his gaze searching hers, before he nodded. "Yes. And I am yours. I will protect you, Mary Ann. You have my word."

The bell rang, and the teacher, already standing in front of the class, began his lecture. She didn't hear a word of it. Oh, she peered straight ahead and pretended to study the board and take notes, but her mind was focused solely on Riley.

Sadly, that's how the rest of the day progressed, as well.

She found herself wondering what he thought of the school, the kids. If he was bored and wanted to be anywhere else. If he liked being with her as much as she liked being with him.

At lunch, they sat together at the back of the cafeteria, and Aden and Victoria joined them. Everyone else stared. Even leaned closer to hear what they were saying. Riley ate from a tray of his own, as well as Mary Ann's and Victoria's. Victoria, Mary Ann noticed, didn't even pretend to eat.

"Well, we won't be discussing anything here," Aden muttered. "Though I will tell you that John, the *real* John," his gaze became pointed, "spoke to me again."

Had he...did he mean... A *ghost?* she mouthed.

He nodded.

First a demon, then a ghost. What would pop up next? Her hand trembled as she spooned a bite of her chocolate pudding. "What did he want?"

"For me to hook him up with Chloe Howard."

Mary Ann pictured the shy girl who rarely spoke up and liked to wear hoodies. "Are you going to do it?" Just how did someone go about hooking up a dead person with the living?

He swallowed a mouthful of soda. "I don't know. What if I screw it up and he gets mad? What if I do it and he sends others my way. And I know there are others. I've seen a few. Didn't know what they were at the time, but in hindsight that's all they could be. Anyway, new subject."

"We can go to my house after school," she said, pushing her tray aside. No way would she be able to wait until tomorrow morning to talk to him again. And maybe, just maybe, her mother was still inside that house. Maybe Aden would see her. Maybe they could talk.

Victoria and Riley nodded, though their expressions were confused. They hadn't followed the thread of conversation. "I'll explain later," she told Riley, and he nodded again.

"I can't." Aden withdrew a sandwich from his lunch bag and peeled back the plastic. "I have a four o'clock curfew at the ranch."

"What about a study group?" She propped her elbows on the table. "Would Dan let you come to my house for a study group?"

First he looked hopeful, then doubtful, then resigned. "I'll ask, but I can guess the answer and it's not a yes."

"Only one way to find out." She withdrew her cell phone from her pocket and turned it on. This was a big no-no, totally against school policy, but she didn't care. She dialed her dad's number. "Daddy," she said when he answered, "would it be all right if I have a few friends over after school to study?"

"Wait. Is this my little girl?" His gruff voice filled the line. "Can't be. She never invites anyone over, even when her dear old dad begs her to do so."

"Dad. Be serious."

"Sure, invite them over. But is that really why you're calling? You almost gave me a heart attack, using this line. Is everything okay?"

"Everything's fine." She was only to call his private work number, the one that interrupted his sessions, for emergencies. She'd never called it before. "I swear. It's just really important that we study." Not a lie. They needed to study each other, the other creatures, figure out what was going on and what needed to be done.

She could just imagine him grinning, nodding his head in satisfaction. "Want me to work late? Wouldn't want my lame self to get in the way."

He really did want her to socialize more, she realized, even if it meant studying. Maybe she *had* been working too hard. "That would be great."

"Then I'll see you around...nine?"

"Perfect. Thanks!"

"I love you, baby."

"Love you, too." Mary Ann disconnected and handed the phone to Aden. She grinned. "Your turn."

"I CAN'T BELIEVE I'm here," Aden said, gazing around Mary Ann's house. Dan had actually said yes. Granted, Victoria had gotten on the line and had told him to agree, but still. Aden was here.

He and Victoria walked around the living room; Riley, who'd already been there, remained beside Mary Ann in the entryway. It was spacious, with soft red couches, a blue-and-green rug, and several tables with orange-and-pink marble tops. Tying it all together was multicolored fringe that dangled from the lampshades.

"My mom decorated the place and my dad just didn't have the heart to change anything after she died," Mary Ann said, and he could hear the affection she still harbored for the woman.

"I love it." It had character and warmth. Livability.

One foster family he'd stayed with had had leather furniture and glass tables. A single smudge had sent the wife into a cleaning frenzy. Another foster family had filled their home with only white and beige furnishings, just like every institution he'd ever been committed to, and though they'd never acted as if they minded, he'd been afraid to even step on the carpet. His favorite foster family hadn't been able to afford anything but mismatched, threadbare stuff and he'd felt most comfortable there.

He would have lived with them forever, if possible, but Eve had transported him back in time and he'd changed the future. When he'd returned to the present, it had been as though he'd never stayed with that wonderful family.

"Riley tried to describe this place to me," Victoria said, "but I didn't believe him. Who could have guessed?" She sighed with longing and joined Aden at the unlit fireplace. Her gaze skidded over his neck, then returned and stayed. More and more, as the day had worn on, her focus had been lingering on his pulse. "Our home is very dark. Colorless." Now her voice was thick, almost slurred.

Was she hungry? Her skin appeared paler than usual, no color in her cheeks. "Where *is* your home, by the way?" If he had to, he would drag her outside and demand she drink from him. "I know you're from Romania, but where have you been staying?"

"A large group of us traveled here, so we had to buy the biggest home we could find. It's far enough away to give us the illusion of privacy, but close enough that we can run into town at a moment's notice." Her gaze never lifted from his neck.

He leaned his head to the side, widening the expanse of skin she could see. Her breath hitched. Oh, yes. She was hungry.

"You can drink from me, you know?" From the corner of his eye, he saw a framed photograph on the mantle and lifted it.

"No," she croaked out.

"You sure?" The photo was of a man, a woman and a little girl. Obviously Mary Ann was the little girl and the adults were her parents. She looked just like her mother. Same dark hair and eyes. Same lean face.

"So, Aden…do you see any ghosts here?" Mary Ann asked hesitantly.

Before he could answer, his companions began chattering frantically.

That man, Eve said on a gasp. *I know him.*

He is familiar, isn't he? Julian said.

Aden drew the picture closer. The man had a clean-shaven face, blue eyes, and was a little boyish, like hundreds of people he'd seen over the years. "It's Mary Ann's dad," Aden said, frowning. "We can't know him."

Yes, yes, we can, Eve replied excitedly. *We've seen him before. In person. Remember? Just add a beard and glasses and you'll—never mind. I'll take you to him.*

No, everyone shouted in his head at once.

"Aden?" Victoria asked. Her hand cupped his shoulder, hot, a brand. "What's wrong?"

"No, Eve, no!" Aden roared, focused only on one thing: survival. "Please don't do this to—"

But it was too late. His entire world faded to black. He was falling down…down…spinning and screaming and flailing for an anchor—an anchor that constantly danced out of reach. His stomach churned and sharp pains tore through him, burning, scorching.

His body began to melt, skin pouring away, muscle disintegrating, bone crumbling until he lost his hold on reality, losing himself completely.

FOURTEEN

"ARE YOU STILL hearing voices, Aden?"

The question jerked Aden from a long, dark tunnel, slamming him into something solid. A brick wall perhaps. His mind was not as quick to reach the wall as his body, so his awareness was gradual. Where was he?

He blinked, the world coming into focus little by little. He sat in a plush leather chair. All around him were bookshelves overflowing with books. In front of him was a desk cluttered with files and papers. To his left was another leather chair, this one occupied by a man with blue eyes, a beard and glasses.

"What's going on?" Aden asked, the words garbled. Was he tanked? He didn't remember drinking.

"We're in my office, having our session." The man smiled indulgently. "Have you forgotten already?"

"Office? Session?" He drew in a deep breath, slowly released it. As the air left him, his memory seeped into center stage. He'd been at Mary Ann's house. Victoria had been looking at his neck with hunger. He'd spied a photo, picked it up. Eve had recognized the man.

I'll take you to him, she'd said.

Eve.

His molars ground together. Obviously she'd tossed him back in time just as she'd threatened. But to when? Where?

He surveyed himself. Ugh. He wore a plain T-shirt, his scrawny, needle-ridden arms poking out of it. There was a sharp, persistent pain in his side. His pants had holes in the knees.

"Aden, is something wrong?" the man asked him.

"No, no," he said, because it seemed like the safest answer. He probed his side, wincing. Were those...stitches? "I'm fine."

"You're still healing," was the gentle reply. "And if you want to keep healing, you have to leave the wound alone."

He forced his hands to settle in his lap.

We're here, Eve exclaimed happily. *You're eleven. Do you remember this office? The doctor?*

Eleven. The year he'd been forked by one of the other patients at the institution where he'd been staying. Dread sprouted wings and flew through him. "The doctor..." he said.

"Yes, Aden?"

His cheeks heated at having been caught talking to himself. The doctor. "Dr...." He couldn't remember the man's name. He was youngish, even though he had a beard—which was probably meant to make him look older. Tall, on the lean side.

"It's Gray." A patient sigh filled the void between them. "Dr. Gray."

He stiffened. Dr. Gray. Mary Ann Gray. Mary Ann's... father? He pulled the photograph to the front of his mind and compared it to the man beside him. Take away the beard and the glasses and the two men were an exact match.

He could have freaked out. He wanted to. But he remained where he was, as if rocks held him down, trying to absorb the shock of what he'd just learned. All those years ago, he'd had a connection to Mary Ann, albeit indirectly, and he hadn't known.

I tried to tell you we knew her, Eve said.

Well, what d'you know, Caleb said.

"I know who you are," Aden told the doctor, more emotion than he'd intended in his tone.

Dr. Gray only smiled. "I should hope so, Aden. Now let's get down to business, shall we?" He propped his elbow on the armrest of his chair and peered over at Aden, expectant.

"I—yes," he said, though he wanted to shout *No!* A thousand questions rushed through his mind, but he couldn't ask them. He had to be careful to appear eleven years old, to answer as he had the first time this meeting had happened.

Losing his favorite foster family the last time Eve had done this wasn't the worst thing to have happened. He'd woken up from that trip in a home he hadn't recognized, with people he'd never seen. That "memory loss" had earned him another stay in another mental hospital. *Everything you do earns you a stay in an institution.*

Sometimes it did seem that way. Upon his return, Eve had promised never to transport him again. Of course, she'd promised that before. Her exuberance always outweighed her qualms, he supposed.

Unlike those other times, though, he couldn't work up a good anger. To see eleven-year-old Mary Ann, to know if she dulled his powers, even as a child, might be worth any price.

Where was she now?

Did Dr. Gray know she was able to mute other people's unnatural abilities? Would he freak if Aden asked? Probably. How much would Aden's future change if he did? Would he ever meet Mary Ann?

Ah. There was his anger. White-hot, bubbling. If this session changed his future so much that he hadn't moved to Crossroads, hadn't met Mary Ann or Victoria...

I sense the direction of your thoughts, Elijah said. *I wish I could reassure you, but...*

Great. He was going to have to do his best to remember every little thing he'd said and exactly how he'd said it. Did eleven-year-olds talk like babies or grown-ups?

"Aden?"

He'd lost the thread of the conversation already; he'd have to be a lot more careful. "Yes?"

"I asked you a question."

"I'm sorry. Will you repeat it, please?"

"I will, but I expect you to pay attention for the rest of our time together. All right?" Only after he nodded did Dr. Gray continue. "There have been reports that you've been arguing loudly with people no one else can hear. So I ask again, are you still hearing voices?"

"I—I—" How had he answered this? "Uh, no." He wouldn't have told the truth. Would he?

"Are you sure?"

Aden focused on the University of Oklahoma Department of Psychology diploma framed proudly between the bookshelves. More calmly, he said, "Yes, I'm sure."

Dr. Gray frowned over at him. "We've had several sessions together, but you always keep me at a distance, telling me nothing more than what can be found within your file. This is a safe space, Aden, where the truth will never be used against you. I hope I've proven that to you."

"You have." The memories of this day, hazy though they were, finally began to flood him. Dr. Gray had been unbelievably nice to him, and for once, he'd been eager to please. "I just—I—I hate this place. I want to leave." There. Now they were on the right track.

"Where would you go? I'm not asking to be cruel, but to make a point. No foster family will have you right now. Everyone thinks you're dangerous, so you can't be allowed to play freely with other children."

Normal children, he meant. There were kids here, but they were all supposedly crazy like him.

"Has someone hurt you?" the doctor persisted. "Is that why you want to leave? Did you have another argument with a patient?"

Silent, he kicked out his stained tennis shoes.

I brought you here for a reason, Eve said. *I don't care what the others say. Ask him what you're dying to know.*

"I just want to go back to the ranch," he said, ignoring Eve. Then he blanched. For a moment he'd forgotten to stick to only what he'd said the first time he was here.

"Ranch?" Dr. Gray sighed again. "To my knowledge, you've never lived at a ranch. For now, this is your home. I'm sorry, but that's just the way it has to be."

Ask him about Mary Ann, Eve insisted.

Don't do it, Ad, Julian said. *I'm happy with the way things are and don't want them to change.*

I mean, we're close to having a girlfriend, Caleb added.

"Aden?"

Dr. Gray. He had to backtrack to remember the direction of their conversation. Had he argued with any of the other patients, was what he'd been asked. "Uh, no. Everyone stays away from me now."

"Oh, really?" The doctor *tsk*ed under his tongue. "I know a few of the patients cornered you yesterday. I know they threatened you, someone hit you and you retaliated. If the orderlies hadn't stopped you… Listen, it's okay, whatever you've done, whatever's going on," he said softly. "You can tell me anything. I won't judge you, son. I only want to help you. Let me help you. Please."

"I—"

Ask him, ask him, ask him! I won't shut up until you do. Eve, proving stubborn.

For God's sake, what if he wakes up in another state, no

Mary Ann, no Victoria, Elijah said, angry. *I hate what Mary Ann does to us, but he's finally out of the hospitals and off the drugs they used to feed him.*

You're the psychic, Caleb said. *Tell us what will happen if he questions the doctor about the girl.*

I told you, I— Elijah stopped abruptly, and everyone held their breath, waiting for him to continue, knowing he'd just gotten something. Several minutes passed, an eternity in which Aden once again lost track of what the doctor was saying. During that time, Elijah gasped, groaned.

"What?" he finally asked, and as Dr. Gray repeated whatever he'd been saying, Elijah said, *You know I usually only predict death but lately I've known, well, more. And right now I know that if you mention Mary Ann, one of two things will happen. Dr. Gray will flip and leave you sooner rather than later. You'll never meet Mary Ann. Or Dr. Gray will flip, still leave as planned, but take an interest in what you've told him. If the second happens, you'll indeed meet Mary Ann— and one of us will be freed.*

Eve gasped. *One of us will be freed? Who? And how?*

I don't know. I wish I did, but... I'm sorry.

If one could be freed, that had to mean they all could be freed. He would have everything he'd ever wanted. Peace, a happily ever after for his companions. A normal life with his new friends. Of course, that normal life wouldn't last long, since his death was steadily approaching, but a mere glimpse of such a life would be better than never knowing it at all.

But, if the other alternative happened, he would have none

of that. He wouldn't even have Mary Ann's friendship. Would he even go to Crossroads, Oklahoma? Would he ever meet Victoria? he couldn't help but wonder again.

He wanted to take some time, figure out the best course of action, maybe sleep on it and weigh the pros versus the cons. That wasn't how this worked, however. He would return to the present the moment this session ended. He didn't have the luxury of time.

If only Eve could control how long they stayed. But she couldn't, not really. When the scene she'd imagined played out, so did his time there. He had to choose now. A chance at getting everything he'd ever wanted or the *loss* of everything he'd ever wanted.

Whatever he decided, he had to act—

"Do you have a daughter?" The question slipped from him before he could stop it. For a moment, he experienced panic. Absolute, blind panic. He'd done it. He'd decided: he'd asked.

All four souls gasped. In astonishment, horror or excitement, he didn't know.

What he did know? There was no going back now.

The good doctor's head tilted to the side, his lips curling in another of those frowns. "I do, yes. How did you know?" No flip out yet.

His heart drummed in his ears, his breathing fast and shallow, as he searched for an answer that wouldn't get him tossed out of the office this very moment. Then he spotted it. A framed picture of a little girl with black-as-night hair, hazel eyes and bronzed skin.

"The, uh, photo on your desk. She's pretty."

"Oh. Thank you. That's my Mary Ann. She's your age. Looks just like her mom." Dr. Gray shook his head, as though he couldn't believe what he'd just admitted. Normal people didn't like to talk about their loved ones with dangerous crazies, Aden knew, no matter how young those dangerous crazies were. Or appeared to be. "Let's get back on track. I need you to talk to me, Aden. That's the only way I can help you."

For the doctor's sake, he said, "You asked me if I was still hearing voices. The answer is yes." Embarrassment he didn't have to force dripped from the undercurrents of his tone. His fingers twisted the fabric of his shirt, wrinkles branching in every direction. He'd bring them back to Mary Ann in a bit. Hopefully Dr. Gray would be more willing to chat once "business" was out of the way. "All the time."

Come on. We're not that bad. Julian.

Stab me in the back, why don't you. Caleb.

"Sorry guys," he wanted to say, but he kept quiet.

"No progress, then." Dr. Gray planted his left ankle atop his right knee. "We can talk to your psychiatrist about changing your medication again."

"All right," he said, even though he suddenly recalled how the new drugs had affected him. Stomach cramps, vomiting. Dehydration and a week hooked to an IV.

Dr. Gray anchored his glasses on his nose. "Let's switch gears for a while. Since you're still hearing voices, I'd like to know what they want from you."

"All kinds of stuff."

"Like?"

What had he told him, all those years ago? "Like…control of the body." Yes, he'd mentioned that. He hadn't usually been so open with his doctors, but something about Dr. Gray had put him at ease.

If only you'd consider it, Eve said.

Really, giving up the captain's hat once in a while isn't unreasonable, Caleb said. *You used to let us take over for a bit and we always gave back control. I never understood why you stopped.*

You'd want control, too, if you were powerless, Elijah said.

Great. They were ganging up on him. "You aren't power-less," he gritted out. He was here, in the past, wasn't he?

"Excuse me?" Dr. Gray said.

"Oh, uh, nothing. Just giving myself a pep talk."

You're well on your way to that flip-out, Elijah said with a sigh.

Frowning, the doctor made a notation in his notebook. "Now, you called it *the body.* Let's explore that a moment. If the voices have to ask for control of your—*the* body, that means they can't take it on their own. You get to decide. That's a good thing, yes? Your being in control?"

His companions might not be able to take over his body without his permission, but they could cause untold damage without it. "Yeah. Sure."

The pen flew over the notebook as the doctor made another notation. "Since you have control, do you ever force the voices to leave you?"

"Me force them? No. But sometimes they do leave."
Because of his daughter.

"And what happens to you when they're gone?"

Aden smiled, though it was laced with guilt. "Peace."

"Oh, Aden." Dr. Gray placed a hand over his heart, expression softening. "That's wonderful."

Bet he feels like a proud papa. Eve actually sounded softer, as though she was warming to the doctor.

That hadn't happened last time. Which meant peace wasn't something he'd admitted to last time. Of course not. Peace wasn't something he'd known about back then. His smile faded. "I'm just kidding. They aren't allowed to leave. They stay with me always."

Dr. Gray rested his hand on the side of his face, the pen poking out between his fingers. "How can I help you if I have to wade through half-truths and lies?"

He glanced down at his feet, hoping he appeared properly shamed. "I won't do it again."

"See that you don't. But why did you do it this time?"

He shrugged, no answer jumping out at him.

"All right. Well, why don't you tell me why you let the voices return to you once they're out? Because I know you were telling the truth about the voices leaving, not about it being a joke. You're in control, remember?"

No way out of this one. He had to cop to the truth. At least some of it. "They're bound to me like…" His head tilted to the side as he considered his next words. "Like pets on a leash. I *can't* keep them out."

That earned him an *Ouch* from Julian and an *I'll make you pay for calling us pets. I hope you know that* from Caleb.

Oh, he knew he'd pay, but now wasn't the time to worry about that. "See, they're people, like you and me, only they weren't given bodies of their own. They were somehow sucked into mine, forcing me to share my head with them."

Dr. Gray took the admission in stride, surprisingly unfazed. "A few days ago, you mentioned that there are four different voices. Or rather, people. Still only four?"

"Yes."

"And they are…" The doctor flipped a page in the notebook. "Your age? All of them?"

"No. I don't know how old they are."

"I see," he muttered and Aden didn't think he knew he'd spoken aloud. "Tell me about them. What they're like."

And while you're at it, Eve said, *ask about his daughter.*

Soon. He didn't want the doctor to have a reason to change the subject back to therapy again. "They're nice. For the most part," he added for their benefit.

That earned him several snorts and another threat from Caleb.

"And do they have names?" Dr. Gray asked.

Aden rattled them off.

His eyes lit with interest at the mention of Eve. "Eve is a female, I'm guessing."

"Yeah. A girl." There was enough disgust in his voice to make the doctor fight a grin.

Oh, hush, Eve said. *You're the luckiest boy on the planet, to have my guidance.*

"I'm most curious about her," the doctor said.

Of course he is, Caleb said, clearly offended. *What am I, dog food? Why doesn't he want to know about me?*

"Aden. I lost you again."

Aden jerked to attention, his head clearing, Caleb and Eve's voices fading as he refocused. "I'm sorry. What?"

"I had asked you a question." Frowning, the doctor eased back in his chair. "What was going on inside your head just then?"

"Nothing," he hedged.

An eyebrow arched. "I thought you weren't going to lie to me anymore."

Aden rubbed his temples and considered his options. He could admit the truth, but at this rate, Dr. Gray would never stop questioning him and he'd never be able to steer the conversation back to Mary Ann. And what if he was whisked away before he even got the chance?

The thought of being whisked away was what finally propelled him into action.

Now or never. "You're most curious about Eve," he said. "Well, she can time travel into younger versions of me. If you'd check my file, you'd see that I've disappeared a few times. From locked rooms. You'll see I've reappeared in places I shouldn't have been able to get inside of. The doctors treating me at the time claimed I was just a great lock picker, that I liked confusing people. The truth is, I traveled into a younger version of myself, like I said, and accidentally changed the future."

Dr. Gray blinked at him. "I know I told you I wanted you

to open up, but I meant I wanted honesty. I believe I mentioned that, as well."

"And that's what I'm giving you. The ability I mentioned is how a sixteen-year-old boy is sitting in front of you now, rather than an eleven-year-old. It's how a sixteen-year-old who knows your—"

"Aden. That's enough."

He gulped, but once again, he didn't allow the doctor to deter him. "You didn't let me finish. I'm really a sixteen-year-old boy who knows your daughter, Mary Ann. We—"

"Aden!" Dr. Gray pinched the bridge of his nose. "You have to stop this. It's not helping your case."

"Just listen to me." What could he say to make this man believe him? "More than time travel, I can raise the dead. Take me to a cemetery and I'll prove it. Just don't bring Mary Ann. She negates my abilities. Corpses will rise. You'll see."

"For the last time, enough!" Dr. Gray was pale, blue veins throbbing under the surface of his skin. He cleared his throat in an effort to collect himself. "I shouldn't have indulged your question about my daughter earlier. I won't tolerate a patient, even a child, dragging my family into a session. Do you understand me?"

"If you won't take me out of this building, fine. I can prove it another way." The words left him in a desperate rush. "Mary Ann has a best friend named Penny. One day she will date a boy named Tucker." Maybe telling the doctor about the future would change it as irrevocably as altering the past. But he was already on this path and couldn't stop himself. "Tucker's a jerk, by the way, and you should put a stop to that before it ever starts. Or maybe she's supposed to date him. I don't know. She will—"

"Okay. I've had it. I want you to leave, Aden. Right now." Dr. Gray pointed to the door. "Clearly you've been through my personal files. Clearly you're trying to compare your life to hers. Well, it's not going to work. I want you out of this office before I do something I'll regret."

Compare his life to whose? Mary Ann's? Or someone else's? Someone equally close to the doctor? "I don't understand. Who are you talking about?"

"I told you to go."

Aden pushed to his feet. His legs were shaky, but he didn't tumble back into his seat. "Tell me who you meant and I will. You'll never have to meet with me again." Well, not here. "Please."

Before the doctor could reply, Aden's mind began fading to black. No. No, no, no. He wasn't ready, had more to say, more to hear. His struggles increased. "For God's sake, just tell…"

Too late.

The tunnel sucked him back in, spinning him round and round, down…down…

The last thought to drift through his mind was a question. Would Mary Ann still be a part of his life when he returned?

We're about to find out, Elijah said grimly.

FIF†EEN

"ADEN. Aden, wake up!"

"Oh, thank God, he's here."

"He popped out of nowhere. Didn't he? Did I imagine that?"

"Aden, can you hear me?"

Aden fought his way out of that long, dark tunnel a second time, afraid of what he'd find. His temples throbbed and blood rushed through his veins too quickly. His muscles were stiff, heavy. At least his companions were quiet as they, too, struggled to orient themselves.

He pried his lashes apart. Muted sunlight streamed in from a large bay window, throwing spots in his line of vision. Subdued though that light was, it still proved to be too bright and his eyes teared.

"Give him space," a deep male voice said. Riley.

Riley was still part of his life, then. That had to mean Victoria was, as well. Please, please let it mean that she was.

Two sets of footsteps shuffled. A girl said, "I can't," then white-hot, trembling hands pressed to his cheeks. He turned his head, sinking into the heat. Victoria loomed over him, dark ponytail falling over her shoulder and tickling his neck.

Thank God.

"Hey you," she said gently. Soft fingers smoothed the hair from his brow.

"Hey. How long was I gone?" He wasn't sure why he didn't just reappear seconds—or even the very moment—after he disappeared, as if he'd never left at all. But no, he didn't. He didn't know why new memories didn't seep into his head, if he had indeed changed his past. But again, no. Time travel and its intricacies simply baffled him. "How long?" he repeated.

"A few hours."

Not good. He tried to pull himself into a sitting position. "Is Mary Ann—" A sharp pain sliced through his head, and he groaned.

"Gently," Victoria said.

When he was up, he dragged his knees to his chest and rested his forehead against them. He was panting. "Is Mary Ann here?"

"I am. What happened?" she'd asked, concern dripping from the words.

All of his friends—plus Riley—were accounted for. Never had he been more relieved. If he'd had the energy, he would have leapt up and hugged them all. "I need a minute to think."

Everything was fuzzy. From more than just traveling back to the present, he suspected. A return had never left him this groggy.

Okay, so. What had happened? Obviously, he'd changed the past. He'd told Dr. Gray things he hadn't told him before.

Dr. Gray had flipped, just as Elijah had predicted. Since Aden had still met Mary Ann, Dr. Gray had later taken an interest in him. Which meant one of the souls would soon be freed.

His lips lifted in a slow grin. They'd done it, then. They'd really done it.

Had anything else changed?

"Do I live at the D and M with Dan Reeves?" he asked Mary Ann.

"You don't remember?"

"Do I?" he insisted.

"Yes. You do." Mary Ann rubbed her arms. "You're scaring me, Aden."

"You will cease scaring her immediately," Riley snapped. So much for his seeming concern about Aden.

"Tell us what happened," Victoria pleaded.

He sighed. "I went back in time, to a therapy session I had when I was eleven." He raised his head, fought the dizziness as he pinned Mary Ann with a tortured gaze. "It was with your father."

She blinked in confusion. "My father? I don't understand."

"He was my doctor for a time, in one of the institutions I stayed at. I don't remember which one. And I didn't realize he was your dad until today. He was nice, truly listened to me. I liked him. I, well, I told him what had happened, that I lived here and you were my friend. That you had dated Tucker. He kind of freaked out, tried to throw me out of his office."

She was shaking her head before he finished. "That doesn't

sound like my dad. He would have considered you delusional, but he would never throw a patient out."

Aden let that go, knowing it would do no good to insist or tarnish her image of her father. "Does he keep records of his patients?" he asked, though he already knew the answer. All doctors did.

"Of course."

"Then he'll have a record of me. I'd like to read his thoughts about me."

She crossed her arms over her chest. "That's not only illegal, it's unethical. He would never give the files to me."

Aden met her stare, unwavering. "I didn't want you to ask for them."

Her mouth floundered open, closed. "That would be stealing."

Victoria's hand traveled the length of his spine, up, then down, a soothing caress meant to comfort him. "Actually, that would be helping a friend in need."

Mary Ann licked her lips and gazed up at Riley, perhaps searching for support. He just shrugged. As innocent as she was and as uneventful a life as she'd probably led, the thought of stealing must frighten her.

"Please, Mary Ann," he said. "Get those files. Something I said caused your dad to compare me to someone else and I want to know who it was. And, because of my confession to him, I could have changed something here in the present. Maybe it was only his mind. His thoughts. But there's only one way to find out."

Still she was silent.

He tried another approach. "Did he ever ask you about a boy named Aden?"

She thought for a moment, gasped. "Not by name, no, but once, right after I introduced him to Tucker, he sat me down and asked about my friends, if I had any new ones and if one liked to talk to himself. At the time, I didn't think anything of it. I thought it was a joke." She scrubbed a hand down her face. "I'll do it," she said in a soft whisper.

"Thank you." His relief was palpable, he was sure.

"It'll be hard, though," she added. "His old files are in storage. And those he's actually put in his computer are in password-protected archives."

"All I ask is that you try." He pushed to his feet, his legs a bit unsteady. Victoria kept her arm around his waist. He didn't need to, not to remain standing, but he leaned against her. "What time is it?"

"Seven-eighteen," Victoria said.

"PM?" He almost moaned. "I need to get back. Dan said my chores and homework had to be done before bed. Otherwise, I'll never be allowed to go anywhere after school again."

"I'll go with you," Victoria said. "I'll change his mind."

Riley sighed, flicked a regretful glance to Mary Ann. "That means I have to go, too."

Victoria gazed at him pleadingly. "I'll be fine. Promise. Besides, you need to look after the human."

With another look to Mary Ann, Riley shifted from one foot to the other, popped his jaw, then finally nodded. "Fine. You've got one hour to return for me."

"Thank you," she said and ushered Aden forward. "Hurry, before he changes his mind."

They quickly reached the line of trees that separated neighborhood from forest. This far away, even someone with Riley's supercharged hearing couldn't detect their words.

"Thank God he stayed behind."

"I know," Victoria said, grinning. "I expected him to balk. As he is charged with my protection, if something were to happen to me, he would be executed." Without breaking her graceful glide, she bent down and picked up several fallen acorns. "He must like Mary Ann more than I realized."

For the first time, Aden was glad about that.

Victoria glanced around. "We have an hour before I have to return. Want to spend it here?"

"Dan—"

"Don't worry. I'll take care of him."

"All right."

She stopped, the acorns balanced perfectly in her hand, not even rolling. Aden stopped, too, facing her. Waning sunlight filtered through the treetops, a haze of pink, violet and gold that worshipped her pale skin.

Skin that couldn't be cut, he recalled. "What could happen to you that would cause Riley to get into trouble?"

"I can be kidnapped," she said, dropping one of the acorns. "Held for ransom by someone who dislikes my father." Another acorn fell. "And I can be hurt." The rest slammed into the ground, forming a pile.

He didn't like the sound of that and found himself

skimming his gaze through the surrounding area, searching
for any threat that might be lurking nearby. But as usual, even
the insects were quiet, perhaps sensing he and Victoria were
more than human and thereby dangerous.

"I want to know how you can be hurt." That way, he, too,
could learn to protect her from harm.

She backed away from him to lean against a tree trunk.
"Telling anyone of a vampire's weakness is punishable by
death, for both the vampire who tells and the one she confides
in. That is why my mother was left in Romania. She spilled
our secrets to a human and is now locked away until my
father decides how best to slay her." There at the end, her
voice trembled.

"I'm sorry about your mom. I don't want anything like that
to happen to you, so please don't tell me." He didn't fear for
himself, but for her. He'd find out some other way. Through
Riley, maybe. They had their moments of civility.

Strangely enough, his companions didn't react to her pronouncement. They'd been silent since he'd woken up in this
new present, actually. Yes, they normally remained silent after
a trip into the past, but not for long. By now, they should have
been back to their normal selves.

He could feel them, so he knew they were in there. Why
weren't they talking?

Victoria peered down at her feet. The slipper shoes were
gone, exposing her black-painted toenails. Black. Huh. She
enjoyed colors; he remembered her wistful smile while she'd
gazed around Mary Ann's home. He wondered if colored

polish was against vampire rules. If so, had she gotten in trouble for dyeing sections of her hair blue?

"I didn't tell you the punishment for sharing vampire secrets to scare you," she said, "only to warn you what can happen to us if you tell anyone else. Even Mary Ann."

"Seriously. You don't have to tell me."

"I want to." Deep breath in, out. "Vampires are vulnerable in our eyes and inside our ears," her hand moved to each place as she spoke, "two places our hardened skin cannot protect." Now she held out that hand to him. "Let me see one of your daggers."

"No way. I don't want a demonstration."

A laugh bubbled from her. "Silly human. I'm not going to poke out one of my own eyes."

Then what was she going to do? His arm was shaky as he handed her the blade.

"Watch." Gaze never leaving his, she raised the weapon and struck herself in the chest.

"No!" he shouted, grabbing for her wrist and jerking it back. He was too late, and he expected to see blood. All he saw was a torn T-shirt. The skin underneath bore not a scratch. Didn't matter to his nervous system, though. His heart was racing uncontrollably, and sweat was beading on his skin. "Don't ever do that again, Victoria. I'm serious."

Another of her carefree laughs drifted between them. "You are sweet. But there can be no stake through the heart for one such as me, so worry not. A blade such as this is nothing to me." She held it up and he saw that the middle was bent. "To kill us, though, to burn through our skin and reach our sensitive organs, all an enemy needs is this." She dropped the knife and lifted her hand, the opal ring she always wore glinting.

Keeping her palm flat, she slid her thumb over the jewel, pushing the opal over the gold and revealing a small tumbler filled with a thick, bright blue paste.

"Je la nune," she said. "This is…well, I guess the best way to describe it is to say that it is fire dipped in acid then wrapped in poison and sprinkled with radiation. Never touch it."

The warning was unnecessary. He'd already backed up a step. "So why do you carry it around?"

"Not all vampires follow my father. There are rebels out there who would love nothing more than to hurt me. This way, *I* can hurt *them.*"

"If it's so corrosive, how does the ring hold it?"

"Just as there are fire-resistant safes for human valuables, there are *je la nune* resistant metals. Not many, but a few. My nails are painted with one of those melted metals to keep them from burning off."

She dipped a long, square-shaped nail into it, closed it, then raised her other arm and slashed her wrist. Flesh sizzled and blood instantly sprang free, trickling down her arm. She was grimacing, pressing her lips together to silence her moans.

"Why did you do that?" he snapped. "I told you I didn't need a demonstration."

A moment passed before she was able to speak, panting as she was. "I wanted you to see. To understand its power."

He wrapped his fingers around her wrist, holding her arm steady for her. "Will you heal?"

"Yes."

He could still hear the pain in her voice. The skin remained broken and torn, the blood still leaking. That blood was redder than any he'd ever seen, brighter, with what looked to be tiny little crystals that caught the fading sunlight and sparkled. "When?"

"Soon." Her eyes closed—but not before he'd seen her gaze stray once more to the pulse hammering in his neck. Her teeth clenched together, sharpened.

Still she continued to bleed, to pant. Why would— Realization hit and he scowled. She'd never planned to tell him. Would have just suffered until they separated. "You'll heal when you drink, won't you?"

She nodded, lids slowly opening, gaze finding his, locking. A shuddering gasp left her. The force of her hunger was like a living thing between them. Thankfully, her resistance was crumbling; he knew it was. Finally.

He released her arm to cup her cheeks. "Drink from me, then. Please. I want you to."

Those sharpened teeth sank into her lower lip. "Don't worry. I can feed later tonight. I'll be fine."

"I want to be the one to help you. To heal you the way you healed my lip that night."

Her hands tangled in his hair, her expression tortured. "What if you hate me for feeding from you? What if I disgust you? What if I become addicted to your blood and try to take from you every day?"

Oh, yes. She was crumbling. He leaned down, slowly, so

slowly she could stop him at any moment, and pressed his lips against hers. "I could never hate you. You could never disgust me. And I'd love to see you every day. I've told you that already."

Her lashes, so impossibly long, fused together as her lids dropped to half-mast. "Aden," she breathed, and then kissed him. Her beautiful lips parted and her tongue flicked out. He opened his mouth, welcoming her inside, then met her tongue with his own.

She tasted of the honeysuckle she smelled like, sweet and floral. Her arms wound around him, holding him close. It was a strong grip, bruising, and he loved it. His hands slid into her hair, one gripping, the other angling her for deeper contact. His first kiss, and it was with the girl he'd dreamed about, wanted for so long, would perhaps want forever.

It was everything he'd craved, yet so much more. She was so soft against him, soft where he was hard, the little moans in the back of her throat so sweet. The rest of the world faded until only she mattered. Until *she* became his world, his anchor in this increasingly wild storm.

Everything Elijah had predicted was coming true. First his meeting with Victoria, then this soul-shattering kiss. He knew what would follow, was expecting it, but nothing could have prepared him for the wondrous moment when she pulled from his lips, lowered her head to his neck and sank her teeth deep. There was a sharp sting, but it was fleeting, an intoxicating warmth soon replacing it, as if she were pumping drugs straight into his vein while she drank from him.

"I'm fine," he told her, in case she worried. He didn't want her to stop. Even when dizziness swirled in his mind, his body becoming weightless, he didn't want her to stop. He stroked her hair, urging her to continue.

Her hands tangled in *his* hair, massaging his scalp. Her tongue pushed against his flesh, urging the blood to flow straight into her mouth. Distantly, he could hear her swallowing. Finally, though, she pulled back, panting.

He moaned at the loss of her. "You shouldn't have feared that," he said. Had he gotten drunk and walked into a tunnel? His words were slurred and he sounded far away. "I loved it. Didn't think you were an animal at all, promise."

"Aden?" she said, horror in her tone. It was the last thing he heard before his knees gave out and he collapsed onto the ground.

SIX+EEN

MARY ANN PICKED at her dinner, Chinese takeout her dad had brought home. He'd only been home for half an hour, and Riley had stayed with her until the very last second possible, having returned after he'd escorted Victoria to their home. She'd wanted to invite him to eat with them, to introduce him to her dad, but she had let him change into his wolf form and jump out her window because she wasn't sure her dad was ready for him. Her dad would have thought the study session had been nothing more than a make-out session.

But she missed Riley already. His intensity, his protectiveness. She valued his opinion and needed a sounding board for what she was considering. She could wait and try to sneak her father's files as Aden had suggested—something she hated doing only because it involved stealing from her dad, her best friend, the man who loved her more than anything and never did things like that to her—or she could ask her father directly, something that could cause him to hide the files Aden wanted just to keep her away from them.

One was unethical, one was just plain risky.

So which path should she take?

The others considered her a bit of a goody-goody, she suspected, but her dad's well-being was just as important to her as Aden's. There had to be a way to please them both.

"Not hungry?" He scooped a small mountain of noodles onto his plate. "I thought orange chicken and beef lo mein could tempt you even if you were full of junk."

Sighing, she pushed her plate away. "I'm just…preoccupied."

His fork paused midair, noodles dangling from the prongs. "Anything you want to talk about?"

"Yes. No." Another sigh. "I don't know."

He laughed and dropped his fork. "Well, which is it?"

"I need to talk to you, but I don't want to."

His smile faded into a frown. "Okay, that sounds serious."

He had no idea. Otherwise, he'd be glaring at her, lecturing her, or perhaps grounding her for life. "I…" Slow and easy. "I have a question."

He reached across the table and patted her hand. "You know you can ask me anything."

They would soon see… "It's about one of your patients."

Now his expression hardened and he shook his head. "Anything except that. Patients trust me to keep their secrets, Mar. Not only that, talking about them would be illegal."

"I know, I know." She'd expected him to say that and didn't

let it derail her. "The thing is, a few weeks ago, I met a boy. We've become really good friends."

Silence.

Her dad leaned back in his chair and folded his arms over his middle. "Okay. Why am I just now hearing about him and what does Tucker think of your friendship with another guy?"

"What Tucker thinks doesn't matter. He and I officially broke up."

Instantly, he shifted from Interrogation Dad to I'm Here For You Dad. "Oh, honey. Are you okay about the breakup? I know I wasn't always supportive of your relationship with him. I mean, there isn't a boy out there who's good enough for you. But I stopped complaining about him because I wanted you happy."

"I'm okay. I'm the one who severed ties. He was cheating on me." Admitting it out loud was easier than she'd thought it would be. Still embarrassing, but not soul-crushing.

"I'm so sorry." Once again he leaned forward and patted her hand. "I counsel couples dealing with infidelity all the time, and the most common response for the victim, and that's what you are, is a feeling of inadequacy. Of being disposable."

Even though she hadn't wanted Tucker anymore, that's exactly what she'd felt. It had even colored her desire to be with Riley, she realized. She'd automatically assumed he'd think she was too boring for him.

"Sometimes it's just a one-time lapse and the culprit learns a valuable lesson," her dad continued, "that what he or she has at home is more precious than any momentary pleasure. Most don't, though they pretend they do so they can have what they think is the best of both worlds."

"Tucker's a pretender for sure." She had no doubts about that. He was a demon, after all. That still shocked her. She'd meant to question Riley about what exactly being a demon entailed, but then Aden had vanished and they'd spent the next few hours searching her house and the forest for him. Riley had even changed into wolf form and raced to the D and M. With his enhanced sense of smell, tracking came easily to him, he'd said, but even he had found no trace.

Then, when they'd been alone, they'd spent their time getting to know each other. He'd asked about her childhood, about her favorite foods, and listened to her fifteen-year plan without rancor. He'd seemed impressed with her goals.

"It's important to know that everyone battles attraction for other people, but it's what they do with those feelings that shows the truth of their character," her dad said. "Did you know the girl he was seeing on the sly?"

Mary Ann nodded but didn't want to admit who it was, so she said, "Thank you for the advice." Penny's parents may not know about her pregnancy and Mary Ann still loved her enough to protect her privacy. "That's actually why I wanted to talk to you about this other boy. He's had a troubled past and is dealing with some things that no one his age should have to deal with."

Her dad tapped a finger against his chin. "I see where you're going with this."

Wait. What? "You do?"

"You want me to talk to him, help him."

"No. I want you to…tell me about him."

His brow furrowed with confusion. "I don't understand. He's your friend. What could I possibly know about him?"

"I think…I think he was once a patient of yours." Here goes. *Just do it, say it.* "His name is Aden Stone."

First, her father's breath hitched. Then the color drained from his face. *Then* he stiffened ever so slightly. She wouldn't have noticed it if she hadn't been studying him so intently. Her stomach twisted into sharp, jagged knots, the points cutting her every time she inhaled.

"You do know him," was all she said.

He looked away from her, a muscle ticking in his jaw. "Once."

"Did you kick him out of your office?"

Rather than answer, he pushed to his feet. The chair skidded loudly against the kitchen tiles. "It's late." There was no emotion in his tone, only distance, as if his thoughts were already someplace else. "You should shower, get some sleep."

"I'd rather talk to you. Aden needs help, Dad. Not the kind you're thinking, though, so please don't tell me never to see him again. I love him like a brother and want to see him happy. And the only way he'll ever truly be happy is if we find a way to free the people—"

"Enough!" He slammed a fist against the table, rattling the dishes. Fire burned in his eyes. They weren't flames of fury or exasperation but of hopelessness. It was a look she'd seen only once. The day her mother died and he'd had to be the one to break it to her. "Enough," he repeated flatly. "We're not going to talk about this."

Startled, she froze in place, unable even to breathe. What was he thinking? What had started that fire? "But he told you we would someday meet, that he would be my friend. Even you can't deny that he wasn't a crazy little boy but a—"

"I said that's enough. You need to go to your room. That isn't a suggestion but an order." With that, he turned on his heel and stalked away. Down the hall, a door slammed. The door to his office, she knew. Never before had he shut her out.

Her dad remembered Aden. That was clear. But *what* did he remember? What had changed her normally mild-mannered father into that distant, snarling beast?

ADEN CAME AWAKE with a jolt, sitting upright, panting. Sweat covered his body, soaking his shirt to his chest. His wild gaze roved his surroundings…he was in his bedroom, he realized, frowning. What time was it? Through the window he could see the crescent moon, so it was late at night. The silence of the house caused his ears to ring. Everyone was asleep.

He was home, yet he didn't remember getting here. He hadn't done his chores, hadn't spoken to Dan. Last thing he remembered was standing in the woods with Victoria, her teeth in his neck.

His head jerked left and right. Where was—

"Shh." Victoria was suddenly sitting beside him, pressing a finger against his lips. "You're all right. You have nothing to worry about. I took care of everything. I cleaned the barn and fed the horses, though the animals weren't happy to see me. I convinced Dan and the others that you came home when you were supposed to. Dan even thinks the two of you had a nice long chat about your study session."

Slowly his muscles loosened their vice-grip on his bones. He eased back down, now noticing the ache in his neck. He reached up, but there were no puncture wounds. She must have healed him. By licking his neck as she'd done to his lip?

"Thank you." He was a little embarrassed that she'd done so much for him. He was the guy and she was the girl. *He* was supposed to take care of *her*. "Did you get in trouble with Riley?"

"No. I returned to him when I promised and he, in turn, took me home. He went back to Mary Ann and I snuck out to return to you. I'm so sorry I took so much of your blood, Aden." She gripped his wrist, her strength enough to crush him. He didn't complain. Any touch of Victoria's was welcome. "I should have pulled back, would have pulled back, but you tasted so sweet, better than anyone, everyone, and all I could think was that I wanted, needed more."

Despite the ache inside him, he shivered in remembrance. His mouth dried and his muscles jerked.

"I told you I was an animal," she cried.

"No, you're not." Whatever she'd pumped into his vein... dear God. He wanted more. He pried her fingers from his arm and twined his own through them. "What you did...I'd be lying if I said I didn't like it."

"Yes, but—"

"No buts. You need blood to survive, and I want to be the

one to give it to you. As long as I'm alive, I want to be the one you come to, the one you feed from." His thumb traced the smooth skin of her wrist. Her pulse raced.

She sniffled. "You speak as if you won't always be around, as if you know you'll be leaving soon."

Should he tell her about Elijah's vision?

He anchored his free hand under his head and stared up at the ceiling. If he told her, she could decide to leave him— for good. A doomed teenager was not exactly good boy-friend material. She could decide to try and save him—which would do her no good and only cause her anguish. Trying to change Elijah's visions was like trying to stop a tidal wave. With the right tools, you could build a dam, but eventually that dam would break and the damage would be a thousand times worse.

Only once had Aden tried to save a person he'd known was going to die. He'd kept one of his doctors from getting into a car he'd seen crash in his mind. Sadly, she'd escaped the crash only to die later that same day. A pole had fallen from the top of a building and slammed its way through her chest, he'd been told. Rather than die instantly as she would have in the car, she'd died slowly, painfully. He shuddered.

Whether Victoria would leave him or not, she deserved to know the truth. She'd stood up for him to her father, had given him the best days of his life, laughing with him in the water, kissing him, drinking from him.

"Come here," he said. He released her hand and held out his arm in open invitation. Eagerly she stretched out beside him, her head burrowing in the hollow of his neck. "I have something to tell you. Something you won't like, something that will probably scare you."

She stiffened against him. "All right."

There was nothing left to do but say it. "I've seen my own death."

"What do you mean?"

He heard the horror in her voice and wished he could take back the words. Instead, he plowed ahead. "Sometimes I know when people will die. Sometimes I know how they'll die. Awhile back I saw my own death, the same as I've seen a thousand others."

Her palm flattened on his chest, just over his heart. She was trembling. "And you've never been wrong?"

"Never."

"When is this supposed to happen? How?"

"I don't know when, only that I won't look much older than I do now. I'll be shirtless and there will be three scars on my right side."

She sat up, silky hair tumbling down her shoulders and back, and gazed down at his stomach. Without asking permission, she lifted his shirt. There were scars, but not the three parallel lines he'd seen in his vision. "To have scars you must first be injured, and that injury must have time to heal."

"Yes."

Her expression hardened with determination. "Once you've rested, you will tell me everything you know about this vision and we will do everything in our power to stop it. For what is the point of knowing something in advance if you can't change it?"

Aden reached up and caressed her cheek. She closed her eyes and leaned into the touch. Some other time, he would tell her the consequences of trying to prevent someone's death. He'd given her enough to deal with for one night. Here, now, there were a thousand other things to talk about, a thousand other things to do.

"Have you noticed anything different about my room?" he asked. "Anything different about the people here at the D and M?" Maybe Ozzie was as sweet as an angel now that the past had been altered. A guy could hope.

She eased back down and once again curled into his side. This time, she wrapped her arm around his middle and held on tightly, as if afraid to let him go. "The only difference I've noticed is the array of pills on your desk. I don't recall ever seeing those before."

Pills?

Amid her protests, he rose from the bed and crossed the room to the desk. At first glance, everything looked normal. There was his iPod. A few weeks ago, someone had left it on a park bench and he'd snatched it up. He swept his gaze across the rest of the desk. Pill bottle after pill bottle greeted him. He picked them up one by one and read the labels. No wonder his companions had been silent since his waking. They were totally and completely drugged.

"Guys?"

No response.

"Guys!" he said to jolt them. What if the drugs had done irreparable damage to them? What if they never returned? He thought he'd taken every kind of medication there was, but he—they—had never reacted this way. He glanced at the label. He hadn't heard of the drug names. Experimental, maybe?

He wanted them out of his head, yes, but he also loved them enough to want them to have lives of their own, fulfilled lives, happy lives. He would rather live with them than see them destroyed.

Elijah had told him one of them would leave him in this new, altered reality. He'd assumed that meant one of them would find a body. What if it meant one of them would be killed inside him? Aden almost threw up then and there. What the hell had he done?

He looked at the name of the doctor printed on the bottles. No longer Dr. Quine, but Dr. Hennessy.

"Guys!"

Finally, Eve spoke. *So tired,* she said.

Can't think, Caleb said.

Just want to sleep, Elijah added.

Julian remained quiet.

"Julian," he demanded in a fierce whisper. Nothing. "Julian!" Louder.

Still quiet.

"Julian, I swear to God if you don't start talking I'm going to—"

Too loud, Julian slurred. *Keep it down.*

His shoulders sagged. Thank God. They were all here and they were all alive and well. As well as they could be, anyway.

What happened? Eve asked.

He explained about the drugs. Like him, they retained the memory of their former selves, not changing even when the past did. They wouldn't know what had happened to them, either.

Aden turned toward the bed, but Victoria was no longer there. He hadn't heard her move, but she was suddenly beside him, arm wrapping around his waist, holding him tight.

"I have to get back," she said, head nuzzling against his neck. "My family is awake this time of night and expects me home. There are werewolves out there, besides Riley, that is, surrounding this property to keep you safe. Mary Ann's house, too."

Aden cupped her cheeks and pressed a soft kiss against her lips. "Will I see you to—" He stopped dead. There was someone at his window, glaring into his bedroom. Glaring at *him.* He shoved Victoria behind him. "Hide," he told her, gaze searching for his blades. Where had she stored them?

"What's—" She stepped around him, gaze following his. A breath hissed between her teeth. "No. No, no, no," she said on a moan. "Not him. Anyone but him."

Why would the wolves have allowed someone Victoria disliked this close to the ranch? "Do you know him?" Aden couldn't stop a tide of jealousy from swimming through him. The man, whoever he was, was tall with blond hair and golden eyes. Who was he? What was he? Aden's gaze sharpened, going deeper, and he froze. A vampire. With skin as pale as Victoria's, his fangs peeking from his lips, gleaming white, that's all he could be.

She moved from behind Aden. He reached for her, planning to draw her back.

"Don't touch me," she said, her voice colder than he'd ever heard it.

"Victoria?"

She glided to the window. "I told you to stay away from me, Aden, and I meant it." With that, she disappeared in a blur of movement.

WHEN RILEY LEAPT through Mary Ann's window at one o'clock in the morning, she was sitting at the edge of her bed, surrounded in darkness, arms hugged to her chest, rocking back and forth.

She didn't say a word as he trotted into her bathroom. Didn't say a word when he emerged fully clothed and crouched in front of her.

"Mary Ann," he whispered. He traced a fingertip over her cheek. "You okay?"

His skin was warm, his hands callused. Comforting. She couldn't stop herself from leaning her head onto his shoulder. At first, he stiffened. Why? Then his free arm wrapped around her waist, tugging her even closer, and she forgot all about that momentary rigidity.

He wore the same shirt and jeans he always wore when over at her house. *And no underwear,* her mind supplied, causing her to blush.

He chuckled, which caused her blush to spread. "Hello, excitement."

"What are you doing back here?" she asked, changing the subject. She did *not* want to tell him what had caused that excitement.

"I took Victoria home. My time is now my own."

"What if she sneaks out again?" There'd been something in Victoria's expression earlier that said such a thing was highly likely. Besides, to be with Riley, Mary Ann would have done just that. *Who are you becoming?* She didn't want Riley in trouble.

He smiled wryly. "There's someone else in charge of her care tonight."

"Who? Why?"

"That is Victoria's secret to share. Not mine," he said, his tone suddenly flat. "Now. Tell me what you were thinking about when I arrived."

She leaned back and looked down at her hands. "My father knew Aden. I just mentioned his name and my dad started acting weird. He locked himself in his office and hasn't come out since."

"Well, at the moment he's asleep."

Her gaze lifted. "You're sure?"

"Very. I peeked in on him and his aura is white, serene. Plus, he's snoring." Once more, Riley traced a fingertip over her cheek.

Her skin tingled.

"More excitement," he said, lips curling in a grin.

She wanted to pull out her hair—or maybe his—in frustration. "Stop reading me."

That grin faded. "Why?"

"It's unfair. I never know how *you're* feeling."

He arched a brow. "In that case, allow me to share. At any given time, it's safe to say I'm thinking about you and equally excited."

"Oh." Wow. The frustration drained. "You...*like me* like me, then?"

"Why else would I hang around like this? Why else would I sometimes want to destroy your *good friend* Aden? Too good a friend, if you ask me. And what about your feelings?"

She watched him, incredulous. "Can't you guess?"

"Just say it," he growled.

"Fine," she said, suddenly wanting to laugh. "Yes. I like you."

His harsh expression evened out. "Good. That's good." He stroked her hair and sighed as he glanced at the alarm clock on her nightstand. "Much as I'd like to continue this conversation, we have to find those files Aden wants. Victoria has insisted I must do what I can."

"I have a feeling they're with my dad."

Frowning, Riley pushed to a stand. "There is only one way to find out."

"I know," she said on a sigh. It's what she'd been debating for hours and had finally decided to do. Wait until her dad fell asleep and then go down there and search.

"Don't worry," he said. "I can get them on my own. You won't have to be involved."

Was that what she wanted? She'd promised to help Aden. And as her history teacher was fond of saying, "A successful future is impossible if you don't know your past." Maybe her dad had seen something in Aden, something that could point them in the right direction.

Their birth certificates hadn't arrived yet, so they didn't know who his parents were and couldn't even visit the hospital where he'd been born to retrieve his medical records. Their only hope at the moment lay in her dad's files.

I am not a coward. I do not welsh on my promises. Besides, it would be better if she took the files rather than someone else. She would be keeping them in the family, so to speak.

She stood, squared her shoulders. "We'll do it. Together." And then she did something that shocked them both. She rose on her tiptoes and pressed a swift kiss on his lips. "Thank you for returning to help me."

When she tried to move away, he latched onto her forearms and held her in place. His eyes were gleaming. "Next time you decide to do that…"

"What?" she said, stiffening. "Give you a little warning?"

"No." He grinned. "Linger."

SEVENTEEN

From the case journal of Dr. Morris Gray
January 23

SUBJECT A. What can I say about him? First time I saw him, I was reminded of my daughter. Not in appearance, of course, they look nothing alike. Not in demeanor, either. Where my daughter is wild and carefree, laughter so easy for her, A is quiet and shy, afraid to look people in the eyes. I have never seen him smile. My daughter is happiest when surrounded by people. A is happiest in the shadows, alone, unnoticed. But I can see the longing in his gaze. He wants to be part of the crowd. He wants to be accepted. That he isn't breaks my heart. And that is where the two are most similar. The love I feel for them, in one case understandable, in the other…not.

Love is exactly what A needs, though. No one has loved him since his parents gave him up, while my daughter has been coddled her entire life. That is why she smiles and he does not. And yet, despite their different pasts and opposing natures, they both possess a bone-deep vulnerability that radiates from them. Something that strikes the heart, like claws digging in and refusing to let go. Something that imprints them in your mind so that you can never forget them.

I've noticed the way some of the other patients look at A. They, too, feel those claws. They, too, are drawn to the young boy without knowing why.

Funny, though, that the only patients concerned with him are those who are here because they see things that aren't there, talk to people who aren't there and think they are spawned from hell itself.

During therapy sessions, I've asked a few of them why they watch A so intently. The answers were the same: he draws me.

That shocked me each time I heard it because I had felt drawn to this institution with the same intensity they were drawn to the boy. I'd driven past it and had been filled with a need to work here, even though I'd already had a job. A well-paying job at a private practice I'd had no intention of leaving. I could have risen up the ladder and eventually become a partner. But none of that had mattered after I drove past Kingsgate Psychiatric Hospital.

I'd wanted to—*had to*—go inside. I'd wanted to be there, to stay there forever. What surprised me most about my determination was that my daughter, also in the car, had cried when we passed it. She'd been perfectly happy there in the backseat of my sedan, applying her favorite flavored ChapStick, when she'd suddenly burst into tears.

I asked her what was wrong, but she'd just rubbed her chest as if it hurt, unable to explain.

I never took her back, but I myself went. The feeling of belonging, of needing to be there had increased. And when I saw A for the first time, I'd been filled with the urge to hug him. To welcome a beloved family member home. Was *I* going crazy?

February 17

Subject A was beaten up today. The patient responsible claimed he'd only wanted the urge to be near A to disappear, that he couldn't live with the invisible tether that bound him to the boy anymore.

I was finally able to give A a hug. He won't remember it, of course, because he was unconscious and drugged with sedatives, and that's best for both of us. I can't really give him what he wants, a place to belong. Still, I hadn't wanted to let go. Tears had even filled my eyes.

Again, I have to wonder what's wrong with me.

February 18

Subject A is recovering nicely. I spoke with him briefly, but the pain medications made him groggy and hard to understand. At one point I think he called me Julian, but I can't be sure.

There has to be a way to help him. There has to be

something I can do. He's a good kid with a kind heart. Another patient had visited with him and had eyeballed his Jell-O. Without any hesitation, A offered up the Jell-O, though it was the only thing he could eat and he wouldn't be given another. Well, shouldn't have been given another. I brought him two an hour later.

February 21

My first true session with Subject A. He's been diagnosed with schizophrenia by several doctors and frankly, though it's highly uncommon in children under sixteen, I understand why. He has a tendency to retreat inside his head during conversation, mumbling to people who aren't there.

Do I believe that myself? I'm not sure. And it's not just because the illness is rare in children. To be honest, my doubt upsets me. Only one other time have I felt it, and that ended in a disaster I have yet to overcome. Grief still eats at me, in fact. But that's a story for another journal.

Before the meeting with A, I perused his file and found something interesting. Since his admittance three months ago, he has escaped a locked room twice—just disappeared from it, leaving no trace of how he managed the feat. In both instances, he reappeared in rooms he shouldn't have been able to access. Everyone thinks he has simply learned how to pick locks and he himself probably thinks it's a fun, harmless game. But I'm upset by it. I've dealt with that before. Not with him, but with someone I love.

I guess I'm not going to wait for another journal entry to veer in this direction after all. My daughter's mother used to do the same thing. Before her pregnancy, that is. She would walk into a room one moment, headed in my direction, and then simply vanish before my eyes. I would search the house but find no sign of her. This happened six times. Six hellish times. Usually she would reappear a few minutes later. Once, though, two days passed before she returned.

Each time I asked her where she had gone, *how* she had gone. Each time, she gave me the same sobbing answer: into a past version of herself. Time travel. I knew it wasn't possible, but she insisted that it was. When I asked for proof, she could give me none.

She is the reason I entered into this field. I'd wanted to understand her, to help her. Oh, did I love her. Still do. I can't hide that, though I should. Too bad I failed her. The only time she claimed to feel normal was the nine months she carried my precious baby girl. And after that, well, I wasn't given a chance to help.

Mary Ann's hand was trembling as she flipped to the next page of her father's journal. She and Riley had pilfered it from the study while her dad slept, head resting on the keyboard nearby. He'd fallen asleep going over his notes about Aden, or rather "Subject A," so they'd had to pry them out from under his head. That he'd kept them here, and so easily transportable, was shocking, but it proved how much they meant to him—and perhaps how often he read them.

She'd been poring over them ever since, nausea churning faster and faster in her stomach. At first, the term Subject A had bothered her, but then she'd realized that had been her father's way of retaining Aden's privacy, even in his personal journals. But she knew it was Aden, and the things he'd endured…the grief her dad felt for some mysterious doubt about the young boy's "illness"…the way her dad had written of her mother as if she were already dead at that time, only speaking of her in past tense all left Mary Ann reeling.

At the time he'd written these journals, her mother had been alive and well and caring for Mary Ann at home. And why couldn't he let others know that he loved her, his own wife? Wasn't that something husbands and wives were supposed to be proud of?

Trembling, Mary Ann read on….

March 1

My second session with Subject A.

A fight had erupted the day before, all of the patients in a frenzy. Seems A told one of the patients he was going to die that day with a fork to the throat. That patient became angered and attacked A. The patients around them jumped into the fray. The hospital staff rushed to the group and began pulling them apart, injecting them with sedatives. But at the bottom of the pile, they found the patient A had predicted would die. He'd had a fork buried deep into his throat, blood pooling around him.

A hadn't done it, that much we know. He'd managed to work himself out of the flailing throng and press himself against the wall, forked himself, in the side. Plus, another patient still had his hand wrapped around the utensil, shoving the metal prongs deeper. Had the patient committed murder because of what Aden had said? How had A known the guy had hidden a fork in his sleeve, though? Had he seen it and hoped the guy would use it the way he described? A self-fulfilling prophecy?

When I asked A these questions, he gave me no answers. Poor kid. He probably thought he'd get in trouble. Or maybe it was guilt. Or pain. I have to reach him, have to gain his trust.

March 4

After my prior encounter with Subject A, I was still a little shaken. Maybe I should have waited to see him again. Maybe then this third session wouldn't have proven to be our last.

A was different today. There was something about him…his eyes had been too old for his age, filled with knowledge no eleven-year-old should have. I had trouble looking at him.

At first, everything progressed as I'd hoped. He'd begun to answer my questions, not evading as usual, but finally allowing me a peek inside his mind and why he does the things that he does. Why he says the things that he says. What he really thinks is going on in his head. His answer— four human souls are trapped inside him.

I dismissed the claim as his way of coping with what was happening to him. Until he mentioned Eve. That intrigued me. Eve was a person who can supposedly time travel. Just as my wife claimed to be able to do.

Everything A said meshed with her accounting. They didn't simply venture to the past, but into their own lives. They changed things. They knew things. Add in their similar disappearances and the fact that A's eyes had flashed to a hazel-brown when they were usually black…for a moment it was as though I was talking to Mary Ann's mother.

The sensation disturbed me, I admit it, disturbed me so much I went a little crazy myself. I even threw A out of my office. The only way he could have known about my wife was by raiding my office, unlocking my file cases and reading my private journals.

Either that, or he was telling the truth.

Part of me, the part that had always longed to prove my wife had not been mentally ill, had wanted to believe him. But how could I believe A when I hadn't believed her? I had hurt her, each and every time she'd tried to explain her experiences to me. I had destroyed her confidence, made *her* think she was crazy. To believe A, a relative stranger, was to admit she'd been right and I'd hurt her for no reason.

How could I live with the guilt of hurting the woman I loved? I couldn't, and I knew it. So I kicked A out and left the institution. I even quit my job. I mean, the kid mentioned my daughter. Had spoken of her with utter confidence—

had spoken of things he couldn't possibly know. Or shouldn't know. I've never been so stunned and upset in my life.

To believe he's right...I can't. I just can't. And even if the things he told me come true...I can't.

May 8

It's like my wife has died all over again. I can't get A out of my head. I find myself thinking about him, wondering how he is, what he's doing, who is treating him. But I won't allow myself to pick up the phone and check on him. I'm not objective about that boy. I couldn't help the love of my life, so I certainly can't help him. A clean break is best. Isn't it? I used to think so. Now, two powerful words haunt me.

What if...

My current wife sees my preoccupation and believes I'm thinking of another woman. One I love more than her. I try to tell her that isn't true, but we both know it is. I have never loved her the way I should. I've always loved another.

I never should have gone to that institution. I never should have taken on A's case.

So many questions, Mary Ann thought, dazed. And so many things no longer made sense. This time her dad had spoken of both a wife and a "current" wife. One was a mentally ill woman who had given birth to her. The other was perfectly sane and had raised her. They were one and the same, though, so two wives shouldn't have been possible. Unless...

Had the woman who raised her not been her birth mother? Again, that didn't make sense. Mary Ann looked like her mother. They shared the same blood type. There was no doubt they were related.

And there was no doubt her mother had loved her more than anything in the world, as a real mother would. The woman had nursed her when sick, held her when she'd cried. Had sung and danced with her when she was happy. They'd had tea parties together and raced Barbie Corvettes. If Mary Ann knew nothing else, she knew she'd been loved.

Was it possible her dad had married two different women who'd looked just alike? The first had given birth to her, and the second had raised her? It was a possibility, she supposed, if far-fetched. But if so, why had he never told her?

Though she didn't want to, she gave the journal to Riley. He stared at the bound leather for a long while before focusing on her. He didn't say anything, just leaned forward and pressed their lips together. Soft, sweet, offering comfort.

Tears burned her eyes. "Take it back to the office, please. I don't want him to know I took it."

Riley nodded and left, his gaze staying on her until he disappeared around the corner. He didn't return to her bedroom. The sun was already rising, and he had to get back. She knew that, but she missed him anyway. He'd held her while she'd read, offering what reassurance he could.

She couldn't go to school today. She was too raw inside. She needed solitude. *That's not the only reason.* Being away from her dad, away from Aden, even away from Riley, would give her the time she needed to think. *Again, you're evading.* This mystery surrounding her mother disturbed her. She needed time to process it. *Liar.*

She wiped a budding tear from the corner of her eye. Fine. She needed Riley. Wanted his arms around her again. Wanted to talk to him, present her questions and hear his thoughts. Why had he gone? *Where* had he gone? To collect Victoria and escort her to school? Wasn't he supposed to protect Mary Ann now? To protect her, he needed to be with her.

At the very least, he should have said goodbye.

God, when had she become so needy?

That doesn't matter right now. Only one thing did, and that was Aden. He'd been right, she thought. Her dad really had thrown him out of his office. Because he'd loved her mom— her real mom? A woman who had been a little bit crazy?— and Aden had awakened memories of her that had sent him into a tailspin of uncertainty?

Pot and pans began banging downstairs and she knew her dad was up. She rose from bed, showered and dressed as if she planned to go to school. In the kitchen, her dad had breakfast prepared and waiting on the table. Scrambled eggs and toast. He was in his usual chair, hidden behind a paper. The thing that proved how upset he was was the colorlessness of his knuckles as he clutched the sports section.

There was nothing she could say to soothe him—not without admitting what she knew. And if she began talking to him, she knew she would ask questions he wasn't yet ready to answer. Questions with answers she would be better off finding on her own. He was hiding something from her, and she didn't want him to have the chance to lie to her.

It was odd, knowing her dad had secrets. Odd, disappointing and yeah, upsetting. He'd promised to be open and honest with her always. *You promised the same,* she thought, but look at her now. Lying about study groups, sneaking around, reading patient files. Guilt was suddenly swallowing her up.

"I don't want you hanging out with that boy, Mary Ann."

The out-of-the-blue statement surprised her; the sternness of his voice jolted her into speechlessness.

"Aden Stone is dangerous." He set the paper down and stared over at her, his eyes devoid of emotion. "I don't know what he's doing in Crossroads or how you met him, but I do know he's no one you should trust. Are you listening to me?"

Nothing in the journal, upsetting as the entries had been to her, had explained such an intense reaction. She cleared her throat. "Yes." She was. But that didn't mean she'd obey. Aden was a part of her life she would not give up. Ever.

"If I have to, I'll call the school and—"

She slapped her palms against the table. "Don't you dare! You would get him in trouble and they would pull him from class, then shove him back into a mental institution. A place he doesn't belong and you know it! Tell me you won't do that to him. Tell me you aren't that cruel."

She'd never spoken to him like that, and he blinked over at her in astonishment.

"Tell me!" Once more she slammed her hands against the table, rattling the dishes.

"I won't," he said softly, "but I need *you* to tell *me* you won't hang out with him anymore."

"Why?"

He pressed his lips together, refusing to answer.

The doorbell rang.

Her dad frowned. "Who's that?"

"I don't know." She unfolded from her chair and strode to the front door, happy for the reprieve. When she opened it and saw the visitor, her heartbeat picked up speed. Riley. He looked as rugged and ruthless as always, wearing a black T-shirt and jeans, his dark hair unkempt from the wind.

"What are you doing here?" she whispered, glancing over her shoulder to ensure that they were alone. They weren't.

"Yes, what are you doing here?" her dad asked rudely from behind her. "And who are you?"

Unperturbed, Riley inclined his head in greeting. "Hello, Dr. Gray. It's nice to finally meet you."

"Dad, this is Riley." Keeping the elation out of her voice was a struggle. "He's new to my school. I've been showing him around and stuff."

"Does he—"

"No," she interjected, knowing he meant to ask if Riley hung with Aden. "He doesn't." *He hangs with me.*

"So I ask again, what are you doing here?"

"Dad!"

"It's fine, Mary Ann." To her dad, Riley said, "I'm here to pick up your daughter for school."

"She likes to walk."

"Not today. I'll be right back. Behave," she said to her dad. She raced into her bedroom, grabbed her backpack and soared back down the stairs. Her dad and Riley were watching each other silently.

She kissed her dad's check, noticed that he appeared older than he ever had before, with lines of tension branching from his eyes. "Bye. Love you."

"I love you, too." He didn't say anything else, didn't try to stop her. She was glad. She didn't know how she would have reacted or what she would have said. She needed Riley right now. Her dad had answers, but Riley had those comforting arms. Inside his shiny red sports car, she buckled.

When they rounded the street corner and were out of sight, he twined their fingers together. Her world suddenly felt right again.

"Where'd you go?" she asked.

"Had to see to Victoria, shower and change."

"Oh."

"I hated to leave, though." He brought her hand to his lips and kissed it.

Goose bumps broke out over her skin. A little bit down the road, the trees thinning, she realized he wasn't leading her toward the school. She frowned. "Where are we going?"

He flicked her a grim smile. "You need to learn how to survive in this new world you've found yourself in. You also need a distraction."

"What does that mean? About surviving."

"You'll see."

EIGHTEEN

VICTORIA SKIPPED SCHOOL. So did Mary Ann, and so did Riley. What kind of students ditched class when it was only their second day at school? And what about supposed rule-follower Mary Ann? She sure was ditching a lot lately.

Were the three of them together? Aden wondered throughout the crapfest of a day. A day that had started with Ozzie threatening to kill him again and worsened when Shannon, coughing and weak, had insisted on coming to school anyway and Aden had practically had to carry him to the building. And then to discover that his friends were gone…

Now he desperately wanted to leave, to head out and look for them, but couldn't. Not if he wanted to return. A single ditch, and Dan would send him packing. Victoria could fix that for him, of course, but only if she still wanted to hang out with him. After last night—*I told you to stay away from me and I meant it,* she'd said after spying the male vampire in the window—he couldn't be sure.

Who had the guy been? Why the sudden change in Victoria?

He had no answers. And hadn't Victoria wanted to protect him from the creatures now in town? Guess that had changed, too.

What made the day even odder was the way everyone waved and smiled at him as if he was their best friend. Guys patted him on the shoulder, girls flashed their pearly whites and giggled as if they were too nervous to talk to him but wanted to be near him all the same. Why?

As if reading his mind, a senior walked by and said, "Way to put Tucker in his place, man," with a nod of approval.

Ahh. Now he understood (the welcome reception, at least). No one had liked Tucker, but they'd pretended to, simply to keep the tyrant from turning all that evil on them. Now they thought Aden was their savior, that he would destroy Tucker if necessary.

No pressure, he thought dryly.

All through chemistry, geometry, and Spanish he half listened to his teachers, half listened to his companions, who were now awake and no longer drugged into a stupor by the meds—though truth be told, he *had* been tempted to take them this morning. During that third class, John O'Conner once more appeared beside him, crouching at his desk.

"Why do you always ambush me here?"

"Because I had this class with Chloe. Speaking of, have you talked to Chloe yet?"

Aden spared him only the briefest of glances. He looked so real. Or perhaps because he was so recently dead. Perhaps because he'd had a power of his own when he'd been alive.

Aden nodded at the rightness of the thought. That made

sense. He drew vampires and werewolves—and goblins, fairies and witches, apparently—so why not ghosts who'd been "gifted" during life? Or did he draw *all* ghosts, gifted or not?

Surely not. Thousands of people died every minute of every day. If all ghosts came to him, he would never see anyone or anything else.

He wanted to question John, but they were in class and surrounded. He'd just have to do so stealthily, he decided, so that the teacher and students around him wouldn't notice.

John babbled about Chloe while Aden considered his options. He couldn't speak out loud, not even in a whisper. He didn't know sign language, and even if he did, John might not. He couldn't leave the classroom; because of his past, he wasn't allowed to roam the halls during class time. What option did that leave him? A note?

A note! Of course. He lifted his pen and began writing. *When you were alive, did you have a*—how should he word this?—*superpower?* He swirled the paper around and slid it toward John.

John continued speaking, oblivious.

Aden tapped the page, keeping his gaze on the teacher.

"What? Oh. You want me to read that?"

He nodded.

A moment passed in silence. Then, "Nah. Not really. I mean, I could sense other people's emotions, which really freaked me out, but that isn't a superpower. It was just me being too sensitive. Like a pansy, as my dad would say. That's why, I, you know, self, uh, medicated."

An empath. John had been an empath. Aden knew about them only because he'd met another boy with a similar ability in one of the institutions and that boy had studied the ability in an effort to stop feeling so much, so strongly.

"What does my pansy factor have to do with anything?" John asked. "Never mind. Don't answer that. It doesn't matter. I need you to talk to Chloe for me. I want you to tell her what I can't."

He could have resisted. He still didn't know what would happen if he failed, or even if he succeeded. But right now he was John's only link to the living, and he knew what it was like to want something desperately but be unable to have it. *Okay,* he wrote.

John sucked in a breath. "Really? You'll talk to her?"

He gave another nod.

"You swear?"

Another nod.

"Today?"

Nod. *What do you want me to tell her?*

"If you're lying…" John balled his fists and slammed them against Aden's desk. The intensity of his emotion must have given him some solidity, because Aden's desk rattled. As the students around him jolted, John said, "I'll follow you. I swear I will. I'll haunt you until you do it."

Aden tapped his finger against the question.

John's anger melted, dejection taking its place. "Tell her I'm sorry. Tell her I didn't use her, that I…loved her. I did."

Aden's brow creased in confusion.

Shame coasted over the boy's face. "We didn't hang with

the same people, but I asked her out on a dare. I never expected to like her. But I did. Her emotions are so pure, you know? Not overpowering. Then she overheard my friends teasing me about her. They wanted her to hear. Planned for her to, I think."

John stared down at his wringing hands. "God, man. Her devastation…I can *still* feel it. It's like I soaked it up and it became a part of me. I tried to talk to her, to explain, but she wanted nothing to do with me. I was desperate to forget, to feel nothing, you know, and did something stupid. Now, here I am." His voice trailed off, perhaps too shaky to work past his throat, and he coughed in renewed embarrassment.

"—Mr. Stone?"

Aden straightened in his seat. The teacher was holding out a piece of chalk. "I'm sorry, what?"

I've been listening to him, Eve said, always the one to his rescue. *He asked you to conjugate the verb run in Spanish.*

"Never mind," Aden muttered, pushing to his feet. He approached the head of the class with trepidation. *"Sí, señor"* was the only Spanish he knew.

Good luck, Caleb said. *I could tell you the color underwear the blonde to your right is wearing—rojo. That means red, by the way. But that's all I know.*

"I'll help," John said, keeping pace beside him.

Thank God. With John telling him what to write, Aden managed to impress the teacher for the first time. He didn't feel guilty about cheating, either. As he'd listened to John and written what he'd heard, he'd learned.

Halfway back to his seat, the bell rang. Crap. He wasn't finished talking to John. He quickened his step, swiped up his backpack, then lifted the pad and pen and wrote, *Since I'm helping you with Chloe, will you help me? I need a bottle of nail polish.*

John barked out a laugh. "Are you kidding me? I didn't peg you as the type."

He shook his head as kids filed past him, jaw locked together, cheeks heating. *It's for a girl.* Last night after Victoria had left him so abruptly, he'd started to think. She had to paint her fingernails with that metal to protect herself from…he couldn't recall the name of the liquid in her ring, but she could paint her toenails and she loved color, so…

Still laughing, John asked, "Any particular color?"

Doesn't matter, he wrote. *As long as it's not black. If you can't, I'll—*

"Oh, I can. I've learned a few tricks these last few months. And I happen to know where Mr. White keeps all the bottles the teachers confiscate from the students."

Has to be unopened, never used.

"Mr. Stone. The bell rang," the teacher, Señor Smith, said impatiently. "You need to leave."

"Never used won't be a problem," John said.

Aden crossed the room to the door. John remained beside him until he hit the hallway, then disappeared.

Time to hunt for Chloe. It was now lunch, so she should be in the cafeteria. He'd planned to sneak off campus and into the forest for an hour—searching for Victoria rather than

Riley this time—but that would have to wait. He'd given John his word. And he wanted that nail polish.

Something slammed into his shoulder, and his bag went flying. Suddenly Tucker loomed in front of him, scowling, pure menace. Determined. "Watch where you're going, Crazy."

He ground his teeth. "Get out of my face, Tucker." He didn't need the threat of Tucker now, on top of the threat Ozzie still presented. Not to mention all the creatures newly arrived in town.

"What'cha gonna do about it, huh? No one's here to save you this time."

The world around him faded, another taking its place. This one was an empty alleyway, redbrick walls colored with graffiti. There was a Dumpster and rats ran along the edges. In the background, he could even hear the wail of a police siren. What the hell?

"It's just you and me now," the jock said, smug.

Aden saw the way Tucker's eyes were swirling, the gray laced with sizzling silver. This had to be an illusion, he realized grimly. Tucker had tried before, but it hadn't worked. This time, Mary Ann wasn't standing next to him. This time, there was nothing to negate Tucker's power. Except…

Riley somehow always negated *Mary Ann's* negation, allowing Aden's companions to talk and act even in her presence. Tucker had tried the spider thing when both had been around him, yet had failed. Shouldn't that mean Tucker simply couldn't use his ability against Aden, no matter who was or was not with him?

Lost in thought as he was, he was unprepared when Tucker shoved him and went flying backward. He tripped over his own feet and fell to the ground. Though his eyes told him he'd hit a brick wall, that wall jumped away from him with a curse. Had he actually hit a person?

Tucker grinned, and there was an evil edge to it. "This is gonna be fun."

As Aden popped to his feet, Tucker launched forward. Back to the ground he went, but this time he rolled, pinning Tucker's shoulders. He drew his knees up, straddling Tucker's waist, holding him down.

"I don't want to fight you," he snarled.

"Chicken?" Tucker jerked his arms free, grabbed hold of his shoulders and tossed him aside.

Just determined to stay here. He stood, fingers curling into fists. "Why can't you just leave me alone? I've never done anything to hurt you."

"Go ahead." Tucker stood, too. "Get up and walk away. I'll just follow you. I'll be your new shadow. Every time you turn around, there I'll be, my fist in your face. Then, when I'm done with you, I'll turn on Mary Ann. After that, I'll go after that new chick, Victoria. She'll—"

Aden roared, his rage springing up, spilling over. Tucker's eyes widened as Aden's fist came at him. Contact. Cartilage snapped and blood poured. Tucker howled in pain.

Stop, Eve said. *You have to stop. He's just taunting you, trying to force you into this fight so you'll be kicked out of school.*

Aden was past the point of listening. No one threatened his

friends. Him, sure. He'd dealt with threats his entire life. But
Mary Ann was too delicate, Victoria too…his. He drew back
his fist for another punch, but stopped when Tucker's image
changed, shifting into Mary Ann's. He blinked in confusion.

Next thing he knew, a fist was connecting with *his* nose.
Again, cartilage snapped and blood poured. His own. He felt
a sharp sting, then nothing as adrenaline surged through his
bloodstream.

Destroy him, Caleb said.

No matter whose face he shows you, attack, Julian added.

Eve is right, Elijah said, trying to be the voice of reason.
*He's provoking you on purpose. Only reason he hit you back
is because his own temper is too volatile to control.*

In the distance, Aden thought he heard kids cheering. He
just couldn't see anyone. So badly he wanted to whip out his
daggers, but he didn't. He didn't want to kill Tucker. He just
wanted to stop him. Perhaps humiliate him in the process.

Aden crouched and leapt, arms wrapping around Tucker's
middle and propelling him into the wall. Cocky laughter filled
his ears. When he straightened, drawing his elbow back, he
saw that Tucker now looked like Victoria.

Not her, not her, not her. Aden threw his punch, Tucker's
eyes widening as it neared. No longer was he fighting fairly.
He hit Tucker in the throat, cutting off his air. The boy
hunched over, trying to breathe. Aden then kneed him in the
face, cracking his cheekbone and sending him to his back,
where he writhed on the ground.

Aden leapt on top of him. Over and over he beat his fists

into Tucker's face. Teeth cut his skin, but he didn't care. After a while, Tucker stopped writhing. Then stopped moving. "You don't ever threaten Mary Ann. You don't ever threaten Victoria. Do you understand me?"

"Aden," Victoria said softly from behind him.

An illusion, he told himself, continuing to punch and punch and punch. Victoria had told him to leave her alone. Victoria wasn't even at school.

Gentle hands settled on his shoulders, inexorably hot. "You have to stop."

He whipped around, ready to attack this new illusion when he noticed the alley had vanished and the halls of the school had once again appeared. Kids were all around him, no longer cheering. Not even smiling. They were gazing at him in horror. In fear.

Today was game day, so many of their faces were painted with *Go Jaguars* and *We're #1*. That paint was stark against the paleness of their skin. His wild gaze flew back to Victoria.

She really was here. She was breathing heavily, her fangs peeking over her lips in a show of absolute hunger. Couldn't be an illusion. Tucker didn't know she was vampire. Aden pushed to shaky legs and reached for her. His hands were covered in blood.

She backed away from him. "Can't…touch you right now," she croaked out.

Did she fear him, too? Or did she simply crave the blood that covered him?

"Oh my God!" Principal White pushed his way through the

crowd and peered down at Tucker's motionless form. "What did you do? What the hell did you do? Someone call 911."

Victoria shook her head, seeming to drag herself out of her stupor, and shouted, "No one move," in that husky voice of hers. Power hummed from her. "Hear me and obey. Except you, Aden."

Everyone froze. Including Shannon, who now stood in the crowd, stopping midcough. *No.* Shannon had been kind to him these past few days, and they'd had each other's backs. Aden hated that the former dreg had seen him like that, bloody and vicious, hated that Victoria now had to use her vampire powers against him.

"A tall, blond stranger came onto campus and fought Tucker," she said, and everyone nodded. "You all saw it. Then you watched as that blond stranger ran off. You didn't follow him because you were too concerned for Tucker. Now go about your day. Principal White will handle things from here."

When she lapsed into silence, everyone started moving at once, backing into the shadows. The kids mumbled fearfully about "some blond stranger," Shannon sneaked away, probably wanting no part of the interrogation that would come, and Principal White bent down and cradled Tucker's head in his lap, feeling for a pulse.

"He's alive," he said with relief.

Aden's shoulders sagged. He hadn't killed him. Thank God.

Victoria cupped his face, forcing his attention on her. "Meet me in the parking lot. I'm going to convince your last three teachers that you are in class, even though you won't be."

"No," John said, suddenly beside him again. "I put the polish in your backpack. Pink, glittery and brand-new. You have to find Chloe now."

Aden flicked him a glance, took in his panicked expression, before turning back to Victoria. She didn't act as if she saw the ghost. "I'll be a few minutes. There's something I have to do first." He didn't give her a chance to ask what. He bent down, kissed her hard—she licked his lips, eyes closed in surrender as the flavor of blood hit her tongue—and raced toward the cafeteria.

"Stop in the bathroom and clean up first," John demanded at his side. "You'll scare her."

Aden quickly obeyed. There was no ridding himself of his bruised nose and hands, so he simply mopped up the blood as best as he could. When he finished, he resumed his journey. Word of the fight was spreading fast. He even heard kids on the phone with their parents, telling them about the unidentified man. Those parents were probably on their way now, meaning to take their precious children home to safety. Would news stations come out? Interview witnesses?

Aden gulped.

Everything will be all right, Elijah said. *You won't be sought and Dan won't be worried.*

You're only encouraging his bad behavior, Eve reprimanded.

"Where is she?" Aden asked John. He scanned the crowded cafeteria, face and hands throbbing. Since learning John was a ghost yesterday, he'd made it a point to find out who Chloe Howard was. She hung with the smart kids, the ones more concerned with grades than appearances. A cute little thing with thick glasses, skin covered in freckles, and braces. She had pen-straight brown hair she always wore in a ponytail.

"There," John said, pointing to the far back corner.

Aden worked his way over. When she spotted him, she ducked her head to her tray. There were three other kids around her, books in front of them as they talked and studied. A moment passed. She glanced up, realizing he was still coming toward her. She looked behind her, saw no one, and her mouth fell open.

"Can I speak with you?" he asked when he reached her.

Her gaze fell to her friends. They, too, were watching him with confusion.

"Alone," he added. "Please. I need to talk to you about something important."

John moved behind her, bent down and breathed her in. He pressed his lips together. To silence a moan? A whimper?

She nodded to her friends, who pushed from their chairs and walked away slowly, eyes never leaving them. Aden sat across from her. John remained behind her, hand brushing her cheek with longing. She didn't seem to notice.

"I'm Aden," he said.

"I know." A blush stained her cheeks. Once again she turned her attention to her food, picking at it with her fork. "What happened to you? And what do you want?"

He ignored her first question. "I have a message for you." There was only one way to present John's case without admitting his own abilities. "John O'Conner and I were friends.

He told me about you, how he loved you." As he spoke, her color became ashen. "He tried to tell you, but—"

She jumped to her feet. Hands shaking, she gathered up her tray. "How dare you!" she whispered fiercely. "Let me guess what happened. You heard the rumor about our...relationship and you decided to taunt me. I thought he was cruel but you..." A pained cry left her.

"Don't let her leave," John rushed out in a panic. "Not until she understands."

Aden, too, stood. "It might have started out as a dare, but he fell in love with you and wanted to be with you."

She turned, ready to stalk away.

"Aden," John said, eyes beseeching him. "Please."

Maybe John's empath powers had somehow transferred to him, because Aden felt his desperation bone-deep. He had to make this right. Had to make this girl understand. Even at his own expense. "Wait. You're right. I didn't know him," he admitted, "not when he was alive. But the past few weeks I've been able to see the dead and he came to me, wanting only one thing. For me to talk to you."

At least she didn't race away. He had her attention, whether she believed him or not.

John must have taken heart, for he jumped in front of her and said, "Tell her I meant what I said the last time I called her. I would have run away with her. I even tried to give her a ring, my grandmother's. I placed it in the glove box of her car to surprise her."

Aden repeated every word.

Slowly she pivoted around and faced him. Tears were streaming down her face. "I don't know how you found out about that ring and I don't care." She closed her eyes, exhaled a shuddering breath, and reached for the chain around her neck, tugging it from under her shirt. A diamond ring hung in the center, the small stones winking in the light. "I just want you to leave me a...lone."

Aden followed her stunned gaze. A beam of light had streamed in through the window, hitting John and outlining the shimmer of his body. Openmouthed, Chloe reached out, fingers misting through him. He leaned into her touch anyway.

"John?"

"Hey, Chlo. God, I miss you."

"Can you hear him?" Aden asked her.

"No," she whispered.

He relayed what had been said. A long while passed in silence. The beam faded, and so did John, but Chloe didn't move.

"What I just saw...that's not possible," she said, shaking her head.

"It's more than possible," Aden told her. "Later, you can tell yourself it was only your mind playing tricks, but for now... What would you say to him if you could?"

She swallowed, licked her lips. "I'd tell him that I forgive him. I'd tell him that when I found the ring, I realized he'd been telling me the truth and that I...I...I loved him, too."

"Thank you. Thank you so much." John pressed a ghostly kiss to her forehead, his image wavering, shimmering and then disappearing altogether.

Would he ever see John again? Aden wondered. Or had fulfilling his last wish ceased the ghost's torment and sent him away for good?

Chloe stood there, crying, and her friends, who hadn't strayed far, closed in on her, offering support and comfort. Aden left her then. Confused but strangely satisfied, he made his way to the parking lot. Victoria was already there, waiting in front of a plain blue car. He stopped. She gave him an unsure smile.

"Where have you been?" he asked, equally unsure. "Where are Riley and Mary Ann?"

She motioned to the car. "Get in and I'll show you."

They settled inside, Aden at the wheel. She handed him the keys and pointed north. Aden had a sinking suspicion that his day was about to take a turn for the worse. As awful as it had already been, that well and truly frightened him.

nineteen

ADEN DIDN'T HAVE MUCH practice behind the wheel of a car, so he wasn't as smooth a driver as he would have liked. He hit the brakes a little too hard and took the turns a little too quickly. At least he didn't have to worry about being pulled over. Not with Victoria in the car. She could talk them out of a ticket. Literally.

They had the music turned low in the background. His fingers tapped against the wheel, keeping the wild beat despite the pain in his knuckles. Just as they'd been during his driving test, the souls were nearly giddy.

When's the last time we were this free? Caleb asked with a laugh.

No doctors, no teachers. Just us and the horses. Julian sighed with contentment.

"This your car?" he asked to break the silence between them and drown out his companions so that he didn't accidentally start talking to them. "'Cause I've never seen you even approach one before."

She shrugged, sheepish. "Let's just say I borrowed it. But don't worry. I'll return it and no one will ever know it was gone."

Borrowed. AKA stolen. Most likely she'd used that commanding voice and the owner had simply handed her the keys. He couldn't help but grin—until his lip split and he winced.

Oh, Aden. Eve *tsked* under her tongue. *Riding around in a stolen car? Whether you'll get in trouble or not, that's not the right thing to do. I'm not sure this girl is the best influence on you. Mary Ann is—*

No, no, no. Elijah banged his head against Aden's skull, rattling his brain. *Mary Ann is a friend only, so don't try to push him on her. And I'm not just saying that because she knocks us into oblivion. Riley would eat us alive.*

Eve huffed. *All I'm saying is she's a better influence.*

Once again, Aden did his best to tune them out. "So…do you know where Riley and Mary Ann are? Were you with them earlier?"

"Yes. They're in Tri City, which is where we're headed."

Tri City. He'd been a few times and knew there were restaurants, lots of clothing stores and a theater. "Why are they there?"

"I—they—" She blew out a frustrated breath. "It's too difficult to explain. It will be easier to show you."

Well, she wasn't the only one dealing with frustration. They had another ten minutes before they reached Tri City, and the wait would *not* be easy. "Have you guys been there all day?"

"Yes."

Yet they'd willingly left him behind. Ouch. "Why not pick me up earlier?"

"You hum with so much power, we wanted to first make sure we could protect you in case something went wrong."

That, he understood. With him, something always went wrong.

A minute passed. Two. He merged off the highway and onto a side road, slowing the car to an acceptable speed. He'd wanted to talk to Victoria all day. And now here she was. He could ask the question he *really* wanted answered. *Just say it. Put it out there.*

"So who was that guy? The one who was at my window yesterday? The one who heard you tell me to leave you alone." The words left his mouth through clenched teeth, each one scraped raw.

She twisted in her seat, facing him, and rested her head against the seat cushion. Her hair was down today, those blue streaks gleaming. "I hated telling you to leave me alone almost as much as I hate that man, but I had to say it. I couldn't let him know how much I…like being with you. He would have challenged you, I would have taken your side, and my father would have punished us all."

Both a comfort—she would have chosen him—and a fright—her father's retribution. Aden would do anything, even stay away from her, to protect her from such a fate. She'd done the right thing; his anger drained.

"Next time, give me a little warning and I'll play along. So who is he?"

"A vampire," she hedged. "Because of him, I have now been forbidden to leave home at night."

Her sudden bitterness matched his own. "Is he another of your bodyguards?"

"You could say that, yes."

He could say that, but she wouldn't? "What's his name? Did he hurt you?"

"His name is Dmitri, and no, he did not hurt me physically."

Emotionally, then? He was beginning to learn her nuances, Aden realized. She didn't want to lie to him, therefore she skirted the edge of the truth with omission. Smart. He did the same with Dan.

Aden wanted her to trust him completely, utterly, no secrets between them. That would take time, though, because he wasn't going to push her the way his doctors had often tried to push him, using promises and assurances. Actions were the true test of a man's integrity. One day she would realize that no matter what she told him, no matter what she did, he would love her.

Love?

His heart skipped a beat, his ears suddenly ringing as blood pumped through his veins. He'd never thought to feel such an emotion himself. He'd always tried to guard himself against it, really. As quickly as he was sometimes taken from foster homes, he'd learned that goodbyes were less painful if he didn't care about the people he was leaving.

This entire experience in Crossroads had been different, though, right from the start. Imagining Dan as his father, be-friending Mary Ann and Shannon, then Victoria (and maybe kinda sorta Riley). Wanting more from Victoria than he'd ever wanted from another, halfway in love with her before he'd ever even met her.

"Are you all right?" she asked, clearly concerned. Could she hear the rush of blood in his veins? Feel the way his heart skidded out of control?

"Yes," he managed to croak out. "Fine." He did. He loved her.

Eve would object. A few of the others, too. But he couldn't help his feelings. They were there, and they were strong. He wanted Victoria safe, he wanted her with him, at night, during the day. He wanted to know everything about her.

She was smart, beautiful, warm. She'd fought for him when no one else ever had. She'd never looked at him as if he were weird or different. No, she'd always looked at him as if he were perfect, even lovable in his own right.

"What are you thinking about?" she asked.

He couldn't tell her. Not yet. How deeply did her feelings for him run?

"About your death?"

He tensed at the reminder.

"It's all I've been able to think about since you told me." Her chin trembled as if she were fighting tears.

Those tears both delighted and sobered him. To cry for him, she must feel deeply for him. But they didn't have much time together. Maybe there was a way to save himself, he thought, though he knew better. He just wasn't ready to give her up yet. "Can I be changed to vampire?"

"Oh, I wish. But unlike what your books and movies portray, it has never been done successfully. Our blood is different than yours, and humans simply cannot tolerate the amount needed to make the transformation. They go insane."

Then there was no better candidate to give the blood to than Aden. According to his doctors, he was halfway there already.

Victoria sighed, and it was a wistful sound. "The first were created in my father's time. When he realized what he was, what had become of him, he forced his elite soldiers and the females of their choosing to drink as he had done, as his pets had done. Some of them changed, some did not. Over the following years, many others tried to change additional humans, but *all* died."

"Seriously? Not a single survivor?"

"Correct. The only new vampires are those that are born from a vampire mother."

"But it stands to reason that if vampires were created once, they could be created again."

"True. But no one knows what recent attempts are lacking. Either the tainted blood my father and his men consumed is no more, or human bodies have evolved, becoming resistant. Sometimes, for reasons we haven't yet figured out, the vampire involved even dies with the human."

So that was out. He wouldn't risk Victoria. He sighed. What was he going to do, then?

"Turn left here," she said.

He did, and soon found himself meandering along a dirt road on the outskirts of the town square, the backs of buildings facing another strip of forested land. Gravel crunched under the tires, and the car bounced. No one was in sight. Only a red corvette.

"Park here."

He eased to a stop and turned off the car. They unbuckled simultaneously, and he peered over at her. She wore a black T-shirt, as usual, and was clutching the hem. Seeing her fingernails reminded him of the polish in his backpack.

Aden reached to the back of the car, unzipped his pack and dug inside. When his fingers curled around the small, cool glass, he tugged it free, praying it was as pink and glittery as John had promised. It was. Thank God.

"Before you show me whatever it is you plan to show me, I wanted you to have this." Gulping, suddenly nervous, he held it out to her. "For you. Well, your toes."

She looked down at it, up at him, then down again, her mouth opening and snapping closed several times. "Me?"

Did that mean she liked it? "You mentioned the colors inside Mary Ann's house and well, I thought maybe you—"

"I love it!" she said, throwing herself into his arms and raining little kisses over his face. When one of those kisses landed on his mouth, she stilled. Her smile fell away. She pressed another kiss to his lips, this one soft and slow, her tongue slipping inside.

He was cut and bruised, and the kiss hurt, but he wouldn't have stopped her for anything. He just wrapped himself around her and held on, savoring the contact. He inhaled deeply, drinking in the floral scent of her hair, enjoying the heady flavor of her. All that heat…

There was a tap at the window.

They jumped apart as if burned. Aden was reaching for his daggers when he spotted Riley's harsh, intense face. Mary Ann stood behind him, paler than he'd ever seen her.

Frowning, he opened the door and emerged. The cool interior of the car gave way to the heat of the day. One thing he hated about Oklahoma was how one day could be bone-chilling and the next a sauna.

He hadn't heard Victoria move, but suddenly she was beside him. "Well?" she asked.

"It's only getting worse," Riley said.

Victoria stiffened, and Aden wrapped an arm around her waist.

"What is?" he asked. He was finally here. Someone needed to tell him what the hell was going on.

"Come. I'll show you."

Aden ran his tongue over his teeth. Would no one give him a straight-up answer?

Riley turned, took Mary Ann's hand and stalked through the alley between two of the buildings, remaining in the shadows. "We shouldn't have brought you here at all, but we needed you to see what's out there and be able to identify the different species at a glance."

Confused, Aden followed, never releasing Victoria. He remained on guard, ready to attack anything that moved. To his surprise, nothing leapt out at them. Also to his surprise, he saw only crowds of people walking in every direction when he reached the front of the buildings. More people than he'd assumed lived in this small tri-city area, sure. But where was the harm in that?

"See that woman?" Victoria pointed to an average-size female with plain brown hair, plain features, a brown top and faded jeans. She would have blended into any crowd, unnoticed, completely forgettable.

"Yes."

"She's a witch and she's cloaked herself in magic. What you see is not what she truly looks like."

His attention sharpened on her, and he noticed the alertness of her gaze as she scanned those around her. There was even a glow that enveloped her, slight though it was, as if the sun was drawn to her more than any other. She studied everyone she neared, even reached out and touched a few, as if expecting to be jolted. When nothing happened, she would frown with disappointment and move on.

"How do you know what she is?" he asked. "How can you tell?"

"You have to train your eyes to look past the surface," Mary Ann said, as if she were quoting something she'd already been told. She probably was.

"Witches can bless with one hand and curse with the other," Victoria explained. "Some wield more magic than others, but all are dangerous."

"I've been listening to a few conversations," Riley said. "The witches want to capture you, Aden, though they don't yet know who you are, to use you to increase their powers. They think whoever summoned them is a mighty wizard. My advice is to avoid capture."

"Oh, really? 'Cause I never would have thought of that on my own," he said dryly.

Riley continued on as if he hadn't spoken. "If you're

captured, when they finish with you, you will be a shell of your former self. They will drain you."

"So noted."

"The man behind her is fairy," said Victoria. The disgust in her voice was palpable.

Aden quickly shifted his focus. The man—or teenager, probably eighteen—was tall and muscled, his skin boasting just a hint of glitter. He had golden hair and golden eyes. Everyone who passed him, male and female alike, stared at him, craning their necks to watch him as long as possible. Except for the witch, Aden noticed. She ran in the opposite direction.

"Like vampires, fairies are drainers," Victoria continued. "Only instead of blood, they live off of energy. Vampire, witch, it doesn't matter. Well, that's not true. They do not drain humans. They consider themselves protectors of humankind, gods among men."

"You mentioned goblins were here, as well." Flesh-eaters. He shuddered, feeling phantom corpses biting at him. "Where are they?" If he could learn to identify them, he could evade them.

"And demons," Mary Ann said with a shudder of her own. "Don't forget those."

"The goblins only emerge at night, their eyesight too sensitive to the sun," Riley said. "Tell your friends to stop going out after dusk. The missing persons count is about to skyrocket. The death toll, as well."

Because of me, Aden thought. Because he'd seen Mary Ann. Because he'd remained in this town.

"Oh, God." Mary Ann covered her mouth with her hand as

if she'd just realized the extent of the danger they were in, tears threatening to spill from her eyes. "People are going to die?"

Riley kissed the top of her head. "Don't worry. We'll do what we can. As for the demons, they are harder to spot. Some have learned to mask their auras."

"How did they get here?" Aden asked. "On earth, I mean. And how long have they been here?"

"They've been here for thousands of years. Before the walls of hell were reinforced, a few escaped their fiery prison. They could not pass themselves off as humans—the scales, horns and forked tongues gave them away—so they passed themselves off as gods. They mated with humans and half demon, half human babies were born. These children still could not pass as humans, nor could their children or their children's children. Eventually, though, the offspring were able to insert themselves into society. Thieves, murderers, those who are purely evil can often trace their lineage back to the first demons."

Purely evil. Like Tucker.

"Tucker," Mary Ann said, clearly mirroring his thoughts.

Riley nodded. "In some way, yes, though we don't know what…"

"What else is out there?" Aden asked. What else wanted to use him?

"Anything, everything, though the others have not yet arrived in Crossroads." Victoria rested her head on Aden's shoulder. "Dragons, angels, valkryies, shape-shifters of every kind. Most live in harmony with the other creatures, but

several of the races are at war. Perhaps that is why they're late
to this party. Or, if we're lucky, they won't come at all."

Mary Ann swiped at her tears with the back of her hand.
"What should we do?"

Aden raised his chin, realizing what had to be done. Mary
Ann worried for her father. Victoria worried for her people.
Riley, well, he probably worried for Mary Ann. The look the
werewolf had given her reminded Aden of how he must surely
regard the vampire princess.

"I'll pack up and leave," he said. "The creatures will follow
me, and everyone here will be safe."

"No!" Victoria straightened with a jolt. "They'll follow
you wherever you go, yes, but that will place more and
more people in danger. You and Mary Ann are both safest
here because the only time your signal is muted is when
you're with her."

"But when she's with Riley, all of my powers remain. Even
now, I can hear my companions in the back of my mind. He
has some kind of effect on her ability to neutralize."

Riley's head tilted to the side. "Maybe I don't affect her at
all. Maybe I affect *you*. I wonder if deep down you sense that
I am a predator, so your defenses and adrenaline work overtime while I'm around, seeping through whatever block Mary
Ann places on you."

They had so much to learn. Too much, it seemed. Where
was he supposed to find the answers?

"Come, we must go," Victoria suddenly said, tugging him
deeper into the shadows.

Why? Aden returned his focus to the town square. The fairy had switched directions and was now headed toward their building. Not good. That fairy had the power to drain Victoria, to hurt her. And staying with her would only place her in more danger.

Aden released her and latched onto Mary Ann. "Riley, get Victoria out of here. We'll meet you at Mary Ann's."

"No, I—" Riley began.

"I'll keep Mary Ann safe," Aden assured him. "But this way, with Mary Ann and me together on our own, there will be no signal for the creatures to follow. So go!" The fairy was closer…closer still.

Riley nodded reluctantly and dragged Victoria away. Or tried to. She managed to wrench free. As she raced to him, she opened her ring and dipped a finger inside. Before he could stop her, she rubbed that finger against her wrist. Immediately the flesh sizzled apart and a gaping wound appeared.

The moment she reached him, she pressed that wound against his mouth. Her grip was so strong, there was no pushing away from her. All he could do was open his mouth to protest—then gulp down the blood flowing through his lips. It was warm and sweet, fizzing like soda, practically alive as it washed over his tongue.

"This tiny amount won't kill you," she said. "Dan can't see you cut up and bruised again. This way, he won't. You'll heal before you reach the house."

Heat spread through him. Heat that intensified with every second that passed, burning, blistering, scorching everything it touched. He felt like he'd caught a fever, or like he was on fire, his entire body erupting before crumbling into ash.

"The aftereffect…" she said. "I'm sorry."

Once more, Riley dragged her away. She held Aden's gaze as long as possible. He tried not to think about what she'd meant by "aftereffect." When they were out of sight, the souls moaned, tossed back into the dark realm they so hated.

The fairy, he noticed, stopped, gazed around with confusion and frowned. Good thing. Aden had to hunch over as he gasped in breath after breath. Finally, his body cooled down.

Mary Ann was patting his back to comfort him, he realized as he straightened.

Deciding to check out the alleyway anyway, the fairy kicked back into motion.

Aden ushered Mary Ann in the opposite direction of their friends. He couldn't worry about the aftereffects of drinking vampire blood right now. No way it would be any worse than corpse venom. And Mary Ann's safety came first.

He increased his pace. If the fairy got a glimpse of him, he didn't know it. He kept moving, never looking backward, until he found an unlocked door. Inside the building—a clothing shop—he ran into an employee who told him no one was supposed to be in the back. He apologized and made his way outside, where he slowed his step. Mary Ann stayed close to him, silent, perhaps too afraid to talk.

There were so many people. Watching them from a distance hadn't done justice to their numbers. They were everywhere. At first glance, they looked as normal as he'd originally assumed, even at this new, close range. But as he stealthily watched them, he began to see past their masks. Most were so beautiful he wanted to gape. Some were so ugly he wanted to vomit. Gaping and vomiting, however, would have given him away.

I'm nothing, he wanted to tell them. *A no one. Don't waste your time tracking me.* They wouldn't have listened. They wanted to use him. Kill him, perhaps. *Would* kill innocents, if he didn't find a way to stop them. Most likely, they were not all evil. Like Victoria and Riley, some of them might be honorable and trustworthy. But he couldn't take a chance. Not now.

"Anyone following us?" Mary Ann asked in a fierce whisper.

Oh, yes. She was afraid. It was there in her voice, layered in every word. He dared a peek behind him. "No. Not that I can tell."

Together, they were like any other kids. Keeping their pace unhurried and normal proved difficult, but they managed it. But if his expression was anything like Mary Ann's, frozen and fearful, they were in trouble.

"Smile as if I just said something funny," he commanded her.

She managed an unconvincing laugh. "Maybe you *should* say something funny."

"I've got nothing." He had to get her mind off their surroundings. If not funny, he'd go with factual. "You ordered our birth certificates, right?"

"Right."

"When will they arrive?"

"Today, I think. I paid for expedited delivery. Actually, they might already be waiting on my front porch."

"That's good." If the certificates were there, they'd have his parents' address. They might be able to head out tomorrow—Saturday—to see of the couple was even still living there. And if not, they might still have time to drive to the hospital where he was born and try to get into their files, find out a little more information about him and his "family."

"So you'll never guess what I did. Because I don't want a conversation lag, I'll just tell you. I snuck into my dad's office and read some of his notes about you," she said as they walked. Blessedly, she sounded calmer, in control. "He remembers you, and really liked you, but what you said about my mother really freaked him out."

She'd done it. She'd truly done it. For him. "First, thank you. Second, I didn't say anything about your mom."

"Yes, you did. The time travel thing."

He'd only mentioned his own time travel. Dr. Gray had been the one to mention another's, a woman's. Could it be? "Did your mom disappear at times?"

"No, never. And I would have known. Most of my childhood I was glued to her side."

"Then I don't understand."

"Me, either. He mentioned both a wife and a current wife, made me think that the woman I thought was my mom wasn't. But I don't see how that's possible."

He led her back to the car Victoria had stolen—the corvette was gone—and they slid inside. He locked the doors. They sat there for several minutes, panting, waiting to see if anyone—or thing—would turn a corner. Nothing did. He heaved a sigh of relief and started the engine.

"Thank you," he told her again. "For everything."

"I plan to talk to him. I just have to do it sometime when he can't avoid me or order me to my room. Otherwise, we'll never get answers. Besides, I need a break from this, you know?"

Hopefully, that time would come before Halloween and the ball he was supposed to attend. Knowledge was power and Aden had a feeling he would need all the power he could get to face Victoria's dad. He loved her, planned to be a part of her life for as long as he had left, and her father's permission would help. As it was, he wasn't likely to gain it. He was a troublemaker, a "schizo."

"We'll learn about you, don't worry," Mary Ann said, probably sensing the direction of his thoughts.

They drove to her house, and this time Aden obeyed the speed laws. He couldn't risk being pulled over. To his disappointment, no package was waiting on Mary Ann's porch, and Riley and Victoria were not there, either. Where were they?

"Your dad's still at work, right?" he asked before stepping foot in the house.

"Yeah. He won't be home for hours yet."

"Then I'll stay. For a little while, at least."

"Just…promise me you won't talk about what's happening, the past, the future. I just can't handle it right now."

She *was* pale. "I promise," he said.

They climbed the stairs and turned on the TV, as if this

were a normal day and they themselves were normal. For the first time in his life, he was able to enjoy a show without any distractions.

The package never arrived. Neither did Riley nor Victoria. He couldn't wait it, or them, out. If he didn't return to school and walk home with Shannon as if he'd been there all day, he'd ruin all of Victoria's hard work.

He glanced out Mary Ann's bedroom window. Victoria's car was still parked there. He'd use it one more time, he decided, but he wouldn't leave it at Crossroads High. He'd park a block away and hide it in the woods until the vampire could retrieve it.

"Lock your doors when I leave," he said. "If you hear from Riley or Victoria, call the D and M. I don't care if it gets me in trouble. I'd rather be punished than worry."

She nodded, hugged him. "Be careful."

"You, too."

TWENTY

OF COURSE, Mary Ann's package came at seven that evening, the last delivery of the day. Her dad was home, in his office, probably poring over his notes about Aden, trying to think up a rational reason he'd been able to claim a friendship with Mary Ann years before he'd actually met her.

She was about to open the package when she realized Penny was tentatively scaling the steps.

"Hey," Penny said.

Mary Ann froze.

They stood facing each other for an eternity, silent, unsure. Mary Ann had avoided her so steadfastly, her friend had eventually stopped calling, stopped seeking her out at school. Or maybe Penny hadn't been there. Sadly, she couldn't be sure. She'd been too preoccupied.

"Hey," Penny said again.

"Hey."

Penny gazed down at her hands, fingers twisting together.

She looked awful. Defeated. How long had it been since Mary Ann had seen the girl's usual sparkle?

"How are you?" Mary Ann asked, not knowing what else to say.

"I could be better. Morning sickness has been a bitch." That flat tone hurt more than it should have, all things considered. "My parents want me to get rid of the baby."

"Are you?"

"Yes. No. Maybe." A sigh. "I don't think so. I hate Tucker, but the baby is also a part of me, you know? I want it. I think."

Tucker was a demon. Would that mean the child Penny carried also carried that taint? She'd wondered before, but now, with Penny right in front of her, that didn't seem to matter. "That's good." Yes or no, a baby was a baby. Innocent and precious.

Silence met her words, heavy, oppressive.

"I miss us," Penny suddenly burst out. "I want us to be the way we were. I'm so sorry for what I did to you. I was drinking, but that's no excuse. I knew better. Oh, God, Mary Ann. I'm so sorry." Tears streamed down her cheeks. "You have to believe me."

Mary Ann waited for the sense of betrayal to surface, but it never did. For all she knew, Tucker could have used his power of illusion on her friend, making her more susceptible to him. Besides, she hated seeing Penny like this, so torn up, so beaten down.

"I believe you," she said. "I don't think we can go back to the way we were, not yet, but I do believe you."

Penny regarded her for a moment, then whimpered and rushed forward, throwing herself against Mary Ann. Mary Ann gasped in surprise. But as Penny cried, she couldn't help but hold her, tracing her free hand along her friend's spine and uttering soothing coos.

As Riley had said, everyone made mistakes. This was Penny's, and if Mary Ann wanted the girl in her life—and she was beginning to think that she did, for she, too, missed their friendship—she had to forgive.

"I'm so sorry. I swear I am. I'll never do anything like that again. You can trust me. I learned my lesson. I swear to God I did."

"Shh, shh. It's okay. I'm not mad at you anymore."

Penny pulled back, though she kept her arms tight around Mary Ann's middle. "You're not?"

"You're an important part of my life. I don't know how long it'll take for me to trust you again, but it no longer seems impossible."

"I don't deserve you." Penny swiped at her face with the back of her wrist. "I know I don't, and I know I should walk away from you and leave you in peace, but I just can't. You're the best thing that's ever happened to me. You understand me in ways no one else ever has, and I've hated myself since this thing with Tucker. I wanted to tell you, I did, but I was so afraid of losing you."

"You're not going to lose me. I need you, too." She saw that now. The tension that had settled on her shoulders since seeing all those creatures in town had just kind of melted away with

Penny's appearance. Was this how Mary Ann made Aden—and Tucker—feel? "Besides, you did me a favor. I'd needed to kick Tucker out of my life. You gave me the push to actually do it."

That earned her a watery smile. "He *is* a jerk, isn't he?"

"Beyond a doubt. Does he plan to help you—"

Penny was shaking her head before Mary Ann could finish the sentence. "He let me know he wants nothing to do with me or the kid." Her chin trembled and the moisture in her eyes once again spilled over. "I'm on my own."

"Well, you've got Aunt Mary Ann. I've never been around kids, but I'm willing to learn."

She was awarded another smile, this one reminiscent of the old Penny. "I have to get back. I'm grounded for being a slut, as my mom says, but I want to get together with you soon. I want to talk."

"Absolutely. *I* want to hear all about the baby."

Penny rubbed the slight bump in her belly, one Mary Ann hadn't noticed before. "I love you, girl." She kissed her cheek and walked away, her step much lighter than when she'd first approached.

Mary Ann watched her until she disappeared inside her house. What a day.

She opened the package eagerly, wishing Aden, Riley and Victoria were with her so they could share this moment together. But she still hadn't heard from the latter two, and didn't want to contact the first without news of their friends.

When she read over Aden's birth certificate, she made note of the hospital where he'd been born—St. Mary's—the names of his parents—Joe and Paula Stone—as well as his birthday—December twelfth. Funny. Her birthday was December twelfth, as well.

She read over her own certificate next. Shook her head. Stared. The words never changed. She stumbled backward, reeling. This wasn't right. Couldn't be right. She'd never thought to ask her dad where she'd been born, but she, too, had entered the world at St. Mary's. Worse, the woman she'd called Mom her entire life was not her mother after all.

Everything suddenly made sense. How she could look like the woman who had raised her, but not be that woman's biological child. How her dad had had two wives.

The warm fuzzies that had filled her while talking to Penny faded completely, leaving a deep chasm filled only with rage. Mary Ann was having trouble catching her breath as she stormed inside her dad's office, each of her limbs trembling. There was a ringing in her ears as the blood rushed, crashing against her skull.

He glanced up, saw her and immediately dropped the journal he held, concern deepening the lines around his eyes. "What's wrong, honey?"

Waiting to talk with her dad until he couldn't escape her or order her away was no longer an option. She had to have the truth. Now. "Explain this," she shouted, slamming the certificate onto his desk.

He looked at it and froze, even stopped breathing, his chest no longer moving. Several long, agonizing beats of silence ensued. "Where did you get that?" he asked softly.

"Doesn't matter. Why don't you tell me why Aunt Anne is my mother, yet you had her sister raise me as her own?" He'd never told her, never even hinted that her aunt, the one she'd never met, the one who had supposedly died *before* her birth, was actually her biological mother.

Her dad's head fell into his upraised hands. He stayed like that, hunched over, for a long while. Silent, dejected. Finally, he said, "I didn't want you to know. I still don't."

"But you're going to tell me. Right. Now!" It was a demand, not a question. Fury and hurt seethed so violently inside her that she couldn't stay still. She paced the room from one side to the other, feet digging into the carpet, pounding against the wood. It was as though the entire expanse of the sky was under her skin right now, making her more than human, making her infinite, while she looked down at everyone, seeing everything clearly for the first time in her life.

"Please, sit down. Let's talk about this like rational human beings."

She was anything but rational just then. "I'll stand. You talk."

He uttered a shuddering sigh. "Does this really matter, Mary Ann? Carolyn was your mother in every way but biologically. She loved you, raised you, held you when you were sick."

"And I loved her for it; I still do. But I deserve to know the truth. I deserve to know about my real mother."

With another of those sighs, he fell back against his chair. He propped his elbow on the arm and rested his temple on one hand. He was pale, the blue veins beneath his skin visible. "I planned to tell you, I did. But I wanted to do so when you were older. Ready. What if you don't like what you hear? What if, once you know, you wish I'd never told you?"

How dare he! "Stop trying to manipulate me. I may not have a degree, but I've read the psychology books you gave me. I am not some patient you can convince to believe as you do, then send on her way. I'm your daughter and I deserve to have what you've always promised me. Honesty."

Once he absorbed her words, he nodded somberly. "All right, Mary Ann. I'll tell you. Honestly. I just hope you're ready."

He paused, clearly waiting for her to tell him she wasn't. When she didn't, he briefly closed his eyes as if praying for guidance.

"I dated your mother—Carolyn, the woman who raised you," he said, "while in high school. I was seventeen. I thought I loved her. Until I went home with her and met her younger sister, Anne. She was sixteen, the age you are now, and it was love at first sight. For both of us. I stopped dating Carolyn immediately. Anne and I weren't going to see each other—that would have hurt Carolyn, and we both loved her in our ways. But we couldn't stay away from each other and all too soon we were dating in secret."

Mary Ann plopped into the seat in front of the desk. Though she was still a mess of turbulent emotions, her legs would no longer hold her up. This was too much to take in.

"Shall I continue?"

She nodded. Too much to take in, but she needed to hear the rest. Why had she never suspected? She didn't even have a picture of Anne in her room. Had barely given the woman, her own mother, a passing thought over the years.

"The more time I spent with Anne, the more I realized she was a bit...unusual. She would disappear for hours and claim—"

Mary Ann's gasp stopped him. "She would claim that she had traveled into a younger version of herself."

His eyes widened; he nodded. "How did you—Aden," he said through clenched teeth. "He's been feeding you his lies, I see."

No. Aden was the only one who'd given her the truth. "This isn't about him. This is about you and the lies you've fed me for years. And I think we both know, deep down, that Aden wasn't lying."

"I thought I'd made it clear that I don't want you hanging out with that boy, Mary Ann. He's dangerous. He was dangerous as a child, beating up the other patients, the guards, and he's dangerous as a teenager. Need proof of that? I did some digging. Found out he's living at the D and M. Everyone knows those kids are bad news. Stay away from him."

"You don't get to tell me what to do right now!" She slammed her fist against her chair. "I know him, better than you ever did, and he wouldn't hurt me. Right now I think I know him better than I know you."

He blanched. "People can turn on you. He—"

"He knew that I would meet him one day. He even told you that. But you, in your stubbornness, didn't believe him. After your experiences with Anne, you're the one person, the one doctor, who should have given Aden a chance to prove he'd told the truth. Yet you're trying to discredit him even now, when the evidence supports him."

Her dad waved a dismissive hand. "Once he had your name, all he had to do was look you up at a later date. Finding people isn't difficult these days."

So *that* was the rationale he had convinced himself of. And she'd once thought him the most intelligent man on earth. "So he waited five years to find me, just to freak you out? His knowing the name of my boyfriend before I started dating the guy was a coincidence, right?" She laughed without humor. "Stop stalling and tell me about my mother. Or so help me, I'll go upstairs, pack my bag and leave. You will never see me again."

He opened his mouth to protest, then closed it with a snap. She'd never threatened him like that, so he had no way of knowing if she'd actually see it through. She didn't, either. Mad as she was, she thought she just might be able to do it.

He gave her a stiff nod. "Anne got pregnant while she was still in high school. Her family was upset, Carolyn most of all, and rightfully so. Anne ended up dropping out, and we got married. The only silver lining was that she stopped disappearing once she was pregnant with you. I thought impending motherhood had changed her. We were so happy those days despite the shotgun wedding. Then your mother began to weaken. No one knew why. She was so weak, in fact, we thought she'd lose you. But she didn't. She held on. Then you were born and Anne…she…she…died, immediately afterwards. The doctors couldn't explain it. She didn't have any condition that placed her at high risk and hadn't weakened further, but the moment they placed you in her arms, she just sort of drifted away from us."

He'd done the right thing, marrying her birth mom, whom he'd loved. Despite everything, Mary Ann was proud of him for that. Tucker wasn't doing the same for Penny. Not that many teenagers would.

Her dad cleared his throat, his chin trembling. "There I was, this eighteen-year-old kid with a baby to raise on his own. As you know, neither of your grandparents are the most supportive of people, so they wanted nothing to do with us. The only person who would help me was Carolyn, but again, her parents hated me, blamed me for Anne's fall from grace and eventual death. So we raised you together. She had always wanted marriage, still loved me, so I did it, I married her.

"I never stopped loving Anne, though, and Carolyn knew it. I didn't deserve her, but still she stayed with me. I owed her so much and she loved you as if you were her own. She was afraid if you knew, you wouldn't love her as much, that you, too, would love Anne more. I promised her I wouldn't tell you, and until now, I kept my word."

So many things made sense now. And yet her entire world had crumbled around her, ceasing to exist, building itself up as something different, something foreign. Truth now, rather than lies.

She'd just forgiven one friend for betraying her, and now she was faced with another betrayal. From someone who was supposed to protect her in all things, someone who had encourage her always to tell the truth, no matter how painful.

Mary Ann pushed to legs that still didn't want to hold her

up. "I'm going upstairs to pack my bag. I'm not running away," she assured her dad when he jumped up. "I just need a little time. I'll stay with a friend. I need to do this, and you owe it to me."

His shoulders slumped. He was in his thirties, but just then he looked like a used up old man on the verge of death. "Which friend? What about school? What about work?"

"I don't know yet, but don't worry. I won't miss a day of school. Work, though, I'm going to call in sick." And it wouldn't be a lie. She'd never been so heartsick.

"Take the car, at least."

"No, I—"

He held up his hand, cutting her off. "Take the car or stay here. Those are your only options." He reached into his desk, withdrew the key and tossed it at her.

She missed and had to bend over to pick it up. Her muscles were protesting so violently she almost couldn't stand back up.

"Take this, too," he said. He unlocked the bottom drawer of his desk. This time he pulled out a yellowed notebook. "It was your mother's. Anne's."

All this time, he'd had something of her mother's, her real mother's, and he'd kept it from her. She claimed it with a shaky hand, wanting to hate him. Silent, she left the office and went to her room to pack. Her backpack was lighter than normal, as it was usually filled with books rather than clothing, but it weighed her down more than ever.

As she drove away, the house she'd lived in most of her life fading from the rearview mirror, tears poured down her cheeks, hot and unceasing. She mourned the mother she'd never met, the father she'd thought she had known, and the innocence that had once surrounded her.

She wanted to blame her dad for it all, but she couldn't, not after reading between the lines of his story. *She* might very well have killed her mother.

Like Aden, her mother had been able to time travel. That meant, also like Aden, her mother had possessed a supernatural ability. Mary Ann negated those abilities. The moment of her conception, her mother had stopped time traveling. That was fact. During the nine months she'd been inside her mother's womb, she'd weakened her, draining her strength bit by bit. Also fact. And then, the moment of her birth, her mother had simply stopped *being*. Because of her?

For hours she drove, fighting to get herself under control—and losing. The journal taunted her. She circled the neighborhood, then drove past the D and M, stopping, realizing she was too emotional to go inside, then backtracking to her own neighborhood. The moon was high, golden. Traffic was thinning by the minute, as were the number of people working on their yards or simply relaxing outside. But what hid in the shadows, waiting to strike? She was afraid of the answer.

She spotted the wolf running alongside the car a few miles from her house. She recognized the black fur, the glowing green eyes, and pulled to the side of the road. Good thing she'd stopped. The tears blurred her vision. Worse, there was a sob lodged in her throat, one she couldn't rid herself of. It was there, scraping against her voice box, sharp and burning, as if covered in acid.

Wait for me, Riley told her inside her head.

She couldn't. She needed him, but she also needed to be alone. Most of all, she needed…she didn't know what. To get away, to forget. Mary Ann jumped from the car and just started running. Running from what she'd learned, running from the pain and the uncertainty. Tears continued to pour from her. The wolf gave chase, paws slapping against the ground.

He caught up to her and jumped on her back, knocking her to the ground. She lay there, without breath and unable to move. *Dangerous out here,* he said in her mind. *Go back to the car. Now.*

He was right, she knew he was, but she stayed where she was, sobbing, choking. His warm tongue stroked her cheek, the corner of her eye.

Please, Mary Ann. You don't want to face a goblin.

She nodded and stood, then tripped her way back to the car. He didn't hop in as she expected but trotted into nearby trees. Only a few minutes passed before he reappeared in human form. He wore a wrinkled shirt and pair of slacks, both obviously pulled on hastily. Hinges squeaked as he entered, and then the lock clicked into place when he was settled.

"I'm sorry if you were hurt back there," he said. "Like I said, goblins are out tonight and I didn't want them to catch your scent. My brethren are tracking them, and I didn't want you in their sights, either."

She turned on him. "Where have you been?" The words were a screech, blazing from her, followed quickly by another sob. Her entire body shook with it, not stopping, only increasing in intensity until she was once again choking, gagging, lost to the grief and the anger. At herself, her father.

"Hey, hey," Riley said, lifting her out of the seat and onto his lap. "What's wrong, sweetheart? Tell me."

Sweetheart. He'd called her sweetheart. It was so wonderful, so welcome, yet it made her cry even harder. Between sobs, she told him what she'd learned. He cradled her the entire time, soothing her with his hands, with the same little coos she'd given Penny. And then he was kissing her, his lips meshed against hers, his tongue warm and sweet and wild, his fingers tangled in her hair.

For a moment, lights illuminated them as a car drove past and they froze. But the moment darkness once more swathed them, they were kissing again. It, too, was wonderful and beautiful and hotter than anything she'd ever done. Her hands were tangled in his hair, his were tangled in hers. They were pressed against each other, soaking each other in. She felt safe, even though she was drowning in sensation, in him; she never wanted it to end. She wanted to linger, as he'd once told her to do.

"We have to stop," he rasped.

Clearly they weren't on the same page. "Don't want to." With his arms around her like this, she didn't have to think, could only feel *him* and the happiness of being with him.

His thumb caressed her cheek. "Trust me. It's for the best. We're in a car and out in the open. But we can—will—pick this up later."

Though she still wanted to protest, she nodded.

"Now, where were you headed?" he asked, his concern returning.

After a deep, shuddering breath, she said, "As soon as I got my emotions under control, I was going to the ranch where Aden lives. I was going to somehow sneak him out and drive him to where his parents live. Or used to live. Did I tell you we were born at the same hospital on the same day?"

"No." Riley's head tilted to the side and his hands, which were still wound around her, stopped drawing circles on her back. "That's odd."

"I know."

"And significant, I'm sure."

"I agree. It can't be a simple coincidence. After we visit his parents, I want to go to the hospital where he—*we*—were born."

"I'll go with you. Victoria is on her way to Aden's now. We can pick them both up." He opened the door and emerged, easily lifting her with him, then walked around and settled her in the passenger seat. "I'll drive."

When he was behind the wheel, she said, "Where did you go when we split? I was worried."

The engine revved and he eased onto the now empty road. He drove so easily it was as if the car were simply an extension of himself. "I had to help Victoria with a problem. And I'm sorry, sweetheart," he added, twining their fingers and lifting her hand to his lips, "I still can't tell you what that problem is. Victoria hasn't told Aden and he should be the first to know."

"I understand."

"Do you?"

"Of course."

He flicked her a glance, his eyes darkening, his lips slightly swollen and red—probably mirrors of hers. "You amaze me. Anyone else would be tossing a stream of questions or accusations my way, hoping to break me."

"Not my style." Or hadn't been until today. People revealed their secrets when they were ready. Pushing them only gave birth to bitterness. As for her dad's secrets, he might not have been ready to reveal them and he might resent her later, but she couldn't bring herself to care. They'd never truly belonged to him.

"For what it's worth, your father loves you," Riley said, clearly catching the crux of her thoughts. "That makes you very lucky. I have no parents. They died not long after my birth, so I was raised by Victoria's father, who believes boys should be warriors, weakness not something to be tolerated. I learned to fight with all manner of weapons at the age of five and killed my first enemy at the age of eight. And when I was injured…" Red stained his cheeks. He looked away from her, cleared his throat. "There was no one to hold me, no one to kiss me and make me better."

She would, she decided. From then on, she would be there to comfort him. As he had comforted her this night. *As Carolyn had done for her.* Knowing he had endured such a terrible childhood only intensified her feelings for him. To have never received a hug or had someone to pat him on the head and tell him how wonderful he was, was criminal. To force him to war, even more so.

Despite the lies, she realized she was lucky to have had her childhood, her parents.

"*You* amaze *me,*" she said. And he liked her. He'd admitted it, kissed her. What did that mean for them, though? "Do you think…could you…has one of your kind ever…you know, dated one of mine?"

His hands tightened on the wheel, his knuckles leaching of color. "No. Werewolves live much longer than humans, so dating one is considered the epitome of stupid."

"Oh." She couldn't hide her disappointment. She'd hoped. And had been looking forward to being stupid.

"But we will find a way to do so," he said.

"Oh," she said again, but this time she was smiling.

+WEN+Y-ONE

IT WAS AFTER Aden finished his nightly chores that he noticed his eyes were shutting down, narrowing his field of vision until he saw only slivers of light. Unsure what was happening, he holed up in his bedroom. He couldn't lock the door because, as of today, Shannon was his new roommate. Apparently Ozzie had been caught sneaking drugs into Aden's room earlier that day (just as Aden had feared).

For once, luck had been on his side and Dan had witnessed what was happening from outside the window. Or maybe it had been an aftereffect of his time traveling. Either way, the police had come out and carted Ozzie off. He was currently being held in a detention center and would not be returning to the ranch.

That eliminated one of Aden's worries.

Dan had noticed the new friendship between Aden and Shannon and, in an apparent effort to encourage it, had moved Shannon into Aden's room. It was weird, no longer being alone at the ranch. Even weirder, Brian, Terry, Ryder and

Seth had been nice to him all day. Without Ozzie's influence, they now seemed to consider him one of their own.

Aden felt as if he'd somehow ended up in a new dimension, or an alternate world.

He stumbled his way to the bed, the bottom bunk, and sprawled out. What was wrong with him? Was he going blind? If so, why? Even as he wondered, what little light he could see was disappearing, leaving only shrouding black.

"What's wrong with me?" he muttered, panicking.

Victoria's blood, maybe, Eve said.

She did warn you there would be complications, Caleb said. Then he whistled. *God, she's hot. When are you going to kiss her again?*

Victoria's blood. Of course. Relief sparked inside him, only to be quickly doused. A dull ache sprang to life in his head, knocking against his temples. How long would the pain and blindness last?

The door squeaked open, then closed. Footsteps shuffled, clothes rustled.

"You okay, man?" Shannon asked. His voice was rough, his throat still clearly raw. "You look awful."

He hadn't stuttered, even a little. Perhaps the lack of Ozzie's constant teasing and the confidence of knowing he had real friends had had an impact.

"Not doing so well." Aden could feel his friend's body heat, and knew he was close. "Are we alone?"

"Yes."

If Victoria came over—where was she? What was she

doing?—he wanted to be ready. Well, as ready as a guy in his condition could be.

"The window…girl…"

"Say no more. I'll leave it unlocked."

A moan escaped him as the ache in his head mutated into a sharp throb, pounding against every inch of his skull like a battering ram, determined to split it open. He almost hoped it did. Then the pain could escape. Pain so intense even his companions felt it, moaning along with him.

Just when he thought he could stand it no longer, multi-hued pinpricks of light suddenly flared—*behind* his eyes. A scene began to take shape: a darkened alleyway, softly lit by the streetlights beyond it. Every so often a car would pass the alley, but hidden as he was, he was safe from observation. He was glad. His keen sense of smell let him know that no one besides him and his meal were present, no one could watch what he was about to do, and that was good, he thought, very good. Only, it wasn't his thought. It didn't spring from his mind. It was a little desperate, a lot hungry. Even shamed.

He was standing behind a man, a man who appeared to be of average height, and yet Aden was at eye level instead of towering over him. He had one pale, dainty hand on the guy's head, angling it to the side, the other on the guy's shoulder, holding him steady.

Pale? Dainty? Those were not his hands, yet they were extensions of his body. He glanced down. Nope. Not his body, either. This one wore a black robe and had sweet curves.

Victoria, he realized. He must be living this scene through

Victoria's eyes. Was it happening now? Or had it happened earlier? Was it a memory?

"You are a naughty boy," Aden said, but it wasn't his voice. It was Victoria's. Never had he heard such a cold, unrelenting tone. He could feel her fury, could still taste her consuming hunger, yet she gave neither away.

Have to stay strong, she was thinking. *Have to protect Aden, Riley and Mary Ann. My friends. My only friends. Oh, God. When Aden learns about Dmitri...don't think about that right now. Eat.*

Aden experienced a jolt. Dmitri, the boy who had come to Aden's window, who had watched him with Victoria, who had scared Victoria enough to send her fleeing. His hands fisted the cotton beneath him.

"You hit your wife and your son, and you think yourself so superior," she sneered. "When the truth is you're really just a sniveling coward who deserves to die in this urine-scented alley."

The man trembled. She'd already commanded his lips to remain sealed, his voice box to cease working, so he couldn't talk, couldn't even whimper.

"But I won't kill you. That would be too easy. Now you'll get to live with the knowledge that you were bested by a little girl." She laughed cruelly. "A little girl who will hunt you down if ever you touch your wife and child in anger again. And if you think I will not know, think again. I saw what you did to them only this morning, didn't I?"

The man's trembling increased.

Having made her point, Victoria savagely bit into his neck.

There was nothing slow and gentle about it, as she'd done to Aden. She dug her fangs deep, hitting tendon. The man's body jerked, his muscles spasmed. She was careful not to allow any of her saliva to seep into his vein, which would have made the experience better for him. It would have drugged him, as Aden had felt drugged.

The metallic smell of blood saturated the air, and Aden breathed it in deeply, exactly as Victoria was doing. She loved it, her hunger luxuriating in it, and he found that through her senses, he loved it too. His mouth was watering, his throat swelling with need.

Why can't I change their natures? Why can I only play with their memories? What good do I do? On and on she drank, until the man's legs buckled. That's when the direction of her thoughts changed. *Thank God Aden isn't here. I'm an animal, an animal with blood all over her face.*

Her teeth pulled free, and she released him. He fell to the pavement, his head knocking against the Dumpster in front of him.

Victoria bent and cupped his chin in her hands. His eyes were closed, his breathing shallow, choppy. Blood dripped from two puncture wounds in his neck.

"You will not remember me or what I did and said to you. You will remember only the fear you felt at my words." And maybe, just maybe, that fear would actually spur him to change his ways. Maybe not. Either way, she'd done all she could. Except kill him, and that she was forbidden to do.

One did not go against her father's laws. The first time she'd accidentally killed, she'd been warned. The next and final time—for she'd learned her lesson well—she'd been flogged with a whip laced with *je la nune,* the substance in her ring.

She opened that ring now, dipped a finger inside and pressed her nail against her fingertip. Instantly her skin sizzled open, creating a pinprick wound. The burn…it rushed through every part of her, blistering, leaving her gasping and out of breath.

Aden cried out, feeling it himself.

Twice she'd done that for him, first to show him that she could and then to feed him her blood, yet she'd never betrayed the brutality of her pain. Because she hadn't wanted him to feel guilty, he realized. Not when she already felt so undeserving of him.

He shook his head in wonder.

Not wanting to put her mouth on the man again and lick him to health, she placed a drop of her blood on each of the punctures. Flesh began to weave back together, pink and healthy as it closed the wounds, leaving no trace of injury. She stood, hunger assuaged, body strong—fury renewed. She hated relying on the depraved for her survival, but preferred them to the innocent and purposely sought them out.

Never again, Aden thought. He would make himself and his blood readily available to her. She would drink from no one but him. He would hide the wounds so that no one saw them or she would heal them. But either way, she wasn't hurting herself like that again.

"Better?" a deep voice asked from behind her.

Slowly she spun. Her gaze lifted and Dmitri came into view. He leaned against the wall, arms crossed over his massive chest. At least six-foot-four, he towered over Victoria. Blond hair was smoothed back from his perfect face. His pale skin seemed to glow. But Aden knew all that beauty hid a monster.

She wiped her face with the back of her wrist and nodded. "You need to return to the house," she said, giving the falling moon a pointed glance. "You have a long run and morning is fast approaching."

Lips cocked in a fond smile, he straightened and closed the distance between them. He reached out and wiped a smear of blood from her chin. She turned her head, dislodging his touch, and his smile flipped into a frown. "From now on, you're supposed to go where I go. That means you return home with me."

Control your anger. Do not challenge him. She smiled sweetly. "Every time you force my hand, I only hate you more."

His eyes narrowed. "Resisting me is pointless, princess."

"Actually, it's not. Anything that keeps you away from me serves a very important purpose."

A red glow seeped into the darkness of his eyes. "This is about the boy, isn't it?"

She raised her chin to hide her tremor of fear. "This is about you and the fact that I want nothing to do with you."

Faster than the eye—even her eye—could see, he leaned down, placing them nose to nose. "I am everything you need. Strong, capable."

"You are just like my father," she countered, refusing to back down. "You see others' spirit as an insult to your prowess. You rule with an iron fist, you punish indiscriminately."

He waved a dismissing hand. "Without order, there would be chaos."

"And what's wrong with that?"

"Is that what the boy offers you? Chaos? I am not as stupid as you must think. I know you want him." He wrapped his hands around her forearms and shook her. "You will not be returning to that mortal school, princess. I forbid it."

Control, control, control. "That is not for you to decide."

"It should be." He gave her one final shake, then released her, doing his best to appear unaffected. "One day, it *will* be."

"But for now, it isn't." She couldn't stop her smile. Putting the bane of her existence in his place was like finding a chalice that never ran out of blood. "You are still answerable to my father."

He bared his sharp teeth in a scowl. His fangs were so long they cut into his bottom lip. "That will not always be the case."

"That sounds like a threat. You know the penalty for that, yes? Even for you, a prince in your own right."

Dmitri stared down at her for a long while. Finally, he said, "Go. Have your fun. Enjoy your chaos. It will end soon whether you want it to or not."

Victoria remained in place as he stalked away, breathing in the night to calm herself. Finally, when he disappeared, she leapt into motion, racing, the wind in her hair, free to be herself, to enjoy. Buildings whizzed past her, then trees. On and on she traveled, worries falling away from her as the leaves fell from their branches. The scents of the night drifted to Aden's nose, dew and dirt and animal.

Only when the D and M came into view did she slow. There, up ahead, was his window. Open for her. Two heart-beats were beyond it. She recognized both: Aden's, a little faster than normal, and Shannon's, slow and steady. One was lost in a vision, she would bet, the other sleeping peacefully.

Almost there... She glided past the glass.

Warm hands banded around Aden's shoulders and shook him. He blinked open his eyes, surprised and disappointed to find the bedroom coming into focus. Even though he should be relieved his blindness had ended, he wasn't ready to leave Victoria's head. He marveled anew at her strength. She had lived through that, had stood toe to toe with Dmitri and hadn't backed down.

Aden had wanted to leap between them, throw the vampire male to the ground and cart Victoria away.

"Aden," she whispered.

Like the first time he'd seen her, she hovered over him, hair cascading around his face and enclosing them in a dark curtain. Unable to stop himself, he reached up and traced a finger over her cheek. She closed her eyes, black lashes casting shadows over her cheeks.

"Shannon is—"

"Sleeping," she told him.

Yes, he'd known that. Because of Victoria, he'd even sensed his friend's heartbeat for a moment. "Thank you. For everything."

She regarded him, unsure, but she didn't pull from his touch. "What did you see?"

He didn't pretend to misunderstand. "You, feeding. You and Dmitri talking."

"Everything, then." She sighed. "You're probably wondering how that's possible."

He nodded.

"Once a vampire ingests human blood, it enters our system and…transforms, I guess is the word. It becomes alive with all that we are. Our thoughts, our emotions, our very essence. The small portion I gave you healed your injuries, but it also linked you to my mind."

"Will I be able to see things through your eyes again?"

"I don't know." A butterfly touch caressed the side of his now healed eye. He felt the fire of her skin and loved it. "While I've heard of a few others doing so, I've never shared my blood with another. Well, I do share droplets to close the puncture wounds, as I told you, but because it isn't ingested, the humans never link to me."

So she'd given him what she'd never given another. His love for her grew, spread. "Who is Dmitri to you?" The guy had spoken as if he owned her, and that had burned Aden up inside.

Her gaze lowered to his chest, and her fingers soon followed, playing over him. "He is someone I despise very much. Someone I—" Her ears perked and she straightened. "Riley is here. His heart is racing." Her brow furrowed, her head tilted and she frowned. "He needs us right away."

Aden rose without hesitation and glanced down at himself. He was dressed in the clothes he'd worn all day, wrinkled and dirty from his work in the barn. "I need five minutes."

"Very well. He says we will be gone all weekend and has even ensured no one will miss us," Victoria said. "Pack a bag and I will take care of Dan and the boys. They'll never know you left. I'll meet you outside." With that, she was off.

He showered quickly, dressed and packed a bag as she'd suggested, throwing in a pair of jeans, a few T-shirts, his toothbrush and toothpaste. Bad breath was not something he wanted to have while around Victoria. Already her senses were better than most.

As promised, she was waiting for him outside. Wet as his hair was, the cool night air gave him a chill and he had to wrap an arm around her to warm back up.

Riley and Mary Ann had a new, probably stolen sedan parked about a half mile from the ranch. Riley stood outside it, tugging a shirt over his head when they emerged from the shadows.

"Get in," the shape-shifter said. "We've got a lot of ground to cover." He slipped into the driver's seat, and Mary Ann leaned into him, head remaining buried in a notebook.

Aden and Victoria claimed the back. Victoria rested her head against his shoulder. Not because she was sleepy—Aden hadn't sensed fatigue in her and wasn't sure she even needed rest—but simply to be near him. He was glad. A part of him feared he could lose her any moment, that someone—Dmitri perhaps—would rip her away from him and he'd never see her again. Did she fear the same thing?

"We won't be parted," he assured them both and she nodded.

We would never let that happen, Julian said.

Elijah sighed. *As if we could stop it. From the very be-*
ginning, I warned you bad things would happen if you
followed Mary Ann.

Yes, he had. Aden had run full speed ahead anyway, and
he still couldn't regret it.

"Where are we going?" he asked.

"I'll let Mary Ann tell you," Riley said.

Mary Ann just mumbled something unintelligible under
her breath and kept reading.

Aden let it drop, not wanting to interrupt whatever had the
girl so entranced. He soon regretted the decision, though. A
long while passed in silence, Mary Ann never looking up
from that book, Riley concentrating on the road and Victoria
lost in thought. Curiosity pounded him.

Aden closed his eyes. With as little rest as he'd gotten
lately, his body constantly wired and ready to fight, a nap
might do him good. In and out he breathed, forcing the tension
to leave him with every exhalation.

After a while, he thought he heard Riley say softly, "You
have to tell him, Vic."

"I will," Victoria replied just as softly, her words barely
audible. "And don't call me that."

Tell him what? He waited for their conversation to
continue, but it never did. "So what's going on?" he asked,
straightening. Victoria jumped, hand fluttering over her heart.

"Oh my God," Mary Ann said, preventing the others
from replying.

"What?" they all asked in unison.

Mary Ann turned and faced him, watery eyes rimmed with red. "You're not going to believe this. Our mothers—wait." She rubbed at her temples. "I think I need to start at the beginning. Otherwise, you'll never believe me. First, our birth certificates came, and it turns out I have two moms. The one who died after giving birth to me and the one who raised me. Second..." She showed Aden the two birth certificates. His eyes widened as he noted their matching birthdays and the exact place of their birth.

"What does it mean?" he asked. "About you and me?"

Her gaze was solemn. "I don't know, but I'm going to find out. All I know right now is that my mother, my real mother, could time travel like you until she got pregnant with me, and that she lived next door to yours. Look here." She held up the certificates again and pointed to their addresses. "I missed it the first few glances because I was so hung up on our birth date and the hospital thing. Actually, I don't think I would have realized it at all if not for my mother's journal.

"In one passage, she talked about her neighbor Paula, who was pregnant, as well, only two weeks ahead of her. She talked about how she'd felt calmer when she was around Paula, after an initial creep-out—her words, not mine—so she talked my dad into giving up their apartment and renting the house next door to Paula. But the more advanced her and Paula's pregnancies became, the more the creep-out feeling returned until they stopped hanging out. She said it became painful for her to be near the woman. Aden, your mother's name is Paula. They were pregnant with *us*."

What did it mean that their mothers had lived next to each other, felt drawn to each other? Enough to have their children on the same day? What did it mean that it had become painful for them to be around each other?

So your parents lived next to each other, and you were born on the same day, Elijah said, *and in the same place.* There was something in his tone, something both hard and soft that Aden couldn't identify. Were they on the same wavelength? *And you can now do what her mother used to do, what* Mary Ann *stopped her mother from doing. What she stops* you *from being able to do.*

Maybe not. "What are you saying?" he demanded.

Everyone in the car eyed him strangely.

"Give me a minute," he said. Their brows remained puckered, but they nodded. He closed his eyes, concentrating only on the people inside his head. "Elijah?"

Think about it, about the similarities.

Similarities. Aden's mom had calmed Mary Ann's mom. Mary Ann now stopped Aden. But the fact that Aden could do so, the fact that he possessed the same ability… Dear God.

Eve gasped. *I've connected the dots. You can't mean—*

I do, Elijah replied flatly.

A tremor moved through Aden. The thought was surreal and wild. Could it be true, though?

"You've felt connected to her since the beginning, Eve," he said.

Yes, I have, but that doesn't mean what you're thinking.

"What if I did indeed draw you into my head the day of my birth? We agree you're human souls without bodies of your own. What if you're actually ghosts? What if you died the day of my birth, in the hospital I was in? What if you, Eve, really are Mary Ann's—

I can't be her mother! I just can't. I would remember my own child.

And there it was. Out in the open. Eve might very well be Mary Ann's mother.

"Had you remained outside my body, yes, you might have. But you didn't. You were sucked into me, or maybe even forced yourself into me for whatever reason, your memories washed. Probably because I was just an infant and my mind wasn't capable of containing or processing four full lifetimes."

No, she said on a trembling breath. *No. There's just no way.*

He didn't give up. Now that the idea had been planted, he couldn't. "That would explain why I've wanted to hug her, why she's wanted to hug me. I think you sensed each other on a soul-deep level."

"What are you saying, Aden?" Mary Ann's voice reached him from the darkness, trembling and unsure.

Just like that, another realization slammed into Aden. If the souls were indeed confused ghosts, then he had only to help them to free them. He had only to help them do the one thing they regretted not being able to do. Like John, they would then float away, presumably to the hereafter. They wouldn't get bodies of their own, but at least they would have peace.

Elijah had already predicted it. One of his companions

would soon go free. Which meant, one of his companions was about to have their last wish granted. As motherly as she was, would Eve's last regret have been not seeing her daughter? Not talking with her, not holding her? Would that be what she'd craved above all else?

There was only one way to find out...

"Pull over, Riley. I think it's time for Mary Ann to meet her mother."

TWENTY-TWO

INSTEAD OF DOING as Aden had asked, Riley kept driving until he reached a motel. Victoria procured a room (free of charge), and the four of them locked themselves inside. Strangely enough, none of them spoke during the twenty minutes it took. Mary Ann was glad; she was a jumble of nerves.

Of all the things she'd come to accept these last few weeks—werewolves, vampires, witches and fairies, flesh-eating goblins and straight-from-hell demons—this would top them all. Her mother, a woman she herself had never known, had been trapped inside of Aden all this time? So close to her, yet so unattainable? Impossible. But that's what Aden had been implying. That's what he wanted her to believe.

Trembling, she stood at the threshold of the room and peered inside. There was a dresser, a nightstand with a TV and two twin beds. Aden crossed over and eased onto the edge of one, facing her but not looking at her. He was as pale as Victoria, who settled next to him.

Riley sat on the other bed and waved Mary Ann over with

a crook of his fingers. Her body didn't want to move; her feet felt rooted in place. *I can do this. I can.* Just the other day she'd hoped to talk to her mother's ghost. A different mother, yeah, but then she hadn't had all the facts.

She just kind of fell forward, forcing her too-heavy legs into action. But when she reached the bed, her knees gave out. Riley caught her and positioned her next to him. She flattened her sweaty palms on her thighs to prevent herself from reaching over and shaking someone. Had to press her lips together to prevent herself from screaming. This was too much, not enough, everything and nothing, hope and defeat all rolled into a beautifully frightening package.

"This can't be right," Riley finally said, breaking the silence. "One of the souls trapped inside you simply can't be Mary Ann's mother."

"Her name is Eve," Aden replied, "and that's what she says, too."

Mary Ann exhaled quickly. "Well, then, it's settled. She's not my mom. Besides, my mother's name was Anne, not Eve." She forced the words past the scream still lodged in her throat. It wasn't that she didn't want Aden's Eve to be her mother. Having her mother nearby would be amazing. It was just that, to hope for the best and then later find out she was wrong…it would be like losing her mom all over again and she wasn't sure she'd survive.

Aden pulled at his shirt collar. "The souls inside of me have no memory of their other lives. Of course their names are different. Besides, I helped pick them."

"What makes you think they're ghosts? I mean, they would have to be for one to be my mother. And I thought ghosts were a possibility for a while, too, but why haven't you drawn other ghosts inside your head? Let's think about this." Did she sound as desperate to them as she did to herself? "My ability to negate others' powers apparently worked while I was inside the womb, not allowing my mother to…time travel." Saying that was hard, made it real. "That means your ability would have shown itself before your birth, as well."

"True. But what if my mother was a neutralizer like you? I wouldn't have drawn anyone until my actual birth, until I was carried away from her. We won't know until we talk to her, if we find her. And as for why I haven't drawn other people—or ghosts, or whatever they are—inside my head, maybe I was only vulnerable at birth. Maybe, even as a baby, I learned to guard myself. Maybe there wasn't room for anyone else. That's something we might not ever learn."

She had no reply. Everything he said made sense and beat at her resolve.

"Right now, you and Eve have the chance to learn the truth. Do you really want to miss out on that?"

Did she? If she continued to hold on to her disbelief, she would remain emotionally guarded. If she opened herself up to the possibilities, she would be risking every ounce of her newfound happiness.

Riley's warm hand curled around the back of her neck and he began massaging the muscles knotted there. With the touch, his strength seeped into her and changed the direction of her thoughts. She wasn't some mouse to be scared away from a dream come true so easily. After all, she had faced down a wolf, befriended a vampire and demanded answers from her father. She could do this, too.

And if, afterward, she needed to pick up the pieces of her shattered life once more, she would.

"No," she said, squaring her shoulders. "I don't want to miss anything."

Aden nodded as though he'd expected such a reply. "I'm going to do something I haven't done in years. Something I hate to do because I become like the souls, trapped inside a body that isn't my own, control no longer mine." His eyes were swirling, all the colors blending together. "I'm going to allow Eve to take control of the body. That means the next time I talk to you, it won't be me. It'll be Eve. Okay?"

Her nervousness intensified but she nodded.

His lids fell, shading those irises. In and out he breathed, every inhalation audible, every exhalation like the calm before a storm. "Eve," he said. "You know what to do."

An eternity passed. Nothing happened, nothing changed. Then he stiffened and a groan parted his lips. *Then,* his eyelids cracked open. The shimmer of colors was gone. Now his eyes were a hazel-brown. Like hers. She could only gape in wonder, the world around her gone. Aden was the only anchor she had at the moment, the only thing keeping her from floating away.

"Hello, Mary Ann," he said. No, Eve said. It was Aden's voice, and yet, there was a gentleness to it that had never been present before.

She shivered, the urge to hug him stronger than ever before. "Hello."

"Should we leave?" Victoria asked.

"You can't," Aden-Eve said. "Without Riley, Mary Ann blocks Aden's abilities. I wouldn't be able to hold on to the body."

They lapsed into an awkward silence.

"This is silly," Mary Ann said. "There's no way we'll figure this out. I don't know anything about my mother, and you don't know anything about her, either. You don't know anything about me." She was surprised by the bitterness in her tone. Not for Eve, but for the things she had missed.

You do know something about her, she reminded herself. The journal. One passage was already burned into her memory.

My friends think I'm stupid. Having a baby at my age when there are ways to "fix" the situation. As if I could part with this miracle. I can feel her already. I love her already. I would die for her.

Sadly, she probably had.

"Do you remember anything about your life?" Mary Ann asked. "Before Aden, I mean?"

A shake of that dark head. "No. I've tried. We've all tried. I think there are memories just waiting to be freed. I mean, I can feel *something* swirling in my consciousness, but I just can't seem to get to it." A sigh. "We all have thoughts and feelings, fears and desires we can't explain any other way."

"What are yours?" she dared to ask.

A fond smile. "I've always been the mother hen, as Aden calls me. The protector. The scolder." That dark gaze lowered, and the smile faded away. "I've always loved children and feared being alone. Perhaps that's why I didn't help Aden try to find a way to free us as doggedly as I should have. But that's my cross to bear."

The nuances of Eve's personality fascinated her, and she found herself comparing her to the little she knew about her mother. So far, they meshed. "You met my father during a therapy session. Do you remember that?"

"Yes."

"Did you feel anything for him? Like an unexplainable need to hug him, the way Aden says you feel for me?" A need Mary Ann still battled herself.

"I felt a fondness for him, a sense of gratitude. At the time, I assumed those feeling were because of his treatment of Aden. He sat down with the boy, listened and didn't judge."

"Now?"

A shrug. "I'm not sure. Like Aden, I was just a child when I first met your father. I wouldn't have known how to interpret something deeper, like what a husband and wife should feel for each other."

Mary Ann threw her arms in the air. "How are we supposed to figure this out then?"

"I have control of the body now. I could travel back, maybe put myself inside a younger version of *me*. This is amazing!" Aden-Eve's head tilted to the side; his lips lifted in another smile. "All the voices. Wow. I had forgotten how difficult it is to tune everyone out. Aden's reminding me that I have to have a specific piece of my life in mind to travel back and as I recall nothing about who I was, if I even was someone else, there's nowhere for me to go but *his* past."

Mary Ann chewed on her bottom lip, thinking. "There might just be a way." Hand still shaking, more so now, she reached into her backpack and withdrew the journal. She clutched it to her chest, not wanting to release it, but after a moment's hesitation, she forced herself to relinquish it. "This belonged to my mother. She wrote about her life. Perhaps, if you truly are her, something in there will spark a memory of your own."

Did she want it to? Did she *not* want it to?

"Wonderful idea." Aden-Eve's hands were shaking just as violently as those strong fingers cracked the spine, settling on a page. "Today I am tired," he read. "There is nothing on TV, but that's okay. I have company. My precious angel, nestled close to my heart. Her kicks are strong today." He rubbed his stomach, as if checking for signs of life. "She's craving apple pie. Maybe I'll bake her one. I can almost smell the cinnamon, almost taste the melted ice cream."

Aden flipped the page, hand shaking, and continued reading. "I was too tired to bake so Morris brought a pie home. The store only had cherry so it'll have to do. I just hope my angel doesn't start kicking up another fuss. She's...he's— Oh, my God." Lips smacked together. "It's almost like I can taste it." Deep breath. "Smell it, too. I can even see it. I can really see it! The cherries are so red." There was an excited gasp, and then suddenly Aden was gone, the only indication he'd been there the dent in the mattress.

Victoria and Riley popped to their feet, both gazing around the room with concern. Mary Ann just clutched her stomach, tears of dread and that silly hope she'd tried so hard to deny pouring down her face, and waited for Aden-Eve to return, telling herself they'd merely gone back into a past version of Aden.

She didn't have to wait long. Within three minutes, Aden was back on the bed as if he'd never left. His eyes were still hazel. Like Mary Ann, he was crying. Or rather, Eve was.

"I remember. I remember." Eve launched herself at Mary Ann, arms wrapping around her. "Oh, darling baby. My darling baby. How I've waited for this day. Dreamed of it, all the days I carried you."

At first, Mary Ann tried to remain immobile. This proved nothing, not to her. No one could remember an entire lifetime that quickly. Right?

"I went back. I was there, in the little house I shared with your dad. I was eight months pregnant and lying on the couch, rubbing my belly and singing you a lullaby, that bowl of cherry pie resting on top of me. I remember now. I remember. The walls had the most horrid floral wallpaper, and the furniture was threadbare, but clean, and I loved every stitch. The orange couch, the yellow loveseat. I'd worked as a waitress to help pay for everything. And since my first memory with Aden isn't as your next-door neighbor, I'm guessing his parents moved him." Her grip tightened. "All this time…if only they had stayed, I could have watched my angel grow up. My beautiful angel."

Mary Ann remembered that floral wallpaper, the carrot couch, as she'd called it, and the sunshine lounge. She'd spent the first ten years of her life inside that house, climbing on that furniture, while her dad put himself through school, then worked like an animal to pay off his debts.

Carolyn could have changed the décor, but she hadn't. She'd left everything the same. A tribute to the sister she'd both envied and mourned?

There was no way Eve could know those details. Unless… Mary Ann stopped breathing. It was true, then. Eve really was her mother. *Eve really was her mother.* For a moment, she was too stunned to react, her emotions numb. Then joy burst through her, joy in its purest form, undiluted, heady, leaving no part of her untouched.

Eve petted her hair. "Tell me your aunt Carolyn treated you well. Tell me your life has been happy."

Her arms moved of their own accord, wrapping around Eve's shoulders. They hugged as tightly as they'd longed to do since the beginning. Just then Mary Ann felt like she was finally home, enveloped in warmth and light and love.

"I was happy," she worked past her throat. "She treated me like her own. And I think—I think she missed you. She changed nothing in the house, even picked up the bright color scheme when we moved, probably so that we'd both feel closer to you."

"So she forgave me. Thank you for telling me that." Eve pulled back and cupped her trembling chin, staring into her watery eyes. "Oh, my darling girl. I adored you from the moment I first learned of you, imagining the two of us tending the garden together, shopping, you styling my hair, painting my nails and doing my makeup as I used to do to my mother. Your father named you after me and the hospital you were born at, I'm guessing."

She nodded. With a whimper, she threw herself back into Eve's arms. The tears were flowing freely now, burning her skin. She had what most people could only dream of: a second chance. A second chance to love, to apologize. "I'm so sorry I killed you. It was my fault. I drained you, stopped you from using your ability."

"Oh, sweet baby, no. Don't ever think that." Eve ran her hands down Mary Ann's back, soft, gentle. "You might have stopped my ability to go back for a redo, as I called it, but I was happy about that. I can't tell you the number of times I screwed up my present by messing something up in the past. For the first time in my life, I couldn't accidentally or even purposely go back, so the amazing future I saw for myself was secure. The nine months I carried you were the happiest of my life. What you gave me...I can never thank you enough. And my sweet darling, it was better for you that I wasn't there. Knowing myself the way I do, I would have tried to go back and fix everything that went wrong in your life. I might have ruined you. Killed you. And I couldn't have lived with that. Your father couldn't have lived with that.

"He was always a good man. Don't be too hard on him for keeping me a secret. I was a difficult part of his life. And a good one." A grin. "We would lie outside for hours, gazing up at the stars, holding each other close."

Mary Ann rested her cheek on her mother's shoulder, the new center of her world. "Was Aden good to you?" She wanted to know everything, every little detail, about her mother's second life.

"The best. He is a treasure, that one. Anyone else would have crumbled thanks to what we put him through, but he managed to flourish. Now, enough about me and the kid for the moment. I want to talk about you. I want to know everything."

They chatted for hours, laughing, crying some more, never letting go of each other. Eventually the sun cast bright rays inside the room. Neither Riley nor Victoria had moved from their places on the beds. They hadn't spoken, either, and Mary Ann assumed they were resting their minds.

She'd never been as happy as she was at that moment, hearing about her mother's childhood and talking about her own. They lay on the bed, in each other's arms, breathing each other in. She didn't want their time together to end. In fact, she no longer saw Aden when she looked at "the body." She saw Eve, with long dark hair, sharp cheekbones, a small nose and a heart-shaped mouth. An illusion of her own making, most likely, but she didn't care.

Eve smoothed a strand of hair from Mary Ann's cheek and hooked it behind her ear. "After I gave birth, they swathed you up and placed you in my arms. I remember looking down at you and thinking how beautiful you were. I could feel myself fading but managed to find the strength to lean down and kiss your forehead. My mind then locked on a single thought: one day. Just give me one day with her. That's all I needed to have led a full life."

"And now we've had that," Mary Ann said with a grin.

Eve returned the grin with another hug. "Now we have."

"And the wonderful thing is, there's so much more we can do! So much more we *will* do. Sure, Aden will look funny when I put makeup on him and style his hair, but he'll—Eve? Anne? Mom?"

Eve had lost her smile, had even closed her eyes. "What's happening?" she asked, and at first Mary Ann thought she was speaking to her. "Aden? Do you know?" Silence, then, "Ahh." Her/his expression crumpled, became resigned. "I understand now. And it's for the best. For you, for Aden."

"What's going on?" Mary Ann peered down at her mother with concern. Those eyes were glazing over, blue seeping into brown. Riley was suddenly behind her, her comfort, her support. "Aden, don't take the body away from her yet. Please."

"I love you, Mary Ann," Eve said softly, sadly, peering over at her with those lovely hazel eyes. "This isn't Aden's doing. It's mine. My time to go. I was granted my final wish, and now it's someone else's turn so that Aden can have the peace he's always wanted. The peace he deserves."

"You plan to go back inside his head, right?" she asked desperately. "You'll still be there. We can still talk."

"I'm so sorry, angel. I'm…leaving the body. I can already feel myself separating. Aden, honey," she said, closing her eyes, "you have to let go. I love you, but this is right. This is how it's supposed to happen. I realize that now. You gave me back my daughter, granted my last wish, and now I'm giving you that which should have always belonged to you. You."

Another of those pauses.

"Aden, my sweet boy. You'll be fine without me. I know you will. You're strong and smart and all a mother could desire in her son. I will miss you more than I can ever say. All I ask is that you take care of my angel."

"Eve. Mom!" Mary Ann gripped her shoulders and shook until Riley pried her hands loose. "Don't do this. Please, don't do this. Stay. I need you. I can't lose you again."

Those lashes flicked open once more, and Eve reached out, touching her face, smiling gently. "I love you so much. You are the best thing I ever did, my greatest joy, and my only reason for living. I will cherish you always. Please don't forget that." She pulled Mary Ann up to her face and kissed her forehead, just as she'd done to her as a newborn. Saying goodbye.

"No. No!" Mary Ann shouted, jerking free of Riley and throwing herself at her mother.

Victoria was suddenly there, moving so quickly she couldn't see her, pushing her back. "You will not hurt him," the vampire said, hovering protectively over Aden's body.

Her gaze moved back to Aden. Aden…no longer Eve.

He sat up in a rush, gaze as wild as hers, a tormented "No" screaming from his lips. "Eve! Can you hear me? Eve! You have to come back. I thought I wanted to be free but I was wrong. I was wrong. I need you."

Mary Ann waited, silent, hoping he would smile at her and

tell her Eve was still there, still talking to him. But the minutes dragged by, time seemingly alive, a presence beside her, constantly whispering in her mind: just a few seconds more. Reality never changed.

Finally, his shoulders slumped and he dropped his head into his upright hands.

"She's gone. She's really gone."

TWENTY-THREE

A week later

ADEN WALKED THROUGH THE FOREST, flanked by Victoria, Mary Ann, Riley and Shannon. School had just ended, but they might as well have remained in class, as quiet as they were.

Everything had changed the night Eve had left him. Afterward, they'd driven to the houses his and Mary Ann's parents had lived in all those years ago. Aden's parents had moved, as Eve had assumed. Mary Ann had kept her eyes squeezed shut the entire time, silent, refusing to even speak about her mother.

So, after that, they had driven to St. Mary's. With some finessing Victoria and Riley were able to get a printout of all the people who died the day of Aden's birth. A list of fifty-three people, many of whom had perished in a bus collision that day.

The list had been in his possession this entire week, but he couldn't seem to make himself care. Depression had settled heavily on his shoulders. He missed Eve, wanted her back.

Which was silly. He had the answers he'd been searching

for all these years. The people inside his head had been ghosts, all killed on the day of his birth. He could free the remaining three now, had always thought he wanted to be alone, but being without Eve made him feel empty. And all too soon, if he figured out who Julian, Elijah and Caleb were and what their last wishes had been, he would be without them, too.

They deserved freedom, their dreams coming true, and so did he, but… This was too hard! Even the other souls missed Eve. They'd been quieter than usual. Something he would have thought he'd enjoy. Until now.

Aden sighed. Poor Mary Ann. Like him, like the others, she had yet to recover.

Sadly, things weren't going to improve for either of them anytime soon. Tomorrow was Halloween. A holiday he'd once enjoyed, since it was the one night of the year that weirdness was actually encouraged. Admired, even. This time, however, Halloween marked the night of—he shuddered—the Vampire Ball. He was finally going to meet Vlad the Impaler. Aden thought having his entire body waxed might have been preferable.

"Did you guys hear about Tucker?" Mary Ann asked, drawing his attention, breaking the silence.

"No." Aden kicked a pebble with the toe of his boot. "Did something happen?"

"He disappeared from the hospital this morning. He was in his room one minute and gone the next, but no one saw him leave."

"Okay, that's freaky. Same thing happened to a boy w-who

lived at the D and M with me and Aden," Shannon said. "This morning, Ozzie disappeared from juvie."

Shannon knew nothing about the events that had transpired recently, nothing about Victoria's and Riley's true identities, but even he recognized that something bizarre was happening. "I hadn't heard that, either," Aden said. Tucker and Ozzie both on their own, both probably gunning for him. What a nightmare. "I've got a therapy session today, but maybe I can talk to Dan about it afterward. See if he's learned anything else."

Therapy. Ugh. His new doctor, the one he now saw because Eve had taken him back in time and he'd changed the future, was…strange. Monotonous, seemingly uncaring and all business. Aden halfway feared the man was going to try and lock him up for a while, just to observe him through those dead, emotionless eyes. He was treading very carefully right now.

"Shannon," Victoria said. "You will race home now and you will remember that Aden walked with you."

Dread beat through Aden as Shannon's eyes glazed over and he picked up speed. Soon, the boy disappeared beyond the trees.

"What's going on?" Aden asked.

"I wish Tucker and Ozzie were the worst of it," Victoria said. "Dmi—another vampire and I found Mr. Applewood, the baseball coach, and his wife, last night. Chewed up." She wrapped her arms around her middle, her ring glittering in the sunlight. "No one knows yet, but when they're discovered, the police will think there's a pack of wild animals on the loose."

"So it has begun," Riley said gravely. He carried two backpacks, his own and Mary Ann's, and now he shifted both to one shoulder, freeing up one of his hands. To better reach for a weapon if needed? "I feared it had when I realized several kids were absent today."

"Goblins?" Aden asked, recalling what they'd told him about the fearsome flesh-eaters. They liked their victims living and fresh. He, too, shifted the two backpacks he carried—his and Victoria's—to one side.

Victoria nodded. "I suspect so."

His stomach rolled. "We've got to stop them."

"I agree," Riley said. "But the only way to do that is to find where they're sleeping during the day and kill them while they're vulnerable."

"Then that's what we'll do," Mary Ann said, kicking a pile of acorns.

Riley opened his mouth to reply, probably to protest and command her away from the actual fighting, but thought the better of it.

"We'll need weapons," Aden said. "We'll also need time. Time I don't have, because of chores and watchful eyes at the ranch. But I don't want you guys going without me." He might not have possessed superstrength like Victoria or superspeed like Riley, but he was not without skills. Plus, he would place Victoria's life before his own, ensuring her safety. Riley, he suspected, would do the same for Mary Ann, perhaps even placing Mary Ann's life before Victoria's. Therefore, they both had to be there.

"I can obtain the weapons," Riley said. "And I will summon my brothers. They will help."

"You have brothers?" Mary Ann asked, eyes wide.

He nodded. "Four by blood, raised by Vlad like me, and many by circumstance."

"Wow."

Aden heard the uncertainty in her voice and wondered what she was thinking.

"They will like you," Riley promised. "Do not worry."

Ah. Now he understood. He looked to Victoria, whose hair was braided in a crown around her head, giving her a regal appearance. "Do you have any siblings?"

"Two older sisters. Lauren and Stephanie. And I'm sorry to tell you this, but they will *not* like you. I tell you only to warn you, since you will be meeting them tomorrow. You are human and they consider humans a food source, nothing more. Already they question my...preoccupation with you."

"You don't have to explain," he said. He'd been despised his entire life. Adding a few names to the list of people who hated him wasn't a big deal. "You're the only one I care about."

Suddenly Victoria threw her arms around him, kissing him hard and deep. He spun her around, despite his surprise, holding her close, kissing her back with everything he had. For that single moment, he was able to forget his troubles, the future. Victoria, too. Laughing, more carefree than he'd ever seen her, she allowed her head to fall back, watching the trees spin above her.

"You're always astounding me," she said. "In all the years

of my life, no one has managed to shock me even once, yet you have time and time again. I expected you to run from danger. You didn't. I expected you to hate me for what I am. You don't. I expected you to be hurt by my family's prejudice. You aren't."

He stilled and gazed down at her, this beautiful girl of his dreams. "Because I, well…" He cleared his throat. He wouldn't admit that he loved her, not with witnesses. "I told you. You're the only one I care about."

Her lids fell to half-mast as she planted another kiss, this one swift but soft, on his lips. "I have a surprise for *you*. It's under your bed."

"What—"

"No. Do not ask, for I will not tell you." Reluctantly, she moved from his embrace and clasped his hand. "I hope you like it, though."

A gift from her? "I know I will." Now, he couldn't wait to get home.

Riley, he saw, had Mary Ann pinned against a tree, a lock of her hair in his hands, whispering to her as she peered up at him shyly.

"Come on, you two," Aden called.

At first they ignored him. Then Mary Ann laughed and shoved him away. Riley gave a mock growl. Aden had never seen the shifter so at ease. "Aden's right," Riley said. "We should go. Dmitri's waiting for you, princess."

The princess in question gasped, stiffened. "Shut up!"

"My bad," Riley muttered.

That reminded him… "So who is Dmitri to you?" he asked Victoria as they all jumped back into motion.

Riley's attention whipped to Victoria, eyes narrowed. Gone was his relaxed demeanor.

There was no color in her cheeks, and she stumbled over her own feet. "Aden," she began.

"It's time," Riley said. "He needs to know."

Oh, no, Elijah suddenly moaned. *Oh, Aden. I'm so sorry. I just heard her answer. She's going to tell you, but please don't react right away. All right?*

Aden stiffened.

Victoria gulped. "Dmitri is my…betrothed."

Betrothed. Took him a moment to recall the meaning of the word. When he did, he stopped. Betrothed—engaged. He'd thought himself stiff before, but now his muscles clamped down on his bones with so much force, his entire body shook.

"I didn't choose him," she rushed out. "My father did. I want nothing to do with him. I hate him. You have to believe that."

"But you *will* marry him?"

Her gaze fell to the ground. A moment passed. She nodded once. "I cannot fight my father on this. He has planned it since my birth."

"What about your sisters?"

"They are promised to others."

Filled with fury, he gripped her upper arms. "Why didn't you tell me?" If she had, he would have fought the urge to love her. Or fought Dmitri when he'd had the chance.

"I wanted to be with you and I didn't want that between us." Slowly her lashes rose until that crystalline gaze was on him, burning deep. "You wouldn't have kissed me."

"You're not marrying him," he gritted out. "You're not."

"My father desires the alliance because Dmitri's family is strong. There is no getting out of it. Not without bloodshed and death. And pain. Oh, God, the pain he can inflict… Not just on me, but on you and everyone you love. I'm sorry, Aden. So sorry."

In the distance, he heard a twig snap. Heard Riley suck in a breath. Heard a gasp as the shape-shifter shoved Mary Ann behind him.

Riley was ripping off his clothing, snarling at the trees. "Sneaky witches." Finally Riley was naked, Mary Ann was looking at him, blushing, and then he was changing from man to wolf, fur sprouting from his skin, bones elongating, reshaping until he was on all fours, sharp teeth bared.

"Witches?" Frowning, Victoria turned.

Aden fought past his emotions and followed suit just as woman after woman stepped between the trees, encircling their group.

"Break the circle before it solidifies," Victoria cried. One moment she was beside him, the next she wasn't, moving so quickly he only saw the blur of her clothing. When she hit the edge of the trees where the women were, she slammed into some type of invisible wall and flew backward, tumbling to the ground.

Aden rushed forward, placing himself in front of her. All

eyes were focused on him as he bent down and drew the daggers out of his boots. He kept the silver hidden by pressing it against his arms, the hilts tight in his hands.

Witches, Riley had called them. He studied them. There were eight of them, all wearing white cloaks that draped their bodies. Hoods covered their heads, casting shadows over their faces. Power hummed from them, coating the air, glistening in the sun like flakes of snow.

"At last we have found you," one of them said in an eerie, almost hypnotic voice. She stepped forward. She had long blond hair that hung over her shoulders, poorly concealed by her cloak. "The source of the summons."

Riley snarled at her.

Inside Aden's head, Caleb was sputtering, something he'd never done before. *I—I think I know her.*

Aden nearly moaned. Eve had said the exact same thing when they'd first seen Mary Ann. Was Caleb somehow connected to the witches? Perhaps Aden should have been studying the list of the dead and figuring out exactly who occupied his head. But he'd been too depressed, too preoccupied. He would remedy that, he decided.

If he lived.

"No way you can know her," he whispered. "You can't even see her."

But I can feeeel *her. Ask her to remove the hood. Please, Aden. Please.*

"Let me see your face," Aden called after only a moment's hesitation.

He was ignored, and Caleb pushed out a frustrated breath.

Again, Riley snarled.

"Which one of you calls us?" another asked, ignoring the wolf, too, as if he were of no importance.

Victoria was on her feet and beside him a second later, panting, leaves falling from her clothing. "You will leave us," she said, "or you will feel my father's wrath."

The word *vampire* rose on the air, voices a mix of fear and fury.

Aden raised his chin and opened his mouth to admit the truth.

"No, Aden," he heard Mary Ann plead. "Don't."

He continued on. "I am the one who summoned you. Let the others go."

Ask her again!

"Now please, show your face."

"He lies," Victoria shouted. "Do not listen to him. I am the one you seek."

As they had done to the wolf, they ignored her.

"Why?" the blonde demanded, concentrating on him. "Why do you call us? If you dared plan to lead us to slaughter—"

"No," he interjected. "Never. I can't help what I am any more than you can help what you are. Though I might wish otherwise, I am the one who summoned you. I didn't want to, didn't mean to, but nonhumans feel the pull of me."

They murmured among themselves, their words too jumbled to hear.

"We have never heard of one such as you," the blonde said when the others quieted.

He shrugged. "I had never seen a real vampire or werewolf until a few weeks ago. That doesn't mean they weren't always real."

Another witch stepped forward, hair red and long. "If you cannot help what you are, how have you masked your pull so often?"

Riley snapped at her, saliva dripping over his lips. She flinched but remained in place.

"That," Aden said, raising his chin yet another notch, "I will not tell you. Unless you let the others go as I asked, of course."

Trade the information for a peek at her, Caleb pleaded. *I have to see her face.*

"I can't," he whispered frantically. Information was the only card he held right now. To play it would end his usefulness—and thereby everyone else's. The witches could attack his friends.

Again, they muttered amongst themselves. Again, he couldn't understand what was being said. This time the words were frantic, determined. Elijah moaned inside his head, perhaps sensing the direction of their conversation.

"We will call a meeting in one week's time, when our elders arrive. You will attend that meeting, human. If you fail to do so, the people in this circle will die. Doubt me not."

In unison, the witches stretched out their arms and began muttering. Riley leapt forward, slamming against the same invisible wall Victoria had met. The power Aden felt pulsing from them grew in intensity, coagulating just above their upraised palms, first white, then blue, then exploding into golden flames.

As one, they tossed those flames into the circle. Several hit Riley, several hit Victoria, but only one hit Mary Ann.

Riley, Victoria and Mary Ann screamed in pain, each of them dropping to their knees, panting, sweating, writhing. As Aden rushed to them, Riley morphed into human form, his bones realigning, his fur retracting under his skin, then switched back to wolf form, then returned to human form again. The sight was at once astonishing and gruesome.

"Until then," the blonde said as if she hadn't a care.

The witches backed up, never giving them their backs, and soon disappeared beyond the trees.

"How will I know where the meeting is?" he shouted. No response. Pushing them and their meeting to the back of his mind, for now, he crouched at Victoria's side, patting her down for injuries. "Are you all right?"

Grimacing, she blinked up at him. He helped her sit up. "Fine, I'm fine."

Riley had already recovered and was helping Mary Ann to her feet. "Come on," he said, striding to his clothes and dressing. "Let's get you guys home. We're done with the woods. Understand? No one is to enter them again."

"My thoughts exactly." He wrapped an arm around Victoria and pulled her to her feet. "What'd they do to you?"

"Bespelled us." A shudder rocked her. "With death."

Breath froze in his lungs, sending frost through his bloodstream. So. His friends really would die if he missed that meeting. A meeting held in a location he didn't know. No pressure. Really. "You'll die? Even if I attend the meeting?"

"No," Riley answered bitterly. "We'll die only if you miss it. Once you attend, the spell will fade."

What a wonderful day this had turned out to be, Aden thought, rubbing his temple to ward off the oncoming ache. His girlfriend was engaged to someone else, he was responsible for his friends' lives, and Caleb might be the next to leave him for a group of witches. Caleb, who was even now pacing the confines of Aden's mind, muttering about the stubborn blond witch who "should have bowed" to him.

Together, they rushed through the forest, jumping over fallen twigs, around rabbits and squirrels trying to rush to their homes, as well. They must have sensed the danger.

There's a way to win Victoria away from Dmitri, Elijah said.

"How?" he rushed out.

"How what?" Victoria asked.

Convince her father that you are more important to his people than Dmitri is.

His heart rate sped up. "Can I do it?"

"Do what—oh." She offered him a faint smile. "You aren't talking to me, are you?"

He shook his head. For once, he wasn't embarrassed to be caught talking to the people in his mind. He was too charged.

Anything is possible, Elijah hedged.

Which meant Elijah couldn't see the results of such an attempt. Which meant Aden would be going in blind. Which meant anything could happen. Good or bad.

TWENTY-FOUR

THAT NIGHT, Riley stayed with Mary Ann. Though her window was shut and locked, she could hear the wolves howling outside as they kept watch. Despite the day's grave events, they talked and laughed, even kissed again. Only when the sun rose did the howls quiet, and only then did she drift off to sleep.

When she woke, the sun was still shining and Riley was still beside her. Her thoughts immediately returned to the wolves, as if her mind had simply been waiting for her to wake back up to continue. She wasn't sure their presence was a good thing. Last night, the news stations had blasted the story of Mr. and Mrs. Applewood and how they had been killed by "wild animals." His brothers—both by blood and circumstance—could be hunted and shot by locals wanting to protect their loved ones.

"Vlad made sure they know how to take care of themselves," he said, as if reading her mind. Perhaps he had. No telling what color her aura was right now. "Besides, they howled to let me know they'd taken out a goblin."

Okay. She hadn't known that. "How many howls have there been?" She'd lost count.

"Twenty-eight."

Wow. "And just how many goblins are out there?"

"Like wolves, they run in packs so it's hard to say."

She snuggled deeper into his side, his heartbeat pounding against her ear. "Maybe the goblins will eat the witches."

"Maybe." He didn't sound convinced that it could happen. Made her wonder exactly how powerful the witches actually were. And if that power was actually a good thing. If the witches died, but their spell didn't die with them, Aden wouldn't be able to attend their meeting. She, Riley and Victoria would then die themselves.

That line of thought had her grimacing. It was beyond confusing and utterly surreal. She didn't feel cursed. Didn't feel like there was a knife hovering over her head, ready to strike her down.

"I negate Aden's powers, so why didn't I negate the witch's spell?"

"I negate your negation, remember? Or maybe I increase his powers. I still don't know. Either way, I think it means we belong together," he said, obviously trying to lighten the mood.

"I like how you think." Because she wanted to be with him. A lot. "Are we really going to die if Aden fails to attend that witches meeting?"

Riley kissed her temple. "Don't worry. I won't let anything happen to you."

Though he'd sidestepped the question, his evasion answered it well enough. Yes, they would. She traced an X over his heart. "Have you ever been bespelled before?"

He nodded reluctantly.

"Tell me about it. Please."

At first, he didn't reply and she figured he planned to ignore her. Then he sighed. "A few years ago I…dated a witch. When I tried to break things off, she became angry and cursed me—as well as my brothers. Until the day we died we were to look amazingly beautiful to everyone we considered friend."

"Uh, that doesn't sound like a curse."

"That's because that was only the beginning of the curse. Anyone we considered more than a friend, anyone we found attractive or wanted to date, would find us plain, even ugly."

"I don't find you ugly." Or plain. He took her breath away. And she knew he found her attractive. He'd kissed her, had said he wanted her. "The curse must have stopped working."

"You're able to see me as I truly am because I died and the curse was broken."

"You d-died? How? How are you here with me, then?"

His hand caressed up and down her rib cage. "I was drained by a fairy trying to get to Victoria. And just as your modern medicine can bring people back from the dead, so, too, can ours. I was brought back. But because I died, the curse was broken. The same is not true of my brothers, innocents in all of this." Guilt layered his voice. Clearly he felt responsible for their pain. "I wish they could die and be revived as I was, but like your medicine, ours is not a guarantee. There is a chance they would not be able to be revived. So they are stuck, unattractive to all the women they desire."

How terrible. Would she have wanted to be with Riley if he'd been unattractive to her? Yes, she thought. She'd liked him, even in wolf form. Liked his strength and his intensity. "Nothing else will free them?"

"No. A curse, once spoken, is unbreakable. Even by the witch who uttered it. It takes on a life of its own, its only purpose enforcing the words that brought it into existence."

So there was no hope for them. Any girl they desired would turn away from them in disgust. And there truly was no breaking the spell that bound her, either. "Poor things." *Poor me. Poor us.*

He laughed with true humor. "Do not let them hear you say such a thing. They despise pity."

As he did, she thought. He was utterly capable and didn't want her or anyone to see him any other way. In fact, he hid his fears so well, she would almost believe he didn't have any. Almost. But she'd seen his expression when the witches first approached them. She'd sensed his torment over his brothers' bleak futures.

"They'll find love one day. I know it."

"I hope you are right." He gave her another kiss and sat up. "What are your plans for today?"

The weekend was here and that meant only one thing. "I have to go to work. I haven't been in weeks."

He flicked her a hard glance over his shoulder. "Nor will you go today. Call in sick. Please," he added as an afterthought.

"I can't. Not again." She anchored a hand behind her neck

to prop herself up and see him better. "I'm already close to being fired."

"Better fired than dead. Do you remember the number of witches and fairies in town? It was dangerous before but it is suicide now. The witches know who you are. I'd prefer it if you stayed home."

He could have forced her. Instead, he was asking. "Fine," she sighed.

He grinned. "Thank you."

"And where will you be?"

"I must prepare for Vlad's awakening," he said, standing. "Well, awakening *ceremony*. I'll return in a few hours to pick you up for the ball."

She jolted upright. "You want me to go?"

"Of course. I wouldn't attend without you."

Whether she sighed dreamily out loud or just inside her head, she didn't know. When he said things like that, she wanted to offer him her heart on a silver platter.

"I don't have a costume."

"Mary Ann," her dad suddenly called through the door. Since her road trip, they hadn't spoken about her mother or his lies. They'd just sort of fallen into a routine, a bit formal with each other and staying out of each other's way whenever possible. "Come down and eat lunch. You missed breakfast."

She'd been in bed that long? "In a minute," she called back. They'd make up, she knew they would. As Anne-Eve had said, he was a good man. Mary Ann had already forgiven him. She just wasn't ready to talk to him about the past again. Losing her mother—a second time—was still too new, too fresh. But soon, she thought. Soon she'd have to tell him she forgave him. She was all he had and he did love her.

Riley hugged her tight, whispering, "Victoria bought you a present. Look under your bed." With that, he untangled himself from her and moved toward the window.

When he was out of sight, she stood and peeked under her bed. There was a medium-size box with a red bow glued to the center. With trembling hands, she slid the cardboard over the carpet and flipped open the lid. When she saw what was inside, she couldn't help but laugh.

Hopefully, the night would end with a smile, as well.

ADEN STOOD in front of his bedroom mirror, studying his reflection. He wore Victoria's gift. A costume. He was a knight in shining armor. The chain mail was thin and light, so it didn't weigh him down. It covered him from neck to ankle, only broken up where the pieces didn't quite meet: his elbows, wrists, stomach and knees.

"How do I look?" he asked Shannon when the boy soared into the room.

"Great, but Dan's never gonna l-let you go to the costume party. We have g-guest. This morning Mr. Sicamore unexpectedly decided to p-pack up and go on an extended vacation, but he recommended someone new. Apparently Dan liked the guy and hired him on the spot. Mrs. Reeves just got done cooking a big dinner for us, so we can all sit down and get to kn-know each other. Dan told me to gather everyone up and bring them over to the main house."

Great.

Victoria will get you out of it, Elijah said.

He relaxed. Tonight he wasn't going to worry about the witches' meeting or losing Caleb. Tonight was about proving himself to Victoria's father and setting her free from her stupid betrothal.

"Tell Dan I'm sick, that I caught what you had," he pleaded. "Tell him you had to help me into bed."

"If I'm caught lying…"

"You won't be. Swear."

Shannon hesitated only a moment more before nodding and taking off. In the hall, Aden could hear the other boys mumbling about the dinner, then their dragging footsteps, then the click of the main door as it shut. He stuffed some pillows under his covers to make it look like he was in bed and switched off all the lights. Where was Victoria? She should have been here by—

A clatter of rocks hit his window. Heartbeat picking up speed, he strode to the glass and peered out. Victoria stood a few feet away, the moon glowing around her. He caught his breath at the sight of her. There were more blue streaks in her hair, half piled on top of her head, the rest curling down her back. She wore a gown of blue velvet that hugged her chest and waist and flowed freely around her ankles. Her sandals showed off her glittery pink toenails.

A damsel in distress to his knight in shining armor, he thought with a grin.

He climbed out the window, surprisingly agile for someone in chain mail, and joined her. Usually she would kiss him in welcome, or he would kiss her, but they just stood peering at each other, unsure. Since her announcement about Dmitri, they had lost some of their ease with each other, and he didn't like it.

Finally, he said, "You look beautiful."

"Thank you. You look…edible."

High praise, from a vampire. "Are you thirsty?"

She licked her lips. "For you? Always."

"Then drink."

Her gaze fell to his neck, and a deep longing entered her crystalline eyes. He'd fed her a lot this past week. "Not tonight. Tonight you need your strength. And mine," she said, lifting the hand that bore that opal ring.

He held up his hands. "Do *not* cut yourself. I can't stand to see you hurt."

Take her up on the offer, Aden, Elijah said. *Please. I have a feeling you'll need it.*

"Aden—" Victoria began.

"No," he told them both. Even if he needed her strength to survive the night, he would not allow her to hurt herself like that.

Slowly she lowered her arm, her eyes narrowing. "I could force you, you know."

"But you won't," he said confidently.

A moment passed. She gave a dejected sigh, the anger leaving her. "But I won't. Not even for your own good."

"Everything will be all right." He hoped. He reached out and stroked her hair, the strands silky against his skin. "You'll see."

"Oh, Aden," she said on a trembling breath. She rested her head on his shoulder. "I'm so afraid. For you, for us."

He gave her the only reassurance he could. "I will never stop wanting you. We'll find a way to be together."

She wanted to believe him; he knew she did, but she gave no response. "So many things are going wrong, all at once. First the witches. Now a fairy is speaking with Dan," she said, taking his hand and leading him to the main house. "Come. Let me show you."

They reached the kitchen and he peered in through the window. Thankfully, it was dark outside and well lit inside, allowing him to see everything clearly without being seen himself. Dan was introducing the boys to a tall, muscled man with silver-white hair who had his back to Aden.

"That's probably the new tutor."

"Let me guess, the old tutor suddenly decided to relocate?"

"Yes. How did you know?"

"Standard operating procedure for a fairy. And with him inside, I can't tell Dan to allow you to go to the party. The fairy would attack me and I would attack him, we wouldn't be able to help ourselves. Our kinds hate each other too much. We would injure each other."

"What does he want with Dan, do you think?"

"He probably followed your energy here. Though it's likely he doesn't know which of you boys has been summoning his kind, or why."

"This is such a mess. I wish—" His voice cut off abruptly as the fairy turned, gazing over at the window.

Aden and Victoria ducked, but not before he'd gotten a glimpse of emerald-green eyes, a face so perfect angels were probably singing to celebrate its creation, and ears that were just a little pointed.

"Let's go," Victoria said.

"I can't leave them with a fairy. I haven't forgotten what you told me, that a fairy's beauty hides its evil."

"Fairies *are* evil. To vampires. As I told you before, they consider themselves protectors of mankind and vampires destroyers of it. That is why they hate us so."

"So the boys will be safe?"

"Without a doubt. The only time a human has to worry is when a fairy thinks it's being usurped. They value power above all things. And you, they won't understand. You, they'll consider a threat. But the others? No."

Okay, then. Off they went, striding around the house and toward the road. Aden would deal with Dan later, if need be. "Is there anything I should know about your dad? Any customs or rituals that I could possibly ruin, thereby bringing a death sentence upon myself?" Like a stabbing, he thought, recalling Elijah's vision.

She twirled a curl around her finger. "He is used to reverence, so bow when you are introduced to him. Do not speak to him unless he asks you a question, and do not look him directly in the eyes. That makes him feel challenged. Believe me, you do not want to challenge him. There is not a crueler living being on earth."

Why was he attending this party again? "And the other vampires? What will they do?"

"Stick to my side. Never leave it. You will be viewed as my property and left alone."

Up ahead, headlights flashed, ending their conversation.

Victoria increased her pace. "That's Riley and Mary Ann."

The car he soon found himself entering did not belong to Mary Ann's father. It was black and sleek and sporty. A model he'd never seen before. Stolen? He and Victoria got in the very small backseat. As he moved back there, he was given a glimpse of Mary Ann's costume. It was a red and white checkered dress that cut off at midthigh, complete with a long red cape and white high heels.

Riley, he noticed, wasn't wearing a costume.

"Little Red Riding Hood and the Big Bad Wolf, I take it," he said with a laugh. "Nice."

On the drive to…wherever they were headed, he lost his amusement in favor of nervousness. Elijah's doom and gloom mutterings didn't help. So much depended on tonight. His life, his time with Victoria. What if he blew it all?

"Will the vampires try to drink from us?" Mary Ann asked.

"They shouldn't, no," Riley told her. "They will have their own meals."

Blood-slaves?

All too soon, they pulled up to a towering monstrosity of a house. It was the only one in sight. Five stories, sprawling, consuming acre after acre, the windows painted black to match the brick. A wrought-iron fence creaked open, allowing them inside. Two wolves stood sentry as the car eased past.

"Wow. I know you said you lived at the edge of town, that your home was hidden and I probably hadn't ever seen it, but I never expected *this*." Mary Ann pressed her nose against the glass.

"We had to renovate it to suit our needs," Riley said.

The moon seemed to shy away from the house, casting its rays elsewhere and leaving the place in total darkness. Because of the car's headlights, he could see that there were no other cars present, and no one but wolves lingered outside. Were they the first to arrive?

"You ran back and forth between school and this place?" Aden asked. "Between the ranch and this place? Every day?"

"Kind of," Victoria answered. "I've been working on my...teleporting skills. I think that's what you humans call it. Moving from one place to another with only a thought. I'm getting better."

Wait. What? She could teleport?

There wasn't time to question her about it. The car stopped at the end of the drive and they emerged. The moment their doors slammed shut, the front doors to the house opened and a tall figure stepped out. Aden recognized the figure immediately and scowled. Dmitri. A red haze of fury clouded Aden's vision.

He stepped in front of Victoria. Dmitri bared his teeth, the only sign he gave of his displeasure.

The vampire closed the distance between them. Victoria's hand slipped into Aden's, squeezed, and then she moved beside him.

"I've been waiting for you." Dmitri leaned down for a kiss but she turned her head. His irritated gaze flicked to Aden. "I see you failed to heed my warning."

"Father commanded his appearance, remember?"

· And she had craved it. He would not allow himself to believe anything else. She wanted Aden, not Dmitri.

"I do," the vampire said. "Which is why I thought you'd be interested in the night's entertainment. Come." He waved his hand and moved off, expecting them to follow.

They did, up the stairs and inside the house. Aden soon found himself standing in a foyer, surrounded by more wealth than he'd dreamed possible. A shiny white bench that looked as if it was made from Mrs. Reeves's pearl necklace, Chinese wall decorations of gold and silver, and glass chests filled with colorful vases.

Victoria pulled him along, so he was only given the barest of glimpses. Mary Ann was just as stunned as he was, cranking her neck to gaze at the spacious entryway until the last possible second.

They didn't climb the spiral staircase, but actually walked straight through the seemingly deserted house to the back door, French doubles that opened before Dmitri could touch them. Suddenly the scent of blood hung in the air, thick and metallic. Chattering voices drifted to his ears, but the words were spoken so quickly they reminded him of crickets chirping.

Dmitri stopped, not exiting the terrace. Twinkling lights were suspended from the trees—trees that flourished with bloodred roses. There was a large silver circle in the center of the yard, flat as the ground but cut into some kind of maze. No one stood upon it.

People were scattered throughout the immaculate lawn. Most of the women wore black robes and most of the men wore black shirts and pants. They drank from chalices, and swayed to a beat of sultry music whisping on the breeze. Those scantily dressed in white were clearly human. They offered their necks, arms, legs, *whatever,* whenever a vampire gestured them over.

Their eyes were glazed, their motions eager, as if they couldn't wait to be bitten. Oh, yes. Blood-slaves.

"My apologies that there isn't time for our two happy couples to dance," Dmitri said, drawing Aden's attention. "There's too much to do, you see."

"Where are my sisters?" Victoria demanded.

"I've had them confined to their rooms."

She stiffened. "You can't do that."

"I can and did." He didn't give her time to respond. "So— is it?—Aden, what do you think of the hors d'oeuvres?" He pointed to the two tables at each side of the yard.

Aden followed the direction of his fingers and sucked in a breath. On one table lay Ozzie. He was clad in jeans but shirtless. He was also bound, motionless, gaze fixed straight ahead. Dead, Aden realized numbly. On the other table was Tucker, again shirtless with his jeans and bound, but still fighting and thrashing as a vampire drank from his wrist. He was gagged yet clearly screaming for help, his eyes bulging from strain. Unconcerned, the vampire continued slurping at him.

Mary Ann noticed, too, and gasped in horror. "What are you doing to him? Stop. Stop!" She tried to race forward but Riley retained a firm grip on her, his face grim.

Aden stepped forward, but Dmitri turned out to be *his* guard, holding out his arm, preventing him from moving a single inch. "The only way to remove a meal is to provide another. Would you like to offer your services, human?"

"How dare you." Victoria's fangs were bared and sharp, her eyes glowing pools of hatred. "You'll pay for this. I'll make sure of it. My father will not be amused."

Dmitri whipped around, his own eyes glowing. "No, you'll thank me for it, my little princess, for I have punished the enemies of your human friend. Doesn't that make you happy?"

She raised her chin. "And after the party? What did you plan to do with the bodies? Call the human police and blame Aden, have him arrested? Out of my reach?"

"That is just an added bonus."

"You disgusting piece of—"

Scowling, Dmitri slammed a fist into his upraised palm. "Do not speak to me so. I am your husband and I—"

"You aren't my husband yet," she shouted. The voices below them tapered to quiet. Heads turned. Attention fixed on them. "And if I have my way, you never will be."

She wasn't taking any crap; Aden wouldn't, either. "You have no idea what you've done, Dmitri," he said flatly. Julian couldn't control his ability to raise the dead, which meant Ozzie wouldn't stay dead much longer.

Even as the thought filled him, Ozzie sat up, dull eyes blinking, tongue flicking out hungrily.

"Oh, thank God. That boy is still alive," Mary Ann cried, clearly relieved. "We have to save him."

"It's too late," Aden told her, still without emotion. He couldn't let himself feel. Not now. Not with what he was about to do. "He's dead, even if he doesn't look it. And there can be no saving him. Dmitri made sure of that."

TWENTY-FIVE

ADEN WITHDREW HIS DAGGERS, pushed past Dmitri and stalked into the midst of the party. Victoria stayed with him every step of the way, head held high. That strengthened him. She could have been embarrassed to be seen with a human, but wasn't. She'd even told her fiancé to get lost. A fiancé who trailed just a few steps behind them.

The rest of the vampires reached for Aden, attempting to touch him in some way, perhaps feeling the tug of his energy. He brushed them aside.

The closer he came to Ozzie, the more Ozzie strained against the ties that bound him, hungry for human flesh. Black saliva soon coated the gag in his mouth and dripped from the corners of his lips. Aden knew Mary Ann was watching him, wanting him to free the boy, the innocent human, but he couldn't. He could only raise his dagger and strike.

Ozzie's body jerked as the head detached, then stilled.

Mary Ann gasped in horror.

The vampires around him laughed.

What did Victoria think?

"Like I said, my father will punish you for this," she told Dmitri with quiet fury. At least she wasn't running from Aden.

Dmitri grinned. "I wouldn't be too sure. You'll find that many things have changed this day, princess."

His amusement gave her pause, destroyed some of her confidence. "What do you mean?"

"You'll see."

Aden might have disliked Ozzie, but he wouldn't have wished such an end for him. For anyone. Even Tucker. He had a feeling Mary Ann felt the same way, despite Tucker's treachery. But that's exactly what would happen if this night continued as it had begun.

"First things first," Dmitri said, moving beside Aden. Aden felt the heat of him, but it didn't energize him as Victoria's did. "Your human has to be dealt with. I warned him. Free a meal and become one himself. Guards," he called, eyes narrowing, humor fading. "Restrain the princess so that I may take care of our guest."

Several male vampires stepped forward, but stopped when Aden raised his now-dripping blades, placing the tip at Dmitri's throat. He knew it would not damage the vampire, not there, but a single shift of his wrist and he could nail Dmitri in his vulnerable eye.

"Touch her and this one will die by my hand."

"And my teeth," Riley added. He was rushing forward, Mary Ann behind him, not stopping until he reached Victoria.

"The princess is mine to protect and I will let no harm befall her. Even at the hands of her betrothed."

He left his brothers behind to protect your friends at the house and Mary Ann's father, Elijah said. *He is alone. And this, my boy, is the end I always feared for you, the evil you cannot escape. You alone will be forced to fight the monster beside you.*

You can't let yourself be killed tonight, Caleb said. *You have a meeting with the witches to attend.*

"I'm not going to die. Not like this." That, at least, he knew. He still lacked those three scars on his side. That didn't mean he wouldn't soon be praying for death.

"Your confidence is misplaced, human," was the angered reply from Dmitri.

Hate to say this, but I think we're screwed, bros, Julian said. *We may not die, but we'll probably wish we had.*

They were on the same page, at least.

Eve would have reassured him of his success, he thought suddenly and wanted to howl. Thankfully, the guards had not moved again. The other vampires were watching intently, even smiling, perhaps thinking this was just another of the night's entertainments.

"My father—" Victoria began, but Dmitri stopped her with a laugh.

"Oh, didn't I tell you?" He splayed his arms and turned. "Allow me to remedy my oversight. Everyone, if I could have your attention, please." All eyes shifted to him. "Welcome, friends, to this magnificent occasion. I'm sure you're wondering where the guest of honor is. Alas, though I hesitate to cast a pall on this splendid gala, I have tragic news to impart. You all know how weak Vlad has been since his premature awakening."

No, Aden thought, sensing what was coming. No, no, no.

A tremor rocked Victoria.

"You all know that even weakened as he was, he was still a formidable soldier. Stronger, still, than most of us. Well, most of *you*. But not," he said, pinning Victoria with a dark stare, "me."

She shifted from one foot to the other, looking like the lost princess she was meant to be in that velvet costume. "What are you saying?"

"I'm saying his decision to allow your human scum to live was wrong. I'm saying he should have had better control of you, for he who cannot control his own daughter has no business reigning over an entire race of vampires. I'm saying…he's dead. Dead by my hand this very morning." His tone reeked of satisfaction as murmurs and cries filled the enclosure. Above the sounds, though, was a whimper from Victoria.

"No. No!"

Yes, Aden thought, *and I helped him. I woke Vlad. I weakened him.* Would Victoria hate him when she realized that?

"Now, take heart, princess. He fought like the king he was and nearly bested me. But in the end, I won. And as his conqueror," Dmitri said, smugger than ever, "I claim all that is his. His people. His daughter—who was always intended to be my bride. I. Am. King. I am now in control of you. A new era has begun!"

Victoria gave a violent shake of her head.

"Shall I prove it?" Dmitri clapped his hands and two vampires emerged from the side of the house, carrying a bejeweled lounge. Atop it lay a body blackened by soot, features indistinguishable. There were three rings on the left hand, all similar to Victoria's, and an intricate crown atop the hairless head.

"No," Victoria gasped. "Father."

Shouts of fury rose up, but only a few, to Aden's surprise. Most of the vampires clapped and cheered.

"I always admired your father," Dmitri said, "but as any worthy warrior, I admired power more. I saw my opportunity and I struck. I like to think Vlad would have understood. And one day, when you have forgotten all about your human scum, you will even thank me. You need a strong hand to guide you, Victoria, and Vlad was not providing it."

"You… You…" Nothing else would seem to fit past her grinding teeth. She was angry, yes, and perhaps in shock. How soon until despair hit her and she crumbled?

"Take them, all but the boy," Dmitri said, and the guards sprang forward. Before Aden could react, Victoria was ripped from his side. Riley, Mary Ann and everyone else who had protested were grabbed, too. There were simply too many soldiers, overwhelming his friends.

Still. He leapt into the fray. Each of them fought with every ounce of strength they possessed. Fought and fought well, and for a moment it appeared that they would win. But no one managed to escape. Not even when Riley morphed into a wolf, biting and clawing. He simply couldn't cut through that hardened vampire skin.

Aden used his daggers, but again, they simply wouldn't cut that skin. He didn't care. Determination was a fire in his blood, burning hot and true. The night would not end in defeat. Not for him, and not for his friends. He wouldn't let it.

He was panting as he turned to Dmitri. "Let's settle this. You and me. Here and now. Winner takes all."

Dmitri grinned slowly as Victoria shouted a denial. Her guards held her immobile or she would have returned to Aden's side, he was sure. "I was hoping you would say that, human."

Before Aden could blink, the vampire was on him. Limbs tangled as they propelled toward the table, knocking it and Ozzie's body to the ground in a loud crash. Aden lost his hold on one of the knives. They rolled, the vampire pinning him down and going for his throat. Thank God for the armor, for it stopped those razor-sharp teeth from hitting their mark.

Arms free, Aden jabbed the remaining dagger into Dmitri's eye. The action was unexpected, and therefore no attempt was made to stop him. His opponent screeched an unholy sound, blood pouring, glittering and fizzing, and Aden cringed, his eardrums probably bleeding, as well. Some of that blood dripped into his mouth and he spit it out automatically. Some managed to trickle down his throat, anyway. And it burned, oh, did it burn.

Reaching out blindly, Dmitri raked his claws over Aden's face. Skin and tissue opened, blood poured, and he released a howl. The vampires around them breathed deeply, collectively, probably savoring both his human blood and Dmitri's vampire blood, and inched closer for a taste.

The blood he'd swallowed, even the minute amount it must have been, must have been working through him, because those wounds soon stopped hurting. But before he could rise, attack, Dmitri was back on top of him, the dagger gone and out of reach, teeth biting at his face, biting at his armor, searching for the weak points. Aden worked his legs between their bodies and pushed. Weak as Dmitri now was, the vampire flew backwards.

Aden stood, lunged. Sensing him, Dmitri swung out his arm, claws moving beneath the armor and into his side. Sinking past skin, into that blistered muscle and bone. Hissing, Aden fell. Spotted the discarded dagger and grabbed it. On his feet a moment later, he dodged to the left and plowed it into Dmitri's ear. There was another unholy screech, this one nearly causing his head to explode.

Dmitri jerked, flailed, clawing at Aden's grip. Soon there was no skin left on Aden's hand, but Dmitri never stilled; he kept fighting, kept flailing. Aden had to end this. Soon. How did one kill a vampire? As Victoria had once told him, the well-known stake through the heart thing wouldn't work because a stake couldn't penetrate their skin. Only the *je la nune* was able—the *je la nune!* he thought. Yes.

"Victoria!" he shouted.

She knew what he wanted, jerked her arm free and tossed him her ring. There was only a little bit of the liquid left inside, but he managed to slide the blade from Dmitri.

"This all you got?" Aden taunted. "I thought you were strong. I thought you were—"

As he'd wanted, Dmitri backhanded him and he went flying. Even though he'd expected it, though, it still hurt, nearly dislocating his jaw. He didn't get up, just waited, allowing the liquid from Victoria's ring to drip onto the metal. He didn't have to wait long. The enraged vampire flew at him, close, so close…Aden merely raised the knife and allowed Dmitri's weight and momentum to do the rest.

The vampire's skin instantly melted, the silver piercing his heart.

There were more screams as Dmitri bucked against him, screams so pain-filled, so agonizing, Aden cringed deep in his soul. Then the screams faded and the body stopped flopping.

As the surrounding vampires gasped in horror, Aden removed the head before the body could rise and fell back, panting, sweating, bleeding. The gasps changed to groans, then to murmurs of disbelief and anger. Then there was only stunned silence.

"Aden," Victoria called, struggling for freedom.

"Let her go," he told the guards, not even having the strength to glance over at them. Wouldn't have mattered, anyway. He was so dizzy he was losing vision with every second that passed.

A moment later, *he* was the one who was stunned. They obeyed without protest, and Victoria rushed to his side, her face hovering above his. She used one of her still-wet nails to cut her wrist and held it to his mouth. This time, he didn't even think about refusing. Without her healing blood, he would fall, crash, vulnerable to those around him, leaving his friends equally vulnerable.

Her blood was hotter than before as it joined Dmitri's, burning through him, consuming him, killing him, helping him rise from the ashes of his former self, new and strong. In a few hours, he would see the world from Victoria's eyes. What about Dmitri's? Now that the vampire was dead, there would likely be nothing to see.

Guess he would have to wait and find out. There were more important things to worry about right now.

"I'm sorry about your dad," he told Victoria, reaching up and thumbing her soft cheek. The dizziness was fading and he could see how pale she was. Paler than normal.

"Thank you." She was trembling, though not as much as before the battle. "But it's you I was most concerned about. Dmitri is—was—a vampire warrior and you, well, are not. I'm just glad you're okay. I thought I had lost you."

A movement behind her caught his eye. The vampires were now bowing in his direction.

He frowned and whispered, "Uh, Victoria. What are they doing?"

She glanced over at them and grimaced. "With the death of my father, Dmitri was indeed king. But you just killed Dmitri, which means…"

"No way." Strong now, he pulled himself into a crouch and shook his head. "Absolutely no way."

"Yes way. My king." Riley knelt and bowed his head, just

like the others. Only Mary Ann remained standing. She was clutching her middle and eyeing the vampires with distaste. "We now live to serve you."

Ridiculous. "Get up, Riley, and stop acting that way. Go free Tucker."

"Yes, my king," Riley said, rushing off to do as he'd been told. This was too weird. Riley was obeying even though he hated Tucker. Aden should have been pleased. Anyone else would have been, he was sure. Instead, he found himself shouting.

"Stop that!" He didn't want his friends treating him any differently, and he certainly didn't want to control the fate of these people. People he didn't know, a race he knew little about.

"Aden," Victoria said.

His attention returned to her and he cupped her face in his hands. "Be honest with me. Are you okay? I never would have wished a parent's death on you, even if it meant losing you."

"I know you wouldn't have," she said softly. "I wasn't close with my father, but I did respect him and I will mourn his passing. But throughout my long years, I have seen death after death. Lost loved one after loved one. I know my sadness will pass." She brushed a strand of hair from his temples. "The only thing I could not live without is you. And now, you can free my mother from her confinement. You can summon her, bring her here." Each new word brought a wider smile.

The only thing I could not live without is you. Words he would cherish. As for her mother, absolutely. He wasn't a king, for God's sake, but he would do whatever was necessary to reunite mother and daughter. Guess that was a new hobby of his.

He stood, dragging Victoria up with him, then winced and grabbed his side. Clearly, not all of his injuries had healed.

She frowned, instantly concerned. "What's wrong?"

"I was cut and didn't know it."

Frown deepening, she helped him out of his armor. Meanwhile, the vampires remained on their knees. Waiting for his command to rise? He wasn't about to issue one, not that he believed they would listen to him. Him, king? Please. Until he learned more about them, and how they would treat Victoria—she'd brought him, Dmitri's killer, to the party, after all—he was keeping his distance.

When he was free of the armor, Victoria raised the hem of his shirt. Her horrified gaze lifted to him. "Oh, Aden. I'm so sorry."

"What is it?" He looked down, not knowing what to expect—and that's when he saw them. Three gashes on his right side. Deep, red and raw.

Eyes wide, she covered her mouth with her hands. "Dmitri must have had the liquid on his nails when he slashed you."

"What does that mean for me, a human?"

She gulped. "Aden, you're going to scar."

That was all? He grinned. "That doesn't upset me, I swear. I have plenty of…scars." The last emerged as a whisper. Understanding had dawned. Three scars on his right side. Just like in the vision Elijah had given him of his own death.

"Oh, Aden!" She threw her arms around him and held tight. He couldn't see her face, it was buried in his neck, but he knew she was crying, the warm droplets landing on his shoulder.

His death was that much closer.

"How much time do we have left?" he asked.

I wish I knew, Elijah said.

A year, perhaps? Maybe months. It would be soon, though. He swallowed the lump in his throat.

"It'll be okay," he told Victoria, and he wished he believed it. For the moment, though, he would do whatever was necessary to make it true. "We have plenty to do before I die. We have a fairy to kick out of the ranch. Maybe Shannon can help with that. We have a witches meeting to attend—" because there was no way he would allow his friends to die for missing it "—a town to save from flesh-hungry creatures, and souls to free."

His vampire princess smiled slowly. "You're right. This will be okay. I wouldn't have believed it before today, but now I see that anything is possible."

They stood as Mary Ann and Riley joined them, Tucker propped up by one of Riley's muscular arms.

"Thank you, thank you, hurt so much, thank you," Tucker babbled. "Hurt, hurt, thank you."

"Just make sure you take advantage of this second chance at life," Mary Ann said as Riley wrapped his free arm around her waist. "It's time to clean up your act. You're going to be a father."

Only time would tell if he would take the advice or not, Aden mused. Only time would reveal what happened to *all* of them. And only time would tell how Aden's life would change now that he was supposedly in charge of the entire vampire society. Not that he had any plans to rule.

His gaze roved over his friends and he nodded in sudden satisfaction. In awe.

He had begun this journey in a cemetery, alone except for the voices in his head, and now he was beginning the next with friends at his side. A guy couldn't ask for more than that.